"A folklorist's eye for telling detail and a front-por...
pace."
　　—*New York Times Book Review*

"A terrifically gifted storyteller."
　　—*Washington Post Book Review*

"A zest for storytelling and a gimlet eye for detail."
　　—*Entertainment Weekly*

"Like 10-alarm chili, Lansdale is pretty strong stuff... He has become a cult
figure."
　　—*People*

"Lansdale i
　　—*Bookl*

"Lansdale is   s...but amped
up to about 100,000 watts."
　　—*Houston Chronicle*

"A great introduction to the raunchy, cheerfully unclassifiable East Texan bon
vivant."
　　—*Publishers Weekly*, starred review

Selected Writings of Joe R. Lansdale

The Drive-In series

The Drive-In: A "B" Movie with Blood
    and Popcorn, Made in Texas (1988)
The Drive-In 2: Not Just One of Them
    Sequels (1989)
The Drive-In: A Double-Feature (1997)
The Drive-In: The Bus Tour (2005)

Ned the Seal trilogy

Zeppelins West (2001)
Flaming London (2006)

Graphic novels and comic books

Lone Ranger & Tonto (1993)
Jonah Hex: Two Gun Mojo (1993)
Jonah Hex: Riders of the Worm and Such
    (1995)
Blood and Shadows (1996)
The Spirit: The New Adventures #8 (1998)
Red Range (1999)
Jonah Hex: Shadows West (1999)
Conan and the Songs of the Dead (2006)
Marvel Adventures: Fantastic Four #32
    (2008)
Pigeons from Hell (2008)

Anthologies edited

The Best of the West (1989)
New Frontier (1989)
Razored Saddles (1989, with Pat Lobrutto)
Dark at Heart (1991, with Karen Lansdale)
Weird Business: A Horror Comics
    Anthology (1995, with Richard Klaw)
West That Was (1994)
    (co-ed: Thomas Knowles)
Wild West Show (1994)
    (co-ed: Thomas Knowles)
Lords of the Razor (2006)
Cross Plains Universe: Texans Celebrate
    Robert E. Howard
    (2006, with Scott A. Cupp)
Retro-Pulp Tales (2007)
Son of Retro-Pulp Tales
    (2009, with Keith Lansdale)

FOR ADAM COATS

The Best of
Joe R. Lansdale

Tachyon

COVER ART © 2005 BY JOHN PICACIO.
APPEARED IN *Texas Parks & Wildlife*,
JANUARY 2005, FOR "THE SECOND HUNT."
COVER DESIGN BY ANN MONN
INTERIOR DESIGN BY JOHN COULTHART

TACHYON PUBLICATIONS
1459 18TH STREET #139
SAN FRANCISCO, CA 94107
(415) 285-5615
WWW.TACHYONPUBLICATIONS.COM
TACHYON@TACHYONPUBLICATIONS.COM

SERIES EDITOR: JACOB WEISMAN

ISBN 13: 978-1-892391-94-0
ISBN 10: 1-892391-94-5

Contents

Crucified Dreams

Introduction by
Joe R. Lansdale

EVENTUALLY, I WILL come to the point as I take you on a spin through the paint mixer of my brain and dip you in the mish-mash of my nostalgia, but not quite yet. For now I speak uncensored, unfiltered, and full of madness.

Thoughts, like electric grasshoppers, jump in space and time.

When I was a child, in the fifties and early sixties, the world was full of magic, but not everyone could see it. For some the world was gray, and it could be that way for me too, unless I turned my head just right and looked for some well-lit crack in my universe so that I might peer into another that was full of color and commotion and a sense of wonder.

My mother opened the secret door first and showed me other worlds were there, and then she backed off and left it up to me to go inside and look around. She showed it to me by reading to me, fairy tales and funny animal stories from comic books, all manner of children's stories, and pretty soon I could read, and I could do this long before I went to school, and for no reason I can clearly explain, once I learned to read, and realized the alphabet helped accomplish what I was reading, I wanted to make letters and find their order and make words and sentences and paragraphs and pages and finally, stories, and books.

But the first things I read with great enthusiasm and wanted to write, and also wanted to illustrate, were comics. I loved DC Comics especially, for here were refugees from another universe, brightly colored in panels with magnificent heroes and rocket ships and monsters and most importantly to me, people who wanted to be honest and good and make the world around them a better place to be.

So I'll say it again, and let me testify: I loved comics, and they introduced me not only to brighter and weirder worlds, but they crossed up worlds. Westerns sometimes blended with horror and science fiction and action and mystery, and sometimes my heroes, like Batman, traveled through space and time, or hung out with my favorite alien, Superman. There were men who were given powers because they were good and just and brave, like Green Lantern. Oh, man. I tried to be good and just and brave for just that reason, hoping some alien dying from a rocket crash might pass to me a power ring and a lamp with which to keep it charged.

"In brightest day and darkest night" and all that. I was primed and ready, waiting on my alien.

I sometimes wished I might find a chemical formula, if just by accident, that could be tasted by me, or that might drench me in such a way (perhaps by lightning bursting through my bedroom window and striking my chemistry set), that when it was all said and done, I would develop the ability to run at top speed, so fast I might have to wear a special red costume compacted inside a ring. I could call myself The Flash. I could vibrate through solid matter, run up walls, dash across the ocean without getting my feet wet, break the sound barrier, the time barrier, and if I was real lucky, I'd get to battle a giant super intelligent gorilla who lived in an invisible city full of other gorillas. Man, the possibilities.

As for Wonder Woman, well, I wanted to be heroic enough that she might like me. Back then I wanted to ride in her invisible plane and go to her secret island. I hadn't yet figured out there was something else about her that attracted me as well. That skimpy costume, for example, or what was under it, and the fact that her island was secret.

But Batman was my favorite hero. He was a regular guy. He learned about all manner of things because not only was he pissed off over the murder of his parents, he was a genius. He studied chemistry, astronomy, all the sciences. He was a gymnast and a martial artist: Judo, Jujitsu, Karate, boxing and wrestling (these were about all the martial arts the reading public knew of in those days), and he was good looking and had money and the women lined up for a mile.

Yeah, baby. I wanted to be Batman.

I didn't have the money. I thought I was okay looking, but nothing to look cool in a tuxedo at a charity benefit. In fact, I had never seen anyone in a tuxedo, or anyone who wanted to wear one. The only charity I knew about was us. We were poorer than the proverbial one-legged church mouse with a respiratory problem. I did study all the disciplines Batman studied, in a small child sort of way. I read books on chemistry and rocks and astronomy and insects and the human body, and before I realized my dad was in fact an excellent wrestler, a fair boxer, and a hell of a former country self-defense fighter, I read the one book I could get on weight training, exercise and self-defense. I don't remember the title, but it was mostly about exercises and lifting weights, and in the back were a few self-defense techniques. I probably got it from the Gladewater library on our trips there to visit with my cousins, returning it when my mother or father went in that direction. My dad tended to do that a lot, as he was a troubleshooter for a company, gone now, called Wanda Petroleum.

But, what I'm trying to tell you in this long-around-the-block manner, via the alleyways with a look in the trashcans and a glance at the sky, is, I wanted to be Batman, and I tried. Even to this day, that character has influenced my life, leading to a thirst for knowledge. I never mastered the disciplines Batman knew. After I found out how to make baking soda boil over, my chemistry skills hit the wall. When it comes to math, once I run out of fingers and toes, I'm done. I still look at the stars, but I remember very little beyond: Oh, pretty.

What Batman did for me, though, was make me understand that the world was bigger than I knew, that there were things beyond getting out of high school and going to work and waiting for retirement. Like Batman, I wanted to be something special.

And, it would be pretty cool too if I could learn to throw a batarang.

One last time, ladies and gentleman, I'll testify, shout it from the roof tops: I loved comic books.

Mae and Pete Green, who ran a kind of general store in my little town, one of the last of its kind, sold me comics on a regular basis, all in color and full of spandex or whatever costumes were made of in the fifties and early sixties, for a dime. Kid crack, jacked to the max. In the back of the store, half the cover page cut off, were unsold comics that were not supposed to be sold, but were in fact raffled off for a nickel a book. There were a few old pulps there too, and a lot of *Popular Science* and *Popular Mechanics* magazines. I thought that store was a little slice of heaven and for a few coins I had been given the keys.

And my mother, bless her heart, she used to sew me Batman suits with cardboard inside the ears, though, in time, this didn't keep them from drooping until I looked a bit like a sad ear-cut Doberman with a constipation problem. She made for my nephew, who was close to my age, as my brother was seventeen when I was born and married not long after, a Robin suit. We were pretty damn cool, right there in Mt. Enterprise, waiting for crime to happen.

We did a lot of waiting. Back then there wasn't much crime in our part of the country, least that we knew about. Though our bank was robbed on occasion, and I remember hearing about that, thinking, well, where the hell were we? Not only did we not know about the robbery, unlike Batman who always seemed to be patrolling at just the right time, we wouldn't even have had our costumes with us if we had. It happened midday — admittedly not a classic time for our Bat hero — but no one sent up a signal or nothing. It was over and done with and we were at the house, enjoying our summer, either watching TV or wrestling in the yard, climbing the apple tree, pretending it was a spaceship. Hell, except for the Bat cowl, when all this happened, my suit was in the wash.

I began to suspect my career as a crime fighter wasn't going to get off the ground.

But that writing thing, creating stories, I began to suspect it had chosen me, and that I had not chosen it, and that bitch was going to be a harsh but delightful mistress. Color poured into the world in a more constant fashion.

The reading of superhero comics led to my reading of other comics, and I suppose you could say more adult comics, like *Classics Illustrated*. These were wonderful and accurate and beautifully drawn and colored versions of classic literature. You'd be surprised what they adapted. Everything from H. G. Wells to Dickens, to all manner of books in-between; things a kid now wouldn't bother to examine, and may never have heard of.

Classics Illustrated led me to read the books from which they were adapted, when I could get my hands on books. They weren't readily available in small town East Texas. In fact, though I was born in Gladewater, my early years were spent in a town of 150 or so, called Mt. Enterprise. There was little enterprise to be found there, but I remember the place fondly, and it was a wonderful place for a kid to grow up. I felt like Huckleberry Finn, who didn't mind going home. And, in fact, I preferred to wind up in my room in my bed at night, perhaps to slip secretly into the living room to watch a late night movie, preferably science fiction, and all the better yet if space aliens were involved. Even better if they were the sort that were frightening and pissed off, and no friend of Earth. It made for a better story, and I was always drawn to that more than the "they don't really mean me any harm" aliens, though, on some level I liked it all.

Forbidden Planet, It Came from Outer Space, This Island Earth, The Day the Earth Stood Still, so many others, including one special bit of creepy nastiness, the original *Invaders from Mars*.

I had a bedroom that reminded me of *Invaders*. It had a back window that looked out on a back yard that also reminded me of the story, and not far away a stretch of woods. The movie came on late one night, on one of the three television stations available back then, one only available when the weather was a certain way and you held your mouth right and shifted your nuts to one side while you turned the antennae by hand.

I snuck into the living room to watch it, and it scared the bejesus out of me, didn't scar me, but tattooed me with deep, bright imagination ink leaking all the colors of the rainbow, and within the colors were dollops of delightful fear, sort you can get away from with the coming of sunlight, the passing of day, the immersion into something else. I liked this sensation.

I've seen the movie since, and it's still cool, but what's really good is the first twenty minutes or so, and the last few minutes. The middle minutes, with the aliens is a little less terrifying than I remember. Now I see the zippers and the men from Mars look a lot like guys in suits, and the mastermind, a telepathic, tentacle-sprouting head in a jar, is like a sad octopus battling depression. And, of course, there's a portion lifted from what looks like an ad for the National Guard. Back then we believed the U.S. military could whip anybody and anything, including a bunch of zipper-suited Martians and their tentacle-headed leader.

Still, I love that movie. The power of the mind is great, and there was less to compare it to. No fantastic *Star Wars* effects and beyond, just simple suggestion and shadow. And now that I think about it, the film was in color, and yet it had a magnificent hint of noir about it, a surrealistic edge that seeps into my work a lot of the time.

Later on, a little older, I was hit the same way by the original black and white *Invasion of the Body Snatchers*, one that time doesn't damage, but in fact, makes creepier.

Wow! Got to get my breath. The memories are like arrows tipped with nostalgia, shooting straight through the heart.

Mt. Enterprise didn't have a library, though one was founded shortly before we moved, partly due to the interest of local women, like my mother, and the kind donation of someone with actual money. But before the library, there were only the occasional books given to me, or loaned to me, or on rare occasions, bought for me, due to their lack of availability in a town so small. There was the Bible, and I read it from cover to cover, and loved it, but realized rather quickly, like the Greek mythology I loved even more, it was nothing more than fantastic stories. Wonderful in their own way, but religion... I was suspicious, and by the time I was seventeen, having read the Bible from cover to cover numerous times, loving the lilt of the language in the same way I love Shakespeare, it was pretty clear to me that there wasn't much reality in those pages. I liked the use of violence and horror and morality play, but for me it was a lot less fascinating and satisfying than the works of Homer. The old blind guy could tell a tale of foul and wounded and imperfect people and gods with the best of them. Better than the Bible. Better than Shakespeare. Homer, he was the bomb.

I lived inside of books — Hardy Boys and Nancy Drew, loaned me by a lady across the street — and moved about in them, as if they were living tissue and I was their aching guts. I was especially fond of Saturday mornings, which for a kid is the magic day. I would get up early on Saturdays, and nothing was more disappointing than sleeping late, losing that wonderful day of the week. I'd jump up and my mother would fix me eggs and toast, and sometimes bacon, and I'd watch things like *Fury*, a story about a horse and the boy who loved him, or better yet, serials like *Flash Gordon* or *Buck Rogers*, both starring Buster Crabbe, with different hair shades. And best of all, Tarzan. I came to love Tarzan as much as Batman.

There were many Tarzans, but Johnny Weissmuller was my favorite, hands down. But I'd take any Tarzan I could get. Gordon Scott, Buster Crabbe (yep, same guy who played Flash Gordon and Buck Rogers, and many other heroes), whichever Tarzan movie and actor that was on Saturday morning TV. It's hard to see those movies now and think they were the same ones I saw. Because in my head, those black and white films, seen then, were in bright color and the jungles were rich and real and full of savagery. Tarzan, for me, was real. Lived in a cool tree house, had a funny chimpanzee for a pet named Cheeta, and a hot wife named Jane. I had some interesting dreams about that tree house and Jane. The chimp, Cheeta, I hasten to add, was not in those dreams.

And then there was the Lone Ranger and Tonto. Loved those guys. I always wanted to be Tonto. Maybe because I had heard we had Indian blood in the family. To this day, I don't know if that's true, but it's always been part of the family story, so perhaps it is; perhaps I am in fact Cherokee and Chickasaw, and perhaps Quanah Parker, the great Comanche War Chief, is kin to me by marriage.

Perhaps not, but these were part of the family stories, along with frontier tales of my kin traveling in covered wagons, going by horse, being pursued by panthers, bitten by snakes, fighting the elements and belligerent people; some of my people perhaps being the most belligerent of all.

Then came the building of that local library, and I read dog stories that told me dogs were noble and true and loyal and fine, and I believed it. I read adventure stories, and mystery stories, and horror stories, and finally, Edgar Rice Burroughs. The world really cracked open then, showed me dimensions that were sideways, threw me on a tilt-a-whirl full of magic that made all the magic before as small and dim as a birthday cake candle. It's hard to beat a world where all the women are beautiful and go naked, and men carry swords, monsters are slain, and it's all a simple morality tale. For boys, swords, naked women, and simple views are way cool. And did I mention naked women?

So you get the idea. I was dipped and battered and buttered and way deep fried in the idea of the hero; the idea that what was noble could stand against anything what was not; that a good man need do no more than put his chest out, keep his eyes lifted, and plod forward; bullies were cowards and dogs were your friends. Right against wrong. Good against evil. America against them.

And then, the sixties rose up over the horizon, head first, long-haired and skeptical, and things went topsy. I learned a valuable lesson. A lot of what I had been taught about right and wrong, the simplicity of it, the American view, was not exactly on the money. Certain dreams and illusions were crucified on the crosses of reality, and though some of those dreams climbed down from the cross, alive and breathing, if a little wounded, the dead ones remained dead, not risen, not reborn, just dead. Same as Jesus, I might add.

So, like the Lone Ranger, I rode on into the shadow of change, the nineteen-sixties, and when I rode out, I was a different person, still masked, still riding, but my clothes were ripped and dirty and the hat was gone, the long-haired head I now possessed was bowed, and the horse, man, he was tired. My view on dogs, though, even tired and barely mounted, has never changed. They're still way cool. And I suppose I have to mention cats in passing. I wish them the best, including my two, but I was never crazy about them.

Backtrack.

The wind of the sixties started to build after the death of John F. Kennedy, who gave our country a big dose of hope and respect for intelligence, education, and longer hairdos. When he was gone something ripped in the fabric of space and time, and from those dimensions something crawled free that could only be seen out of the corner of the eye during a certain moment in the day when the light was right (or wrong), and that something was a reality check.

Even the good can die.

Even the young can die.

Nothing happens to you if you wear white after Labor Day.

I started reading Hemingway and Fitzgerald and Faulkner and Flannery O'Connor, bless her violent heart, and Carson McCullers and William S.

Burroughs (interesting, but no fan here), and so many others, and they touched me, because they were about people, they were about ideas; and then came Chandler and Hammett and Cain with people who talked like people I knew. Complex stories, not necessarily always better, but different, and there was a bleed over in my mind between literary and pulp, comics and the art of Peter Max, Remington, and Dalí, men on horses and melting clocks.

A wind started to blow, turned sour and hot, picked up in force. At first the wind just brought us tie-dyed T-shirts and longer hair than even Kennedy wore, some cool music with loud guitars, The Beatles, by God, and there were good things in this strong wind, like civil rights, and recognition that the Vietnam War might not be one of America's good wars. For a brief romantic moment it looked as if the world could change, that we could be those brave and good and heroic people of our comic book dreams... But it was just a moment. That door slammed, and then came too many disappointments, the stupidity of drugs, and finally hate, on both sides, and the wind became a tornado of confusion. Our country split between straights and freaks, liberals and conservatives. Kind of the way it is now, only worse.

I dropped out of college.

I was drafted.

I refused to go.

I was told I'd go to prison.

I didn't. Thank goodness.

They ended up giving me a rating called 1-Y, which meant they drafted criminals before they drafted me. I didn't think right. I didn't agree. There was, according to them, something wrong with my head. I was against America's absolute and certain rightness, which, I no longer believed. Not because I had lost the ethics I had learned from my heroes, but because I suddenly realized our country, not as a whole, but in many places and a variety of ways, didn't abide by the ethics, the goodness that it presented in its comics and TV shows. I was shocked to discover that life was more complicated and full of liars and back-stabbing assholes. Not just the obvious villains, but the folks we were supposed to respect.

I learned from my mother that racial hatred was wrong. That women could be trained to do what men could do; that they weren't inferior, just different. My father taught me to be a skeptic, not a paranoid, but someone who wasn't afraid to question the "facts." I dropped out. I didn't drink and didn't take drugs, but I did find a place to farm and relax and to avoid the world for a while. I went back to the land with a stack of books and a wonderful wife. I love my country, but not blindly. I love my wife blindly. I love my family blindly. And, of course, the dog.

I began to write. I found it to be the best way to deal with life, all of my anger and disappointment went into the work; a reason so much of it is violent and weird, dear hearts.

Life and literature and film and comics and race relations (or lack there of) and my disappointment over lying politicians and stupid wars and hatred of anything different or strange or not of America all rolled together with my new found interests in anthropology and archeology and sociology and psychology, surrealism and experimental ideas, and what first came out was just some re-hash of things that had gone before, and then at some point, the scab popped off and the pus that was me leaked out, and it produced...

Stories...so many stories. It's hard to believe that it was me who wrote them. Or some version of me, the me that was me at the time.

I apologize for the trip to get you here, to tell you some of the things that I loved that led to these stories based on my crucified dreams. Many of my early truths were sabotaged, but not entirely lost. Some, like a broken boat, are still floating on the surface of the water, but amidst a howling storm with nothing left but the devil and the deep blue sea.

This is some of the refuse left from my boat, scooped out with a net. My childhood passions remain in the fragments, sometimes in the ripped cloth of the sails, and even those pieces of the boat that are intact are not without stains. This then is an overview of my work over the past thirty-five years. Little is presented here from the very early years, but nothing here is without the experience of those years. These stories are all of me and I am all of them. They are not the totality of my life, but they are a portion of my life, and my life is often expressed in them, if only metaphorically and symbolically. I hope at least some of them will appeal to you, that in many cases sparks will fly and they will serve as some kind of fuel for your internal combustion engine. I hope there might be an insight, an occasional profundity. And if there are none of these things, may they at least entertain you, the most important part of any story.

These stories are only a few of the stories I have produced. There are many more out there, some good, some better, a few, if you'll pardon the conceit, that are very good, and a few that are like obnoxious relatives whose kinship you'd rather not admit to. But these are the ones we have chosen. These are the ones that allow readers interested in my work to stand back and look at the variety.

How should you feel about them? Obviously, I leave that to you. I hope you will like them enough to seek out others, and I hope, there will be many more to come.

And so the paint mixer winds down and the nostalgia dries up, and in the end, what I have written is probably nothing more than the old saw about the sound and the fury signifying nothing.

But it's my nothing.

Godzilla's Twelve-Step Program

ONE: HONEST WORK

Godzilla, on his way to work at the foundry, sees a large building that seems to be mostly made of shiny copper and dark, reflecting solar glass. He sees his image in the glass and thinks of the old days, wonders what it would be like to stomp on the building, to blow flames at it, kiss the windows black with his burning breath, then dance rapturously in the smoking debris.

One day at a time, he tells himself. One day at a time.

Godzilla makes himself look at the building hard. He passes it by. He goes to the foundry. He puts on his hard hat. He blows his fiery breath into the great vat full of used car parts, turns the car parts to molten metal. The metal runs through pipes and into new molds for new car parts. Doors. Roofs. Etc.

Godzilla feels some of the tension drain out.

TWO: RECREATION

After work Godzilla stays away from downtown. He feels tense. To stop blowing flames after work is difficult. He goes over to the BIG MONSTER RECREATION CENTER.

Gorgo is there. Drunk from oily seawater, as usual. Gorgo talks about the old days. She's like that. Always the old days.

They go out back and use their breath on the debris that is deposited there daily for the center's use. Kong is out back. Drunk as a monkey. He's playing with Barbie dolls. He does that all the time. Finally, he puts the Barbies away in his coat pocket, takes hold of his walker and wobbles past Godzilla and Gorgo.

Gorgo says, "Since the fall he ain't been worth shit. And what's with him and the little plastic broads anyway? Don't he know there's real women in the world?"

Godzilla thinks Gorgo looks at Kong's departing walker-supported ass a little too wistfully. He's sure he sees wetness in Gorgo's eyes.

Godzilla blows some scrap to cinders for recreation, but it doesn't do much for him, as he's been blowing fire all day long and has, at best, merely taken the edge off his compulsions. This isn't even as satisfying as the foundry. He goes home.

THREE: SEX AND DESTRUCTION

That night there's a monster movie on television. The usual one. Big beasts wrecking havoc on city after city. Crushing pedestrians under foot.

Godzilla examines the bottom of his right foot, looks at the scar there from stomping cars flat. He remembers how it was to have people squish between his toes. He thinks about all of that and changes the channel. He watches twenty minutes of *Mr. Ed*, turns off the TV, masturbates to the images of burning cities and squashing flesh.

Later, deep into the night, he awakens in a cold sweat. He goes to the bathroom and quickly carves crude human figures from bars of soap. He mashes the soap between his toes, closes his eyes and imagines. Tries to remember.

FOUR: BEACH TRIP AND THE BIG TURTLE

Saturday, Godzilla goes to the beach. A drunk monster that looks like a big turtle flies by and bumps Godzilla. The turtle calls Godzilla a name, looking for a fight. Godzilla remembers the turtle is called Gamera.

Gamera is always trouble. No one liked Gamera. The turtle was a real asshole.

Godzilla grits his teeth and holds back the flames. He turns his back and walks along the beach. He mutters a secret mantra given him by his sponsor. The giant turtle follows after, calling him names.

Godzilla packs up his beach stuff and goes home. At his back he hears the turtle, still cussing, still pushing. It's all he can do not to respond to the big dumb bastard. All he can do. He knows the turtle will be in the news tomorrow. He will have destroyed something, or will have been destroyed himself.

Godzilla thinks perhaps he should try and talk to the turtle, get him on the twelve-step program. That's what you're supposed to do. Help others. Maybe the turtle could find some peace.

The Best of Joe R. Lansdale

But then again, you can only help those who help themselves. Godzilla realizes he cannot save all the monsters of the world. They have to make these decisions for themselves. But he makes a mental note to go armed with leaflets about the twelve-step program from now on.

Later, he calls in to his sponsor. Tells him he's had a bad day. That he wanted to burn buildings and fight the big turtle. Reptilicus tells him it's okay. He's had days like that. Will have days like that once again.

Once a monster, always a monster. But a recovering monster is where it's at. Take it one day at a time. It's the only way to be happy in the world. You can't burn and kill and chew up humans and their creations without paying the price of guilt and multiple artillery wounds.

Godzilla thanks Reptilicus and hangs up. He feels better for a while, but deep down he wonders just how much guilt he really harbors. He thinks maybe it's the artillery and the rocket-firing jets he really hates, not the guilt.

FIVE: OFF THE WAGON

It happens suddenly. He falls off the wagon. Coming back from work he sees a small doghouse with a sleeping dog sticking halfway out of a doorway. There's no one around. The dog looks old. It's on a chain. Probably miserable anyway. The water dish is empty. The dog is living a worthless life. Chained. Bored. No water.

Godzilla leaps and comes down on the doghouse and squashes dog in all directions. He burns what's left of the doghouse with a blast of his breath. He leaps and spins on tip-toe through the wreckage. Black cinders and cooked dog slip through his toes and remind him of the old days.

He gets away fast. No one has seen him. He feels giddy. He can hardly walk he's so intoxicated. He calls Reptilicus, gets his answering machine. "I'm not in right now. I'm out doing good. But please leave a message, and I'll get right back to you."

The machine beeps. Godzilla says, "Help."

SIX: HIS SPONSOR

The doghouse rolls around in his head all the next day. While at work he thinks of the dog and the way it burned. He thinks of the little house and the way it crumbled. He thinks of the dance he did in the ruins.

The day drags on forever. He thinks maybe when work is through he might find another doghouse, another dog.

On the way home he keeps an eye peeled, but no doghouses or dogs are seen.

When he gets home his answering machine light is blinking. It's a message from Reptilicus. Reptilicus's voice says, "Call me."

Godzilla does. He says, "Reptilicus. Forgive me, for I have sinned."

SEVEN: DISILLUSIONED. DISAPPOINTED.

Reptilicus's talk doesn't help much. Godzilla shreds all the twelve-step program leaflets. He wipes his butt on a couple and throws them out the window. He puts the scraps of the others in the sink and sets them on fire with his breath. He burns a coffee table and a chair, and when he's through, feels bad for it. He knows the landlady will expect him to replace them.

He turns on the radio and lies on the bed listening to an Oldies station. After a while, he falls asleep to Martha and the Vandellas singing "Heat Wave."

EIGHT: UNEMPLOYED

Godzilla dreams. In it God comes to him, all scaly and blowing fire. He tells Godzilla he's ashamed of him. He says he should do better. Godzilla awakes covered in sweat. No one is in the room.

Godzilla feels guilt. He has faint memories of waking up and going out to destroy part of the city. He really tied one on, but he can't remember everything he did. Maybe he'll read about it in the papers. He notices he smells like charred lumber and melted plastic. There's gooshy stuff between his toes, and something tells him it isn't soap.

He wants to kill himself. He goes to look for his gun, but he's too drunk to find it. He passes out on the floor. He dreams of the Devil this time. He looks just like God except he has one eyebrow that goes over both eyes. The Devil says he's come for Godzilla

Godzilla moans and fights. He dreams he gets up and takes pokes at the Devil, blows ineffective fire on him.

Godzilla rises late the next morning, hung over. He remembers the dream. He calls in to work sick. Sleeps off most of the day. That evening, he reads about himself in the papers. He really did some damage. Smoked a large part of the city. There's a very clear picture of him biting the head off of a woman.

He gets a call from the plant manager that night. The manager's seen the paper. He tells Godzilla he's fired.

NINE: ENTICEMENT

Next day some humans show up. They're wearing black suits and white shirts and polished shoes and they've got badges. They've got guns, too. One of them says, "You're a problem. Our government wants to send you back to Japan."

"They hate me there," says Godzilla. "I burned Tokyo down."

"You haven't done so good here either. Lucky that was a colored section of town you burned, or we'd be on your ass. As it is, we've got a job proposition for you."

"What?" Godzilla asks.

"You scratch our back, we'll scratch yours." Then the men tell him what they have in mind.

TEN: CHOOSING

Godzilla sleeps badly that night. He gets up and plays the "Monster Mash" on his little record player. He dances around the room as if he's enjoying himself, but knows he's not. He goes over to the BIG MONSTER RECREATION CENTER. He sees Kong there, on a stool, undressing one of his Barbies, fingering the smooth spot between her legs. He sees that Kong has drawn a crack there, like a vagina. It appears to have been drawn with a blue ink pen. He's feathered the central line with ink-drawn pubic hair. Godzilla thinks he should have got someone to do the work for him. It doesn't look all that natural.

God, he doesn't want to end up like Kong. Completely spaced. Then again, maybe if he had some dolls he could melt, maybe that would serve to relax him.

No. After the real thing, what was a Barbie? Some kind of form of Near Beer. That's what the debris out back was. Near Beer. The foundry. The Twelve-Step Program. All of it. Near Beer.

ELEVEN: WORKING FOR THE GOVERNMENT

Godzilla calls the government assholes. "All right," he says. "I'll do it."

"Good," says the government man. "We thought you would. Check your mail box. The map and instructions are there."

Godzilla goes outside and looks in his box. There's a manila envelope there. Inside are instructions. They say: "Burn all the spots you see on the map. You finish those, we'll find others. No penalties. Just make sure no one escapes. Any rioting starts, you finish them. To the last man, woman and child."

Godzilla unfolds the map. On it are red marks. Above the red marks are listings: *Nigger Town. Chink Village. White Trash Enclave. A Clutch of Queers. Mostly Democrats.*

Godzilla thinks about what he can do now. Unbidden. He can burn without guilt. He can stomp without guilt. Not only that, they'll send him a check. He has been hired by his adopted country to clean out the bad spots as they see them.

TWELVE: THE FINAL STEP

Godzilla stops near the first place on the list: *Nigger Town.* He sees kids playing in the streets. Dogs. Humans looking up at him, wondering what the hell he's doing here.

Godzilla suddenly feels something move inside him. He knows he's being used. He turns around and walks away. He heads toward the government section of town. He starts with the governor's mansion. He goes wild. Artillery is brought out, but it's no use, he's rampaging. Like the old days.

Reptilicus shows up with a megaphone, tries to talk Godzilla down from the top of the Great Monument Building, but Godzilla doesn't listen. He's burning the top of the building off with his breath, moving down, burning some more, moving down, burning some more, all the way to the ground.

Kong shows up and cheers him on. Kong drops his walker and crawls along the road on his belly and reaches a building and pulls himself up and starts climbing. Bullets spark all around the big ape.

Godzilla watches as Kong reaches the summit of the building and clings by one hand and waves the other, which contains a Barbie doll.

Kong puts the Barbie doll between his teeth. He reaches in his coat and brings out a naked Ken doll. Godzilla can see that Kong has made Ken some kind of penis out of silly putty or something. The penis is as big as Ken's leg.

Kong is yelling, "Yeah, that's right. That's right. I'm AC/DC, you sonsofa-bitches."

Jets appear and swoop down on Kong. The big ape catches a load of rocket right in the teeth. Barbie, teeth and brains decorate the graying sky. Kong falls.

Gorgo comes out of the crowd and bends over the ape, takes him in her arms and cries. Kong's hand slowly opens, revealing Ken, his penis broken off.

The flying turtle shows up and starts trying to steal Godzilla's thunder, but Godzilla isn't having it. He tears the top off the building Kong had mounted and beats Gamera with it. Even the cops and the army cheer over this.

Godzilla beats and beats the turtle, splattering turtle meat all over the place, like an overheated poodle in a microwave. A few quick pedestrians gather up chunks of the turtle meat to take home and cook, 'cause the rumor is it tastes just like chicken.

Godzilla takes a triple shot of rockets in the chest, staggers, goes down. Tanks gather around him.

Godzilla opens his bloody mouth and laughs. He thinks: If I'd have gotten finished here, then I'd have done the black people too. I'd have gotten the yellow people and the white trash and the homosexuals. I'm an equal opportunity destroyer. To hell with the twelve-step program. To hell with humanity.

Then Godzilla dies and makes a mess on the street. Military men tip-toe around the mess and hold their noses.

Later, Gorgo claims Kong's body and leaves.

Reptilicus, being interviewed by television reporters, says, "Zilla was almost there, man. Almost. If he could have completed the program, he'd have been all right. But the pressures of society were too much for him. You can't blame him for what society made of him."

On the way home, Reptilicus thinks about all the excitement. The burning buildings. The gunfire. Just like the old days when he and Zilla and Kong and that goon-ball turtle were young.

Reptilicus thinks of Kong's defiance, waving the Ken doll, the Barbie in his teeth. He thinks of Godzilla, laughing as he died.

Reptilicus finds a lot of old feelings resurfacing. They're hard to fight. He locates a lonesome spot and a dark house and urinates through an open window, then goes home.

Bubba Ho-Tep

ELVIS DREAMED HE had his dick out, checking to see if the bump on the head of it had filled with pus again. If it had, he was going to name the bump Priscilla, after his ex-wife, and bust it by jacking off. Or he liked to think that's what he'd do. Dreams let you think like that. The truth was, he hadn't had a hard-on in years.

That bitch, Priscilla. Gets a new hairdo and she's gone, just because she caught him fucking a big tittied gospel singer. It wasn't like the singer had mattered. Priscilla ought to have understood that, so what was with her making a big deal out of it?

Was it because she couldn't hit a high note the same and as good as the singer when she came?

When had that happened anyway, Priscilla leaving?

Yesterday? Last year? Ten years ago?

Oh God, it came to him instantly as he slipped out of sleep like a soft turd squeezed free of a loose asshole, for he could hardly think of himself or life in any context other than sewage, since so often he was too tired to do anything other than let it all fly in his sleep, wake up in an ocean of piss or shit, waiting for the nurses or the aides to come in and wipe his ass. But now it came to him. Suddenly he realized it had been years ago that he had supposedly died, and longer years than that since Priscilla left, and how old was she anyway? Sixty-five? Seventy?

And how old was he?

Christ! He was almost convinced he was too old to be alive, and had to be dead, but he wasn't convinced enough, unfortunately. He knew where he was now, and in that moment of realization, he sincerely wished he was dead. This was worse than death.

From across the room, his roommate, Bull Thomas, bellowed and coughed and moaned and fell back into painful sleep, the cancer gnawing at his insides like a rat plugged up inside a watermelon.

Bull's bellow of pain and anger and indignation at growing old and diseased was the only thing bullish about him now, though Elvis had seen photographs of him when he was younger, and Bull had been very bullish indeed. Thick-chested, slab-faced and tall. Probably thought he'd live forever, and happily. A boozing, pill-popping, swinging dick until the end of time.

Now Bull was shrunk down, was little more than a wrinkled sheet-white husk that throbbed with occasional pulses of blood while the carcinoma fed.

Elvis took hold of the bed's lift button, eased himself upright. He glanced at Bull. Bull was breathing heavily and his bony knees rose up and down like he was peddling a bicycle; his kneecaps punched feebly at the sheet, making puptents that rose up and collapsed, rose up and collapsed.

Elvis looked down at the sheet stretched over his own bony knees. He thought: *My God, how long have I been here? Am I really awake now, or am I dreaming I'm awake? How could my plans have gone so wrong? When are they going to serve lunch, and considering what they serve, why do I care? And if Priscilla discovered I was alive, would she come see me, would she want to see me, and would we still want to fuck, or would we have to merely talk about it? Is there finally, and really, anything to life other than food and shit and sex?*

Elvis pushed the sheet down to do what he had done in the dream. He pulled up his gown, leaned forward, and examined his dick. It was wrinkled and small. It didn't look like something that had dive-bombed movie starlet pussies or filled their mouths like a big zucchini or pumped forth a load of sperm frothy as cake icing. The healthiest thing about his pecker was the big red bump with the black ring around it and the pus-filled white center. Fact was, that bump kept growing, he was going to have to pull a chair up beside his bed and put a pillow in it so the bump would have some place to sleep at night. There was more pus in that damn bump than there was cum in his loins. The old diddlebopper was no longer a flesh cannon loaded for bare ass. It was a peanut too small to harvest; wasting away on the vine. His nuts were a couple of darkening, about-to-rot grapes, too limp to produce juice for life's wine. His legs were stick-and-paper things with over-large, vein-swollen feet on the ends. His belly was such a bloat, it was a pain for him to lean forward and scrutinize his dick and balls.

Pulling his gown down and the sheet back over himself, Elvis leaned back and wished he had a peanut butter and banana sandwich fried in butter. There had been a time when he and his crew would board his private jet and fly clean across country just to have a special made fried peanut butter and 'nanner sandwich. He could still taste the damn things.

Elvis closed his eyes and thought he would awake from a bad dream, but didn't. He opened his eyes again, slowly, and saw that he was still where he had been, and things were no better. He reached over and opened his dresser drawer and got out a little round mirror and looked at himself.

He was horrified. His hair was white as salt and had receded dramatically. He had wrinkles deep enough to conceal outstretched earthworms, the big ones, the night crawlers. His pouty mouth no longer appeared pouty. It looked like the drooping waddles of a bulldog, seeming more that way because he was slobbering a mite. He dragged his tired tongue across his lips to daub the slobber, revealed to himself in the mirror that he was missing a lot of teeth.

Goddamn it! How had he gone from King of Rock and Roll to this? Old guy in a rest home in East Texas with a growth on his dick?

And what was that growth? Cancer? No one was talking. No one seemed to know. Perhaps the bump was a manifestation of the mistakes of his life, so many of them made with his dick.

He considered on that. Did he ask himself this question every day, or just now and then? Time sort of ran together when the last moment and the immediate moment and the moment forthcoming were all alike.

Shit, when was lunch time? Had he slept through it?

Was it about time for his main nurse again? The good looking one with the smooth chocolate skin and tits like grapefruits? The one who came in and sponge bathed him and held his pitiful little pecker in her gloved hands and put salve on his canker with all the enthusiasm of a mechanic oiling a defective part?

He hoped not. That was the worst of it. A doll like that handling him without warmth or emotion. Twenty years ago, just twenty, he could have made with the curled lip smile and had her eating out of his asshole. Where had his youth gone? Why hadn't fame denied old age and death, and why had he left his fame in the first place, and did he want it back, and could he have it back, and if he could, would it make any difference?

And finally, when he was evacuated from the bowels of life into the toilet bowl of the beyond and was flushed, would the great sewer pipe flow him to the other side where God would — in the guise of a great all-seeing turd with corn kernel eyes — be waiting with open turd arms, and would there be amongst the sewage his mother (bless her fat little heart) and father and friends, waiting with fried peanut butter and 'nanner sandwiches and ice cream cones, predigested, or course?

He was reflecting on this, pondering the afterlife, when Bull gave out with a hell of a scream, pooched his eyes damn near out of his head, arched his back, grease-farted like a blast from Gabriel's trumpet, and checked his tired old soul out of the Mud Creek Shady Grove Convalescence Home; flushed it on out and across the great shitty beyond.

Later that day, Elvis lay sleeping, his lips fluttering the bad taste of lunch — steamed zucchini and boiled peas — out of his belly. He awoke to a noise, rolled over to see a young attractive woman cleaning out Bull's dresser drawer. The curtains over the window next to Bull's bed were pulled wide open, and the sunlight was cutting through it and showing her to great advantage. She was blonde and Nordic-featured and her long hair was tied back with a big red bow and she wore big, gold, hoop earrings that shimmered in the sunlight. She was dressed in a white blouse and a short black skirt and dark hose and high heels. The heels made her ass ride up beneath her skirt like soft bald baby heads under a thin blanket.

She had a big, yellow plastic trashcan and she had one of Bull's dresser drawers pulled out, and she was picking through it, like a magpie looking for bright things. She found a few coins, a pocket knife, a cheap watch. These were plucked free and laid on the dresser top, then the remaining contents of the drawer — Bull's photographs of himself when young, a rotten pack of rubbers (wishful thinking never deserted Bull), a bronze star and a Purple Heart from his performance in the Vietnam War — were dumped into the trashcan with a bang and a flutter.

Elvis got hold of his bed lift button and raised himself for a better look. The woman had her back to him now, and didn't notice. She was replacing the dresser drawer and pulling out another. It was full of clothes. She took out the few shirts and pants and socks and underwear, and laid them on Bull's bed remade now, and minus Bull, who had been toted off to be taxidermied, embalmed, burned up, whatever.

"You're gonna toss that stuff," Elvis said. "Could I have one of them pictures of Bull? Maybe that Purple Heart? He was proud of it."

The young woman turned and looked at him, "I suppose," she said. She went to the trashcan and bent over it and showed her black panties to Elvis as she rummaged. He knew the revealing of her panties was neither intentional or unintentional. She just didn't give a damn. She saw him as so physically and sexually non-threatening, she didn't mind if he got a bird's-eye view of her; it was the same to her as a house cat sneaking a peek.

Elvis observed the thin panties straining and slipping into the caverns of her ass cheeks and felt his pecker flutter once, like a bird having a heart attack, then it laid down and remained limp and still.

Well, these days, even a flutter was kind of reassuring.

The woman surfaced from the trashcan with a photo and the Purple Heart, went over to Elvis's bed and handed them to him.

Elvis dangled the ribbon that held the Purple Heart between his fingers, said, "Bull your kin?"

"My daddy," she said.

"I haven't seen you here before."

"Only been here once before," she said. "When I checked him in."

"Oh," Elvis said. "That was three years ago, wasn't it?"

"Yeah. Were you and him friends?"

Elvis considered the question. He didn't know the real answer. All he knew was Bull listened to him when he said he was Elvis Presley and seemed to believe him. If he didn't believe him, he at least had the courtesy not to patronize. Bull always called him Elvis, and before Bull grew too ill, he always played cards and checkers with him.

"Just roommates," Elvis said. "He didn't feel good enough to say much. I just sort of hated to see what was left of him go away so easy. He was an all right guy. He mentioned you a lot. You're Callie, right?"

"Yeah," she said. "Well, he was all right."

"Not enough you came and saw him though."

"Don't try to put some guilt trip on me, Mister. I did what I could. Hadn't been for Medicaid, Medicare, whatever that stuff was, he'd have been in a ditch somewhere. I didn't have the money to take care of him."

Elvis thought of his own daughter, lost long ago to him. If she knew he lived, would she come to see him? Would she care? He feared knowing the answer.

"You could have come and seen him," Elvis said.

"I was busy. Mind your own business. Hear?"

The chocolate-skin nurse with the grapefruit tits came in. Her white uniform crackled like cards being shuffled. Her little white nurse hat was tilted on her head in a way that said she loved mankind and made good money and was getting regular dick. She smiled at Callie and then at Elvis. "How are you this morning, Mr. Haff?"

"All right," Elvis said. "But I prefer Mr. Presley. Or Elvis. I keep telling you that. I don't go by Sebastian Haff anymore. I don't try to hide anymore."

"Why, of course," said the pretty nurse. "I knew that. I forgot. Good morning, Elvis."

Her voice dripped with sorghum syrup. Elvis wanted to hit her with his bed pan.

The nurse said to Callie: "Did you know we have a celebrity here, Miss Jones? Elvis Presley. You know, the rock and roll singer?"

"I've heard of him," Callie said. "I thought he was dead."

Callie went back to the dresser and squatted and set to work on the bottom drawer. The nurse looked at Elvis and smiled again, only she spoke to Callie. "Well, actually, Elvis is dead, and Mr. Haff knows that, don't you, Mr. Haff?"

"Hell no," said Elvis. "I'm right here. I ain't dead, yet."

"Now, Mr. Haff, I don't mind calling you Elvis, but you're a little confused, or like to play sometimes. You were an Elvis impersonator. Remember? You fell off a stage and broke your hip. What was it...Twenty years ago? It got infected and you went into a coma for a few years. You came out with a few problems."

"I was impersonating myself," Elvis said. "I couldn't do nothing else. I haven't got any problems. You're trying to say my brain is messed up, aren't you?"

Callie quit cleaning out the bottom drawer of the dresser. She was interested now, and though it was no use, Elvis couldn't help but try and explain who he was, just one more time. The explaining had become a habit, like wanting to smoke a cigar long after the enjoyment of it was gone.

"I got tired of it all," he said. "I got on drugs, you know. I wanted out. Fella named Sebastian Haff, an Elvis imitator, the best of them. He took my place. He had a bad heart and he liked drugs, too. It was him died, not me. I took his place."

"Why would you want to leave all that fame," Callie said, "all that money?" and she looked at the nurse, like *Let's humor the old fart for a lark.*

"'Cause it got old. Woman I loved, Priscilla, she was gone. Rest of the women...were just women. The music wasn't mine anymore. I wasn't even me anymore. I was this thing they made up. Friends were sucking me dry. I got away and liked it, left all the money with Sebastian, except for enough to sustain me if things got bad. We had a deal, me and Sebastian. When I wanted to come back, he'd let me. It was all written up in a contract in case he wanted to give me a hard time, got to liking my life too good. Thing was, copy of the contract I had got lost in a trailer fire. I was living simple. Way Haff had been. Going from town to town doing the Elvis act. Only I felt like I was really me again. Can you dig that?"

"We're digging it, Mr. Haff...Mr. Presley," said the pretty nurse.

"I was singing the old way. Doing some new songs. Stuff I wrote. I was getting attention on a small but good scale. Women throwing themselves at me, 'cause they could imagine I was Elvis — only I was Elvis, playing Sebastian

Haff playing Elvis… It was all pretty good. I didn't mind the contract being burned up. I didn't even try to go back and convince anybody. Then I had the accident. Like I was saying, I'd laid up a little money in case of illness, stuff like that. That's what's paying for here. These nice facilities. Ha!"

"Now, Elvis," the nurse said. "Don't carry it too far. You may just get way out there and not come back."

"Oh fuck you," Elvis said.

The nurse giggled.

Shit, Elvis thought. *Get old, you can't even cuss somebody and have it bother them. Everything you do is either worthless or sadly amusing.*

"You know, Elvis," said the pretty nurse, "we have a Mr. Dillinger here too. And a President Kennedy. He says the bullet only wounded him and his brain is in a fruit jar at the White House, hooked up to some wires and a battery, and as long as the battery works, he can walk around without it. His brain, that is. You know, he says everyone was in on trying to assassinate him. Even Elvis Presley."

"You're an asshole," Elvis said.

"I'm not trying to hurt your feelings, Mr. Haff," the nurse said. "I'm merely trying to give you a reality check."

"You can shove that reality check right up your pretty black ass," Elvis said.

The nurse made a sad little snicking sound. "Mr. Haff, Mr. Haff. Such language."

"What happened to get you here?" said Callie. "Say you fell off a stage?"

"I was gyrating," Elvis said. "Doing 'Blue Moon,' but my hip went out. I'd been having trouble with it." Which was quite true. He'd sprained it making love to a blue-haired old lady with ELVIS tattooed on her fat ass. He couldn't help himself from wanting to fuck her. She looked like his mother, Gladys.

"You swiveled right off the stage?" Callie said. "Now that's sexy."

Elvis looked at her. She was smiling. This was great fun for her, listening to some nut tell a tale. She hadn't had this much fun since she put her old man in the rest home.

"Oh, leave me the hell alone," Elvis said.

The women smiled at one another, passing a private joke. Callie said to the nurse: "I've got what I want." She scraped the bright things off the top of Bull's dresser into her purse. "The clothes can go to Goodwill or the Salvation Army."

The pretty nurse nodded to Callie. "Very well. And I'm very sorry about your father. He was a nice man."

"Yeah," said Callie, and she started out of there. She paused at the foot of Elvis's bed. "Nice to meet you, Mr. Presley."

"Get the hell out," Elvis said.

"Now, now," said the pretty nurse, patting his foot through the covers, as if it were a little cantankerous dog. "I'll be back later to do that…little thing that has to be done. You know?"

"I know," Elvis said, not liking the words "little thing."

Callie and the nurse started away then, punishing him with the clean lines of their faces and the sheen of their hair, the jiggle of their asses and tits. When they were out of sight, Elvis heard them laugh about something in the hall, then they were gone, and Elvis felt as if he were on the far side of Pluto without a jacket. He picked up the ribbon with the Purple Heart and looked at it.

Poor Bull. In the end, did anything really matter?

Meanwhile…

The Earth swirled around the sun like a spinning turd in the toilet bowl (to keep up with Elvis's metaphors) and the good old abused Earth clicked about on its axis and the hole in the ozone spread slightly wider, like a shy lady fingering open her vagina, and the South American trees that had stood for centuries, were visited by the dozer, the chainsaw and the match, and they rose up in burned black puffs that expanded and dissipated into minuscule wisps, and while the puffs of smoke dissolved, there were IRA bombings in London, and there was more war in the Mideast. Blacks died in Africa of famine, the HIV virus infected a million more, the Dallas Cowboys lost again, and that Ole Blue Moon that Elvis and Patsy Cline sang so well about, swung around the Earth and came in close and rose over the Shady Grove Convalescent Home, shone its bittersweet, silver-blue rays down on the joint like a flashlight beam shining through a blue-haired lady's 'do, and inside the rest home, evil waddled about like a duck looking for a spot to squat, and Elvis rolled over in his sleep and awoke with the intense desire to pee.

All right, thought Elvis. *This time I make it.* No more piss or crap in the bed. (Famous last words.)

Elvis sat up and hung his feet over the side of the bed and the bed swung far to the left and around the ceiling and back, and then it wasn't moving at all. The dizziness passed.

Elvis looked at his walker and sighed, leaned forward, took hold of the grips and eased himself off the bed and clumped the rubber padded tips forward, and made for the toilet.

He was in the process of milking his bump-swollen weasel, when he heard something in the hallway — a kind of scrambling, like a big spider scuttling about in a box of gravel.

There was always some sound in the hallway, people coming and going, yelling in pain or confusion, but this time of night, three A.M., was normally quite dead.

It shouldn't have concerned him, but the truth of the matter was, now that he was up and had successfully pissed in the pot, he was no longer sleepy; he was still thinking about that bimbo, Callie, and the nurse (What the hell was her name?) with the tits like grapefruits, and all they had said.

Elvis stumped his walker backwards out of the bathroom, turned it, made his way forward into the hall. The hall was semi-dark, with every other light out, and the lights that were on were dimmed to a watery egg yoke yellow. The black and white tile floor looked like a great chessboard, waxed and buffed for the next game of life, and here he was, a semi-crippled pawn, ready to go.

Off in the far wing of the home, Old Lady McGee, better known in the home as The Blue Yodeler, broke into one of her famous yodels (she claimed to have sung with a country and western band in her youth), then ceased abruptly. Elvis swung the walker forward and moved on. He hadn't been out of his room in ages, and he hadn't been out of his bed much either. Tonight, he felt invigorated because he hadn't pissed his bed, and he'd heard the sound again, the spider in the box of gravel. (Big spider. Big box. Lots of gravel.) And following the sound gave him something to do.

Elvis rounded the corner, beads of sweat popping out on his forehead like heat blisters. Jesus. He wasn't invigorated now. Thinking about how invigorated he was had bushed him. Still, going back to his room to lie on his bed and wait for morning so he could wait for noon, then afternoon and night, didn't appeal to him.

He went by Jack McLaughlin's room, the fellow who was convinced he was John F. Kennedy, and that his brain was in the White House running on batteries. The door to Jack's room was open. Elvis peeked in as he moved by, knowing full well that Jack might not want to see him. Sometimes he accepted Elvis as the real Elvis, and when he did, he got scared, saying it was Elvis who had been behind the assassination.

Actually, Elvis hoped he felt that way tonight. It would at least be some acknowledgment that he was who he was, even if the acknowledgment was a fearful shriek from a nut.

'Course, Elvis thought, *maybe I'm nuts too. Maybe I am Sebastian Haff and I fell off the stage and broke more than my hip, cracked some part of my brain that lost my old self and made me think I'm Elvis.*

No. He couldn't believe that. That's the way they wanted him to think. They wanted him to believe he was nuts and he wasn't Elvis, just some sad old fart who had once lived out part of another man's life because he had none of his own.

He wouldn't accept that. He wasn't Sebastian Haff. He was Elvis Goddamn Aaron Fucking Presley with a boil on his dick.

'Course, he believed that, maybe he ought to believe Jack was John F. Kennedy, and Mums Delay, another patient here at Shady Grove, was Dillinger. Then again, maybe not. They were kind of scanty on evidence. He at least looked like Elvis gone old and sick. Jack was black — he claimed The Powers That Be had dyed him that color to keep him hidden — and Mums was a woman who claimed she'd had a sex change operation.

Jesus, was this a rest home or a nut house?

Jack's room was one of the special kind. He didn't have to share. He had money from somewhere. The room was packed with books and little luxuries. And though Jack could walk well, he even had a fancy electric wheelchair that he rode about in sometimes. Once, Elvis had seen him riding it around the outside circular drive, popping wheelies and spinning doughnuts.

When Elvis looked into Jack's room, he saw him lying on the floor. Jack's gown was pulled up around his neck, and his bony black ass appeared to be made of licorice in the dim light. Elvis figured Jack had been on his way to the shitter, or was coming back from it, and had collapsed. His heart, maybe.

"Jack," Elvis said.

Elvis clumped into the room, positioned his walker next to Jack, took a deep breath and stepped out of it, supporting himself with one side of it. He got down on his knees beside Jack, hoping he'd be able to get up again. God, but his knees and back hurt.

Jack was breathing hard. Elvis noted the scar at Jack's hairline, a long scar that made Jack's skin lighter there, almost grey. ("That's where they took the brain out," Jack always explained, "put it in that fucking jar. I got a little bag of sand up there now.")

Elvis touched the old man's shoulder. "Jack. Man, you okay?"

No response.

Elvis tried again. "Mr. Kennedy."

"Uh," said Jack (Mr. Kennedy).

"Hey, man. You're on the floor," Elvis said.

"No shit? Who are you?"

Elvis hesitated. This wasn't the time to get Jack worked up.

"Sebastian," he said. "Sebastian Haff."

Elvis took hold of Jack's shoulder and rolled him over. It was about as difficult as rolling a jelly roll. Jack lay on his back now. He strayed an eyeball at Elvis. He started to speak, hesitated. Elvis took hold of Jack's nightgown and managed to work it down around Jack's knees, trying to give the old fart some dignity.

Jack finally got his breath. "Did you see him go by in the hall? He scuttled like."

"Who?"

"Someone they sent."

"Who's they?"

"You know. Lyndon Johnson. Castro. They've sent someone to finish me. I think maybe it was Johnson himself. Real ugly. Real goddamn ugly."

"Johnson's dead," Elvis said.

"That won't stop him," Jack said.

Later that morning, sunlight shooting into Elvis's room through Venetian blinds, Elvis put his hands behind his head and considered the night before while the pretty black nurse with the grapefruit tits salved his dick. He had reported Jack's fall and the aides had come to help Jack back in bed, and him back on his walker. He had clumped back to his room (after being scolded for being out there that time of night) feeling that an air of strangeness had blown into the rest home, an air that wasn't there the day before. It was at low ebb now, but certainly still present, humming in the background like some kind of generator ready to buzz up to a higher notch at a moment's notice.

And he was certain it wasn't just his imagination. The scuttling sound he'd heard last night, Jack had heard it, too. What was that all about? It wasn't the sound of a walker, or a crip dragging their foot, or a wheelchair creeping along, it was something else, and now that he thought about it, it wasn't exactly spider legs in gravel, more like a roll of barbed wire tumbling across tile.

Elvis was so wrapped up in these considerations, he lost awareness of the nurse until she said, "Mr. Haff!"

"What...?" He saw that she was smiling and looking down at her hands. He looked too. There, nestled in one of her gloved palms was a massive, blue-veined hooter with a pus-filled bump on it the size of a pecan. It was *his* hooter and *his* pus-filled bump.

"You ole rascal," she said, and gently lowered his dick between his legs. "I think you better take a cold shower, Mr. Haff."

Elvis was amazed. That was the first time in years he'd had a boner like that. What gave here?

Then he realized what gave. He wasn't thinking about not being able to do it. He was thinking about something that interested him, and now, with something clicking around inside his head besides old memories and confusions, concerns about his next meal and going to the crapper, he had been given a dose of life again. He grinned his gums and what teeth were in them at the nurse.

"You get in there with me," he said, "and I'll take that shower."

"You silly thing," she said, and pulled his nightgown down and stood and removed her plastic gloves and dropped them in the trash can beside his bed.

"Why don't you pull on it a little," Elvis said.

"You ought to be ashamed," the nurse said, but she smiled when she said it.

She left the room door open after she left. This concerned Elvis a little, but he felt his bed was at such an angle no one could look in, and if they did, tough luck. He wasn't going to look a gift hard-on in the pee-hole. He pulled the sheet over him and pushed his hands beneath the sheets and got his gown pulled up over his belly. He took hold of his snake and began to choke it with one hand, running his thumb over the pus-filled bump. With his other hand, he fondled his balls. He thought of Priscilla and the pretty black nurse and Bull's daughter and even the blue-haired fat lady with ELVIS tattooed on her butt, and he stroked harder and faster, and goddamn but he got stiffer and stiffer, and the bump on his cock gave up its load first, exploded hot pus down his thighs, and then his balls, which he thought forever empty, filled up with juice and electricity, and finally he threw the switch. The dam broke and the juice flew. He heard himself scream happily and felt hot wetness jetting down his legs, splattering as far as his big toes.

"Oh God," he said softly. "I like that. I like that."

He closed his eyes and slept. And for the first time in a long time, not fitfully.

Lunchtime. The Shady Grove lunch room.

Elvis sat with a plate of steamed carrots and broccoli and flaky roast beef in front of him. A dry roll, a pat of butter and a short glass of milk soldiered on the side. It was not inspiring.

Next to him, The Blue Yodeler was stuffing a carrot up her nose while she expounded on the sins of God, the Heavenly Father, for knocking up that nice Mary in her sleep, slipping up her ungreased poontang while she snored, and — bless her little heart — not even knowing it, or getting a clit throb from it, but waking up with a belly full of baby and no memory of action.

Elvis had heard it all before. It used to offend him, this talk of God as rapist, but he'd heard it so much now he didn't care. She rattled on.

Across the way, an old man who wore a black mask and sometimes a white stetson, known to residents and staff alike as Kemosabe, snapped one of his two capless cap pistols at the floor and called for an invisible Tonto to bend over so he could drive him home.

At the far end of the table, Dillinger was talking about how much whisky he used to drink, and how many cigars he used to smoke before he got his dick cut off at the stump and split so he could become a she and hide out as a woman. Now she said she no longer thought of banks and machine guns, women and fine cigars. She now thought about spots on dishes, the colors of curtains and drapes as coordinated with carpets and walls.

Even as the depression of his surroundings settled over him again, Elvis deliberated last night, and glanced down the length of the table at Jack (Mr. Kennedy) who headed its far end. He saw the old man was looking at him, as if they shared a secret. Elvis's ill mood dropped a notch; a real mystery was at work here, and come nightfall, he was going to investigate.

Swing the Shady Grove Convalescent Home's side of the Earth away from the sun again, and swing the moon in close and blue again. Blow some gauzy clouds across the nasty, black sky. Now ease on into three A.M.

Elvis awoke with a start and turned his head toward the intrusion. Jack stood next to the bed looking down at him. Jack was wearing a suit coat over his nightgown and he had on thick glasses. He said, "Sebastian. It's loose."

Elvis collected his thoughts, pasted them together into a not-too-scattered collage. "What's loose?"

"It," said Jack. "Listen."

Elvis listened. Out in the hall he heard the scuttling sound of the night before. Tonight, it reminded him of great locust wings beating frantically inside a small cardboard box, the tips of them scratching at the cardboard, cutting it, ripping it apart.

"Jesus Christ, what is it?" Elvis said.

"I thought it was Lyndon Johnson, but it isn't. I've come across new evidence that suggests another assassin."

"Assassin?"

Jack cocked an ear. The sound had gone away, moved distant, then ceased.

"It's got another target tonight," said Jack. "Come on. I want to show you something. I don't think it's safe if you go back to sleep."

"For Christ's sake," Elvis said. "Tell the administrators."

"The suits and the white starches," Jack said. "No thanks. I trusted them back when I was in Dallas, and look where that got my brain and me. I'm thinking with sand here, maybe picking up a few waves from my brain. Someday, who's to say they won't just disconnect the battery at the White House?"

"That's something to worry about, all right," Elvis said.

"Listen here," Jack said. "I know you're Elvis, and there were rumors, you know…about how you hated me, but I've thought it over. You hated me, you could have finished me the other night. All I want from you is to look me in the eye and assure me you had nothing to do with that day in Dallas, and that you never knew Lee Harvey Oswald or Jack Ruby."

Elvis stared at him as sincerely as possible. "I had nothing to do with Dallas, and I knew neither Lee Harvey Oswald or Jack Ruby."

"Good," said Jack. "May I call you Elvis instead of Sebastian?"

"You may."

"Excellent. You wear glasses to read?"

"I wear glasses when I really want to see," Elvis said.

"Get 'em and come on."

Elvis swung his walker along easily, not feeling as if he needed it too much tonight. He was excited. Jack was a nut, and maybe he himself was nuts, but there was an adventure going on.

They came to the hall restroom. The one reserved for male visitors. "In here," Jack said.

"Now wait a minute," Elvis said. "You're not going to get me in there and try and play with my pecker, are you?"

Jack stared at him. "Man, I made love to Jackie and Marilyn and a ton of others, and you think I want to play with your nasty ole dick?"

"Good point," said Elvis.

They went into the restroom. It was large, with several stalls and urinals.

"Over here," said Jack. He went over to one of the stalls and pushed open the door and stood back by the commode to make room for Elvis's walker. Elvis eased inside and looked at what Jack was now pointing to.

Graffiti.

"That's it?" Elvis said. "We're investigating a scuttling in the hall, trying to discover who attacked you last night, and you bring me in here to show me stick pictures on the shit house wall?"

"Look close," Jack said.

Elvis leaned forward. His eyes weren't what they used to be, and his glasses probably needed to be upgraded, but he could see that instead of writing, the graffiti was a series of simple pictorials.

A thrill, like a shot of good booze, ran through Elvis. He had once been a fanatic reader of ancient and esoteric lore, like *The Egyptian Book of the Dead* and *The Complete Works of H. P. Lovecraft,* and straight away he recognized what he was staring at. "Egyptian hieroglyphics," he said.

"Right-a-reen-O," Jack said. "Hey, you're not as stupid as some folks made you out."

"Thanks," Elvis said.

Jack reached into his suit coat pocket and took out a folded piece of paper and unfolded it. He pressed it to the wall. Elvis saw that it was covered with the same sort of figures that were on the wall of the stall.

"I copied this down yesterday. I came in here to shit because they hadn't cleaned up my bathroom. I saw this on the wall, went back to my room and looked it up in my books and wrote it all down. The top line translates something like: *Pharaoh gobbles donkey goober.* And the bottom line is: *Cleopatra does the dirty.*"

"What?"

"Well, pretty much," Jack said.

Elvis was mystified. "All right," he said. "One of the nuts here, present company excluded, thinks he's Tutankhamun or something, and he writes on the wall in hieroglyphics. So what? I mean, what's the connection? Why are we hanging out in a toilet?"

"I don't know how they connect exactly," Jack said. "Not yet. But this... thing, it caught me asleep last night, and I came awake just in time to...well, he had me on the floor and had his mouth over my asshole."

"A shit eater?" Elvis said.

"I don't think so," Jack said. "He was after my soul. You can get that out of any of the major orifices in a person's body. I've read about it."

"Where?" Elvis asked. *"Hustler?"*

"The Everyday Man or Woman's Book of the Soul by David Webb. It has some pretty good movie reviews about stolen soul movies in the back, too."

"Oh, that sounds trustworthy," Elvis said.

They went back to Jack's room and sat on his bed and looked through his many books on astrology, the Kennedy assassination, and a number of esoteric tomes, including the philosophy book, *The Everyday Man or Woman's Book of the Soul.*

Elvis found that book fascinating in particular; it indicated that not only did humans have a soul, but that the soul could be stolen, and there was a section concerning vampires and ghouls and incubi and succubi, as well as related soul suckers. Bottom line was, one of those dudes was around, you had to watch your holes. Mouth hole. Nose hole. Asshole. If you were a woman, you needed to watch a different hole. Dick pee-holes and ear holes — male or female — didn't matter. The soul didn't hang out there. They weren't considered major orifices for some reason.

In the back of the book was a list of items, related and not related to the book, that you could buy. Little plastic pyramids. Hats you could wear while channeling. Subliminal tapes that would help you learn Arabic. Postage was paid.

"Every kind of soul eater is in that book except politicians and science fiction fans," Jack said. "And I think that's what we got here in Shady Grove. A soul eater. Turn to the Egyptian section."

Elvis did. The chapter was prefaced by a movie still from *The Ten Commandments* with Yul Brynner playing Pharaoh. He was standing up in his chariot looking serious, which seemed a fair enough expression, considering the Red Sea, which had been parted by Moses, was about to come back together and drown him and his army.

Elvis read the article slowly while Jack heated water with his plug-in heater and made cups of instant coffee. "I get my niece to smuggle this stuff in," said Jack. "Or she claims to be my niece. She's a black woman. I never saw her before I was shot that day in Dallas and they took my brain out. She's part of the new identity they've given me. She's got a great ass."

"Damn," said Elvis. "What it says here, is that you can bury some dude, and if he gets the right tanna leaves and spells said over him and such bullshit, he can come back to life some thousands of years later, and to stay alive, he has to suck on the souls of the living, and that if the souls are small, his life force doesn't last long. Small. What's that mean?"

"Read on... No, never mind, I'll tell you." Jack handed Elvis his cup of coffee and sat down on the bed next to him. "Before I do, want a Ding Dong? Not mine. The chocolate kind. Well, I guess mine is chocolate, now that I've been dyed."

"You got Ding Dongs?" Elvis asked.

The Best of Joe R. Lansdale

"Couple of PayDays and Baby Ruth too," Jack said. "Which will it be? Let's get decadent."

Elvis licked his lips. "I'll have a Ding Dong."

While Elvis savored the Ding Dong, gumming it sloppily, sipping his coffee between bites, Jack, coffee cup balanced on his knee, a Baby Ruth in one mitt, expounded.

"Small souls means those without much fire for life," Jack said. "You know a place like that?"

"If souls were fires," Elvis said, "they couldn't burn much lower without being out than here. Only thing we got going in this joint is the pilot light."

"Exactamundo," Jack said. "What we got here in Shady Grove is an Egyptian soul sucker of some sort. A mummy hiding out, coming in here to feed on the sleeping. It's perfect, you see. The souls are little, and don't provide him with much. If this thing comes back two or three times in a row to wrap his lips around some elder's asshole, that elder is going to die pretty soon, and who's the wiser? Our mummy may not be getting much energy out of this, way he would with big souls, but the prey is easy. A mummy couldn't be too strong, really. Mostly just husk. But we're pretty much that way ourselves. We're not too far off being mummies."

"And with new people coming in all the time," Elvis said, "he can keep this up forever, this soul robbing."

"That's right. Because that's what we're brought here for. To get us out of the way until we die. And the ones don't die first of disease, or just plain old age, he gets."

Elvis considered all that. "That's why he doesn't bother the nurses and aides and administrators? He can go unsuspected."

"That, and they're not asleep. He has to get you when you're sleeping or unconscious."

"All right, but the thing throws me, Jack, is how does an ancient Egyptian end up in an East Texas rest home, and why is he writing on shit house walls?"

"He went to take a crap, got bored, and wrote on the wall. He probably wrote on pyramid walls, centuries ago."

"What would he crap?" Elvis said. "It's not like he'd eat, is it?"

"He eats souls," Jack said, "so I assume, he craps soul residue. And what that means to me is, you die by his mouth, you don't go to the other side, or wherever souls go. He digests the souls 'til they don't exist anymore —"

"And you're just so much toilet-water decoration," Elvis said.

"That's the way I've got it worked out," Jack said. "He's just like anyone else when he wants to take a dump. He likes a nice clean place with a flush. They didn't have that in his time, and I'm sure he finds it handy. The writing on the walls is just habit. Maybe, to him, Pharaoh and Cleopatra were just yesterday."

Elvis finished off the Ding Dong and sipped his coffee. He felt a rush from the sugar and he loved it. He wanted to ask Jack for the PayDay he had mentioned, but restrained himself. Sweets, fried foods, late nights and drugs had been the beginning of his original downhill spiral. He had to keep himself collected this time. He had to be ready to battle the Egyptian soul-sucking menace.

Soul-sucking menace?

God. He was really bored. It was time for him to go back to his room and to bed so he could shit on himself, get back to normal.

But Jesus and Ra, this was different from what had been going on up until now! It might all be bullshit, but considering what was going on in his life right now, it was absorbing bullshit. It might be worth playing the game to the hilt, even if he was playing it with a black guy who thought he was John F. Kennedy and believed an Egyptian mummy was stalking the corridors of Shady Grove Convalescent Home, writing graffiti on toilet stalls, sucking people's souls out through their assholes, digesting them, and crapping them down the visitors' toilet.

Suddenly, Elvis was pulled out of his considerations. There came from the hall the noise again. The sound that each time he heard it reminded him of something different. This time it was dried corn husks being rattled in a high wind. He felt goose bumps travel up his spine and the hairs on the back of his neck and arms stood up. He leaned forward and put his hands on his walker and pulled himself upright.

"Don't go in the hall," Jack said.

"I'm not asleep."

"That doesn't mean it won't hurt you.

"'It' my ass, there isn't any mummy from Egypt."

"Nice knowing you, Elvis."

Elvis inched the walker forward. He was halfway to the open door when he spied the figure in the hallway.

As the thing came even with the doorway, the hall lights went dim and sputtered. Twisting about the apparition, like pet crows, were flutters of shadows. The thing walked and stumbled, shuffled and flowed. Its legs moved like Elvis' own, meaning not too good, and yet, there was something about its locomotion that was impossible to identify. Stiff, but ghostly smooth. It was dressed in nasty looking jeans, a black shirt and a black cowboy hat that came down so low it covered where the thing's eyebrows should be. It wore large cowboy boots with the toes curled up, and there came from the thing a kind of mixed-stench: a compost pile of mud, rotting leaves, resin, spoiled fruit, dry dust and gassy sewage.

Elvis found that he couldn't scoot ahead another inch. He froze. The thing stopped and cautiously turned its head on its apple stem neck and looked at Elvis with empty eye sockets, revealing that it was, in fact, uglier than Lyndon Johnson.

Surprisingly, Elvis found he was surging forward as if on a zooming camera dolly, and that he was plunging into the thing's right eye socket, which swelled speedily to the dimensions of a vast canyon bottomed by blackness.

Down Elvis went, spinning and spinning, and out of the emptiness rushed resin-scented memories of pyramids and boats on a river, hot, blue skies, and a great silver bus lashed hard by black rain, a crumbling bridge and a charge of dusky water and a gleam of silver. Then there was a darkness so caliginous it was beyond being called dark, and Elvis could feel and taste mud in his mouth and a sensation of claustrophobia beyond expression. And he could perceive the thing's hunger, a hunger that prodded him like hot pins, and then —

— there came a *popping* sound in rapid succession, and Elvis felt himself whirling even faster, spinning backwards out of that deep memory canyon of the dusty head, and now he stood once again within the framework of his walker, and the mummy — for Elvis no longer denied to himself that it was such — turned its head away and began to move again, to shuffle, to flow, to stumble, to glide, down the hall, its pet shadows screeching with rusty throats around its head. *Pop! Pop! Pop!*

As the thing moved on, Elvis compelled himself to lift his walker and advance into the hall. Jack slipped up beside him, and they saw the mummy in cowboy clothes traveling toward the exit door at the back of the home. When it came to the locked door, it leaned against where the door met the jam and twisted and writhed, squeezed through the invisible crack where the two connected. Its shadows pursued it, as if sucked through by a vacuum cleaner.

The popping sound went on, and Elvis turned his head in that direction, and there, in his mask, his double concho-studded holster belted around his waist, was Kemosabe, a silver Fanner Fifty in either hand. He was popping caps rapidly at where the mummy had departed, the black spotted red rolls flowing out from behind the hammers of his revolvers in smoky relay.

"Asshole!" Kemosabe said. "Asshole!"

And then Kemosabe quivered, dropped both hands, popped a cap from each gun toward the ground, stiffened, collapsed.

Elvis knew he was dead of a ruptured heart before he hit the black and white tile; gone down and out with both guns blazing, soul intact.

The hall lights trembled back to normal.

The administrators, the nurses and the aides came then. They rolled Kemosabe over and drove their palms against his chest, but he didn't breathe again. No more Hi-Yo-Silver. They sighed over him and clucked their tongues, and finally an aide reached over and lifted Kemosabe's mask, pulled it off his head and dropped it on the floor, nonchalantly, and without respect, revealed his identity.

It was no one anyone really knew.

Once again, Elvis got scolded, and this time he got quizzed about what had happened to Kemosabe, and so did Jack, but neither told the truth. Who was going to believe a couple of nuts? Elvis and Jack Kennedy explaining that Kemosabe was gunning for a mummy in cowboy duds, a Bubba Ho-Tep with a flock of shadows roiling about his cowboy-hatted head?

So, what they did was lie.

"He came snapping caps and then he fell," Elvis said, and Jack corroborated his story and when Kemosabe had been carried off, Elvis, with some difficulty, using his walker for support, got down on his knee and picked up the discarded mask and carried it away with him. He had wanted the guns, but an aide had taken those for her four-year-old son.

Later, he and Jack learned through the grapevine that Kemosabe's roommate, an eighty-year-old man who had been in a semi-comatose condition for several years, had been found dead on the floor of his room. It was assumed Kemosabe had lost it and dragged him off his bed and onto the floor and the eighty-year-old man had kicked the bucket during the fall. As for Kemosabe, they figured he had then gone nuts when he realized what he had done, and had wandered out in the hall firing, and had a heart attack.

Elvis knew different. The mummy had come and Kemosabe had tried to protect his roommate in the only way he knew how. But instead of silver bullets, his gun smoked sulphur. Elvis felt a rush of pride in the old fart.

He and Jack got together later, talked about what they had seen, and then there was nothing left to say.

Night went away and the sun came up, and Elvis, who had slept not a wink, came up with it and put on khaki pants and a khaki shirt and used his walker to go outside. It had been ages since he had been out, and it seemed strange out there, all that sunlight and the smells of flowers and the Texas sky so high and the clouds so white.

It was hard to believe he had spent so much time in his bed. Just the use of his legs with the walker these last few days had tightened the muscles, and he found he could get around better.

The pretty nurse with the grapefruit tits came outside and said: "Mr. Presley, you look so much stronger. But you shouldn't stay out too long. It's almost time for a nap and for us, to, you know…"

"Fuck off, you patronizing bitch," said Elvis. "I'm tired of your shit. I'll lube my own transmission. You treat me like a baby again, I'll wrap this goddamn walker around your head."

The pretty nurse stood stunned, then went away quietly.

Elvis inched his way with the walker around the great circular drive that surrounded the home. It was a half hour later when he reached the back of the home and the door through which the mummy had departed. It was still locked, and he stood and looked at it amazed. How in hell had the mummy done that, slipping through an indiscernible chink between door and frame?

Elvis looked down at the concrete that lay at the back of the door. No clues there. He used the walker to travel toward the growth of trees out back, a growth of pin-oaks and sweet gums and hickory nut trees that shouldered on either side of the large creek that flowed behind the home.

The ground tipped sharply there, and for a moment he hesitated, then reconsidered. *Well, what the fuck?* he thought.

He planted the walker and started going forward, the ground sloping ever more dramatically. By the time he reached the bank of the creek and came to a gap in the trees, he was exhausted. He had the urge to start yelling for help, but didn't want to belittle himself, not after his performance with the nurse. He knew that he had regained some of his former confidence. His cursing and abuse had not seemed cute to her that time. The words had bitten her, if only slightly. Truth was, he was going to miss her greasing his pecker.

He looked over the bank of the creek. It was quite a drop there. The creek itself was narrow, and on either side of it was a gravel-littered six feet of shore. To his left, where the creek ran beneath a bridge, he could see where a mass of weeds and mud had gathered over time, and he could see something shiny in their midst.

Elvis eased to the ground inside his walker and sat there and looked at the water churning along. A huge woodpecker laughed in a tree nearby and a jay yelled at a smaller bird to leave his territory.

Where had ole Bubba Ho-Tep gone? Where did he come from? How in hell did he get here?

He recalled what he had seen inside the mummy's mind. The silver bus, the rain, the shattered bridge, the wash of water and mud.

Well, now wait a minute, he thought. Here we have water and mud and a bridge, though it's not broken, and there's something shiny in the midst of all those leaves and limbs and collected debris. All these items were elements of what he had seen in Bubba Ho-Tep's head. Obviously there was a connection.

But what was it?

When he got his strength back, Elvis pulled himself up and got the walker turned, and worked his way back to the home. He was covered in sweat and stiff as wire by the time he reached his room and tugged himself into bed. The blister on his dick throbbed and he unfastened his pants and eased down his underwear. The blister had refilled with pus, and it looked nastier than usual.

It's a cancer, he determined. He made the conclusion in a certain final rush. They're keeping it from me because I'm old and to them it doesn't matter. They think age will kill me first, and they are probably right.

Well, fuck them. I know what it is, and if it isn't, it might as well be.

He got the salve and doctored the pus-filled lesion, and put the salve away, and pulled up his underwear and pants, and fastened his belt.

Elvis got his TV remote off the dresser and clicked it on while he waited for lunch. As he ran the channels, he hit upon an advertisement for Elvis Presley week. It startled him. It wasn't the first time it had happened, but at the moment it struck him hard. It showed clips from his movies, *Clambake, Roustabout,* several others. All shit movies. Here he was complaining about loss of pride and how life had treated him, and now he realized he'd never had any pride and much of how life had treated him had been quite good, and the bulk of the bad had been his own fault. He wished now he'd fired his manager, Colonel Parker, about the time he got into films. The old fart had been a fool, and he had been a bigger fool for following him. He wished too he had treated Priscilla right. He wished he could tell his daughter he loved her.

Always the questions. Never the answers. Always the hopes. Never the fulfillments.

Elvis clicked off the set and dropped the remote on the dresser just as Jack came into the room. He had a folder under his arm. He looked like he was ready for a briefing at the White House.

"I had the woman who calls herself my niece come get me," he said. "She took me downtown to the newspaper morgue. She's been helping me do some research."

"On what?" Elvis said.

"On our mummy."

"You know something about him?" Elvis asked.

"I know plenty."

Jack pulled a chair up next to the bed, and Elvis used the bed's lift button to raise his back and head so he could see what was in Jack's folder.

Jack opened the folder, took out some clippings, and laid them on the bed. Elvis looked at them as Jack talked.

"One of the lesser mummies, on loan from the Egyptian government, was being circulated across the United States. You know, museums, that kind of stuff. It wasn't a major exhibit, like the King Tut exhibit some years back, but it was of interest. The mummy was flown or carried by train from state to state. When it got to Texas, it was stolen.

"Evidence points to the fact that it was stolen at night by a couple of guys in a silver bus. There was a witness. Some guy walking his dog or something. Anyway, the thieves broke in the museum and stole it, hoping to get a ransom probably. But in came the worst storm in East Texas history. Tornadoes. Rain. Hail. You name it. Creeks and rivers overflowed. Mobile homes were washed away. Livestock drowned. Maybe you remember it... No matter. It was one hell of a flood.

"These guys got away, and nothing was ever heard from them. After you told me what you saw inside the mummy's head — the silver bus, the storm, the bridge, all that — I came up with a more interesting, and I believe, considerably more accurate scenario."

"Let me guess. The bus got washed away. I think I saw it today. Right out back in the creek. It must have washed up there years ago."

"That confirms it. The bridge you saw breaking, that's how the bus got in the water, which would have been as deep then as a raging river. The bus was carried downstream. It lodged somewhere nearby, and the mummy was imprisoned by debris, and recently it worked its way loose."

"But how did it come alive?" Elvis asked. "And how did I end up inside its memories?"

"The speculation is broader here, but from what I've read, sometimes mummies were buried without their names, a curse put on their sarcophagus, or coffin, if you will. My guess is our guy was one of those. While he was in the coffin, he was a drying corpse. But when the bus was washed off the road, the coffin was overturned, or broken open, and our boy was freed of coffin and curse. Or more likely, it rotted open in time, and the holding spell was broken. And think about him down there all that time, waiting for freedom, alive, but not alive. Hungry, and no way to feed. I said he was free of his curse, but that's not entirely true. He's free of his imprisonment, but he still needs souls.

"And now, he's free to have them, and he'll keep feeding unless he's finally destroyed... You know, I think there's a part of him, oddly enough, that wants to fit in. To be human again. He doesn't entirely know what he's become. He responds to some old desires and the new desires of his condition. That's why he's taken on the illusion of clothes, probably copying the dress of one of his victims.

"The souls give him strength. Increase his spectral powers. One of which was to hypnotize you, kinda, draw you inside his head. He couldn't steal your soul that way, you have to be unconscious to have that done to you, but he could weaken you, distract you."

"And those shadows around him?"

"His guardians. They warn him. They have some limited powers of their own. I've read about them in *The Everyday Man or Woman's Book of the Soul*."

"What do we do?" Elvis asked.

"I think changing rest homes would be a good idea," Jack said. "I can't think of much else. I will say this. Our mummy is a nighttime kind of guy. Three A.M. actually. So, I'm going to sleep now, and again after lunch. Set my alarm for before dark so I can fix myself a couple cups of coffee. He comes tonight, I don't want him slapping his lips over my asshole again. I think he heard you coming down the hall about the time he got started on me the other night, and he ran. Not because he was scared, but because he didn't want anyone to find out he's around. Consider it. He has the proverbial bird's nest on the ground here."

After Jack left, Elvis decided he should follow Jack's lead and nap. Of course, at his age, he napped a lot anyway, and could fall asleep at any time, or toss restlessly for hours. There was no rhyme or reason to it.

He nestled his head into his pillow and tried to sleep, but sleep wouldn't come. Instead, he thought about things. Like, what did he really have left in life but this place? It wasn't much of a home, but it was all he had, and he'd be damned if he'd let a foreign, graffiti-writing, soul-sucking sonofabitch in an oversized hat and cowboy boots (with elf toes) take away his family members' souls and shit them down the visitors' toilet.

In the movies he had always played heroic types. But when the stage lights went out, it was time for drugs and stupidity and the coveting of women. Now it was time to be a little of what he had always fantasized being.

A hero.

Elvis leaned over and got hold of his telephone and dialed Jack's room. "Mr. Kennedy," Elvis said when Jack answered. "Ask not what your rest home can do for you. Ask what you can do for your rest home."

"Hey, you're copping my best lines," Jack said.

"Well then, to paraphrase one of my own, 'Let's take care of business.'"

"What are you getting at?"

"You know what I'm getting at. We're gonna kill a mummy."

The sun, like a boil on the bright blue ass of day, rolled gradually forward and spread its legs wide to reveal the pubic thatch of night, a hairy darkness in which stars crawled like lice, and the moon crabbed slowly upward like an albino dog tick striving for the anal gulch.

During this slow rolling transition, Elvis and Jack discussed their plans, then they slept a little, ate their lunch of boiled cabbage and meatloaf, slept some more, ate a supper of white bread and asparagus and a helping of shit on a shingle without the shingle, slept again, awoke about the time the pubic thatch appeared and those starry lice began to crawl.

And even then, with night about them, they had to wait until midnight to do what they had to do.

Jack squinted through his glasses and examined his list. "Two bottles of rubbing alcohol?" Jack said.

"Check," said Elvis. "And we won't have to toss it. Look here." Elvis held up a paint sprayer. "I found this in the storage room."

"I thought they kept it locked." Jack said.

"They do. But I stole a hair pin from Dillinger and picked the lock."

"Great!" Jack said. "Matches?"

"Check. I also scrounged a cigarette lighter."

"Good. Uniforms?"

Elvis held up his white suit, slightly greyed in spots with a chili stain on the front. A white silk scarf and the big gold and silver and ruby-studded belt that went with the outfit lay on the bed. There were zippered boots from K-Mart. "Check."

Jack held up a grey business suit on a hanger. "I've got some nice shoes and a tie to go with it in my room."

"Check," Elvis said.

"Scissors?"

"Check."

"I've got my motorized wheelchair oiled and ready to roll," Jack said, "and I've looked up a few words of power in one of my magic books. I don't know if they'll stop a mummy, but they're supposed to ward off evil. I wrote them down on a piece of paper."

"We use what we got," Elvis said. "Well then. 2:45 out back of the place."

"Considering our rate of travel, better start moving about 2:30," Jack said.

"Jack," Elvis asked. "Do we know what we're doing?"

"No, but they say fire cleanses evil. Let's hope they, whoever they are, are right."

"Check on that, too," said Elvis. "Synchronize watches."

They did, and Elvis added: "Remember. The key words for tonight are *Caution* and *Flammable*. And *Watch Your Ass*."

The front door had an alarm system, but it was easily manipulated from the inside. Once Elvis had the wires cut with the scissors, they pushed the compression lever on the door, and Jack shoved his wheelchair outside, and held the door while Elvis worked his walker through. Elvis tossed the scissors into the shrubbery, and Jack jammed a paperback book between the doors to allow them re-entry, should re-entry be an option at a later date.

Elvis was wearing a large pair of glasses with multi-colored gem-studded chocolate frames and his stained white jumpsuit with scarf and belt and zippered boots. The suit was open at the front and hung loose on him, except at the belly. To make it even tighter there, Elvis had made up an Indian medicine bag of sorts, and stuffed it inside his jumpsuit. The bag contained Kemosabe's mask, Bull's Purple Heart, and the newspaper clipping where he had first read of his alleged death.

Jack had on his grey business suit with a black-and-red-striped tie knotted carefully at the throat, sensible black shoes, and black nylon socks. The suit fit him well. He looked like a former president.

In the seat of the wheelchair was the paint sprayer, filled with rubbing alcohol, and beside it, a cigarette lighter and a paper folder of matches. Jack handed Elvis the paint sprayer. A strap made of a strip of torn sheet had been added to the device. Elvis hung the sprayer over his shoulder, reached inside his belt and got out a flattened, half-smoked stogie he had been saving for a special occasion. An occasion he had begun to think would never arrive. He clenched the cigar between his teeth, picked the matches from the seat of the wheelchair, and lit his cigar. It tasted like a dog turd, but he puffed it anyway. He tossed the folder of matches back on the chair and looked at Jack, said, "Let's do it, amigo."

Jack put the matches and the lighter in his suit pocket. He sat down in the wheelchair, kicked the foot stanchions into place and rested his feet on them. He leaned back slightly and flicked a switch on the arm rest. The electric motor hummed, the chair eased forward.

"Meet you there," said Jack. He rolled down the concrete ramp, on out to the circular drive, and disappeared around the edge of the building.

Elvis looked at his watch. It was nearly 2:45. He had to hump it. He clenched both hands on the walker and started truckin'.

Fifteen exhaustive minutes later, out back, Elvis settled in against the door, the place where Bubba Ho-Tep had been entering and exiting. The shadows fell over him like an umbrella. He propped the paint gun across the walker and used his scarf to wipe the sweat off his forehead.

In the old days, after a performance, he'd wipe his face with it and toss it to some woman in the crowd, watch as she creamed on herself. Panties and hotel keys would fly onto the stage at that point, bouquets of roses.

Tonight, he hoped Bubba Ho-Tep didn't use the scarf to wipe his ass after shitting him down the crapper.

Elvis looked where the circular concrete drive rose up slightly to the right, and there, seated in the wheelchair, very patient and still, was Jack. The moonlight spread over Jack and made him look like a concrete yard gnome.

Apprehension spread over Elvis like a dose of the measles. He thought: *Bubba Ho-Tep comes out of that creek bed, he's going to come out hungry and pissed, and when I try to stop him, he's going to jam this paint gun up my ass, then jam me and that wheelchair up Jack's ass.*

He puffed his cigar so fast it made him dizzy He looked out at the creek bank, and where the trees gaped wide, a figure rose up like a cloud of termites, scrabbled like a crab, flowed like water, chunked and chinked like a mass of oil-field tools tumbling downhill.

Its eyeless sockets trapped the moonlight and held it momentarily before permitting it to pass through and out the back of its head in irregular gold beams. The figure that simultaneously gave the impression of shambling and gliding, appeared one moment as nothing more than a shadow surrounded by more active shadows, then it was a heap of twisted brown sticks and dried mud molded into the shape of a human being, and in another moment, it was a cowboy-hatted, booted thing taking each step as if it were its last.

Halfway to the rest home it spotted Elvis, standing in the dark framework of the door. Elvis felt his bowels go loose, but he was determined not to shit his only good stage suit. His knees clacked together like stalks of ribbon cane rattling in a high wind. The dog-turd cigar fell from his lips.

He picked up the paint gun and made sure it was ready to spray. He pushed the butt of it into his hip and waited.

Bubba Ho-Tep didn't move. He had ceased to come forward. Elvis began to sweat more than before. His face and chest and balls were soaked. If Bubba Ho-Tep didn't come forward, their plan was fucked. They had to get him in range of the paint sprayer. The idea was he'd soak him with the alcohol, and Jack would come wheeling down from behind, flipping matches or the lighter at Bubba, catching him on fire.

Elvis said softly, "Come and get it, you dead piece of shit."

Jack had nodded off for a moment, but now he came awake. His flesh was tingling. It felt as if tiny ball bearings were being rolled beneath his skin. He looked up and saw Bubba Ho-Tep paused between the creek bank, himself, and Elvis at the door.

Jack took a deep breath. This was not the way they had planned it. The mummy was supposed to go for Elvis because he was blocking the door. But, no soap.

Jack got the matches and the cigarette lighter out of his coat pocket and put them between his legs on the seat of the chair. He put his hand on the gear box of the wheelchair, gunned it forward. He had to make things happen; had to get Bubba Ho-Tep to follow him, come within range of Elvis' spray gun.

Bubba Ho-Tep stuck out his arm and clotheslined Jack Kennedy. There was a sound like a rifle crack (no question Warren Commission, this blow was from the front), and over went the chair, and out went Jack, flipping and sliding across the driveway, the cement tearing his suit knees open, gnawing into his hide. The chair, minus its rider, tumbled over and came upright, and still rolling, veered downhill toward Elvis in the doorway, leaning on his walker, spray gun in hand.

The wheelchair hit Elvis' walker. Elvis bounced against the door, popped forward, grabbed the walker just in time, but dropped his spray gun.

He glanced up to see Bubba Ho-Tep leaning over the unconscious Jack. Bubba Ho-Tep's mouth went wide, and wider yet, and became a black toothless vacuum that throbbed pink as a raw wound in the moonlight; then Bubba Ho-Tep turned his head and the pink was not visible. Bubba Ho-Tep's mouth went down over Jack's face, and as Bubba Ho-Tep sucked, the shadows about it thrashed and gobbled like turkeys.

Elvis used the walker to allow him to bend down and get hold of the paint gun. When he came up with it, he tossed the walker aside, eased himself around, and into the wheelchair. He found the matches and the lighter there. Jack had done what he had done to distract Bubba Ho-Tep, to try and bring him down closer to the door. But he had failed. Yet by accident, he had provided Elvis with the instruments of mummy destruction, and now it was up to him to do what he and Jack had hoped to do together. Elvis put the matches inside his open chested outfit, pushed the lighter tight under his ass.

Elvis let his hand play over the wheelchair switches, as nimbly as he had once played with studio keyboards. He roared the wheelchair up the incline toward Bubba Ho-Tep, terrified, but determined, and as he rolled, in a voice cracking, but certainly reminiscent of him at his best, he began to sing "Don't Be Cruel," and within instants, he was on Bubba Ho-Tep and his busy shadows.

Bubba Ho-Tep looked up as Elvis roared into range, singing. Bubba Ho-Tep's open mouth irised to normal size, and teeth, formerly non-existent, rose up in his gums like little, black stumps. Electric locusts crackled and hopped in his empty sockets. He yelled something in Egyptian. Elvis saw the words jump out of Bubba Ho-Tep's mouth in visible hieroglyphics like dark beetles and sticks:

 *

Elvis bore down on Bubba Ho-Tep. When he was in range, he ceased singing, and gave the paint sprayer trigger a squeeze. Rubbing alcohol squirted from the sprayer and struck Bubba Ho-Tep in the face.

Elvis swerved, screeched around Bubba Ho-Tep in a sweeping circle, came back, the lighter in his hand. As he neared Bubba, the shadows swarming around the mummy's head separated and flew high up above him like startled bats.

The black hat Bubba wore wobbled and sprouted wings and flapped away from his head, becoming what it had always been, a living shadow. The shadows came down in a rush, screeching like harpies. They swarmed over Elvis' face, giving him the sensation of skinned animal pelts — blood-side in — being dragged over his flesh.

Bubba bent forward at the waist like a collapsed puppet, bopped his head against the cement drive. His black bat hat came down out of the dark in a swoop, expanding rapidly and falling over Bubba's body, splattering it like spilled ink. Bubba blob-flowed rapidly under the wheels of Elvis' mount and rose up in a dark swell beneath the chair and through the spokes of the wheels and billowed over the front of the chair and loomed upwards, jabbing his ravaged, ever-changing face through the flittering shadows, poking it right at Elvis.

* *"By the unwinking red eye of Ra!"*

Elvis, through gaps in the shadows, saw a face like an old jack-o'-lantern gone black and to rot, with jagged eyes, nose and mouth. And that mouth spread tunnel wide, and down that tunnel-mouth Elvis could see the dark and awful forever that was Bubba's lot, and Elvis clicked the lighter to flame, and the flame jumped, and the alcohol lit Bubba's face, and Bubba's head turned baby-eye blue, flowed jet-quick away, splashed upward like a black wave carrying a blazing oil slick. Then Bubba came down in a shuffle of blazing sticks and dark mud, a tar baby on fire, fleeing across the concrete drive toward the creek. The guardian shadows flapped after it, fearful of being abandoned.

Elvis wheeled over to Jack, leaned forward and whispered: "Mr. Kennedy."

Jack's eyelids fluttered. He could barely move his head, and something grated in his neck when he did. "The President is soon dead," he said, and his clenched fist throbbed and opened, and out fell a wad of paper. "You got to get him."

Jack's body went loose and his head rolled back on his damaged neck and the moon showed double in his eyes. Elvis swallowed and saluted Jack. "Mr. President," he said.

Well, at least he had kept Bubba Ho-Tep from taking Jack's soul. Elvis leaned forward, picked up the paper Jack had dropped. He read it aloud to himself in the moonlight: "You nasty thing from beyond the dead. No matter what you think and do, good things will never come to you. If evil is your black design, you can bet the goodness of the Light Ones will kick your bad behind."

That's it? thought Elvis. That's the chant against evil from the *Book of the Soul*? Yeah, right, boss. And what kind of decoder ring does that come with? Shit, it doesn't even rhyme well.

Elvis looked up. Bubba Ho-Tep had fallen down in a blue blaze, but he was rising up again, preparing to go over the lip of the creek, down to wherever his sanctuary was.

Elvis pulled around Jack and gave the wheelchair full throttle. He gave out with a rebel cry. His white scarf fluttered in the wind as he thundered forward.

Bubba Ho-Tep's flames had gone out. He was on his feet. His head was hissing grey smoke into the crisp night air. He turned completely to face Elvis, stood defiant, raised an arm and shook a fist. He yelled, and once again Elvis saw the hieroglyphics leap out of his mouth. The characters danced in a row, briefly —

* *"Eat the dog dick of Anubis, you ass wipe!"*

The Best of Joe R. Lansdale

— and vanished.

Elvis let go of the protective paper. It was dog shit. What was needed here was action.

When Bubba Ho-Tep saw Elvis was coming, chair geared to high, holding the paint sprayer in one hand, he turned to bolt, but Elvis was on him.

Elvis stuck out a foot and hit Bubba Ho-Tep in the back, and his foot went right through Bubba. The mummy squirmed, spitted on Elvis' leg. Elvis fired the paint sprayer, as Bubba Ho-Tep, himself, and chair, went over the creek bank in a flash of moonlight and a tumble of shadows.

Elvis screamed as the hard ground and sharp stones snapped his body like a piñata. He made the trip with Bubba Ho-Tep still on his leg, and when he quit sliding, he ended up close to the creek.

Bubba Ho-Tep, as if made of rubber, twisted around on Elvis' leg, and looked at him.

Elvis still had the paint sprayer. He had clung to it as if it were a life preserver. He gave Bubba another dose. Bubba's right arm flopped way out and ran along the ground and found a hunk of wood that had washed up on the edge of the creek, gripped it, and swung the long arm back. The arm came around and hit Elvis on the side of the head with the wood.

Elvis fell backwards. The paint sprayer flew from his hands. Bubba Ho-Tep was leaning over him. He hit Elvis again with the wood. Elvis felt himself going out. He knew if he did, not only was he a dead sonofabitch, but so was his soul. He would be just so much crap; no afterlife for him; no reincarnation; no angels with harps. Whatever lay beyond would not be known to him. It would all end right here for Elvis Presley. Nothing left but a quick flush.

Bubba Ho-Tep's mouth loomed over Elvis' face. It looked like an open manhole. Sewage fumes came out of it.

Elvis reached inside his open jumpsuit and got hold of the folder of matches. Laying back, pretending to nod out so as to bring Bubba Ho-Tep's ripe mouth closer, he thumbed back the flap on the matches, thumbed down one of the paper sticks, and pushed the sulphurous head of the match across the black strip.

Just as Elvis felt the cloying mouth of Bubba Ho-Tep falling down on his kisser like a Venus flytrap, the entire folder of matches ignited in Elvis' hand, burned him and made him yell.

The alcohol on Bubba's body called the flames to it, and Bubba burst into a stalk of blue flame, singeing the hair off Elvis' head, scorching his eyebrows down to nubs, blinding him until he could see nothing more than a scalding white light.

Elvis realized that Bubba Ho-Tep was no longer on or over him, and the white light became a stained white light, then a grey light, and eventually, the world, like a Polaroid negative developing, came into view, greenish at first, then full of the night's colors.

Elvis rolled on his side and saw the moon floating in the water. He saw too a scarecrow floating in the water, the straw separating from it, the current carrying it away.

No, not a scarecrow. Bubba Ho-Tep. For all his dark magic and ability to shift, or to appear to shift, fire had done him in, or had it been the stupid words from Jack's book on souls? Or both?

It didn't matter. Elvis got up on one elbow and looked at the corpse. The water was dissolving it more rapidly and the current was carrying it away.

Elvis fell over on his back. He felt something inside him grate against something soft. He felt like a water balloon with a hole poked in it.

He was going down for the last count, and he knew it.

But I've still got my soul, he thought. Still mine. All mine. And the folks in Shady Grove, Dillinger, the Blue Yodeler, all of them, they have theirs, and they'll keep 'em.

Elvis stared up at the stars between the forked and twisted boughs of an oak. He could see a lot of those beautiful stars, and he realized now that the constellations looked a little like the outlines of great hieroglyphics. He turned away from where he was looking, and to his right, seeming to sit on the edge of the bank, were more stars, more hieroglyphics.

He rolled his head back to the figures above him, rolled to the right and looked at those. Put them together in his mind.

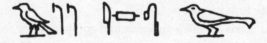

He smiled. Suddenly, he thought he could read hieroglyphics after all, and what they spelled out against the dark beautiful night was simple, and yet profound.

ALL IS WELL.

Elvis closed his eyes and did not open them again.

The Best of Joe R. Lansdale

THE END

Thanks to

(Mark Nelson) for translating East Texas "Egyptian" Hieroglyphics.

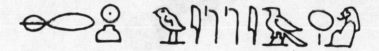

Mad Dog Summer

News, as opposed to rumor, didn't travel the way it does now. Not back then. Not by radio or newspaper it didn't. Not in East Texas. Things were different. What happened in another county was often left to that county.

World news was just that, something that was of importance to us all. We didn't have to know about terrible things that didn't affect us in Bilgewater, Oregon, or even across the state in El Paso, or up northern state way in godforsaken Amarillo.

All it takes now for us to know all the gory details about some murder is for it to be horrible, or it to be a slow news week, and it's everywhere, even if it's some grocery clerk's murder in Maine that hasn't a thing to do with us.

Back in the thirties a killing might occur several counties over and you'd never know about it unless you were related, because as I said, news traveled slower then, and law enforcement tried to take care of their own.

On the other hand, there were times it might have been better had news traveled faster, or traveled at all. If we had known certain things, perhaps some of the terrible experiences my family and I went through could have been avoided.

What's done is done though, and even now in my eighties, as I lie here in the old folks' home, my room full of the smell of my own decaying body, awaiting a meal of whatever, mashed and diced and tasteless, a tube in my shank, the television tuned to some talk show peopled by idiots, I've got the memories of then, nearly eighty years ago, and they are as fresh as the moment.

It all happened in the years of nineteen thirty-one and -two.

I suppose there were some back then had money, but we weren't among them. The Depression was on, and if we had been one of those with money, there really wasn't that much to buy, outside of hogs, chickens, vegetables, and the staples, and since we raised the first three, with us it was the staples.

Daddy farmed a little, had a barbershop he ran most days except Sunday and Monday, and was a community constable.

We lived back in the deep woods near the Sabine River in a three-room white house he had built before we were born. We had a leak in the roof, no electricity, a smoky wood stove, a rickety barn, and an outhouse prone to snakes.

We used kerosene lamps, hauled water from the well, and did a lot of hunting and fishing to add to the larder. We had about four acres cut out of the woods, and owned another twenty-five acres of hard timber and pine. We farmed the cleared four acres of sandy land with a mule named Sally Redback. We had a car, but Daddy used it primarily for his constable business and Sunday church. The rest of the time we walked, or me and my sister rode Sally Redback.

The woods we owned, and the hundreds of acres of it that surrounded our land, was full of game, chiggers, and ticks. Back then in East Texas, all the big woods hadn't been timbered out and they didn't all belong to somebody. There were still mighty trees and lots of them, lost places in the forest and along the riverbanks that no one had touched but animals.

Wild hogs, squirrels, rabbits, coons, possums, some armadillo, and all manner of birds and plenty of snakes were out there. Sometimes you could see those darn water moccasins swimming in a school down the river, their evil heads bobbing up like knobs on logs. And woe unto the fella fell in amongst them, and bless the heart of the fool who believed if he swam down under them he'd be safe because a moccasin couldn't bite underwater. They not only could, but would.

Deer roamed the woods too. Maybe fewer than now, as people grow them like crops these days and harvest them on a three-day drunk during season from a deer stand with a high-powered rifle. Deer they've corn fed and trained to be like pets so they can get a cheap, free shot and feel like they've done some serious hunting. It costs them more to shoot the deer, ride its corpse around and mount its head, than it would cost to go to the store and buy an equal amount of beefsteak. Then they like to smear their faces with the blood after the kill and take photos, like this makes them some kind of warrior.

But I've quit talking, and done gone to preaching. I was saying how we lived. And I was saying about all the game. Then too, there was the Goat Man. Half goat, half man, he liked to hang around what was called the swinging bridge. I had never seen him, but sometimes at night, out possum hunting, I thought maybe I heard him, howling and whimpering down there near the cable bridge that hung bold over the river, swinging with the wind in the moonlight, the beams playing on the metal cables like fairies on ropes.

He was supposed to steal livestock and children, and though I didn't know of any children that had been eaten, some farmers claimed the Goat Man had taken their livestock, and there were some kids I knew claimed they had cousins taken off by the Goat Man, never to be seen again.

It was said he didn't go as far as the main road because Baptist preachers traveled regular there on foot and by car, making the preaching rounds, and therefore making the road holy. It was said he didn't get out of the woods that made up the Sabine bottoms. High land was something he couldn't tolerate. He needed the damp, thick leaf mush beneath his feet, which were hooves.

Dad said there wasn't any Goat Man. That it was a wives' tale heard throughout the South. He said what I heard out there was water and animal sounds, but I tell you, those sounds made your skin crawl, and they did remind you of a hurt goat. Mr. Cecil Chambers, who worked with my daddy at the barbershop, said it was probably a panther. They showed up now and then in the deep woods, and they could scream like a woman, he said.

Me and my sister Tom — well, Thomasina, but we all called her Tom 'cause it was easier to remember and because she was a tomboy — roamed those woods from daylight to dark. We had a dog named Toby that was part hound, part terrier, and part what we called feist.

Toby was a hunting sonofagun. But the summer of nineteen thirty-one, while rearing up against a tree so he could bark at a squirrel he'd tracked, the oak he was under lost a rotten limb and it fell on him, striking his back so hard he couldn't move his back legs or tail. I carried him home in my arms. Him whimpering, me and Tom crying.

Daddy was out in the field plowing with Sally, working the plow around a stump that was still in the field. Now and then he chopped at its base with an ax and had set fire to it, but it was stubborn and remained.

Daddy stopped his plowing when he saw us, took the looped lines off his shoulders and dropped them, left Sally Redback standing in the field hitched up to the plow. He walked part of the way across the field to meet us, and we carried Toby out to him and put him on the soft plowed ground and Daddy looked him over. Daddy moved Toby's paws around, tried to straighten Toby's back, but Toby would whine hard when he did that.

After a while, as if considering all possibilities, he told me and Tom to get the gun and take poor Toby out in the woods and put him out of his misery.

"It ain't what I want you to do," Daddy said. "But it's the thing has to be done."

"Yes sir," I said.

These days that might sound rough, but back then we didn't have many vets, and no money to take a dog to one if we wanted to. And all a vet would have done was do what we were gonna do.

Another thing different was you learned about things like dying when you were quite young. It couldn't be helped. You raised and killed chickens and hogs, hunted and fished, so you were constantly up against it. That being the case, I think we respected life more than some do now, and useless suffering was not to be tolerated.

And in the case of something like Toby, you were often expected to do the deed yourself, not pass on the responsibility. It was unspoken, but it was pretty well understood that Toby was our dog, and therefore, our responsibility. Things like that were considered part of the learning process.

We cried awhile, then got a wheelbarrow and put Toby in it. I already had my .22 for squirrels, but for this I went in the house and swapped it for the single-shot sixteen-gauge shotgun, so there wouldn't be any suffering. The thought of shooting Toby in the back of the head like that, blasting his skull all over creation, was not something I looked forward to.

Our responsibility or not, I was thirteen and Tom was only nine. I told her she could stay at the house, but she wouldn't. She said she'd come on with me. She knew I needed someone to help me be strong.

Tom got the shovel to bury Toby, put it over her shoulder, and we wheeled old Toby along, him whining and such, but after a bit he quit making noise. He just lay there in the wheelbarrow while we pushed him down the trail, his back slightly twisted, his head raised, sniffing the air.

In short time he started sniffing deeper, and we could tell he had a squirrel's scent. Toby always had a way of turning to look at you when he had a squirrel, then he'd point his head in the direction he wanted to go and take off running and yapping in that deep voice of his. Daddy said that was his way of letting us know the direction of the scent before he got out of sight. Well, he had his head turned like that, and I knew what it was I was supposed to do, but I decided to prolong it by giving Toby his head.

We pushed in the direction he wanted to go, and pretty soon we were racing over a narrow trail littered with pine needles, and Toby was barking like crazy. Eventually we run the wheelbarrow up against a hickory tree.

Up there in the high branches two big fat squirrels played around as if taunting us. I shot both of them and tossed them into the wheelbarrow with Toby, and darned if he didn't signal and start barking again.

It was rough pushing that wheelbarrow over all that bumpy wood debris and leaf and needle-littered ground, but we did it, forgetting all about what we were supposed to do for Toby.

By the time Toby quit hitting on squirrel scent, it was near nightfall and we were down deep in the woods with six squirrels — a bumper crop — and we were tuckered out.

There Toby was, a dadburn cripple, and I'd never seen him work the trees better. It was like Toby knew what was coming and was trying to prolong things by treeing squirrels.

We sat down under a big, old sweetgum and left Toby in the wheelbarrow with the squirrels. The sun was falling through the trees like a big, fat plum coming to pieces. Shadows were rising up like dark men all around us. We didn't have a hunting lamp. There was just the moon and it wasn't up good yet.

"Harry," Tom said. "What about Toby?"

I had been considering on that.

"He don't seem to be in pain none," I said. "And he treed six dadburn squirrels."

"Yeah," Tom said, "but his back's still broke."

"Reckon so," I said.

"Maybe we could hide him down here, come every day, feed and water him."

"I don't think so. He'd be at the mercy of anything came along. Darn chiggers and ticks would eat him alive." I'd thought of that because I could feel bites all over me and knew tonight I'd be spending some time with a lamp, some tweezers and such myself, getting them off all kinds of places, bathing myself later in kerosene, then rinsing. During the summer me and Tom ended up doing that darn near every evening.

"It's gettin' dark," Tom said.

"I know."

"I don't think Toby's in all that much pain now."

"He does seem better," I said. "But that don't mean his back ain't broke."

"Daddy wanted us to shoot him to put him out of his misery. He don't look so miserable to me. It ain't right to shoot him he ain't miserable, is it?"

I looked at Toby. There was mostly just a lump to see, lying there in the wheelbarrow covered by the dark. While I was looking he raised his head and his tail beat on the wooden bottom of the wheelbarrow a couple of times.

"Don't reckon I can do it," I said. "I think we ought to take him back to Daddy, show how he's improved. He may have a broke back, but he ain't in pain like he was. He can move his head and even his tail now, so his whole body ain't dead. He don't need killin'."

"Daddy may not see it that way, though."

"Reckon not, but I can't just shoot him without trying to give him a chance. Heck, he treed six dadburn squirrels. Mama'll be glad to see them squirrels. We'll just take him back."

We got up to go. It was then that it settled on us. We were lost. We had been so busy chasing those squirrels, following Toby's lead, we had gotten down deep in the woods and we didn't recognize anything. We weren't scared, of course, least not right away. We roamed these woods all the time, but it had grown dark, and this immediate place wasn't familiar.

The moon was up some more, and I used that for my bearings. "We need to go that way," I said. "Eventually that'll lead back to the house or the road."

We set out, pushing the wheelbarrow, stumbling over roots and ruts and fallen limbs, banging up against trees with the wheelbarrow and ourselves. Near us we could hear wildlife moving around, and I thought about what Mr. Chambers had said about panthers, and I thought about wild hogs and wondered if we might come up on one rootin' for acorns, and I remembered that Mr. Chambers had also said this was a bad year for the hydrophobia, and lots of animals were coming down with it, and the thought of all that made me nervous enough to feel around in my pocket for shotgun shells. I had three left.

As we went along, there was more movement around us, and after a while I began to think whatever it was was keeping stride with us. When we slowed, it slowed. We sped up, it sped up. And not the way an animal will do, or even the way a coach whip snake will sometimes follow and run you. This was something bigger than a snake. It was stalking us, like a panther. Or a man.

Toby was growling as we went along, his head lifted, the hair on the back of his neck raised.

I looked over at Tom, and the moon was just able to split through the trees and show me her face and how scared she was. I knew she had come to the same conclusion I had.

I wanted to say something, shout out at whatever it was in the bushes, but I was afraid that might be like some kind of bugle call that set it off, causing it to come down on us.

I had broken open the shotgun earlier for safety's sake, laid it in the wheelbarrow and was pushing it, Toby, the shovel, and the squirrels along. Now I stopped, got the shotgun out, made sure a shell was in it, snapped it shut and put my thumb on the hammer.

Toby had really started to make noise, had gone from growling to barking.

I looked at Tom, and she took hold of the wheelbarrow and started pushing.

I could tell she was having trouble with it, working it over the soft ground, but I didn't have any choice but to hold on to the gun, and we couldn't leave Toby behind, not after what he'd been through.

Whatever was in those bushes paced us for a while, then went silent. We picked up speed, and didn't hear it anymore. And we didn't feel its presence no more neither. Earlier it was like we was walking along with the Devil beside us.

I finally got brave enough to break open the shotgun and lay it in the wheelbarrow and take over the pushing again.

"What was that?" Tom asked.

"I don't know," I said.

"It sounded big."

"Yeah."

"The Goat Man?"

"Daddy says there ain't any Goat Man."

"Yeah, but he's sometimes wrong, ain't he?"

"Hardly ever," I said.

We went along some more, and found a narrow place in the river, and crossed, struggling with the wheelbarrow. We shouldn't have crossed, but there was a spot, and someone or something following us had spooked me, and I had just wanted to put some space between us and it.

We walked along a longer time, and eventually came up against a wad of brambles that twisted in amongst the trees and scrubs and vines and made a wall of thorns. It was a wall of wild rosebushes. Some of the vines on them were thick as well ropes, the thorns like nails, and the flowers smelled strong and sweet in the night wind, almost sweet as sorghum syrup cooking.

The bramble patch ran some distance in either direction, and encased us on all sides. We had wandered into a maze of thorns too wide and thick to go around, and too high and sharp to climb over, and besides they had wound together with low hanging limbs, and it was like a ceiling above. I thought of Brer Rabbit and the briar patch, but unlike Brer Rabbit, I had not been born and raised in a briar patch, and unlike Brer Rabbit, it wasn't what I wanted.

I dug in my pocket and got a match I had left over from when me and Tom tried to smoke some corn silk cigarettes and grapevines, and I struck the match with my thumb and waved it around, saw there was a wide space in the brambles, and it didn't take a lot of know-how to see the path had been cut in them. I bent down and poked the match forward, and I could see the brambles were a kind of tunnel, about six feet high and six feet wide. I couldn't tell how far it went, but it was a goodly distance.

I shook the match out before it burned my hand, said to Tom, "We can go back, or we can take this tunnel."

Tom looked to our left, saw the brambles were thick and solid, and in front of us was a wall of them too. "I don't want to go back because of that thing, whatever it is. And I don't want to go down that tunnel neither. We'd be like rats in a pipe. Maybe whatever it is knew it'd get us boxed in like this, and it's just waitin' at the other end of that bramble trap for us, like that thing Daddy read to us about. The thing that was part man, part cow."

"Part bull, part man," I said. "The Minotaur."

"Yeah. A minutetar. It could be waitin' on us, Harry."

I had, of course, thought about that. "I think we ought to take the tunnel. It can't come from any side on us that way. It has to come from front or rear."

"Can't there be other tunnels in there?"

I hadn't thought of that. There could be openings cut like this anywhere.

"I got the gun," I said. "If you can push the wheelbarrow, Toby can sort of watch for us, let us know something's coming. Anything jumps out at us, I'll cut it in two."

"I don't like any of them choices."

I picked up the gun and made it ready. Tom took hold of the wheelbarrow handles. I went on in and Tom came after me.

The smell of roses was thick and overwhelming. It made me sick. The thorns sometimes stuck out on vines you couldn't see in the dark. They snagged my old shirt and cut my arms and face. I could hear Tom back there behind me, cussing softly under her breath as she got scratched. I was glad for the fact that Toby was silent. It gave me some kind of relief.

The bramble tunnel went on for a good ways, then I heard a rushing sound, and the bramble tunnel widened and we came out on the bank of the roaring Sabine. There were splits in the trees above, and the moonlight came through strong and fell over everything and looked yellow and thick like milk that had turned sour. Whatever had been pacing us seemed to be good and gone.

I studied the moon a moment, then thought about the river. I said, "We've gone some out of the way. But I can see how we ought to go. We can follow the river a ways, which ain't the right direction, but I think it's not far from here to the swinging bridge. We cross that, we can hit the main road, walk to the house."

"The swinging bridge?"

"Yeah," I said.

"Think Momma and Daddy are worried?" Tom asked.

"Yeah," I said. "Reckon they are. I hope they'll be glad to see these squirrels as I think they'll be."

"What about Toby?"

"We just got to wait and see."

The bank sloped down, and near the water there was a little trail ran along the edge of the river.

"Reckon we got to carry Toby down, then bring the wheelbarrow. You can push it forward, and I'll get in front and boost it down."

I carefully picked up Toby, who whimpered softly, and Tom, getting ahead of herself, pushed the wheelbarrow. It, the squirrels, shotgun, and shovel went over the edge, tipped over near the creek.

"Damn it, Tom," I said.

"I'm sorry," she said. "It got away from me. I'm gonna tell Mama you cussed."

"You do and I'll whup the tar out of you. 'Sides, I heard you cussin' plenty."

I gave Toby to Tom to hold till I could go down a ways, get a footing and have him passed to me.

I slid down the bank, came up against a huge oak growing near the water. The brambles had grown down the bank and were wrapped around the tree. I went around it, put my hand out to steady myself, and jerked it back quick. What I had touched hadn't been tree trunk, or even a thorn, but something soft.

When I looked I saw a gray mess hung up in brambles, and the moonlight was shining across the water and falling on a face, or what had been a face, but was more like a jack-o'-lantern now, swollen and round with dark sockets for eyes. There was a wad of hair on the head like a chunk of dark lamb's wool, and the body was swollen up and twisted and without clothes. A woman.

I had seen a couple of cards with naked women on them that Jake Sterning had shown me. He was always coming up with stuff like that 'cause his daddy was a traveling salesman and sold not only Garrett Snuff but what was called novelties on the side.

But this wasn't like that. Those pictures had stirred me in a way I didn't understand but found somehow sweet and satisfying. This was stirring me in a way I understood immediately. Horror. Fear.

Her breasts were split like rotted melons cracked in the sun. The brambles were tightly wrapped around her swollen flesh and her skin was gray as cigar ash. Her feet weren't touching the ground. She was held against the tree by the brambles. In the moonlight she looked like a fat witch bound to a massive post by barbed wire, ready to be burned.

"Jesus," I said.

"You're cussin' again," Tom said.

I climbed up the bank a bit, took Toby from Tom, laid him on the soft ground by the riverbank, stared some more at the body. Tom slid down, saw what I saw.

"Is it the Goat Man?" she asked.

"No," I said. "It's a dead woman."

"She ain't got no clothes on."

"No, she ain't. Don't look at her, Tom."

"I can't help it."

"We got to get home, tell Daddy."

"Light a match, Harry. Let's get a good look."

I considered on that, finally dug in my pocket. "I just got one left."

"Use it."

I struck the match with my thumb and held it out. The match wavered as my hand shook. I got up as close as I could stand to get. It was even more horrible by match light.

"I think it's a colored woman," I said.

The match went out. I righted the wheelbarrow, shook mud out of the end of the shotgun, put it and the squirrels and Toby back in the wheelbarrow. I couldn't find the shovel, figured it had slid on down into the river and was gone. That was going to cost me.

"We got to get on," I said.

Tom was standing on the bank, staring at the body. She couldn't take her eyes off of it.

"Come on!"

Tom tore herself away. We went along the bank, me pushing that wheelbarrow for all I was worth, it bogging in the soft dirt until I couldn't push it anymore. I bound the squirrels' legs together with some string Tom had, and tied them around my waist.

"You carry the shotgun, Tom, and I'll carry Toby."

Tom took the gun, I picked Toby up, and we started toward the swinging bridge, which was where the Goat Man was supposed to live.

Me and my friends normally stayed away from the swinging bridge, all except Jake. Jake wasn't scared of anything. Then again, Jake wasn't smart enough to be scared of much. Story on him and his old man was you cut off their head they wouldn't be any dumber.

Jake said all the stories you heard about the swinging bridge were made up by our parents to keep us off of it 'cause it was dangerous. And maybe that was true.

The bridge was some cables strung across the Sabine from high spots on the banks. Some long board slats were fastened to the cables by rusty metal clamps and rotting ropes. I didn't know who had built it, and maybe it had been a pretty good bridge once, but now a lot of the slats were missing and others were rotten and cracked and the cables were fastened to the high bank on either side by rusty metal bars buried deep in the ground. In places, where the water had washed the bank, you could see part of the bars showing through the dirt. Enough time and water, the whole bridge would fall into the river.

When the wind blew, the bridge swung, and in a high wind it was something. I had crossed it only once before, during the day, the wind dead calm, and that had been scary enough. Every time you stepped, it moved, threatened to dump you. The boards creaked and ached as if in pain. Sometimes little bits of rotten wood came loose and fell into the river below. I might add that below was a deep spot and the water ran fast there, crashed up against some rocks, fell over a little falls, and into wide, deep water.

Now, here we were at night, looking down the length of the bridge, thinking about the Goat Man, the body we'd found, Toby, and it being late, and our parents worried.

"We gotta cross, Harry?" Tom asked.

"Yeah," I said. "Reckon so. I'm gonna lead, and you watch where I step. The boards hold me, they're liable to hold you."

The bridge creaked above the roar of the river, swaying ever so slightly on its cables, like a snake sliding through tall grass.

It had been bad enough trying to cross when I could put both hands on the cables, but carrying Toby, and it being night, and Tom with me, and her trying to carry the shotgun… Well, it didn't look promising.

The other choice was to go back the way we had come, or to try another path on down where the river went shallow, cross over there, walk back to the road and our house. But the river didn't shallow until some miles away, and the woods were rough, and it was dark, and Toby was heavy, and there was something out there that had been tracking us. I didn't see any other way but the bridge.

I took a deep breath, got a good hold on Toby, stepped out on the first slat.

When I did the bridge swung hard to the left, then back even more violently. I had Toby in my arms, so the only thing I could do was bend my legs and try to ride the swing. It took a long time for the bridge to quit swinging, and I took the next step even more gingerly. It didn't swing as much this time. I had gotten a kind of rhythm to my stepping.

I called back to Tom, "You got to step in the middle of them slats. That way it don't swing so much."

"I'm scared, Harry."

"It's all right," I said. "We'll do fine."

I stepped on a slat, and it cracked and I pulled my foot back. Part of the board had broken loose and was falling into the river below. It hit with a splash, was caught up in the water, flickered in the moonlight, and was whipped away. It churned under the brown water, went over the little falls and was gone.

I stood there feeling as if the bottom of my belly had fell out. I hugged Toby tight and took a wide step over the missing slat toward the next one. I made it, but the bridge shook and I heard Tom scream. I turned and looked over my shoulder as she dropped the shotgun and grabbed at the cable. The shotgun fell longways and hung between the two lower cables. The bridge swung violently, threw me against one of the cables, then to the other side, and I thought I was a goner for sure.

When the bridge slowed, I lowered to one knee on the slat, pivoted and looked at Tom. "Easy," I said.

"I'm too scared to let go," Tom said.

"You got to, and you got to get the gun."

It was a long time before Tom finally bent over and picked up the gun. After a bit of heavy breathing, we started on again. That was when we heard the noise down below and saw the thing in the shadows.

It was moving along the bank on the opposite side, down near the water, under the bridge. You couldn't see it good, because it was outside of the moonlight, in the shadows. Its head was huge and there was something like horns on it and the rest of it was dark as a coal bin. It leaned a little forward, as if trying to get a good look at us, and I could see the whites of its eyes and chalky teeth shining in the moonlight.

"Jesus, Harry," Tom said. "It's the Goat Man. What do we do?"

I thought about going back. That way we'd be across the river from it, but then again, we'd have all the woods to travel through, and for miles. And if it crossed over somewhere, we'd have it tracking us again, because now I felt certain that's what had been following us in the brambles.

If we went on across, we'd be above it, on the higher bank, and it wouldn't be that far to the road. It was said the Goat Man didn't ever go as far as the road. That was his quitting place. He was trapped here in the woods and along the banks of the Sabine, and the route them preachers took kept him away from the road.

"We got to go on," I said. I took one more look at those white eyes and teeth, and started pushing on across. The bridge swung, but I had more motivation now, and I was moving pretty good, and so was Tom.

When we were near to the other side, I looked down, but I couldn't see the Goat Man no more. I didn't know if it was the angle, or if it had gone on. I kept thinking when I got to the other side it would have climbed up and would be waiting.

But when we got to the other side, there was only the trail that split the deep woods standing out in the moonlight. Nothing on it.

We started down the trail. Toby was heavy and I was trying not to jar him too much, but I was so frightened, I wasn't doing that good of a job. He whimpered some.

After we'd gone on a good distance, the trail turned into shadow where the limbs from trees reached out and hid it from the moonlight and seemed to hold the ground in a kind of dark hug.

"I reckon if it's gonna jump us," I said, "that'd be the place."

"Then let's don't go there."

"You want to go back across the bridge?"

"I don't think so."

"Then we got to go on. We don't know he's even followed."

"Did you see those horns on his head?"

"I seen somethin'. I think what we oughta do, least till we get through that bend in the trail there, is swap. You carry Toby and let me carry the shotgun."

"I like the shotgun."

"Yeah, but I can shoot it without it knocking me down. And I got the shells."

Tom considered this. "Okay," she said.

She put the shotgun on the ground and I gave her Toby. I picked up the gun and we started around the dark curve in the trail.

I had been down this trail many times in the daylight. Out to the swinging bridge, but except for that one other time, I had never crossed the bridge until now. I had been in the woods at night before, but not this deep, and usually with Daddy.

When we were deep in the shadow of the trail nothing leaped out on us or bit us, but as we neared the moonlit part of the trail we heard movement in the woods. The same sort of movement we had heard back in the brambles. Calculated. Moving right along with us.

We finally reached the moonlit part of the trail and felt better. But there really wasn't any reason for it. It was just a way of feeling. Moonlight didn't change anything. I looked back over my shoulder, into the darkness we had just left, and in the middle of the trail, covered in shadow, I could see it. Standing there. Watching.

I didn't say anything to Tom about it. Instead I said, "You take the shotgun now, and I'll take Toby. Then I want you to run with everything you got to where the road is."

Tom, not being any dummy, and my eyes probably giving me away, turned and looked back in the shadows. She saw it too. It crossed into the woods. She turned and gave me Toby and took the shotgun and took off like a bolt of lightning. I ran after her, bouncing poor Toby, the squirrels slapping against my legs. Toby whined and whimpered and yelped. The trail widened, the moonlight grew brighter, and the red clay road came up and we hit it, looked back.

Nothing was pursuing us. We didn't hear anything moving in the woods.

"Is it okay now?" Tom asked.

"Reckon so. They say he can't come as far as the road."

"What if he can?"

"Well, he can't… I don't think."

"You think he killed that woman?"

"Figure he did."

"How'd she get to lookin' like that?"

"Somethin' dead swells up like that."

"How'd she get all cut? On his horns?"

"I don't know, Tom."

We went on down the road, and in time, after a number of rest stops, after helping Toby go to the bathroom by holding up his tail and legs, in the deepest part of the night, we reached home.

It wasn't entirely a happy homecoming. The sky had grown cloudy and the moon was no longer bright. You could hear the cicadas chirping and frogs bleating off somewhere in the bottoms. When we entered into the yard carrying Toby, Daddy spoke from the shadows, and an owl, startled, flew out of the oak and was temporarily outlined against the faintly brighter sky.

"I ought to whup y'all's butts," Daddy said.

"Yes sir," I said.

Daddy was sitting in a chair under an oak in the yard. It was sort of our gathering tree, where we sat and talked and shelled peas in the summer. He was smoking a pipe, a habit that would kill him later in life. I could see its glow as he puffed flames from a match into the tobacco. The smell from the pipe was woody and sour to me.

We went over and stood beneath the oak, near his chair.

"Your mother's been terrified," he said. "Harry, you know better than to stay out like that, and with your sister. You're supposed to take care of her."

"Yes sir."

"I see you still have Toby."

"Yes sir. I think he's doing better."

"You don't do better with a broken back."

"He treed six squirrels," I said. I took my pocketknife out and cut the string around my waist and presented him with the squirrels. He looked at them in the darkness, laid them beside his chair.

"You have an excuse?" he said.

"Yes sir," I said.

"All right, then," he said. "Tom, you go on up to the house and get the tub and start filling it with water. It's warm enough you won't need to heat it. Not tonight. You bathe, then you get after them bugs on you with the kerosene and such, then hit the bed."

"Yes sir," she said. "But Daddy…"

"Go to the house, Tom," Daddy said.

Tom looked at me, laid the shotgun down on the ground and went on toward the house.

Daddy puffed his pipe. "You said you had an excuse."

"Yes sir. I got to runnin' squirrels, but there's something else. There's a body down by the river."

He leaned forward in his chair. "What?"

I told him everything that had happened. About being followed, the brambles, the body, the Goat Man. When I was finished, he said, "There isn't any Goat Man, Harry. But the person you saw, it's possible he was the killer. You being out like that, it could have been you or Tom."

"Yes sir."

"Suppose I'll have to take a look early morning. You think you can find her again?"

"Yes sir, but I don't want to."

"I know, but I'm gonna need your help. You go up to the house now, and when Tom gets through, you wash up and get the bugs off of you. I know you're covered. Hand me the shotgun and I'll take care of Toby."

I started to say something, but I didn't know what to say. Daddy got up, cradled Toby in his arms and I put the shotgun in his hand.

"Damn rotten thing to happen to a good dog," he said.

Daddy started walking off toward the little barn we had out back of the house by the field.

"Daddy," I said. "I couldn't do it. Not Toby."

"That's all right, son," he said, and went on out to the barn.

When I got up to the house, Tom was on the back porch in the tub and Mama was scrubbing her vigorously by the light of a lantern hanging on a porch beam. When I came up, Mama, who was on her knees, looked over her shoulder at me. Her blonde hair was gathered up in a fat bun and a tendril of it had come loose and was hanging across her forehead and eye. She pushed it aside with a soapy hand. "You ought to know better than to stay out this late. And scaring Tom with stories about seeing a body."

"It ain't a story, Mama," I said.

I told her about it, making it brief.

When I finished, she was quiet for a long moment. "Where's your daddy?"

"He took Toby out to the barn. Toby's back is broken."

"I heard. I'm real sorry."

I listened for the blast of the shotgun, but after fifteen minutes it still hadn't come. Then I heard Daddy coming down from the barn, and pretty soon he stepped out of the shadows and into the lantern light, carrying the shotgun.

"I don't reckon he needs killin'," Daddy said. I felt my heart lighten, and I looked at Tom, who was peeking under Mama's arm as Mama scrubbed her head with lye soap. "He could move his back legs a little, lift his tail. You might be right, Harry. He might be better. Besides, I wasn't any better doin' what ought to be done than you, son. He takes a turn for the worse, stays the same, well… In the meantime, he's yours and Tom's responsibility. Feed and water him, and you'll need to manage him to do his business somehow."

"Yes sir," I said. "Thanks, Daddy."

Daddy sat down on the porch with the shotgun cradled in his lap. "You say the woman was colored?"

"Yes sir."

Daddy sighed. "That's gonna make it some difficult," he said.

Next morning I led Daddy out there by means of the road and the trail up to the swinging bridge. I didn't want to cross the bridge again. I pointed out from the bank the spot across and down the river where the body could be found.

"All right," Daddy said. "I'll manage from here. You go home. Better yet, get into town and open up the barbershop. Cecil will be wondering where I am."

I went home, out to the barn to check on Toby. He was crawling around on his belly, wiggling his back legs some. I left Tom with the duty to look after Toby being fed and all, then I got the barbershop key, saddled up Sally Redback, rode her the five miles into town.

Marvel Creek wasn't much of a town really, not that it's anything now, but back then it was pretty much two streets. Main and West. West had a row of houses, Main had the General Store, a courthouse, post office, the doctor's office, the barbershop my daddy owned, a couple other businesses, and sometimes a band of roving hogs that belonged to Old Man Crittendon.

The barbershop was a little, one-room white building built under a couple of oaks. It was big enough for one real barber chair and a regular chair with a cushion on the seat and a cushion fastened to the back. Daddy cut hair out of the barber chair, and Cecil used the other.

During the summer the door was open, and there was just a screen door between you and the flies. The flies liked to gather on the screen and cluster like grapes. The wind was often hot.

Cecil was sitting on the steps reading the Tyler newspaper when I arrived. I tied Sally to one of the oaks, went over to unlock the door, and as I did, I gave Cecil a bit of a rundown, letting him know what Daddy was doing.

Cecil listened, shook his head, made a clucking noise with his tongue, then we were inside.

I loved the aroma of the shop. It smelled of alcohol, disinfectants, and hair oils. The bottles were in a row on a shelf behind the barber chair, and the liquid in them was in different colors, red and yellow and a blue liquid that smelled faintly of coconut.

There was a long bench along the wall near the door and a table with a stack of magazines with bright covers. Most of the magazines were detective stories. I read them whenever I got a chance, and sometimes Daddy brought the worn ones home.

When there weren't any customers, Cecil read them too, sitting on the bench with a hand-rolled cigarette in his mouth, looking like one of the characters out of the magazines. Hard-boiled, carefree, efficient.

Cecil was a big man, and from what I heard around town and indirectly from Daddy, ladies found him good-looking. He had a well-tended shock of reddish hair, bright eyes, and a nice face with slightly hooded eyes. He had come to Marvel Creek about two months back, a barber looking for work. Daddy, realizing he might have competition, put him in the extra chair and gave him a percentage.

Daddy had since halfway regretted it. It wasn't that Cecil wasn't a good worker, nor was it Daddy didn't like him. It was the fact Cecil was too good. He could really cut hair, and pretty soon, more and more of Daddy's customers were waiting for Cecil to take their turn. More mothers came with their sons and waited while Cecil cut their boys' hair and chatted with them while he pinched their kids' cheeks and made them laugh. Cecil was like that. He could chum up to anyone in a big-city minute.

Though Daddy never admitted it, I could see it got his goat, made him a little jealous. There was also the fact that when Mama came down to the shop she always wilted under Cecil's gaze, turned red. She laughed when he said things that weren't that funny.

Cecil had cut my hair a few times, when Daddy was busy, and the truth was, it was an experience. Cecil loved to talk, and he told great stories about places he'd been. All over the United States, all over the world. He had fought in World War I, seen some of the dirtiest fighting. Beyond admitting that, he didn't say much about it. It seemed to pain him. He did once show me a French coin he wore around his neck on a little chain. It had been struck by a bullet and dented. The coin had been in his shirt pocket, and he credited it with saving his life.

But if he was fairly quiet on the war, on everything else he'd done he was a regular blabbermouth. He kidded me some about girls, and sometimes the kidding was a little too far to one side for Daddy, and he'd flash a look at Cecil, and I could see them in the mirror behind the bench, the one designed for the customer to look in while the barber snipped away. Cecil would take the look, wink at Daddy and change the subject. But Cecil always seemed to come back around to it, taking a real interest in any girlfriend I might have, even if I didn't really have any. Doing that, he made me feel as if I were growing up, taking part in the rituals and thoughts of men.

Tom liked him too, and sometimes she came down to the barbershop just to hang around him and hear him flatter and kid her. He loved to have her sit on his knee and tell her stories about all manner of things, and if Tom was interested in the stories I can't say, but she was certainly interested in Cecil, who was like a wild uncle to both her and me.

But what was most amazing about Cecil was the way he could cut hair. His scissors were like an extension of himself. They flashed and turned and snipped with little more than a flex of his wrist. When I was in his chair pruned hair haloed around me in the sunlight and my head became a piece of sculpture, transformed from a mass of unruly hair to a work of art. Cecil never missed a beat, never poked you with the scissor tips — which Daddy couldn't say — and when he was finished, when he had rubbed spiced oil into your scalp and parted and combed your hair, when he spun you around to look in the closer mirror behind the chairs, you weren't the same guy anymore. I felt I looked older, more manly, when he was finished. Maybe a little like those guys on the magazine covers myself.

When Daddy did the job, parted my hair, put on the oil, and let me out of the chair (he never spun me for a look like he did his adult customers), I was still just a kid. With a haircut.

Since on this day I'm talking about, Daddy was out, and haircuts for me were free, I asked Cecil if he would cut my hair, and he did, finishing with hand-whipped shaving cream and a razor around my ears to get those bits of hair too contrary for scissors. Cecil used his hands to work oil into my scalp, and he massaged the back of my neck with his thumb and fingers. It felt warm and tingly in the heat and made me sleepy.

No sooner had I climbed down from the chair than Old Man Nation drove up in his mule-drawn wagon and he and his two boys came in. Mr. Ethan Nation was a big man in overalls with tufts of hair in his ears and crawling out of his nose. His boys were big, redheaded, jug-eared versions of him. They all chewed tobacco, had brown teeth, and spat when they spoke. Most of their conversation was tied to or worked around cuss words not often spoken in that day and time. They never came in to get a haircut. They cut their own hair with a bowl and scissors. They liked to sit in the chairs and read what words they could out of the magazines and talk about how bad things were.

Cecil, though no friend of theirs, always managed to be polite, and, as Daddy often said, he was a man liked to talk, even if he was talking to the Devil.

No sooner had Old Man Nation taken a seat than Cecil said, "Harry says there's been a murder." It was like it was a fact he was proud to spread around, but since I'd been quick to tell him and was about to burst with the news myself, I couldn't blame him none.

Once the word was out, there was nothing for me to do but tell it all. Well, almost all. For some reason I left the Goat Man out of it. I don't know exactly why, but I did.

When I was finished, Mr. Nation said, "Well, one less nigger wench ain't gonna hurt the world none. I was down in the bottoms, came across one of them burr-head women, I don't know, I might be inclined to do her in myself. They're the ones make the little ones. Drop babies like the rest of us drop turds. I might want her to help me out some first, though, you know what I mean. I mean, hell, they're niggers, but for about five minutes the important thing is they're all pink on the inside."

His boys smirked. Cecil said, "Watch your language," and moved his head in my direction.

"Sorry, son," Mr. Nation said. "Your pa's looking in on this, huh?"

"Yes sir," I said.

"Well, he's probably upset about it. He was always one to worry about the niggers. It's just another shine killin', boy, and he ought to leave it alone, let them niggers keep on killin' each other, then the rest of us won't have to worry with it."

At that moment, something changed for me. I had never really thought about my father's personal beliefs, but suddenly it occurred to me his were opposite those of Mr. Nation, and that Mr. Nation, though he liked our barbershop for wasting time, spouting his ideas and reading our magazines, didn't really like my daddy. The fact that he didn't, that Daddy had an opposite point of view to this man, made me proud.

In time, Mr. Johnson, a preacher, came in, and Mr. Nation, feeling the pressure, packed him and his two boys in their wagon and went on down the road to annoy someone else. Late in the day, Daddy came in, and when Cecil asked him about the murder, Daddy looked at me, and I knew then I should have kept my mouth shut.

Daddy told Cecil what I had told him, and little else, other than he thought the woman hadn't gotten caught up there by high water but had been bound there with those briars, like she was being showcased. Daddy figured the murderer had done it.

That night, back at the house, lying in bed, my ear against the wall, Tom asleep across the way, I listened. The walls were thin, and when it was good and quiet, and Mama and Daddy were talking, I could hear them.

"Doctor in town wouldn't even look at her," Daddy said.

"Because she was colored?"

"Yeah. I had to drive her over to Mission Creek's colored section to see a doctor there."

"She was in our car?"

"It didn't hurt anything. After Harry showed me where she was, I came back, drove over to Billy Gold's house. He and his brother went down there with me, helped me wrap her in a tarp, carry her out and put her in the car."

"What did the doctor say?"

"He reckoned she'd been raped. Her breasts had been split from top to bottom."

"Oh, my goodness."

"Yeah. And worse things were done. Doctor didn't know for sure, but when he got through looking her over, cutting on her, looking at her lungs, he thought maybe she'd been dumped in the river still alive, had drowned, been washed up and maybe a day or so later, someone, most likely the killer, had gone down there and found her, maybe by accident, maybe by design, and had bound her against that tree with the briars."

"Who would do such a thing?"

"I don't know. I haven't even an idea."

"Did the doctor know her?"

"No, but he brought in the colored preacher over there, Mr. Bail. He knew her. Name was Jelda May Sykes. He said she was a local prostitute. Now and then she came to the church to talk to him about getting out of the trade. He said she got salvation about once a month and lost it the rest of the time. She worked some of the black juke joints along the river. Picked up a little white trade now and then."

"So no one has any ideas who could have done it?"

"Nobody over there gives a damn, Marilyn. No one. The coloreds don't have any high feelings for her, and the white law enforcement let me know real quick I was out of my jurisdiction. Or as they put it, 'We take care of our own niggers.' Which, of course, means they don't take care of them at all."

"If it's out of your jurisdiction, you'll have to leave it alone."

"Taking her to Mission Creek was out of my jurisdiction, but where she was found isn't out of my jurisdiction. Law over there figures some hobo ridin' the rails got off over there, had his fun with her, dumped her in a river and caught the next train out. They're probably right. But if that's so, who bound her to the tree?"

"It could have been someone else, couldn't it?"

"I suppose, but it worries me mightily to think that there's that much cruelty out there in the world. And besides, I don't buy it. I think the same man killed her and displayed her. I did a little snoopin' while I was over in Mission Creek. I know a newspaperman over there, Cal Fields."

"He the older man with the younger wife? The hot patootie?"

"Yeah. He's a good guy. The wife ran off with a drummer, by the way. That doesn't bother Cal any. He's got a new girlfriend. But what he was tellin' me was interestin'. He said this is the third murder in the area in eighteen months. He didn't write about any of 'em in the paper, primarily because they're messy, but also because they've all been colored killings, and his audience don't care about colored killings. All the murders have been of prostitutes. One happened there in Mission Creek. Her body was found stuffed in a big, ole drainpipe down near the river. Her legs had been broken and pulled up and tied to her head."

"Goodness."

"Cal said he'd just heard the rumor of the other. Cal gave me the name of the editor of the colored paper. I went over and talked to him, a fella named Max Greene. They did do a report on it. He gave me a back issue. The first one was killed January of last year, a little farther up than Mission Creek. They found her in the river too. Her private parts had been cut out and stuffed in her mouth."

"My God. But those murders are some months apart. It wouldn't be the same person, would it?"

"I hope so. Like I said, I don't want to think there's two or three just like this fella runnin' around. Way the bodies are mistreated, sort of displayed, something terribly vulgar done to them. I think it's the same man.

"Greene was of the opinion the murderer likes to finish 'em by drowning 'em. Even the one found in the drainpipe was in water. And the law over there is probably right about it being someone rides the rails. Every spot was near the tracks, close to some little jumping-off point with a juke joint and a working girl. But that don't mean he's a hobo or someone leaves the area much. He could just use the trains to go to the murder sites."

"The body Harry found. What happened to it? Who took it?"

"No one. Honey, I paid to have her buried in the colored cemetery over there. I know we don't have the money, but…"

"Shush. That's all right. You did good."

They grew quiet, and I rolled on my back and looked at the ceiling. When I closed my eyes I saw the woman's body, ruined and swollen, fixed to the tree by vines and thorns. And I saw the bright eyes and white teeth in the dark face of the horned Goat Man. I remembered looking over my shoulder and seeing the Goat Man standing in shadow in the middle of the wooded trail, watching me.

Eventually, in my dream I reached the road, and then I fell asleep.

After a while, things drifted back to normal for Tom and me. Time is like that. Especially when you're young. It can fix a lot of things, and what it doesn't fix, you forget, or at least push back and only bring out at certain times, which is what I did, now and then, late at night, just before sleep claimed me. Eventually it was all a distant memory.

Daddy looked around for the Goat Man awhile, but except for some tracks along the bank, some signs of somebody scavenging around down there, he didn't find anyone. But I heard him telling Mama how he felt he was being watched, and that he figured there was someone out there knew the woods as well as any animal.

But making a living took the lead over any kind of investigation, and my daddy was no investigator anyway. He was just a small-town constable who mainly delivered legal summonses and picked up dead bodies with the justice of the peace. And if they were colored, he picked them up without the justice of the peace. So, in time the murder and the Goat Man moved into our past.

By that fall, Toby had actually begun to walk again. His back wasn't broken, but the limb had caused some kind of nerve damage. He never quite got back to normal, but he could get around with a bit of stiffness, and from time to time, for no reason we could see, his hips would go dead and he'd end up dragging his rear end. Most of the time, he was all right, and ran with a kind of limp, and not very fast. He was still the best squirrel dog in the county.

Late October, a week short of Halloween, when the air had turned cool and the nights were crisp and clear and the moon was like a pumpkin in the sky, Tom and me played late, chasing lightning bugs and each other. Daddy had gone off on a constable duty, and Mama was in the house sewing, and when we got good and played out, me and Tom sat out under the oak talking about this and that, and suddenly we stopped, and I had a kind of cold feeling. I don't know if a person really has a sixth sense. Maybe it's little things you notice unconsciously. Something seen out of the corner of the eye. Something heard at the back of a conversation. But I had that same feeling Daddy had spoken of, the feeling of being watched.

I stopped listening to Tom, who was chattering on about something or another, and slowly turned my head toward the woods, and there, between two trees, in the shadows, but clearly framed by the light, was a horned figure, watching us.

Tom, noticing I wasn't listening to her, said, "Hey."

"Tom," I said, "be quiet a moment and look where I'm lookin'."

"I don't see any —" Then she went quiet, and after a moment, whispered, "It's him… It's the Goat Man."

The shape abruptly turned, crunched a stick, rustled some leaves, and was gone. We didn't tell Daddy or Mama what we saw. I don't exactly know why, but we didn't. It was between me and Tom, and the next day we hardly mentioned it.

A week later, Janice Jane Willman was dead.

We heard about it Halloween night. There was a little party in town for the kids and whoever wanted to come. There were no invitations. Each year it was understood the party would take place and you could show up. The women brought covered dishes and the men brought a little bit of hooch to slip into their drinks.

The party was at Mrs. Canerton's. She was a widow, and kept books at her house as a kind of library. She let us borrow them from her, or we could come and sit in her house and read or even be read to, and she always had some cookies or lemonade, and she wasn't adverse to listening to our stories or problems. She was a sweet-faced lady with large breasts and a lot of men in town liked her and thought she was pretty.

Every year she had a little Halloween party for the kids. Apples. Pumpkin pie and such. Everyone who could afford a spare pillowcase made a ghost costume. A few of the older boys would slip off to West Street to soap some windows, and that was about it for Halloween. But back then, it seemed pretty wonderful.

Daddy had taken us to the party. It was another fine, cool night with lots of lightning bugs and crickets chirping, and me and Tom got to playing hide and go seek with the rest of the kids, and while the person who was it was counting, we went to hide. I crawled up under Mrs. Canerton's house, under the front porch. I hadn't no more than got up under there good, than Tom crawled up beside me.

"Hey," I whispered. "Go find your own place."

"I didn't know you was under here. It's too late for me to go anywhere."

"Then be quiet," I said.

While we were sitting there, we saw shoes and pants legs moving toward the porch steps. It was the men who had been standing out in the yard smoking. They were gathering on the porch to talk. I recognized a pair of boots as Daddy's, and after a bit of moving about on the porch above us, we heard the porch swing creak and some of the porch chairs scraping around, and then I heard Cecil speak.

"How long she been dead?"

"About a week I reckon," Daddy said.

"She anyone we know?"

"A prostitute," Daddy said. "Janice Jane Willman. She lives near all them juke joints outside of Mission Creek. She picked up the wrong man. Ended up in the river."

"She drown?" someone else asked.

"Reckon so. But she suffered some before that."

"You know who did it?" Cecil asked. "Any leads?"

"No. Not really."

"Niggers." I knew that voice. Old Man Nation. He showed up wherever there was food and possibly liquor, and he never brought a covered dish or liquor. "Niggers find a white woman down there in the bottoms, they'll get her."

"Yeah," I heard a voice say. "And what would a white woman be doin' wanderin' around down there?"

"Maybe he brought her there," Mr. Nation said. "A nigger'll take a white woman he gets a chance. Hell, wouldn't you if you was a nigger? Think about what you'd be gettin' at home. Some nigger. A white woman, that's prime business to 'em. Then, if you're a nigger and you've done it to her, you got to kill her so no one knows. Not that any self-respectin' white woman would want to live after somethin' like that."

"That's enough of that," Daddy said.

"You threatenin' me?" Mr. Nation said.

"I'm sayin' we don't need that kind of talk," Daddy said. "The murderer could have been white or black."

"It'll turn out to be a nigger," Mr. Nation said. "Mark my words."

"I heard you had a suspect," Cecil said.

"Not really," Daddy said.

"Some colored fella, I heard," Cecil said.

"I knew it," Nation said. "Some goddamn nigger."

"I picked a man up for questioning, that's all."

"Where is he?" Nation asked.

"You know," Daddy said, "I think I'm gonna have me a piece of that pie."

The porch creaked, the screen door opened, and we heard boot steps entering into the house.

"Nigger lover," Nation said.

"That's enough of that," Cecil said.

"You talkin' to me, fella?" Mr. Nation said.

"I am, and I said that's enough."

There was some scuttling movement on the porch, and suddenly there was a smacking sound and Mr. Nation hit the ground in front of us. We could see him through the steps. His face turned in our direction, but I don't think he saw us. It was dark under the house, and he had his mind on other things. He got up quick like, leaving his hat on the ground, then we heard movement on the porch and Daddy's voice. "Ethan, don't come back on the porch. Go on home."

"Who do you think you are to tell me anything?" Mr. Nation said.

"Right now, I'm the constable, and you come up on this porch, you do one little thing that annoys me, I will arrest you."

"You and who else?"

"Just me."

"What about him? He hit me. You're on his side because he took up for you."

"I'm on his side because you're a loudmouth spoiling everyone else's good time. You been drinkin' too much. Go on home and sleep it off, Ethan. Let's don't let this get out of hand."

Mr. Nation's hand dropped down and picked up his hat. He said, "You're awfully high and mighty, aren't you?"

"There's just no use fighting over something silly," Daddy said.

"You watch yourself, nigger lover," Mr. Nation said.

"Don't come by the barbershop no more," Daddy said.

"Wouldn't think of it, nigger lover."

Then Mr. Nation turned and we saw him walking away.

Daddy said, "Cecil. You talk too much."

"Yeah, I know," Cecil said.

"Now, I was gonna get some pie," Daddy said. "I'm gonna go back inside and try it again. When I come back out, how's about we talk about somethin' altogether different?"

"Suits me," someone said, and I heard the screen door open again. For a moment I thought they were all inside, then I realized Daddy and Cecil were still on the porch, and Daddy was talking to Cecil.

"I shouldn't have spoken to you like that," Daddy said.

"It's all right. You're right. I talk too much."

"Let's forget it."

"Sure… Jacob, this suspect. You think he did it?"

"No. I don't."

"Is he safe?"

"For now. I may just let him go and never let it be known who he is. Bill Smoote is helping me out with him right now."

"Again, I'm sorry, Jacob."

"No problem. Let's get some of that pie."

On the way home in the car our bellies were full of apples, pie, and lemonade. The windows were rolled down and the October wind was fresh and ripe with the smell of the woods. As we wound through those woods along the dirt road that led to our house, I began to feel sleepy.

Tom had already nodded off. I leaned against the side of the car and began to halfway doze. In time, I realized Mama and Daddy were talking.

"He had her purse?" Mama said.

"Yeah." Daddy said. "He had it, and he'd taken money from it."

"Could it be him?"

"He says he was fishing, saw the purse and her dress floating, snagged the purse with his fishing line. He saw there was money inside, and he took it. He said he figured a purse in the river wasn't something anyone was going to find, and there wasn't any name in it, and it was just five dollars going to waste. He said he didn't even consider that someone had been murdered. It could have happened that way. Personally, I believe him. I've known old Mose all my life. He taught me how to fish. He practically lives on that river in that boat of his. He wouldn't harm a fly. Besides, the man's seventy years old and not in the best of health. He's had a hell of a life. His wife ran off forty years ago and he's never gotten over it. His son disappeared when he was a youngster. Whoever raped this woman had to be pretty strong. She was young enough, and from the way her body looked, she put up a pretty good fight. Man did this had to be strong enough to... Well, she was cut up pretty bad. Same as the other women. Slashes along the breasts. Her hand hacked off at the wrist. We didn't find it."

"Oh dear."

"I'm sorry, honey. I didn't mean to upset you."

"How did you come by the purse?"

"I went by to see Mose. Like I always do when I'm down on the river. It was layin' on the table in his shack. I had to arrest him. I don't know I should have now. Maybe I should have just taken the purse and said I found it. I mean, I believe him. But I don't have evidence one way or the other."

"Hon, didn't Mose have some trouble before?"

"When his wife ran off some thought he'd killed her. She was fairly loose. That was the rumor. Nothing ever came of it."

"But he could have done it?"

"I suppose."

Mad Dog Summer

85

"And wasn't there something about his boy?"

"Telly was the boy's name. He was addleheaded. Mose claimed that's why his wife run off. She was embarrassed by that addleheaded boy. Kid disappeared four or five years later and Mose never talked about it. Some thought he killed him too. But that's just rumor. White folks talkin' about colored folks like they do. I believe his wife ran off. The boy wasn't much of a thinker, and he may have run off too. He liked to roam the woods and river. He might have drowned, fallen in some hole somewhere and never got out."

"But none of that makes it look good for Mose, does it?"

"No, it doesn't."

"What are you gonna do, Jacob?"

"I don't know. I was afraid to lock him up over at the courthouse. It isn't a real jail anyway, and word gets around a colored man was involved, there won't be any real thinking on the matter. I talked Bill Smoote into letting me keep Mose over at his bait house."

"Couldn't Mose just run away?"

"I suppose. But he's not in that good a health, hon. And he trusts me to investigate, clear him. That's what makes me nervous. I don't know how. I thought about talking to the Mission Creek police, as they have more experience, but they have a tendency to be a little emotional themselves. Rumor is, sheriff over there is in the Klan, or used to be. Frankly, I'm not sure what to do."

I began to drift off again. I thought of Mose. He was an old colored man who got around on shore with use of a cane. He had white blood in him. Red in his hair, and eyes as green as spring leaves. Mostly you saw him in his little rowboat fishing. He lived in a shack alongside the river not more than three miles from us. Living off the fish he caught, the squirrels he shot. Sometimes, when we had a good day hunting or fishing, Daddy would go by there and give Mose a squirrel or some fish. Mose was always glad to see us, or seemed to be. Up until a year ago, I used to go fishing with him. It was then Jake told me I ought not. That it wasn't right to be seen with a nigger all the time.

Thinking back on that, I felt sick to my stomach, confused. Mose had taught my daddy to fish, I had gone fishing with him, and suddenly I deserted him because of what Jake had said.

I thought of the Goat Man again. I recalled him standing below the swinging bridge, looking up through the shadows at me. I thought of him near our house, watching. The Goat Man had killed those women, I knew it. And Mose was gonna take the blame for what he had done.

It was there in the car, battered by the cool October wind, that I began to formulate a plan to find the Goat Man and free Mose. I thought on it for several days after, and I think maybe I had begun to come up with something that seemed like a good idea to me: It probably wasn't. Just some thirteen-year-old's idea of a plan. But it didn't really matter. Shortly thereafter, things turned for the worse.

It was a Monday, a couple days later, and Daddy was off from the barbershop that day. He had already gotten up and fed the livestock, and as daybreak was making through the trees, he come and got me up to help tote water from the well to the house. Mama was in the kitchen cooking grits, biscuits, and fatback for breakfast.

Me and Daddy had a bucket of water apiece and were carrying them back to the house, when I said, "Daddy. You ever figure out what you're gonna do with Ole Mose?"

He paused a moment. "How'd you know about that?"

"I heard you and Mama talkin'."

He nodded, and we started walking again. "I can't leave him where he is for good. Someone will get onto it. I reckon I'm gonna have to take him to the courthouse or let him go. There's no real evidence against him, just some circumstantial stuff. But a colored man, a white woman, and a hint of suspicion... He'll never get a fair trial. I got to be sure myself he didn't do it."

"Ain't you?"

We were on the back porch now, and Daddy set his bucket down and set mine down too. "You know, I reckon I am. If no one ever knows who it was I arrested, he can go on about his business. I ain't got nothin' on him. Not really. Something else comes up, some real evidence against him, I know where he is."

"Mose couldn't have killed those women. He hardly gets around, Daddy."

I saw his face redden. "Yeah. You're right."

He picked up both buckets and carried them into the house. Mama had the food on the table, and Tom was sitting there with her eyes squinted, looking as if she were going to fall face forward in her grits any moment. Normally, there'd be school, but the schoolteacher had quit and they hadn't hired another yet, so we had nowhere to go that day, me and Tom.

I think that was part of the reason Daddy asked me to go with him after breakfast. That, and I figured he wanted some company. He told me he had decided to go down and let Mose loose.

We drove over to Bill Smoote's. Bill owned an icehouse down by the river. It was a big room really, with sawdust and ice packed in there, and people came and bought it by car or by boat on the river. He sold right smart of it. Up behind the icehouse was the little house where Bill lived with his wife and two daughters that looked as if they had fallen out of an ugly tree, hit every branch on the way down, then smacked the dirt solid. They was always smilin' at me and such, and it made me nervous.

Behind Mr. Smoote's house was his barn, really more of a big ole shed. That's where Daddy said Mose was kept. As we pulled up at Mr. Smoote's place alongside the river, we saw the yard was full of cars, wagons, horses, mules, and people. It was early morning still, and the sunlight fell through the trees like Christmas decorations, and the river was red with the morning sun, and the people in the yard were painted with the same red light as the river.

At first I thought Mr. Smoote was just having him a big run of customers, but as we got up there, we saw there was a wad of people coming from the barn. The wad was Mr. Nation, his two boys, and some other man I'd seen around town before but didn't know. They had Mose between them. He wasn't exactly walking with them. He was being half dragged, and I heard Mr. Nation's loud voice say something about "damn nigger," then Daddy was out of the car and pushing through the crowd.

A heavyset woman in a print dress and square-looking shoes, her hair wadded on top of her head and pinned there, yelled, "To hell with you, Jacob, for hidin' this nigger out. After what he done."

It was then I realized we was in the middle of the crowd, and they were closing around us, except for a gap that opened so Mr. Nation and his bunch could drag Mose into the circle.

Mose looked ancient, withered and knotted like old cowhide soaked in brine. His head was bleeding, his eyes were swollen, his lips were split. He had already taken quite a beating.

When Mose saw Daddy, his green eyes lit up. "Mr. Jacob, don't let them do nothin'. I didn't do nothin' to nobody."

"It's all right, Mose," he said. Then he glared at Mr. Nation. "Nation, this ain't your business."

"It's all our business," Mr. Nation said. "When our womenfolk can't walk around without worrying about some nigger draggin' 'em off, then it's our business."

There was a voice of agreement from the crowd.

"I only picked him up 'cause he might know something could lead to the killer," Daddy said. "I was comin' out here to let him go. I realized he don't know a thing."

"Bill here says he had that woman's purse," Nation said.

Daddy turned to look at Mr. Smoote, who didn't acknowledge Daddy's look. He just said softly under his breath, "I didn't tell 'em he was here, Jacob. They knew. I just told 'em why you had him here. I tried to get them to listen, but they wouldn't."

Daddy just stared at Mr. Smoote for a long moment. Then he turned to Nation, said, "Let him go."

"In the old days, we took care of bad niggers prompt like," Mr. Nation said. "And we figured out somethin' real quick. A nigger hurt a white man or woman, you hung him, he didn't hurt anyone again. You got to take care of a nigger problem quick, or ever' nigger around here will be thinkin' he can rape and murder white women at will."

Daddy spoke calmly. "He deserves a fair trial. We're not here to punish anyone."

"Hell we ain't," someone said.

The crowd grew tighter around us. I turned to look for Mr. Smoote, but he was gone from sight.

Mr. Nation said, "You ain't so high and mighty now, are you, Jacob? You and your nigger-lovin' ways aren't gonna cut the mustard around here."

"Hand him over," Daddy said. "I'll take him. See he gets a fair trial."

"You said you were gonna turn him loose," Nation said.

"I thought about it. Yes."

"He ain't gonna be turned loose, except at the end of the rope."

"You're not gonna hang this man," Daddy said.

"That's funny," Nation said. "I thought that's exactly what we were gonna do."

"This ain't the wild west," Daddy said.

"No," Nation said. "This here is a riverbank with trees, and we got us a rope and a bad nigger."

One of Mr. Nation's boys had slipped off while Daddy and Mr. Nation were talking, and when he reappeared, he had a rope tied in a noose. He slipped it over Mose's head.

Daddy stepped forward then, grabbed the rope and jerked it off of Mose. The crowd let out a sound like an animal in pain, then they were all over Daddy, punching and kicking. I tried to fight them, but they hit me too, and the next thing I knew I was on the ground and legs were kicking at us and then I heard Mose scream for my daddy, and when I looked up they had the rope around his neck and were dragging him along the ground.

One man grabbed the end of the rope and threw it over a thick oak limb, and in unison the crowd grabbed the rope and began to pull, hoisting Mose up. Mose grabbed at the rope with his hands and his feet kicked.

Daddy pushed himself up, staggered forward, grabbed Mose's legs and ducked his head under Mose and lifted him. But Mr. Nation blindsided Daddy with a kick to the ribs, and Daddy went down and Mose dropped with a snapping sound, started to kick and spit foam. Daddy tried to get up, but men and women began to kick and beat him. I got up and ran for him. Someone clipped me in the back of the neck, and when I come to everyone was gone except me and Daddy, still unconscious, and Mose hung above us, his tongue long and black and thick as a sock stuffed with paper. His green eyes bulged out of his head like little green persimmons.

On hands and knees I threw up until I didn't think I had any more in me. Hands grabbed my sides, and I was figuring on more of a beating, but then I heard Mr. Smoote say, "Easy, boy. Easy."

He tried to help me up, but I couldn't stand. He left me sitting on the ground and went over and looked at Daddy. He turned him over and pulled an eyelid back.

I said, "Is he...?"

"No. He's all right. He just took some good shots."

Daddy stirred. Mr. Smoote sat him up. Daddy lifted his eyes to Mose. He said, "For Christ's sake, Bill, cut him down from there."

Mose was buried on our place, between the barn and the field. Daddy made him a wooden cross and carved MOSE on it, and swore when he got money he'd get him a stone.

After that, Daddy wasn't quite the same. He wanted to quit being a constable, but the little money the job brought in was needed, so he stayed at it, swearing anything like this came up again he was gonna quit.

Fall passed into winter, and there were no more murders. Those who had helped lynch Mose warmed themselves by their self-righteousness. A bad nigger had been laid low. No more women would die — especially white women.

Many of those there that day had been Daddy's customers, and we didn't see them anymore at the shop. As for the rest, Cecil cut most of the hair, and Daddy was doing so little of it, he finally gave Cecil a key and a bigger slice of the money and only came around now and then. He turned his attention to working around the farm, fishing, and hunting.

When spring came, Daddy went to planting, just like always, but he didn't talk about the crops much, and I didn't hear him and Mama talking much, but sometimes late at night, through the wall, I could hear him cry. There's no way to explain how bad it hurts to hear your father cry.

They got a new schoolmaster come that spring, but it was decided school wouldn't pick up until the fall, after all the crops had been laid by. Cecil started teaching me how to cut hair, and I even got so I could handle a little trade at the shop, mostly kids my age that liked the idea of me doing it. I brought the money home to Mama, and when I gave it to her, she nearly always cried.

For the first time in my life, the Depression seemed like the Depression to me. Tom and I still hunted and fished together, but there was starting to be more of a gulf between our ages. I was about to turn fourteen and I felt as old as Mose had been.

That next spring came and went and was pleasant enough, but the summer set in with a vengeance, hot as hell's griddle, and the river receded some and the fish didn't seem to want to bite, and the squirrels and rabbits were wormy that time of year, so there wasn't much use in that. Most of the crops burned up, and if that wasn't bad enough, mid July, there was a bad case of the hydrophobia broke out. Forest animals, domesticated dogs and cats were the victims. It was pretty awful. Got so people shot stray dogs on sight. We kept Toby close to the house, and in the cool, as it was believed by many that an animal could catch rabies not only by being bitten by a diseased animal but by air when it was hot.

Anyway, it got so folks were calling it a mad dog summer, and it turned out that in more ways than one they were right.

Clem Sumption lived some ten miles down the road from us, right where a little road forked off what served as a main highway then. You wouldn't think of it as a highway now, but it was the main road, and if you turned off of it, trying to cross through our neck of the woods on your way to Tyler, you had to pass his house, which was situated alongside the river.

Clem's outhouse was over near the river, and it was fixed up so what went out of him and his family went into the river. Lot of folks did that, though some like my daddy were appalled at the idea. It was that place and time's idea of plumbing. The waste dropped down a slanted hole onto the bank and when the water rose, the mess was carried away. When it didn't, flies lived there on mounds of dark mess, buried in it, glowing like jewels in rancid chocolate.

Clem ran a little roadside stand where he sold a bit of vegetables now and then, and on this hot day I'm talking about, he suddenly had the urge to take care of a mild stomach disorder, and left his son, Wilson, in charge of the stand.

After doing his business, Clem rolled a cigarette and went out beside the outhouse to look down on the fly-infested pile, maybe hoping the river had carried some of it away. But dry as it was, the pile was bigger and the water was lower, and something pale lay facedown in the pile.

Clem, first spying it, thought it was a huge, bloated, belly-up catfish. One of those enormous bottom crawler types that were reputed by some to be able to swallow small dogs and babies.

But a catfish didn't have legs.

Clem said later, even when he saw the legs, it didn't register with him that it was a human being. It looked too swollen, too strange to be a person.

But as he eased carefully down the side of the hill, mindful not to step in what his family had been dropping along the bank all summer, he saw that it was indeed a woman's bloated body lying facedown in the moist blackness, and the flies were as delighted with the corpse as they were with the waste.

Clem saddled up a horse and arrived in our yard sometime after that. This wasn't like now, when medical examiners show up and cops measure this and measure that, take fingerprints and photos. My father and Clem pulled the body out of the pile and dipped it into the river for a rinse, and it was then that Daddy saw the face of Marla Canerton buried in a mass of swollen flesh, one cold dead eye open, as if she were winking.

The body arrived at our house wrapped in a tarp. Daddy and Clem hauled it out of the car and toted it up to the barn. As they walked by, me and Tom, out under the big tree, playing some game or another, could smell that terrible dead smell through the tarp, and with no wind blowing, it was dry and rude to the nostrils and made me sick.

When Daddy came out of the barn with Clem, he had an ax handle in his hand. He started walking briskly down to the car, and I could hear Clem arguing with him. "Don't do it, Jacob. It ain't worth it."

We ran over to the car as Mama came out of the house. Daddy calmly laid the ax handle in the front seat, and Clem stood shaking his head. Mama climbed into the car and started on Daddy. "Jacob, I know what you're thinkin'. You can't."

Daddy started up the car. Mama yelled out, "Children. Get in. I'm not leavin' you here."

We did just that, and roared off leaving Clem standing in the yard bewildered. Mama fussed and yelled and pleaded all the way over to Mr. Nation's house, but Daddy never said a word. When he pulled up in Nation's yard, Mr. Nation's wife was outside hoeing at a pathetic, little garden, and Mr. Nation and his two boys were sitting in rickety chairs under a tree.

Daddy got out of the car with his ax handle and started walking toward Mr. Nation. Mama was hanging on his arm, but he pulled free. He walked right past Mrs. Nation, who paused and looked up in surprise.

Mr. Nation and his boys spotted Daddy coming, and Mr. Nation slowly rose from his chair. "What the hell you doin' with that ax handle?" he asked.

Daddy didn't answer, but the next moment what he was doing with that ax handle became clear. It whistled through the hot morning air like a flaming arrow and caught Mr. Nation alongside the head about where the jaw meets the ear, and the sound it made was, to put it mildly, akin to a rifle shot.

Mr. Nation went down like a windblown scarecrow, and Daddy stood over him swinging the ax handle, and Mr. Nation was yelling and putting up his arms in a pathetic way, and the two boys came at Daddy, and Daddy turned and swatted one of them down, and the other tackled him. Instinctively, I started kicking at that boy, and he came off Daddy and climbed me, but Daddy was up now, and the ax handle whistled, and that ole boy went out like a light and the other one, who was still conscious, started scuttling along the ground on all fours with a motion like a crippled centipede. He finally got upright and ran for the house.

Mr. Nation tried to get up several times, but every time he did that ax handle would cut the air, and down he'd go. Daddy whapped on Mr. Nation's sides and back and legs until he was worn out, had to back off and lean on the somewhat splintered handle.

Nation, battered, ribs surely broken, lip busted, spitting teeth, looked at Daddy, but he didn't try to get up. Daddy, when he got his wind back, said, "They found Marla Canerton down by the river. Dead. Cut the same way. You and your boys and that lynch mob didn't do nothin' but hang an innocent man."

"You're supposed to be the law?" Nation said.

"If'n I was any kind of law, I'd have had you arrested for what you did to Mose, but that wouldn't have done any good. No one around here would convict you, Nation. They're scared of you. But I ain't. I ain't. And if you ever cross my path again, I swear to God, I'll kill you."

Daddy tossed the ax handle aside, said "Come on," and we all started back to the car. As we passed Mrs. Nation, she looked up and leaned on her hoe. She had a black eye and a swollen lip and some old bruises on her cheek. She smiled at us.

We all went to Mrs. Canerton's funeral. Me and my family stood in the front row. Cecil was there. Just about everyone in town and around about, except the Nations and some of the people who had been in the lynch mob that killed Mose.

Within a week Daddy's customers at the barbershop returned, among them members of the lynch party, and the majority of them wanted him to cut their hair. He had to go back to work regularly. I don't know how he felt about that, cutting the hair of those who had beaten me and him that day, that had killed Mose, but he cut their hair and took their money. Maybe Daddy saw it as a kind of revenge. And maybe we just needed the money.

Mama took a job in town at the courthouse. With school out, that left me to take care of Tom, and though we were supposed to stay out of the woods that summer, especially knowing there was a murderer on the loose, we were kids and adventurous and bored.

One morning me and Tom and Toby went down to the river and walked along the bank, looking for a place to ford near the swinging bridge. Neither of us wanted to cross the bridge, and we used the excuse that Toby couldn't cross it, but that was just an excuse.

We wanted to look at the briar tunnel we had been lost in that night, but we didn't want to cross the bridge to get there. We walked a long ways and finally came to the shack where Mose had lived, and we just stood there looking at it. It had never been much, just a hovel made of wood and tin and tarpaper. Mose mostly set outside of it in an old chair under a willow tree that overlooked the river.

The door was wide open, and when we looked in there, we could see animals had been prowling about. A tin of flour had been knocked over and was littered with bugs. Other foodstuff was not recognizable. They were just glaze matted into the hard dirt floor. A few pathetic possessions were lying here and there. A wooden child's toy was on a shelf and next to it a very faded photograph of a dark black woman that might have been Mose's wife.

The place depressed me. Toby went inside and sniffed about and prowled in the flour till we called him out. We walked around the house and out near the chair, and it was then, looking back at the house, I noted there was something hanging on a nail on the outside wall. It was a chain, and from the chain hung a number of fish skeletons, and one fresh fish.

We went over and looked at it. The fresh fish was very fresh, and in fact, it was still damp. Someone had hung it there recently, and the other stack of fish bones indicated that someone had been hanging fish there on a regular basis, and for some time, like an offering to Mose. An offering he could no longer take.

On another nail nearby, strings tied together, was a pair of old shoes that had most likely been fished from the river, and hung over them was a water-warped belt. On the ground, leaning against the side of the house below the nail with the shoes, was a tin plate and a bright blue river rock and a mason jar. All of it laid out like gifts.

I don't know why, but I took the dead fish down, all the old bones, and cast them into the river and put the chain back on the nail. I tossed the shoes and belt, the plate, rock and mason jar into the river. Not out of meanness, but so the gifts would seem to be taken.

Mose's old boat was still up by the house, laid up on rocks so it wouldn't rot on the ground. A paddle lay in its bottom. We decided to take it and float it upriver to where the briar tunnels were. We loaded Toby in the boat, pushed it into the water and set out. We floated the long distance back to the swinging bridge and went under it, looking for the Goat Man under there, waiting like Billy Goat Gruff.

In shadow, under the bridge, deep into the bank, was a dark indention, like a cave. I imagined that was where the Goat Man lived, waiting for prey.

We paddled gently to the riverbank where we had found the woman bound to the tree by the river. She was long gone, of course, and the vines that had held her were no longer there.

We pulled the boat onto the dirt and gravel bank and left it there as we went up the taller part of the bank, past the tree where the woman had been, and into the briars. The tunnel was the same, and it was clear in the daytime that the tunnel had, as we suspected, been cut into the briars. It was not as large or as long a tunnel as it had seemed that night, and it emptied out into a wider tunnel, and it too was shorter and smaller than we had thought. There were little bits of colored cloth hung on briars all about and there were pictures from Sears catalogs of women in underwear and there were a few of those playing cards like I had seen hung on briars. We hadn't seen all that at night, but I figured it had been there all along.

In the middle of the tunnel was a place where someone had built a fire, and above us the briars wrapped so thick and were so intertwined with low-hanging branches, you could imagine much of this place would stay almost dry during a rainstorm.

Toby was sniffing and running about as best his poor old damaged back and legs would allow him.

"It's like some kind of nest," Tom said, "The Goat Man's nest."

A chill came over me then, and it occurred to me that if that was true, and if this was his den instead of the cave under the bridge, or one of his dens, he might come home at any time. I told Tom that, and we called up Toby and got out of there, tried to paddle the boat back upriver, but couldn't.

We finally got out and made to carry it along the bank, but it was too heavy. We gave up and left it by the river. We walked past the swinging bridge and for a long ways till we found a sandbar. We used that to cross, and went back home, finished the chores, cleaned ourselves and Toby up before Mama and Daddy came chugging home from work in our car.

Next morning, when Mama and Daddy left for town and work, me and Tom and Toby went at it again. I had a hunch about Mose's old shack, and I wanted to check it out. But my hunch was wrong. There was nothing new hung from the nails or leaned against the wall. But there was something curious. The boat we had left on the bank was back in its place atop the rocks with the paddle inside.

It was that night, lying in bed, that I heard Mama and Daddy talking. After Daddy had beaten Mr. Nation and his boys with the ax handle, his spirit had been restored. I heard him tell Mama: "There's this thing I been thinking, honey. What if the murderer wanted people to think it was Mose, so he made a big to-do about it to hide the fact he done it. Maybe he was gonna quit doin' it, but he couldn't. You know, like some of them diseases that come back on you when you think you're over it."

"You mean Mr. Nation, don't you?" Mama said.

"Well, it's a thought. And it come to me it might be one of them boys, Esau or Uriah. Uriah has had a few problems. There's lots of talk about him torturin' little animals and such, stomping the fish he caught on the bank, for no good reason other than he wanted to."

"That doesn't mean he killed those women."

"No. But he likes to hurt things and cut them up. And the other'n, Esau. He starts fires, and not like some kids will do, but regular like. He's been in trouble over it before. Folks like that worry me."

"That still don't mean they're murderers."

"No. But if Nation was capable of such a thing, it would be like him to blame it on a colored. Most people in these parts would be quick to accept that. I've heard a couple of lawmen say when you don't know who did it, go out and get you a nigger. It calms people down, and it's one less nigger."

"That's terrible."

"Of course it is. But there's some like that. If Nation didn't do it, and he knows one or both of them worthless boys did it, he might have been coverin' up for him."

The Best of Joe R. Lansdale

"You really think that's possible, Jacob?"

"I think it's possible. I don't know it's likely, but I'm gonna keep my eye on 'em."

Daddy made sense about Mr. Nation and his boys. I had seen Mr. Nation a couple of times since the day Daddy gave him his beating, and when he saw me, he gave me a look that could have set fire to rocks, then went his way. Esau had even followed me down Main Street one day, scowling, but by the time I reached the barbershop, he had turned and gone between a couple of buildings and out of sight.

But all that aside, I still put my odds on the Goat Man. He had been near the site of the body me and Tom had found, and he had followed us out to the road, as if we were to be his next victims. And I figured only something that wasn't quite human would be capable of the kind of things that had happened in those bottoms with those women.

Poor Mrs. Canerton had always been so nice. All those books. The Halloween parties. The way she smiled.

As I drifted off to sleep I thought of telling Daddy about the Sears catalog pictures and the cloth and such in the briar tunnel, but being young like I was then, I was more worried about getting in trouble for being where I wasn't supposed to be, so I kept quiet. Actually, thinking back now, it wouldn't have mattered.

That summer, from time to time, me and Tom slipped off and went down to Mose's old cabin. Now and then there would be a fish on the nail, or some odd thing from the river, so my hunch had been right all along. Someone was bringing Mose gifts, perhaps unaware he was dead. Or maybe they had been left there for some other reason.

We dutifully took down what was there and returned it to the river, wondering if maybe it was the Goat Man leaving the goods. But when we looked around for sign of him, all we could find were prints from someone wearing large-sized shoes. No hoof prints.

As the summer moved on, it got hotter and hotter, and the air was like having a blanket wrapped twice around your head. Got so you hardly wanted to move midday, and for a time we quit slipping off down to the river and stayed close at home.

That Fourth of July, our little town decided to have a celebration. Me and Tom were excited because there was to be firecrackers and some Roman candles and all manner of fireworks, and, of course, plenty of home-cooked food.

Folks were pretty leery, thinking that the killer was probably still out there somewhere, and the general thinking had gone from him being some traveling fellow to being someone among us.

Fact was, no one had ever seen or heard of anything like this, except for Jack the Ripper, and we had thought that kind of murder was only done in some big city far away.

The town gathered late afternoon before dark. Main Street had been blocked off, which was no big deal as traffic was rare anyway, and tables with covered dishes and watermelons on them were set up in the street, and after a preacher said a few words, everyone got a plate and went around and helped themselves. I remember eating a little of everything that was there, zeroing in on mashed potatoes and gravy, mincemeat, apple, and pear pies. Tom ate pie and cake and nothing else except watermelon that Cecil helped her cut.

There was a circle of chairs between the tables and behind the chairs was a kind of makeshift stage, and there were a handful of folks with guitars and fiddles playing and singing now and then, and the men and womenfolk would gather in the middle and dance to the tunes. Mama and Daddy were dancing too, and Tom was sitting on Cecil's knee and he was clapping and keeping time to the music, bouncing her up and down.

I kept thinking Mr. Nation and his boys would show, as they were always ones to be about when there was free food or the possibility of a drink, but they didn't. I figured that was because of Daddy. Mr. Nation might have looked tough and had a big mouth, but that ax handle had tamed him.

As the night wore on, the music was stopped and the fireworks were set. The firecrackers popped and the candles and such exploded high above Main Street, burst into all kinds of colors, pinned themselves against the night, then went wide and thin and faded. I remember watching as one bright swath did not fade right away, but dropped to earth like a falling star, and as my eyes followed it down, it dipped behind Cecil and Tom, and in the final light from its burst, I could see Tom's smiling face, and Cecil, his hands on her shoulders, his face slack and beaded with sweat, his knee still bouncing her gently, even though there was no music to keep time to, the two of them looking up, awaiting more bright explosions.

Worry about the murders, about there being a killer amongst us, had withered. In that moment, all seemed right with the world.

When we got home that night we were all excited, and we sat down for a while under the big oak outside and drank some apple cider. It was great fun, but I kept having that uncomfortable feeling of being watched. I scanned the woods, but didn't see anything. Tom didn't seem to have noticed, and neither had my parents. Not long after a possum presented itself at the edge of the woods, peeked out at our celebration and disappeared back into the darkness.

Daddy and Mama sang a few tunes as he picked his old guitar, then they told stories awhile, and a couple of them were kind of spooky ones, then we all took turns going out to the outhouse, and finally to bed.

Tom and I talked some, then I helped her open the window by her bed, and the warm air blew in carrying the smell of rain brewing.

As I lay in bed that night, my ear to the wall, I heard Mama say: "The children will hear, honey. These walls are paper thin."

"Don't you want to?"

"Of course. Sure."

"The walls are always paper thin."

"You're not always like you are tonight. You know how you are when you're like this."

"How am I?"

Mama laughed. "Loud."

"Listen, honey. I really, you know, need to. And I want to be loud. What say we take the car down the road a piece. I know a spot."

"Jacob. What if someone came along?"

"I know a spot they won't come along. It'll be real private."

"Well, we don't have to do that. We can do it here. We'll just have to be quiet."

"I don't want to be quiet. And even if I did, it's a great night. I'm not sleepy."

"What about the children?"

"It's just down the road, hon. It'll be fun."

"All right... All right. Why not?"

I lay there wondering what in the world had gotten into my parents, and as I lay there I heard the car start up and glide away down the road.

Where could they be going?

And why?

It was really some years later before I realized what was going on. At the time it was a mystery. But back then I contemplated it for a time, then nodded off, the wind turning from warm to cool by the touch of oncoming rain.

Sometime later I was awakened by Toby barking, but it didn't last and I went back to sleep. After that, I heard a tapping sound. It was as if some bird were pecking corn from a hard surface. I gradually opened my eyes and turned in my bed and saw a figure at the open window. When the curtains blew I could see the shape standing there, looking in. It was a dark shape with horns on its head, and one hand was tapping on the windowsill with long fingernails. The Goat Man was making a kind of grunting sound.

I sat bolt upright in bed, my back to the wall.

"Go away!" I said.

But the shape remained and its gruntings changed to whimpers. The curtains blew in, back out, and the shape was gone. Then I noticed that Tom's bed, which was directly beneath the window, was empty.

I had helped open that window.

I eased over to her bed and peeked outside. Out by the woods I could see the Goat Man. He lifted his hand and summoned me.

I hesitated. I ran to Mama and Daddy's room, but they were gone. I dimly remembered before dropping off to sleep they had driven off in the car, for God knows what. I went back to our little room and assured myself I was not dreaming. Tom was gone, stolen by the Goat Man, most likely, and now the thing was summoning me to follow. A kind of taunt. A kind of game.

I looked out the window again, and the Goat Man was still there. I got the shotgun and some shells and pulled my pants on, tucked in my nightshirt, and slipped on my shoes. I went back to the window and looked out. The Goat Man was still in his spot by the woods. I slid out the window and went after him. As soon as he saw my gun, he ducked into the shadows.

As I ran, I called for Mama and Daddy and Tom. But no one answered. I tripped and went down. When I rose to my knees I saw that I had tripped over Toby. He lay still on the ground. I put the shotgun down and picked him up. His head rolled limp to one side. His neck was broken.

Oh God. Toby was dead. After all he had been through, he had been murdered. He had barked earlier, to warn me about the Goat Man, and now he was dead and Tom was missing, and Mama and Daddy had gone off somewhere in the car, and the Goat Man was no longer in sight.

I put Toby down easy, pushed back the tears, picked up the shotgun and ran blindly into the woods, down the narrow path the Goat Man had taken, fully expecting at any moment to fall over Tom's body, her neck broken like Toby's.

But that didn't happen.

There was just enough moon for me to see where I was going, but not enough to keep every shadow from looking like the Goat Man, coiled and ready to pounce. The wind was sighing through the trees and there were bits of rain with it, and the rain was cool.

I didn't know if I should go on or go back and try and find Mama and Daddy. I felt that no matter what I did, valuable time was being lost. There was no telling what the Goat Man was doing to poor Tom. He had probably tied her up and put her at the edge of the woods before coming back to taunt me at the window. Maybe he had wanted me too. I thought of what had been done to all those poor women, and I thought of Tom, and a kind of sickness came over me, and I ran faster, deciding it was best to continue on course, hoping I'd come up on the monster and would get a clear shot at him and be able to rescue Tom.

It was then that I saw a strange thing in the middle of the trail. A limb had been cut, and it was forced into the ground, and it was bent to the right at the top and whittled on to make it sharp. It was like a kind of arrow pointing the way.

The Goat Man was having his fun with me. I decided I had no choice other than to go where the arrow was pointing, a little trail even more narrow than the one I was on.

I went on down it, and in the middle of it was another limb, this one more hastily prepared, just broken off and stuck in the ground, bent over at the middle and pointing to the right again.

Where it pointed wasn't hardly even a trail, just a break here and there in the trees. I went that way, spider webs twisting into my hair, limbs slapping me across the face, and before I knew it my feet had gone out from under me and I was sliding over the edge of an embankment, and when I hit on the seat of my pants and looked out, I was at the road, the one the preachers traveled. The Goat Man had brought me to the road by a shortcut and had gone straight down it, because right in front of me, drawn in the dirt of the road, was an arrow. If he could cross the road or travel down it, that meant he could go anywhere he wanted. There wasn't any safe place from the Goat Man.

I ran down the road, and I wasn't even looking for sign anymore. I knew I was heading for the swinging bridge, and across from that the briar tunnels, where I figured the Goat Man had taken her. That would be his place, I reckoned. Those tunnels, and I knew then that the tunnels were where he had done his meanness to those women before casting them into the river. By placing that dead colored woman there, he had been taunting us all, showing us not only the place of the murder but the probable place of all the murders. A place where he could take his time and do what he wanted for as long as he wanted.

When I got to the swinging bridge, the wind was blowing hard and it was starting to rain harder. The bridge lashed back and forth, and I finally decided I'd be better off to go down to Mose's cabin and use his boat to cross the river.

I ran down the bank as fast as I could go, and when I got to the cabin my sides hurt from running. I threw the shotgun into the boat, pushed the boat off its blocks, let it slide down to the edge of the river. It got caught up in the sand there, and I couldn't move it. It had bogged down good in the soft sand. I pushed and pulled, but no dice. I started to cry. I should have crossed the swinging bridge.

I grabbed the shotgun out of the boat and started to run back toward the bridge, but as I went up the little hill toward the cabin, I saw something hanging from the nail there that gave me a start.

There was a chain over the nail, and hanging from the chain was a hand, and part of a wrist. I felt sick. Tom. Oh God. Tom.

I went up there slowly and bent forward and saw that the hand was too large to be Tom's, and it was mostly rotten with only a bit of flesh on it. In the shadows it had looked whole, but it was anything but. The chain was not tied to the hand, but the hand was in a half fist and the chain was draped through its fingers, and in the partial open palm I could see what it held was a coin. A French coin with a dent in it. Cecil's coin.

I knew I should hurry, but it was as if I had been hit with a stick. The killer had chopped off one of his victim's hands. I remembered that. I decided the woman had grabbed the killer, and the killer had chopped at her with something big and sharp, and her hand had come off.

This gave me as many questions as answers. How did Cecil's coin get in the hand, and how did it end up here? Who was leaving all these things here, and why? Was it the Goat Man?

Then there was a hand on my shoulder.

As I jerked my head around I brought up the shotgun, but another hand came out quickly and took the shotgun away from me, and I was looking straight into the face of the Goat Man.

The moon rolled out from behind a rain cloud, and its light fell into the Goat Man's eyes, and they shone, and I realized they were green. Green like Ole Mose's eyes.

The Goat Man made a soft grunting sound and patted my shoulder. I saw then his horns were not horns at all but an old straw hat that had rotted, leaving a gap in the front, like something had taken a bite out of it, and it made him look like he had horns. It was just a straw hat. A dadburn straw hat. No horns. And those eyes. Ole Mose's eyes.

And in that instant I knew. The Goat Man wasn't any goat man at all. He was Mose's son, the one wasn't right in the head and was thought to be dead. He'd been living out here in the woods all this time, and Mose had been taking care of him, and the son in his turn had been trying to take care of Mose by bringing him gifts he had found in the river, and now that Mose was dead and gone, he was still doing it. He was just a big dumb boy in a man's body, wandering the woods wearing worn-out clothes and shoes with soles that flopped.

The Goat Man turned and pointed upriver. I knew then he hadn't killed anyone, hadn't taken Tom. He had come to warn me, to let me know Tom had been taken, and now he was pointing the way. I just knew it. I didn't know how he had come by the hand or Cecil's chain and coin, but I knew the Goat Man hadn't killed anybody. He had been watching our house, and he had seen what had happened, and now he was trying to help me.

I broke loose from him and ran back to the boat, tried to push it free again. The Goat Man followed me down and put the shotgun in the boat and grabbed it and pushed it out of the sand and into the river and helped me into it, waded and pushed me out until the current had me good. I watched as he waded back toward the shore and the cabin. I picked up the paddle and went to work, trying not to think too much about what was being done to Tom.

Dark clouds passed over the moon from time to time, and the raindrops became more frequent and the wind was high and slightly cool with the dampness. I paddled so hard my back and shoulders began to ache, but the current was with me, pulling me fast. I passed a whole school of water moccasins swimming in the dark, and I feared they might try to climb up into the boat, as they liked to do, thinking it was a floating log and wanting a rest.

I paddled quickly through them, spreading the school, and one did indeed try to climb up the side, but I brought the boat paddle down on him hard and he went back in the water, alive or dead I couldn't say.

As I paddled around a bend in the river, I saw where the wild briars grew, and in that moment I had a strange sinking feeling. Not only for fear of what I might find in the briar tunnels, but fear I might find nothing at all. Fear I was all wrong. Or that the Goat Man did indeed have Tom. Perhaps in Mose's cabin, and had been keeping her there, waiting until I was out of sight. But if that was true, why had he given my gun back? Then again, he wasn't bright.

He was a creature of the woods, same as a coon or a possum. He didn't think like regular folks.

All of this went through my head and swirled around and confused itself with my own fears and the thought of actually cutting down on a man with a shotgun. I felt like I was in a dream, like the kind I'd had when I'd had the flu the year before and everything had swirled and Mama and Daddy's voices had seemed to echo and there were shadows all around me, trying to grab at me and pull me away into who knows where.

I paddled up to the bank and got out and pulled the boat up on shore best I could. I couldn't quite get it out of the water since I was so tuckered out from paddling. I just hoped it would hang there and hold.

I got the shotgun out and went up the hill quietly and found the mouth of the tunnel just beyond the tree, where me and Tom and Toby had come out that night.

It was dark inside the briars, and the moon had gone away behind a cloud and the wind rattled the briars and clicked them together and bits of rain sliced through the briars and mixed with the sweat in my hair, ran down my face and made me shiver. July the Fourth, and I was cold.

As I sneaked down the tunnel, an orange glow leaped and danced and I could hear a crackling sound. I trembled and eased forward and came to the end of the tunnel, and froze. I couldn't make myself turn into the other tunnel. It was as if my feet were nailed the ground.

I pulled back the hammer on the shotgun, slipped my face around the edge of the briars, and looked.

There was a fire going in the center of the tunnel, in the spot where Tom and I had seen the burn marks that day, and I could see Tom lying on the ground, her clothes off and strewn about, and a man was leaning over her, running his hands over her back and forth, making a sound like an animal eating after a long time without food. His hands flowed over her as if he was playing a piano. A huge machete was stuck up in the dirt near Tom's head, and Tom's face was turned toward me. Her eyes were wide and full of tears, and tied around her mouth was a thick bandanna, and her hands and feet were bound with rope, and as I looked the man rose and I saw that his pants were undone and he had hold of himself, and he was walking back and forth behind the fire, looking down at Tom, yelling, "I don't want to do this. You make me do this. It's your fault, you know? You're getting just right. Just right."

The voice was loud, but not like any voice I'd ever heard. There was all the darkness and wetness of the bottom of the river in that voice, as well as the mud

The Best of Joe R. Lansdale

down there, and anything that might collect in it.

I hadn't been able to get a good look at his face, but I could tell from the way he was built, the way the fire caught his hair, it was Mr. Nation's son, Uriah.

Then he turned slightly, and it wasn't Uriah at all. I had merely thought it was Uriah because he was built like Uriah, but it wasn't.

I stepped fully into the tunnel and said, "Cecil?"

The word just came out of my mouth, without me really planning to say it. Cecil turned now, and when he saw me his face was like it had been earlier, when Tom was being bounced on his knee and the fireworks had exploded behind him. He had the same slack-jawed look, his face was beaded in sweat.

He let go of his privates and just let them hang out for me to see, as if he were proud of them and that I should be too.

"Oh, boy," he said, his voice still husky and animal-like. "It's just gone all wrong. I didn't want to have to have Tom. I didn't. But she's been ripenin', boy, right in front of my eyes. Every time I saw her, I said, no, you don't shit where you eat, but she's ripenin', boy, and I thought I'd go to your place, peek in on her if I could, and then I seen her there, easy to take, and I knew tonight I had to have her. There wasn't nothing else for it."

"Why?"

"Oh, son. There is no why. I just have to. I have to do them all. I tell myself I won't, but I do. I do."

He eased toward me.

I lifted the shotgun.

"Now, boy," he said. "You don't want to shoot me."

"Yes, sir. I do."

"It ain't something I can help. Listen here. I'll let her go, and we'll just forget about this business. Time you get home, I'll be out of here. I got a little boat hid out, and I can take it downriver to where I can catch a train. I'm good at that. I can be gone before you know it."

"You're wiltin'," I said.

His pee-dink had gone limp.

Cecil looked down. "So I am."

He pushed himself inside his pants and buttoned up as he talked. "Look here. I wasn't gonna hurt her. Just feel her some. I was just gonna get my finger wet. I'll go on, and everything will be all right."

"You'll just go down the river and do it again," I said. "Way you come down the river to us and did it here. You ain't gonna stop, are you?"

"There's nothing to say about it, Harry. It just gets out of hand sometime."

"Where's your chain and coin, Cecil?"

He touched his throat. "It got lost."

"That woman got her hand chopped off, she grabbed it, didn't she?"

"I reckon she did."

"Move to the left there, Cecil."

He moved to the left, pointed at the machete. "She grabbed me, I chopped her with that, and her hand came off. Damndest thing. I got her down here and she got away from me and I chased her. And she grabbed me, fought back. I chopped her hand off and it went in the river. Can you imagine that... How did you know?"

"The Goat Man finds things in the river. He hangs them on Mose's shack."

"Goat Man?"

"You're the real Goat Man."

"You're not making any sense, boy."

"Move on around to the side there."

I wanted him away from the exit on that other side, the one me and Tom had stumbled into that night we found the body.

Cecil slipped to my left, and I went to the right. We were kind of circling each other. I got over close to Tom and I squatted down by her, still pointing the shotgun at Cecil.

"I could be gone for good," Cecil said. "All you got to do is let me go."

I reached out with one hand and got hold of the knot on the bandanna and pulled it loose. Tom said, "Shoot him! Shoot him! He stuck his fingers in me. Shoot him! He took me out of the window and stuck his fingers in me."

"Hush, Tom," I said. "Take it easy."

"Cut me loose. Give me the gun and I'll shoot him."

"All the time you were bringin' those women here to kill, weren't you?" I said.

"It's a perfect place. Already made by hobos. Once I decided on a woman, well, I can easily handle a woman. I always had my boat ready, and you can get almost anywhere you need to go by river. The tracks aren't far from here. Plenty of trains run. It's easy to get around. Now and then I borrowed a car. You know whose? Mrs. Canerton. One night she loaned it to me, and well, I asked her if she wanted to go for a drive with me while I ran an errand. And she liked me, boy, and I just couldn't contain myself. All I had to do was bring them here, and when I finished, I tossed out the trash."

"Daddy trusted you. You told where Mose was. You told Mr. Nation."

"It was just a nigger, boy. I had to try and hide my trail. You understand. It wasn't like the world lost an upstanding citizen."

"We thought you were our friend," I said.

"I am. I am. Sometimes friends make you mad, though, don't they? They do wrong things. But I don't mean to."

"We ain't talkin' about stealin' a piece of peppermint, here. You're worse than the critters out there with hydrophobia, 'cause you ain't as good as them. They can't help themselves."

"Neither can I."

The fire crackled, bled red colors across his face. Some of the rain leaked in through the thick wad of briars and vines and limbs overhead, hit the fire and it hissed. "You're like your daddy, ain't you? Self-righteous."

"Reckon so."

I had one hand holding the shotgun, resting it against me as I squatted down and worked the knots free on Tom's hands. I wasn't having any luck with that, so I got my pocketknife out of my pants and cut her hands loose, then her feet.

I stood up, raised the gun, and he flinched some, but I couldn't cut down on him. It just wasn't in me, not unless he tried to lay hands on us.

I didn't know what to do with him. I decided I had no choice but to let him go, tell Daddy and have them try and hunt him down.

Tom was pulling on her clothes when I said, "You'll get yours eventually."

"Now you're talkin', boy."

"You stay over yonder, we're goin' out."

He held up his hands. "Now you're using some sense."

Tom said, "You can't shoot him, I can."

"Go on, Tom."

She didn't like it, but she turned down the tunnel and headed out. Cecil said, "Remember, boy. We had some good times."

"We ain't got nothin'. You ain't never done nothing with me but cut my hair, and you didn't know how to cut a boy's hair anyway." I turned and went out by the tunnel. "And I ought to blow one of your legs off for what you done to Toby."

We didn't use the opening in the tunnel that led to the woods because I wanted to go out the way I'd come and get back to the boat. We got on the river it would be hard for him to track us, if that was his notion.

When we got down to the river, the boat, which I hadn't pulled up good on the shore, had washed out in the river, and I could see it floating away with the current.

"Damn," I said.

"Was that Mose's boat?" Tom asked.

"We got to go by the bank, to the swinging bridge."

"It's a long ways," I heard Cecil say.

I spun around, and there he was up on the higher bank next to the tree where me and Tom had found the body. He was just a big shadow next to the tree, and I thought of the Devil come up from the ground, all dark and evil and full of bluff. "You got a long ways to go, children. A long ways."

I pointed the shotgun at him and he slipped behind the tree out of sight, said, "A long ways."

I knew then I should have killed him. Without the boat, he could follow alongside us easy, back up in the woods there, and we couldn't even see him.

Me and Tom started moving brisk like along the bank, and we could hear Cecil moving through the woods on the bank above us, and finally we didn't hear him anymore. It was the same as that night when we heard the sounds near and in the tunnel. I figured it had been him, maybe come down to see his handiwork at the tree there, liking it perhaps, wanting it to be seen by someone. Maybe we had come down right after he finished doing it. He had been stalking us, or Tom, maybe. He had wanted Tom all along.

We walked fast and Tom was cussing most of it, talking about what Cecil had done with his fingers, and the whole thing was making me sick.

"Just shut up, Tom. Shut up."

She started crying. I stopped and got down on one knee, let the shotgun lay against me as I reached out with both hands and took hold of her shoulders.

"I'm sorry, Tom, really. I'm scared too. We got to keep ourselves together, you hear me?"

"I hear you," she said.

"We got to stay the course here. I got a gun. He don't. He may have already given up."

"He ain't give up, and you know it."

"We got to keep moving."

Tom nodded, and we started out again, and pretty soon the long, dark shadow of the swinging bridge was visible across the river, and the wind was high, and the bridge thrashed back and forth and creaked and groaned like hinges on rusty doors.

"We could go on down a ways, Tom, I think we got to cross by the bridge here. It's quicker, and we can be home sooner."

"I'm scared, Harry."

"So am I."

"Can you do it?"

Tom sucked in her top lip and nodded. "I can."

We climbed up the bank where the bridge began and looked down on it. It swung back and forth. I looked down at the river. White foam rose with the dark water and it rolled away and crashed over the little falls into the broader, deeper, slower part of the river. The rain came down on us and the wind was chilly, and all around the woods seemed quiet, yet full of something I couldn't put a name to. Now and again, in spite of the rain, the clouds would split and the moon would shine down on us, looking as if it were something greasy.

I decided to cross first, so if a board gave out Tom would know. When I stepped on the bridge, the wind the way it was, and now my weight, made it swing way up and I darn near tipped into the water. When I reached out to grab the cables, I let go of the shotgun. It went into the water without any sound I could hear and was instantly gone.

"You lost it, Harry," Tom yelled from the bank.

"Come on, just hang to the cables."

Tom stepped onto the bridge, and it swung hard and nearly tipped again.

"We got to walk light," I said, "and kind of together. Where I take a step, you take one, but if a board goes, or I go, you'll see in time."

"If you fall, what do I do?"

"You got to go on across, Tom."

We started on across, and we seemed to have gotten the movement right, because we weren't tipping quite so bad, and pretty soon we were halfway done.

I turned and looked down the length of the bridge, past Tom. I didn't see anyone tryin' to follow.

It was slow going, but it wasn't long before we were six feet from the other side. I began to breathe a sigh of relief. Then I realized I still had a ways to go yet till we got to the wide trail, then the road, and now I knew there wasn't any road would stop Cecil or anyone else. It was just a road. If we got that far, we still had some distance yet, and Cecil would know where we were going, and Mama and Daddy might not even be home yet.

I thought if we got to the road I might try and fool him, go the other way, but it was a longer distance like that to someone's house, and if he figured what we were doin', we could be in worse trouble.

I decided there wasn't nothing for it but to head home and stay cautious. But while all this was on my mind, and we were about to reach the opposite bank, a shadow separated from the brush and dirt there and became Cecil.

He held the machete in his hand. He smiled and stuck it in the dirt, stayed on solid ground, but took hold of both sides of the cables that held up the swinging bridge. He said, "I beat you across, boy. Just waited. Now you and little Tom, you're gonna have to take a dip. I didn't want it this way, but that's how it is. You see that, don't you? All I wanted was Tom. You give her to me, to do as I want, then you can go. By the time you get home, me and her, we'll be on our way."

"You ain't got your dough done in the middle," I said.

Cecil clutched the cables hard and shook them. The bridge swung out from under me and I found my feet hanging out in midair. Only my arms wrapped around one of the cables was holding me. I could see Tom. She had fallen and was grabbing at one of the board steps, and I could see bits of rotten wood splintering. The board and Tom were gonna go.

Cecil shook the cables again, but I hung tight, and the board Tom clung to didn't give. I glanced toward Cecil and saw another shape coming out of the shadows. A huge one, with what looked like goat horns on its head.

Mose's boy, Telly.

Telly grabbed Cecil around the neck and jerked him back, and Cecil spun loose and hit him in the stomach, and they grappled around there for a moment, then Cecil got hold of the machete and slashed it across Telly's chest. Telly let out with a noise like a bull bellowing, leaped against Cecil, and the both of them went flying onto the bridge. When they hit, boards splintered, the bridge swung to the side and up and there was a snapping sound as one of the cables broke in two, whipped out and away from us and into the water. Cecil and Telly fell past us into the Sabine. Me and Tom clung for a moment to the remaining cable, then it snapped, and we fell into the fast rushing water after them.

I went down deep, and when I came up, I bumped into Tom. She screamed and I screamed and I grabbed her. The water churned us under again, and I fought to bring us up, all the while clinging to Tom's collar. When I broke the surface of the water I saw Cecil and Telly in a clench, riding the blast of the Sabine over the little falls, flowing out into deeper, calmer waters.

The next thing I knew, we were there too, through the falls, into the deeper, less rapid flowing water. I got a good grip on Tom and started trying to swim toward shore. It was hard in our wet clothes, tired like we were; and me trying to hang on to and pull Tom, who wasn't helping herself a bit, didn't make it any easier.

I finally swam to where my feet were touching sand and gravel, and I waded us on into shore, pulled Tom up next to me. She rolled over and puked.

I looked out at the water. The rain had ceased and the sky had cleared momentarily, and the moon, though weak, cast a glow on the Sabine like grease starting to shine on a hot skillet. I could see Cecil and Telly gripped together, a hand flying up now and then to strike, and I could see something else all around them, something that rose up in a dozen silvery knobs that gleamed in the moonlight, then extended quickly and struck at the pair, time after time.

Cecil and Telly had washed into that school of water moccasins, or another just like them, had stirred them up, and now it was like bull whips flying from the water, hitting the two of them time after time.

They washed around a bend in the river with the snakes and went out of sight.

I was finally able to stand up, and I realized I had lost a shoe. I got hold of Tom and started pulling her on up the bank. The ground around the bank was rough, and then there were stickers and briars, and my one bare foot took a beating. But we went on out of there, onto the road and finally to the house, where Daddy and Mama were standing in the yard yelling our names.

The next morning they found Cecil on a sandbar. He was bloated up and swollen from water and snakebites. His neck was broken, Daddy said. Telly had taken care of him before the snakebite.

Caught up in some roots next to the bank, his arms spread and through them and his feet wound in vines, was Telly. The machete wound had torn open his chest and side. Daddy said that silly hat was still on his head, and he discovered that it was somehow wound into Telly's hair. He said the parts that looked like horns had washed down and were covering his eyes, like huge eyelids.

I wondered what had gotten into Telly, the Goat Man. He had led me out there to save Tom, but he hadn't wanted any part of stopping Cecil. Maybe he was afraid. But when we were on the bridge, and Cecil was getting the best of us, he had come for him.

Had it been because he wanted to help us, or was he just there already and frightened? I'd never know. I thought of poor Telly living out there in the woods all that time, only his daddy knowing he was there, and maybe keeping it secret just so folks would leave him alone, not take advantage of him because he was addleheaded.

In the end, the whole thing was one horrible experience. I remember mostly just lying in bed for two days after, nursing all the wounds in my foot from stickers and such, trying to get my strength back, weak from thinking about what almost happened to Tom.

Mama stayed by our side for the next two days, leaving us only long enough to make soup. Daddy sat up with us at night. When I awoke, frightened, thinking I was still on the swinging bridge, he would be there, and he would smile and put out his hand and touch my head, and I would lie back and sleep again.

Over a period of years, picking up a word here and there, we would learn that there had been more murders like those in our area, all the way down from Arkansas and over into Oklahoma and some of North Texas. Back then no one pinned those on one murderer. The law just didn't think like that then. The true nature of serial killers was unknown. Had communication been better, had knowledge been better, perhaps some, or all, of what happened that time long ago might have been avoided.

And maybe not. It's all done now, those long-ago events of nineteen thirty-one and -two.

Now, I lie here, not much longer for the world, and with no desire to be here or to have my life stretched out for another moment, just lying here with this tube in my shank, waiting on mashed peas and corn and some awful thing that will pass for meat, all to be hand-fed to me, and I think of then and how I lay in bed in our little house next to the woods, and how when I awoke Daddy or Mama would be there, and how comforting it was.

So now I close my eyes with my memories of those two years, and that great and horrible mad dog summer, and I hope this time when I awake I will no longer be of this world, and Mama and Daddy, and even poor Tom, dead before her time in a car accident, will be waiting, and perhaps even Mose and the Goat Man and good old Toby.

Fire Dog

When Jim applied for the dispatcher job the fire department turned him down, but the Fire Chief offered him something else.

"Our fire dog, Rex, is retiring. You might want that job. Pays good and the retirement is great."

"Fire dog?" Jim said.

"That's right."

"Well, I don't know…"

"Suit yourself."

Jim considered. "I suppose I could give it a try —"

"Actually, we prefer greater dedication than that. We don't just want someone to give it a try. Being fire dog is an important job."

"Very well," Jim said. "I'll take it."

"Good."

The Chief opened a drawer, pulled out a spotted suit with tail and ears, pushed it across the desk.

"I have to wear this?"

"How the hell you gonna be the fire dog, you don't wear the suit?"

"Of course."

Jim examined the suit. It had a hole for his face, his bottom, and what his mother had called his pee-pee.

"Good grief," Jim said. "I can't go around with my…well, you know, my stuff hanging out."

"How many dogs you see wearing pants?"

"Well, Goofy comes to mind."

"Those are cartoons. I haven't got time to screw around here. You either want the job, or you don't."

"I want it."

"By the way. You sure Goofy's a dog?"

"Well, he looks like a dog. And he has that dog, Pluto."

"Pluto, by the way, doesn't wear pants."

"You got me there."

"Try on the suit, let's see if it needs tailoring."

The suit fit perfectly, though Jim did feel a bit exposed. Still, he had to admit there was something refreshing about the exposure. He wore the suit into the break room, following the Chief.

Rex, the current fire dog, was sprawled on the couch watching a cop show. His suit looked worn, even a bit smoke stained. He was tired around the eyes. His jowls drooped.

"This is our new fire dog," the Chief said.

Rex turned and looked at Jim, said, "I'm not out the door, already you got a guy in the suit?"

"Rex, no hard feelings. You got what, two, three days? We got to be ready. You know that."

Rex sat up on the couch, adjusted some pillows and leaned into them. "Yeah, I know. But, I've had this job nine years."

"And in dog years that's a lot."

"I don't know why I can't just keep being the fire dog. I think I've done a good job."

"You're our best fire dog yet. Jim here has a lot to live up to."

"I only get to work nine years?" Jim said.

"In dog years you'd be pretty old, and it's a decent retirement."

"Is he gonna take my name too?" Rex said.

"No," the Chief said, "of course not. We'll call him Spot."

"Oh, that's rich," said Rex. "You really worked on that one."

"It's no worse than Rex."

"Hey, Rex is a good name."

"I don't like Spot," Jim said. "Can't I come up with something else?"

"Dogs don't name themselves," the Chief said. "Your name is Spot."

"Spot," Rex said, "don't you think you ought to get started by coming over here and sniffing my butt?"

The first few days at work Spot found riding on the truck to be uncomfortable. He was always given a tool box to sit on so that he could be seen, as this was the fire department's way. They liked the idea of the fire dog in full view, his ears flapping in the wind. It was very promotional for the mascot to be seen.

Spot's exposed butt was cold on the tool box, and the wind not only blew his ears around, it moved another part of his anatomy about. That was annoying.

He did, however, enjoy the little motorized tail-wagging device he activated with a touch of a finger. He found that got him a lot of snacks from the fire men. He was especially fond of the liver snacks.

After three weeks on the job, Spot found his wife Shella to be very friendly. After dinner one evening, when he went to the bedroom to remove his dog suit, he discovered Shella lying on their bed wearing a negligee and a pair of dog ears attached to a hair band.

"Feel frisky, Spot?"

"Jim."

"Whatever. Feel frisky?"

"Well, yeah. Let me shed the suit, take a shower…"

"You don't need a shower… And baby, leave the suit on, will you?"

They went at it.

"You know how I want it," she said.

"Yeah. Doggie style."

"Good boy."

After sex, Shella liked to scratch his belly and behind his ears. He used the tail-wagging device to show how much he appreciated it. This wasn't so bad, he thought. He got less when he was a man.

Though his sex life had improved, Spot found himself being put outside a lot, having to relieve himself in a corner of the yard while his wife looked in the other direction, her hand in a plastic bag, ready to use to pick up his deposits.

He only removed his dog suit now when Shella wasn't around. She liked it on him at all times. At first he was insulted, but the sex was so good, and his life was so good, he relented. He even let her call him Spot all the time.

When she wasn't around, he washed and dried his suit carefully, ironed it. But he never wore anything else. When he rode the bus to work, everyone wanted to pet him. One woman even asked if he liked poodles because she had one.

At work he was well respected, and enjoyed being taken to schools with the Fire Chief. The Chief talked about fire prevention. Spot wagged his tail, sat up, barked, looked cute by turning his head from side to side.

He was even taken to his daughter's class once. He heard her say proudly to a kid sitting next to her, "That's my Daddy. He's the fire dog."

His chest swelled with pride. He made his tail wag enthusiastically.

The job really was the pip. You didn't have fires every day, so Spot laid around all day most days, on the couch sometimes, though some of the fireman would run him off and make him lie on the floor when they came in. But the floor had rugs on it and the television was always on, though he was not allowed to change the channels. Some kind of rule, a union thing. The fire dog can not and will not change channels.

He did hate having to take worm medicine, and the annual required trips to the vet were no picnic either. Especially the thermometer up the ass part.

But, hell, it was a living, and not a bad one. Another plus was after several months of trying, he was able to lick his balls.

At night, when everyone was in their bunks and there were no fires, Spot would read from *Call of the Wild*, *White Fang*, *Dog Digest*, or such, or lie on his back with all four feet in the air, trying to look cute.

He loved it the when the firemen came in and caught him that way and *ooohheeed* and *ahhhhhed* and scratched his belly or patted his head.

This went on for just short of nine years. Then, one day, while he was lying on the couch, licking his ass — something he cultivated after three years on the job — the Fire Chief and a guy in a dog suit came in.

"This is your replacement, Spot," the Chief said.

"What?"

"Well, it has been nine years."

"You didn't tell me. Has it been? You're sure? Aren't you supposed to warn me? Rex knew his time was up. Remember?"

"Not exactly. But if you say so. Spot, meet Hal."

"Hal? What kind of dog's name is that? Hal?"

But it was no use. By the end of the day he had his personal dog biscuits, pin-ups from *Dog Digest*, and his worm-away medicine packed. There was also a spray can the firemen used to mist on his poop to keep him from eating it. The can of spray didn't really belong to him, but he took it anyway.

He picked up his old clothes, went into the changing room. He hadn't worn anything but the fire dog suit in years, and it felt odd to try his old clothes on. He could hardly remember ever wearing them. He found they were a bit moth-eaten, and he had gotten a little too plump for them. The shoes fit, but he couldn't tolerate them.

He kept the dog suit on.

He caught the bus and went home.

"What? You lost your job?" his wife said.

"I didn't lose anything. They retired me."

"You're not the fire dog?"

"No. Hal is the fire dog."

"I can't believe it. I give you nine great years —"

"We've been married eleven."

"I only count the dog years. Those were the good ones, you know."

"Well, I don't have to quit being a dog. Hell, I am a dog."

"You're not the fire dog. You've lost your position, Spot. Oh, I can't even stand to think about it. Outside. Go on. Git. Outside."

Spot went.

After a while he scratched on the door, but his wife didn't let him in. He went around back and tried there. That didn't work either. He looked in the windows, but couldn't see her.

He laid down in the yard.

That night it rained, and he slept under the car, awakened just in time to keep his wife from backing over him on her way to work.

That afternoon he waited, but his wife did not return at the usual time. Five o'clock was when he came home from the fire house, and she was always waiting, and he had a feeling it was at least five o'clock, and finally the sun went down and he knew it was late.

Still, no wife.

Finally, he saw headlights and a car pulled into the drive. Shella got out. He ran to meet her. To show he was interested, he hunched her leg.

She kicked him loose. He noticed she was holding a leash. Out of the car came Hal.

"Look who I got. A real dog."

Spot was dumbfounded.

"I met him today at the fire house, and well, we hit it off."

"You went by the fire house?"

"Of course."

"What about me?" Spot asked.

"Well, Spot, you are a little old. Sometimes, things change. New blood is necessary."

"Me and Hal, we're going to share the house?"

"I didn't say that."

She took Hal inside. Just before they closed the door, Hal slipped a paw behind Shella's back and shot Spot the finger.

When they were inside, Spot scratched on the door in a half-hearted way. No soap.

Next morning Shella hustled him out of the shrubbery by calling his name. She didn't have Hal with her.

Great! She had missed him. He bounded out, his tongue dangling like a wet sock. "Come here, Spot."

He went. That's what dogs did. When the master called, you went to them. He was still her dog. Yes sirree, Bob.

"Come on, boy." She hustled him to the car.

As he climbed inside on the back seat and she shut the door, he saw Hal come out of the house stretching. He looked pretty happy. He walked over to the car and slapped Shella on the butt.

"See you later, baby."

"You bet, you dog you."

Hal walked down the street to the bus stop. Spot watched him by turning first to the back glass, then rushing over to the side view glass.

Shella got in the car.

"Where are we going?" Spot asked.

"It's a surprise," she said.

"Can you roll down the window back here a bit?"

"Sure."

Spot stuck his head out as they drove along, his ears flapping, his tongue hanging.

They drove down a side street, turned and tooled up an alley.

Spot thought he recognized the place.

Why yes, the vet. They had come from another direction and he hadn't spotted it right off, but that's where he was.

He unhooked the little tag that dangled from his collar. Checked the dates of his last shots.

No. Nothing was overdue.

They stopped and Shella smiled. She opened the back door and took hold of the leash. "Come on, Spot."

Spot climbed out of the car, though carefully. He wasn't as spry as he once was.

Two men were at the back door. One of them was the doctor. The other an assistant.

"Here's Spot," she said.

"He looks pretty good," said the doctor.

"I know. But... Well, he's old and has his problems. And I have too many dogs."

She left him there.

The vet checked him over and called the animal shelter. "There's nothing really wrong with him," he told the attendant that came for him. "He's just old, and well, the woman doesn't want to care for him. He'd be great with children."

"You know how it is, Doc," said the attendant. "Dogs all over the place."

Later, at the animal shelter he stood on the cold concrete and smelled the other dogs. He barked at the cats he could smell. Fact was, he found himself barking anytime anyone came into the corridor of pens.

Sometimes men and woman and children came and looked at him.

None of them chose him. The device in his tail didn't work right, so he couldn't wag as ferociously as he liked. His ears were pretty droopy and his jowls hung way too low.

"He looks like his spots are fading," said one woman whose little girl had stuck her fingers through the grating so Spot could lick her hand.

"His breath stinks," she said.

As the days went by, Spot tried to look perky all the time. Hoping for adoption.

But one day, they came for him, wearing white coats and grim faces, brandishing a leash and a muzzle and a hypodermic needle.

The Big Blow

TUESDAY, SEPTEMBER 4, 1900, 4:00 P.M.

Telegraphed Message from Washington, D.C., Weather Bureau, Central Office, to Issac Cline, Galveston, Texas, Weather Bureau:

Tropical storm disturbance moving northward over Cuba.

6:38 P.M.

On an afternoon hotter than two rats fucking in a wool sock, John McBride, six-foot one-and-a-half inches, 220 pounds, ham-handed, built like a wild boar and of similar disposition, arrived by ferry from mainland Texas to Galveston Island, a six-gun under his coat and a razor in his shoe.

As the ferry docked, McBride set his suitcase down, removed his bowler, took a crisp, white handkerchief from inside his coat, wiped the bowler's sweatband with it, used it to mop his forehead, ran it over his thinning black hair, and put the hat back on.

An old Chinese guy in San Francisco told him he was losing his hair because he always wore hats, and McBride decided maybe he was right, but now he wore the hats to hide his baldness. At thirty he felt he was too young to lose his hair. The Chinaman had given him a tonic for his problem at a considerable sum. McBride used it religiously, rubbed it into his scalp. So far, all he could see it had done was shine his bald spot. He ever got back to Frisco, he was gonna look that Chinaman up, maybe knock a few knots in his head.

As McBride picked up his suitcase and stepped off the ferry with the others, he observed the sky. It appeared green as a pool table cloth. As the sun dipped down to drink from the Gulf, McBride almost expected to see steam rise up from beyond the island. He took in a deep breath of sea air and thought it tasted all right. It made him hungry. That was why he was here. He was hungry. First on the menu was a woman, then a steak, then some rest before the final meal — the thing he had come for. To whip a nigger.

He hired a buggy to take him to a poke house he had been told about by his employers, the fellows who had paid his way from Chicago. According to what they said, there was a redhead there so good and tight she'd make you sing soprano. Way he felt, if she was redheaded, female, and ready, he'd be all right, and to hell with the song. It was on another's tab anyway.

As the coach trotted along, McBride took in Galveston. It was a Southerner's version of New York, with a touch of the tropics. Houses were upraised on stilts — thick support posts actually — against the washing of storm waters, and in the city proper the houses looked to be fresh off Deep South plantations.

City Hall had apparently been designed by an architect with a Moorish background. It was ripe with domes and spirals. The style collided with a magnificent clock housed in the building's highest point, a peaked tower. The clock was like a miniature Big Ben. England meets the Middle East.

Electric streetcars hissed along the streets, and there were a large number of bicycles, carriages, buggies, and pedestrians. McBride even saw one automobile.

The streets themselves were made of buried wooden blocks that McBride identified as ships' ballast. Some of the side streets were made of white shell, and some were hardened sand. He liked what he saw, thought: Maybe, after I do in the nigger, I'll stick around awhile. Take in the sun at the beach. Find a way to get my fingers in a little solid graft of some sort.

When McBride finally got to the whorehouse, it was full dark. He gave the black driver a big tip, cocked his bowler, grabbed his suitcase, went through the ornate iron gate, up the steps, and inside to get his tumblers clicked right.

After giving his name to the plump madam, who looked as if she could still grind out a customer or two herself, he was given the royalty treatment. The madam herself took him upstairs, undressed him, bathed him, fondled him a bit.

When he was clean, she dried him off, nestled him in bed, kissed him on the forehead as if he were her little boy, then toddled off. The moment she left, he climbed out of bed, got in front of the mirror on the dresser and combed his hair, trying to push as much as possible over the bald spot. He had just gotten it arranged and gone back to bed when the redhead entered.

She was green-eyed and a little thick-waisted, but not bad to look at. She had fire-red hair on her head and a darker fire between her legs, which were white as sheets and smooth as a newborn pig.

He started off by hurting her a little, tweaking her nipples, just to show her who was boss. She pretended to like it. Kind of money his employers were paying, he figured she'd dip a turd in gravel and push it around the floor with her nose and pretend to like it.

McBride roughed her bottom some, then got in the saddle and bucked a few. Later on, when she got a little slow about doing what he wanted, he blacked one of her eyes.

When the representatives of the Galveston Sporting Club showed up, he was lying in bed with the redhead, uncovered, letting a hot wind blow through the open windows and dry his and the redhead's juices.

The madam let the club members in and went away. There were four of them, all dressed in evening wear with top hats in their hands. Two were gray-haired and gray-whiskered. The other two were younger men. One was large, had a face that looked as if it regularly stopped cannonballs. Both eyes were black from a recent encounter. His nose was flat and strayed to the left of his face. He did his breathing through his mouth. He didn't have any top front teeth.

The other young man was slight and a dandy. This, McBride assumed, would be Ronald Beems, the man who had written him on behalf of the Sporting Club.

Everything about Beems annoyed McBride. His suit, unlike the wrinkled and drooping suits of the others, looked fresh-pressed, unresponsive to the afternoon's humidity. He smelled faintly of mothballs and naphtha, and some sort of hair tonic that had ginger as a base. He wore a thin little moustache and the sort of hair McBride wished he had. Black, full, and longish, with muttonchop sideburns. He had perfect features. No fist had ever touched him. He stood stiff, as if he had a hoe handle up his ass.

Beems, like the others, looked at McBride and the redhead with more than a little astonishment. McBride lay with his legs spread and his back propped against a pillow. He looked very big there. His legs and shoulders and arms were thick and twisted with muscle and glazed in sweat. His stomach protruded a bit, but it was hard-looking.

The whore, sweaty, eye blacked, legs spread, breasts slouching from the heat, looked more embarrassed than McBride. She wanted to cover, but she didn't move. Fresh in her memory was that punch to the eye.

"For heaven's sake, man," Beems said. "Cover yourself."

"What the hell you think we've been doin' here?" McBride said. "Playin' checkers?"

"There's no need to be open about it. A man's pleasure is taken in private."

"Certainly you've seen balls before," McBride said, reaching for a cigar that lay on the table next to his revolver and a box of matches. Then he smiled and studied Beems. "Then maybe you ain't... And then again, maybe, well, you've seen plenty and close up. You look to me the sort that would rather hear a fat boy fart than a pretty girl sing."

"You disgusting brute," Beems said.

"That's telling me," McBride said. "Now I'm hurt. Cut to the goddamn core." McBride patted the redhead's inner thigh. "You recognize this business, don't you? You don't, I got to tell you about it. We men call it a woman, and that thing between her legs is the ole red snapper."

"We'll not conduct our affairs in this fashion," Beems said.

McBride smiled, took a match from the box, and lit the cigar. He puffed, said, "You dressed-up pieces of dirt brought me all the way down here from Chicago. I didn't ask to come. You offered me a job, and I took it, and I can untake it, it suits me. I got round-trip money from you already. You sent for me, and I came, and you set me up with a paid hair hole, and you're here for a meeting at a whorehouse, and now you're gonna tell me you're too special to look at my balls. Too prudish to look at pussy. Go on out, let me finish what I really want to finish. I'll be out of here come tomorrow, and you can whip your own nigger."

There was a moment of foot shuffling, and one of the elderly men leaned over and whispered to Beems. Beems breathed once, like a fish out of water, said, "Very well. There's not that much needs to be said. We want this nigger whipped, and we want him whipped bad. We understand in your last bout, the man died."

"Yeah," McBride said. "I killed him and dipped my wick in his old lady. Same night."

This was a lie, but McBride liked the sound of it. He liked the way their faces looked when he told it. The woman had actually been the man's half sister, and the man had died three days later from the beating.

"And this was a white man?" Beems said.

"White as snow. Dead as a stone. Talk money."

"We've explained our financial offer."

"Talk it again. I like the sound of money."

"Hundred dollars before you get in the ring with the nigger. Two hundred more if you beat him. A bonus of five hundred if you kill him. This is a short fight. Not forty-five rounds. No prizefighter makes money like that for so little work. Not even John L. Sullivan."

"This must be one hated nigger. Why? He mountin' your dog?"

"That's our business."

"All right. But I'll take half of that money now."

"That wasn't our deal."

"Now it is. And I'll be runnin' me a tab while I'm here, too. Pick it up."

More foot shuffling. Finally, the two elderly men got their heads together, pulled out their wallets. They pooled their money, gave it to Beems. "These gentlemen are our backers," Beems said. "This is Mr. —"

"I don't care who they are," McBride said. "Give me the money."

Beems tossed it on the foot of the bed.

"Pick it up and bring it here," McBride said to Beems.

"I will not."

"Yes, you will, 'cause you want me to beat this nigger. You want me to do it bad. And another reason is this: You don't, I'll get up and whip your dainty little ass all over this room."

Beems shook a little. "But why?"

"Because I can."

Beems, his face red as infection, gathered the bills from the bed, carried them around to McBride. He thrust them at McBride. McBride, fast as a duck on a June bug, grabbed Beems's wrist and pulled him forward, causing him to let go of the money and drop it onto McBride's chest. McBride pulled the cigar from his mouth with his free hand, stuck it against the back of Beems's thumb. Beems let out a squeal, said, "Forrest!"

The big man with no teeth and black eyes started around the bed toward McBride. McBride said, "Step back, Charlie, or you'll have to hire someone to yank this fella out of your ass."

Forrest hesitated, looked as if he might keep coming, then stepped back and hung his head.

McBride pulled Beems's captured hand between his legs and rubbed it over his sweaty balls a few times, then pushed him away. Beems stood with his mouth open, stared at his hand.

"I'm bull of the woods here," McBride said, "and it stays that way from here on out. You treat me with respect. I say, hold my rope while I pee, you hold it, I say, hold my sacks off the sheet while I get a piece, you hold 'em."

Beems said, "You bastard. I could have you killed."

"Then do it. I hate your type. I hate someone I think's your type. I hate someone who likes your type or wants to be your type. I'd kill a dog liked to be with you. I hate all of you expensive bastards with money and no guts. I hate you 'cause you can't whip your own nigger, and I'm glad you can't, 'cause I can. And you'll pay me. So go ahead, send your killers around. See where it gets them. Where it gets you. And I hate your goddamn hair, Beems."

"When this is over," Beems said, "you leave immediately!"

"I will, but not because of you. Because I can't stand you or your little pack of turds."

The big man with missing teeth raised his head, glared at McBride. McBride said, "Nigger whipped your ass, didn't he, Forrest?"

Forrest didn't say anything, but his face said a lot. McBride said, "You can't whip the nigger, so your boss sent for me. I can whip the nigger. So don't think for a moment you can whip me."

"Come on," Beems said. "Let's leave. The man makes me sick."

Beems joined the others, his hand held out to his side. The elderly gentlemen looked as if they had just realized they were lost in the forest. They organized themselves enough to start out the door. Beems followed, turned before exiting, glared at McBride.

McBride said, "Don't wash that hand, Beems. You can say, 'Shake the hand of the man who shook the balls of John McBride.' "

"You go to hell," Beems said.

"Keep me posted," McBride said. Beems left. McBride yelled after him and his crowd, "And gentlemen, enjoyed doing business with you."

9:12 P.M.

Later in the night the redhead displeased him and McBride popped her other eye, stretched her out, lay across her, and slept. While he slept, he dreamed he had a head of hair like Mr. Ronald Beems.

Outside, the wind picked up slightly, blew hot, brine-scented air down Galveston's streets and through the whorehouse window.

9:34 P.M.

Bill Cooper was working outside on the second-floor deck he was building. He had it completed except for a bit of trim work. It had gone dark on him sometime back, and he was trying to finish by lantern light. He was hammering a sidewall board into place when he felt a drop of rain. He stopped hammering and looked up. The night sky had a peculiar appearance, and for a moment it gave him pause. He studied the heavens a moment longer, decided it didn't look all that bad. It was just the starlight that gave it that look. No more drops fell on him.

Bill tossed the hammer on the deck, leaving the nail only partially driven, picked up the lantern, and went inside the house to be with his wife and baby son. He'd had enough for one day.

11:01 P.M.

The waves came in loud against the beach and the air was surprisingly heavy for so late at night. It lay hot and sweaty on "Lil" Arthur John Johnson's bare chest. He breathed in the air and blew it out, pounded the railroad tie with all his might for the hundredth time. His right fist struck it, and the tie moved in the sand. He hooked it with a left, jammed it with a straight right, putting his entire six-foot, two-hundred-pound frame into it. The tie went backward, came out of the sand, and hit the beach.

Arthur stepped back and held out his broad, black hands and examined them in the moonlight. They were scuffed, but essentially sound. He walked down to the water and squatted and stuck his hands in, let the surf roll over them. The salt didn't even burn. His hands were like leather. He rubbed them together, being sure to coat them completely with seawater. He cupped water in his palms, rubbed it on his face, over his shaved, bullet head.

Along with a number of other pounding exercises, he had been doing this for months, conditioning his hands and face with work and brine. Rumor was, this man he was to fight, this McBride, had fists like razors, fists that cut right through the gloves and tore the flesh.

"Lil" Arthur took another breath, and this one was filled not only with the smell of saltwater and dead fish, but of raw sewage, which was regularly dumped offshore in the Gulf.

He took his shovel and redug the hole in the sand and dropped the tie back in, patted it down, went back to work. This time, two socks and it came up. He repeated the washing of his hands and face, then picked up the tie, placed it on a broad shoulder and began to run down the beach. When he had gone a good distance, he switched shoulders and ran back. He didn't even feel winded.

He collected his shovel, and with the tie on one shoulder, headed toward his family's shack in the Flats, also known as Nigger Town.

"Lil" Arthur left the tie in front of the shack and put the shovel on the sagging porch. He was about to go inside when he saw a man start across the little excuse of a yard. The man was white. He was wearing dress clothes and a top hat.

When he was near the front porch, he stopped, took off his hat. It was Forrest Thomas, the man "Lil" Arthur had beaten unconscious three weeks back. It had taken only till the middle of the third round.

Even in the cloud-hazy moonlight, "Lil" Arthur could see Forrest looked rough. For a moment, a fleeting moment, he almost felt bad about inflicting so much damage. But then he began to wonder if the man had a gun.

"Arthur," Forrest said. "I come to talk a minute, if'n it's all right."

This was certainly different from the night "Lil" Arthur had climbed into the ring with him. Then, Forrest Thomas had been conceited and full of piss and vinegar and wore the word nigger on his lips as firmly as a mole. He was angry he had been reduced by his employer to fighting a black man. To hear him tell it, he deserved no less than John L. Sullivan, who refused to fight a Negro, considering it a debasement to the heavyweight title.

"Yeah," "Lil" Arthur said. "What you want?"

"I ain't got nothing against you," Forrest said.

"Don't matter you do," "Lil" Arthur said.

"You whupped me fair and square."

"I know, and I can do it again."

"I didn't think so before, but I know you can now."

"That's what you come to say? You got all dressed up, just to come talk to a nigger that whupped you?"

"I come to say more."

"Say it. I'm tired."

"McBride's come in."

"That ain't tellin' me nothin'. I reckoned he'd come in sometime. How'm I gonna fight him, he don't come in?"

"You don't know anything about McBride. Not really. He killed a man in the ring, his last fight in Chicago. That's why Beems brought him in, to kill you. Beems and his bunch want you dead 'cause you whipped a white man. They don't care you whipped me. They care you whipped a white man. Beems figures it's an insult to the white race, a white man being beat by a colored. This McBride, he's got a shot at the Championship of the World. He's that good."

"You tellin' me you concerned for me?"

"I'm tellin' you Beems and the members of the Sportin' Club can't take it. They lost a lot of money on bets, too. They got to set it right, see. I ain't no friend of yours, but I figure I owe you that. I come to warn you this McBride is a killer."

"Lil" Arthur listened to the crickets saw their legs a moment, then said, "If that worried me, this man being a killer, and I didn't fight him, that would look pretty good for your boss, wouldn't it? Beems could say the bad nigger didn't show up. That he was scared of a white man."

"You fight this McBride, there's a good chance he'll kill you or cripple you. Boxing bein' against the law, there won't be nobody there legal to keep check on things. Not really. Audience gonna be there ain't gonna say nothin'. They ain't supposed to be there anyway. You died, got hurt bad, you'd end up out there in the Gulf with a block of granite tied to your dick, and that'd be that."

"Sayin' I should run?"

"You run, it gives Beems face, and you don't take a beatin', maybe get killed. You figure it."

"You ain't doin' nothin' for me. You're just pimpin' for Beems. You tryin' to beat me with your mouth. Well, I ain't gonna take no beatin'. White. Colored. Striped. It don't matter. McBride gets in the ring, I'll knock him down. You go on back to Beems. Tell him I ain't scared, and I ain't gonna run. And ain't none of this workin'."

Forrest put his hat on. "Have it your way, nigger." He turned and walked away.

"Lil" Arthur started inside the house, but before he could open the door, his father, Henry, came out. He dragged his left leg behind him as he came, leaned on his cane. He wore a ragged undershirt and work pants. He was sweaty. Tired. Gray. Grayer yet in the muted moonlight.

"You ought not talk to a white man that way," Henry said. "Them Ku Kluxers'll come 'round."

"I ain't afraid of no Ku Kluxers."

"Yeah, well I am, and we be seein' what you say when you swingin' from a rope, a peckerwood cuttin' off yo balls. You ain't lived none yet. You ain't nothin' but twenty-two years. Sit down, boy."

"Papa, you ain't me. I ain't got no bad leg. I ain't scared of nobody."

"I ain't always had no bad leg. Sit down."

"Lil" Arthur sat down beside his father. Henry said, "A colored man, he got to play the game, to win the game. You hear me?"

"I ain't seen you winnin' much."

Henry slapped "Lil" Arthur quickly. It was fast, and "Lil" Arthur realized where he had inherited his hand speed. "You shut yo face," Henry said. "Don't talk to your papa like that."

"Lil" Arthur reached up and touched his cheek, not because it hurt, but because he was still a little amazed. Henry said, "For a colored man, winnin' is stayin' alive to live out the time God give you."

"But how you spend what time you got, Papa, that ain't up to God. I'm gonna be the Heavyweight Champion of the World someday. You'll see."

"There ain't never gonna be no colored Champion of the World, 'Lil' Arthur. And there ain't no talkin' to you. You a fool. I'm gonna be cuttin' you down from a tree some morning, yo neck all stretched out. Help me up. I'm goin' to bed."

"Lil" Arthur helped his father up, and the old man, balanced on his cane, dragged himself inside the shack.

A moment later, "Lil" Arthur's mother, Tina, came out. She was a broad-faced woman, short and stocky, nearly twenty years younger than her husband.

"You don't need talk yo papa that way," she said.

"He don't do nothin', and he don't want me to do nothin'," "Lil" Arthur said.

"He know what he been through, Arthur. He born a slave. He made to fight for white mens like he was some kinda fightin' rooster, and he got his leg paralyzed cause he had to fight for them Rebels in the war. You think on that. He in one hell of a fix. Him a colored man out there shootin' at Yankees, 'cause if he don't, they gonna shoot him, and them Rebels gonna shoot him he don't fight the Yankees."

"I ain't all that fond of Yankees myself. They ain't likin' niggers any more than anyone else."

"That's true. But, yo papa, he right about one thing. You ain't lived enough to know nothin' about nothin'. You want to be a white man so bad it hurt you. You is African, boy. You is born of slaves come from slaves come from Africa."

"You sayin' what he's sayin'?"

"Naw, I ain't. I'm sayin', you whup this fella, and you whup him good. Remember when them bullies used to chase you home, and I tell you, you come back without fightin', I'm gonna whup you harder than them?"

"Yes ma'am."

"And you got so you whupped 'em good, just so I wouldn't whup yo ass?"

"Yes ma'am."

"Well, these here white men hire out this man against you, threaten you, they're bullies. You go in there, and you whup this fella, and you use what God give you in them hands, and you make your way. But you remember, you ain't gonna have nothin' easy. Only way a white man gonna get respect for you is you knock him down, you hear? And you can knock him down in that ring better than out here, 'cause then you just a bad nigger they gonna hang. But you don't talk to yo papa that way. He better than most. He got him a steady job, and he hold this family together."

"He's a janitor."

"That's more than you is."

"And you hold this family together."

"It a two-person job, son."

"Yes, ma'am."

"Good night, son."

"Lil" Arthur hugged her, kissed her cheek, and she went inside. He followed, but the smallness of the two-room house, all those bodies on pallets — his parents, three sisters, two brothers, and a brother-in-law — made him feel crowded. And the pigeons sickened him. Always the pigeons. They had found a hole in the roof — the one that had been covered with tar paper — and now they were roosting inside on the rafters. Tomorrow, half the house would be covered in bird shit. He needed to get up there and put some fresh tar paper on the roof. He kept meaning to. Papa couldn't do it, and he spent his own time training. He had to do more for the family besides bring in a few dollars from fighting.

"Lil" Arthur got the stick they kept by the door for just such an occasion, used it to roust the pigeons by poking at them. In the long run, it wouldn't matter. They would fly as high as the roof, then gradually creep back down to roost. But the explosion of bird wings, their rise to the sky through the hole in the roof, lifted his spirits.

His brother-in-law, Clement, rose up on an elbow from his pallet, and his wife, "Lil" Arthur's sister Lucy, stirred and rolled over, stretched her arm across Clement's chest, but didn't wake up.

"What you doin', Arthur?" Clement whispered. "You don't know a man's got to sleep? I got work to do 'morrow. Ain't all of us sleep all day."

"Sleep then. And stay out of my sister. Lucy don't need no kids now. We got a house full a folks."

"She my wife. We supposed to do that. And multiply."

"Then get your own place and multiply. We packed tight as turds here."

"You crazy, Arthur."

Arthur cocked the pigeon stick. "Lay down and shut up."

Clement lay down, and Arthur put the stick back and gathered up his pallet and went outside. He inspected the pallet for bird shit, found none, stretched out on the porch, and tried to sleep. He thought about getting his guitar, going back to the beach to strum it, but he was too tired for that. Too tired to do anything, too awake to sleep.

His mother had told him time and again that when he was a baby, an old Negro lady with the second sight had picked up his little hand and said, "This child gonna eat his bread in many countries."

It was something that had always sustained him. But now, he began to wonder. Except for trying to leave Galveston by train once, falling asleep in the boxcar, only to discover it had been making circles in the train yard all night as supplies were unloaded, he'd had no adventures, and was still eating his bread in Galveston.

All night he fought mosquitoes, the heat, and his own ambition. By morning he was exhausted.

WEDNESDAY, SEPTEMBER 5, 10:20 A.M.

Telegraphed Message from Washington, D.C., Weather Bureau, Central Office, to Issac Cline, Galveston, Texas, Weather Bureau:

Disturbance center near Key West moving northwest. Vessels bound for Florida and Cuban ports should exercise caution. Storm likely to become dangerous.

10:23 A.M.

McBride awoke, fucked the redhead, sat up in bed, and cracked his knuckles, said, "I'm going to eat and train, Red. You have your ass here when I get back, and put it on the Sportin' Club's bill. And wash yourself, for heaven's sake."

"Yes sir, Mr. McBride," she said.

McBride got up, poured water into a washbasin, washed his dick, under his arms, splashed water on his face. Then he sat at the dresser in front of the mirror and spent twenty minutes putting on the Chinaman's remedy and combing his hair. As soon as he had it just right, he put on a cap.

He got dressed in loose pants, a short-sleeved shirt, soft shoes, wrapped his knuckles with gauze, put a little notebook and pencil in his back pocket, then pulled on soft leather gloves. When the redhead wasn't looking, he wrapped his revolver and razor in a washrag, stuffed them between his shirt and his stomach.

Downstairs, making sure no one was about, he removed the rag containing his revolver and razor, stuck them into the drooping greenness of a potted plant, then went away.

He strolled down the street to a café and ordered steak and eggs and lots of coffee. He ate with his gloves and hat on. He paid for the meal, but got a receipt.

Comfortably full, he went out to train.

He began at the docks. There were a number of men hard at work. They were loading bags of cottonseed onto a ship. He stood with his hands behind his back and watched. The scent of the sea was strong. The water lapped at the pilings enthusiastically, and the air was as heavy as a cotton sack.

After a while, he strolled over to a large, bald man with arms and legs like plantation columns. The man wore faded overalls without a shirt, and his chest was as hairy as a bear's ass. He had on heavy work boots with the sides burst out. McBride could see his bare feet through the openings. McBride hated a man that didn't keep up his appearance, even when he was working. Pride was like a dog. You didn't feed it regularly, it died.

McBride said, "What's your name?"

The man, a bag of cottonseed under each arm, stopped and looked at him, taken aback. "Ketchum," he said. "Warner Ketchum."

"Yeah," McBride said. "Thought so. So, you're the one."

The man glared at him. "One what?"

The other men stopped working, turned to look.

"I just wanted to see you," McBride said. "Yeah, you fit the description. I just never thought there was a white man would stoop to such a thing. Fact is, hard to imagine any man stooping to such a thing."

"What are you talkin' about, fella?"

"Well, word is, Warner Ketchum that works at the dock has been known to suck a little nigger dick in his time."

Ketchum dropped the cottonseed bags. "Who the hell are you? Where you hear that?"

McBride put his gloved hands behind his back and held them. "They say, on a good night, you can do more with a nigger's dick than a cat can with a ball of twine."

The man was fuming. "You got me mixed up with somebody else, you Yankee-talkin' sonofabitch."

"Naw, I ain't got you mixed up. Your name's Warner Ketchum. You look how you was described to me by the nigger whose stick you slicked."

Warner stepped forward with his right foot and swung a right punch so looped it looked like a sickle blade. McBride ducked it without removing his hands from behind his back, slipped inside and twisted his hips as he brought a right uppercut into Warner's midsection.

Warner's air exploded and he wobbled back, and McBride was in again, a left hook to the ribs, a straight right to the solar plexus. Warner doubled and went to his knees.

McBride leaned over and kissed him on the ear, said, "Tell me. Them nigger dicks taste like licorice?"

Warner came up then, and he was wild. He threw a right, then a left. McBride bobbed beneath them. Warner kicked at him. McBride turned sideways, let the kick go by, unloaded a left hand that caught Warner on the jaw, followed it with a right that struck with a sound like the impact of an artillery shell.

Warner dropped to one knee. McBride grabbed him by the head and swung his knee into Warner's face, busting his nose all over the dock. Warner fell face forward, caught himself on his hands, almost got up. Then, very slowly, he collapsed, lay down, and didn't move.

McBride looked at the men who were watching him. He said, "He didn't suck no nigger dicks. I made that up." He got out his pad and pencil and wrote: Owed me. Price of one sparring partner, FIVE DOLLARS.

He put the pad and pencil away. Got five dollars out of his wallet, folded it, put it in the man's back pocket. He turned to the other men who stood staring at him as if he were one of Jesus' miracles.

"Frankly, I think you're all a bunch of sorry assholes, and I think, one at a time, I can lick every goddamn one of you Southern white trash pieces of shit. Any takers?"

"Not likely," said a stocky man at the front of the crowd. "You're a ringer." He picked up a sack of cottonseed he had put down, started toward the ship. The other men did the same.

McBride said, "Okay," and walked away.

He thought, maybe, on down the docks he might find another sparring partner.

5:23 P.M.

By the end of the day, near dark, McBride checked his notepad for expenses, saw the Sporting Club owed him forty-five dollars in sparring partners, and a new pair of gloves, as well as breakfast and dinner to come. He added money for a shoeshine. A clumsy sonofabitch had scuffed one of his shoes.

He got the shoeshine and ate a steak, flexed his muscles as he arrived at the whorehouse. He felt loose still, like he could take on another two or three yokels.

He went inside, got his goods out of the potted plant, and climbed the stairs.

THURSDAY, SEPTEMBER 6, 6:00 P.M.

Telegraphed Message from Washington, D.C., Weather Bureau, Central Office, to Issac Cline, Galveston, Texas, Weather Bureau:

Storm center just northwest of Key West.

7:30 P.M.

"Lil" Arthur ran down to the Sporting Club that night and stood in front of it, his hands in his pants pockets. The wind was brisk, and the air was just plain sour.

Saturday, he was going to fight a heavyweight crown contender, and though it would not be listed as an official bout, and McBride was just in it to pick up some money, "Lil" Arthur was glad to have the chance to fight a man who might fight for the championship someday. And if he could beat him, even if it didn't affect McBride's record, "Lil" Arthur knew he'd have that; he would have beaten a contender for the Heavyweight Championship of the World.

It was a far cry from the Battle Royales he had first participated in. There was a time when he looked upon those degrading events with favor.

He remembered his first Battle Royale. His friend Ernest had talked him into it. Once a month, sometimes more often, white "sporting men" liked to get a bunch of colored boys and men to come down to the club for a free-for-all. They'd put nine or ten of them in a ring, sometimes make them strip naked and wear Sambo masks. He'd done that once himself.

While the coloreds fought, the whites would toss money and yell for them to kill one another. Sometimes they'd tie two coloreds together by the ankles, let them go at it. Blood flowed thick as molasses on flapjacks. Bones were broken. Muscles torn. For the whites, it was great fun, watching a couple of coons knock each other about.

"Lil" Arthur found he was good at all that fighting, and even knocked Ernest out, effectively ending their friendship. He couldn't help himself. He got in there, got the battling blood up, he would hit whoever came near him.

He started boxing regularly, gained some skill. No more Battle Royales. He got a reputation with the colored boxers, and in time that spread to the whites.

The Sporting Club, plumb out of new white contenders for their champion, Forrest Thomas, gave "Lil" Arthur twenty-five dollars to mix it up with their man, thinking a colored and a white would be a novelty, and the superiority of the white race would be proved in a match of skill and timing.

Right before the fight, "Lil" Arthur said his prayers, and then considering he was going to be fighting in front of a bunch of angry, mean-spirited whites, and for the first time, white women — sporting women, but women — who wanted to see a black man knocked to jelly, he took gauze and wrapped his dick. He wrapped it so that it was as thick as a blackjack. He figured he'd give them white folks something to look at. The thing they feared the most. A black as coal stud nigger.

He whipped Forrest Thomas like he was a redheaded stepchild; whipped him so badly, they stopped the fight so no one would see a colored man knock a white man out.

Against their wishes, the Sporting Club was forced to hand the championship over to "Lil" Arthur John Johnson, and the fact that a colored now held the club's precious boxing crown was like a chicken bone in the club's throat. Primarily Beems's throat. As the current president of the Sporting Club, the match had been Beems's idea, and Forrest Thomas had been Beems's man.

Enter McBride. Beems, on the side, talked a couple of the Sporting Club's more wealthy members into financing a fight. One where a true contender to the heavyweight crown would whip "Lil" Arthur and return the local championship to a white man, even if that white man relinquished the crown when he returned to Chicago, leaving it vacant. In that case, "Lil" Arthur was certain he'd never get another shot at the Sporting Club championship. They wanted him out, by hook or crook.

"Lil" Arthur had never seen McBride. Didn't know how he fought. He'd just heard he was as tough as stone and had balls like a brass monkey. He liked to think he was the same way. He didn't intend to give the championship up. Saturday, he'd find out if he had to.

9:00 P.M.

The redhead, nursing a fat lip, two black eyes, and a bruise on her belly, rolled over gingerly and put her arm across McBride's hairy chest. "You had enough?"

"I'll say when I've had enough."

"I was just thinking, I might go downstairs and get something to eat. Come back in a few minutes."

"You had time to eat before I got back. You didn't eat, you just messed up. I'm paying for this. Or rather the Sporting Club is."

"An engine's got to have coal, if you want that engine to go."

"Yeah?"

"Yeah." The redhead reached up and ran her fingers through McBride's hair.

McBride reached across his chest and slapped the redhead. "Don't touch my hair. Stay out of my hair. And shut up. I don't care you want to fuck or not. I want to fuck, we fuck. Got it?"

"Yes, sir."

"Listen here, I'm gonna take a shit. I get back, I want you to wash that goddamn nasty hole of yours. You think I like stickin' my wick in that, it not being clean? You got to get clean."

"It's so hot. I sweat. And you're just gonna mess me up again."

"I don't care. You wash that thing. I went around with my johnson like that, it'd fall off. I get a disease, girl, I'll come back here, kick your ass so hard your butthole will swap places with your cunt."

"I ain't got no disease, Mr. McBride."

"Good."

"Why you got to be so mean?" the redhead asked suddenly, then couldn't believe it had come out of her mouth. She realized, not only would a remark like that anger McBride, but the question was stupid. It was like asking a chicken why it pecked shit. It just did. McBride was mean because he was, and that was that.

But even as the redhead flinched, McBride turned philosophical. "It isn't a matter of mean. It's because I can do what I want, and others can't. You got that, sister?"

"Sure. I didn't mean nothing by it."

"Someone can do to me what I do to them, then all right, that's how it is. Isn't a man, woman, or animal on Earth that's worth a damn. You know that?"

"Sure. You're right."

"You bet I am. Only thing pure in this world is a baby. Human or animal, a baby is born hungry and innocent. It can't do a thing for itself. Then it grows up and gets just like everyone else. A baby is all right until it's about two. Then, it ought to just be smothered and save the world the room. My sister, she was all right till she was about two, then it wasn't nothing but her wanting stuff and my mother giving it to her. Later on, Mama didn't have nothing to do with her either, same as me. She got over two years old, she was just trouble. Like I was. Like everybody else is."

"Sure," the redhead said.

"Oh, shut up, you don't know your ass from a pig track."

McBride got up and went to the john. He took his revolver and his wallet and his razor with him. He didn't trust a whore — any woman for that matter — far as he could hurl one.

While he was in the can trying out the new flush toilet, the redhead eased out of bed wearing only a sheet. She slipped out the door, went downstairs and outside, into the streets. She flagged down a man in a buggy, talked him into a ride, for a ride, then she was out of there, destination unimportant.

9:49 P.M.

Later, pissed at the redhead, McBride used the madam herself, blacked both her eyes when she suggested that a lot of sex before a fight might not be a good idea for an athlete.

The madam, lying in bed with McBride's muscular arm across her ample breasts, sighed and watched the glow of the gas streetlights play on the ceiling.

Well, she thought, *it's a living.*

FRIDAY, SEPTEMBER 7, 10:35 A.M.

Telegraphed Message from Washington, D.C., Weather Bureau, Central Office, to Issac Cline, Galveston, Texas, Weather Bureau:

Storm warning. Galveston, Texas. Take precautions.

Issac Cline, head of the Galveston Weather Bureau, sat at his desk on the third floor of the Levy Building and read the telegram. He went downstairs and outside for a look-see.

The weather was certainly in a stormy mood, but it didn't look like serious hurricane weather. He had been with the Weather Bureau for eight years, and he thought he ought to know a hurricane by now, and this wasn't it. The sky wasn't the right color.

He walked until he got to the beach. By then the wind was picking up, and the sea was swelling. The clouds were like wads of duck down ripped from a pillow. He walked a little farther down the beach, found a turtle wrapped in seaweed, poked it with a stick. It was dead as a stone.

Issac returned to the Levy Building, and by the time he made his way back, the wind had picked up considerably. He climbed the stairs to the roof. The roof barometer was dropping quickly, and the wind was serious. He revised his opinion on how much he knew about storms. He estimated the wind to be blowing at twenty miles an hour, and growing. He pushed against it, made his way to the weather pole, hoisted two flags. The top flag was actually a white pennant. It whipped in the wind like a gossip's tongue. Anyone who saw it knew it meant the wind was coming from the northwest. Beneath it was a red flag with a black center; this flag meant the wind was coming ass over teakettle, and that a seriously violent storm was expected within hours.

The air smelled dank and fishy. For a moment, Cline thought perhaps he had actually touched the dead turtle and brought its stink back with him. But no, it was the wind.

At about this same time, the steamship *Pensacola*, commanded by Captain James Slater, left the port of Galveston from Pier 34, destination Pensacola, Florida.

Slater had read the hurricane reports of the day before, and though the wind was picking up and was oddly steamy, the sky failed to show what he was watching for. A dusty, brick red color, a sure sign of a hurricane. He felt the whole Weather Bureau business was about as much guess and luck as it was anything else. He figured he could do that and be as accurate.

He gave orders to ease the *Pensacola* into the Gulf.

1:06 P.M.

The pigeons fluttered through the opening in the Johnsons' roof. Tar paper lifted, tore, blew away, tumbled through the sky as if they were little black pieces of the structure's soul.

"It's them birds again," his mother said.

"Lil" Arthur stopped doing push-ups, looked to the ceiling. Pigeons were thick on the rafters. So was pigeon shit. The sky was very visible through the roof. And very black. It looked venomous.

"Shit," "Lil" Arthur said.

"It's okay," she said. "Leave 'em be. They scared. So am I."

"Lil" Arthur stood up, said, "Ain't nothin' be scared of. We been through all kinda storms. We're on a rise here. Water don't never get this high."

"I ain't never liked no storm. I be glad when yo daddy and the young'uns gets home."

"Papa's got an old tarp I might can put over that hole. Keep out the rain."

"You think you can, go on."

"I already shoulda," "Lil" Arthur said.

"Lil" Arthur went outside, crawled under the upraised porch, and got hold of the old tarp. It was pretty rotten, but it might serve his purpose, at least temporarily. He dragged it into the yard, crawled back under, tugged out the creaking ladder and a rusty hammer. He was about to go inside and get the nails when he heard a kind of odd roaring. He stopped, listened, recognized it.

It was the surf. He had certainly heard it before, but not this loud and this far from the beach. He got the nails and put the ladder against the side of the house and carried the tarp onto the roof. The tarp nearly took to the air when he spread it, almost carried him with it. With considerable effort he got it nailed over the hole, trapping what pigeons didn't flee inside the house.

2:30 P.M.

Inside the whorehouse, the madam, a fat lip added to her black eyes, watched from the bed as McBride, naked, seated in a chair before the dresser mirror, carefully oiled and combed his hair over his bald spot. The windows were closed, and the wind rattled them like dice in a gambler's fist. The air inside the whorehouse was as stuffy as a minister's wife.

"What's that smell?" she asked.

It was the tonic the Chinaman had given him. He said, "You don't want your tits pinched, shut the fuck up."

"All right," she said.

The windows rattled again. Pops of rain flecked the glass.

McBride went to the window, his limp dick resting on the windowsill, almost touching the glass, like a large, wrinkled grub looking for a way out.

"Storm coming," he said.

The madam thought: *No shit.*

McBride opened the window. The wind blew a comb and hairbrush off the dresser. A man, walking along the sandy street, one hand on his hat to save it from the wind, glanced up at McBride. McBride took hold of his dick and wagged it at him. The man turned his head and picked up his pace.

McBride said, "Spread those fat legs, honey-ass, 'cause I'm sailing into port, and I'm ready to drop anchor."

Sighing, the madam rolled onto her back, and McBride mounted her. "Don't mess up my hair this time," he said.

4:30 P.M.

The study smelled of stale cigar smoke and sweat, and faintly of baby oil. The grandfather clock chimed four-thirty. The air was humid and sticky as it shoved through the open windows and fluttered the dark curtains. The sunlight, which was tinted with a green cloud haze, flashed in and out, giving brightness to the false eyes and the yellowed teeth of a dozen mounted animal heads on the walls. Bears. Boar. Deer. Even a wolf.

Beems, the source of much of the sweat smell, thought: It's at least another hour before my wife gets home. Good.

Forrest drove him so hard Beems's forehead slammed into the wall, rocking the head of the wild boar that was mounted there, causing the boar to look as if it had turned its head in response to a distant sound, a peculiar sight.

"It's not because I'm one of them kind I do this," Beems said. "It's just, oh yeah, honey... The wife, you know, she don't do nothing for me. I mean, you got to get a little pleasure where you can. A man's got to get his pleasure, don't you think... Oh, yes. That's it... A man, he's got to get his pleasure, right? Even if there's nothing funny about him?"

Forrest rested his hands on Beems's naked shoulders, pushing him down until his head rested on top of the couch cushion. Forrest cocked his hips, drove forward with teeth clenched, penetrating deep into Beems's ass. He said, "Yeah. Sure."

"You mean that? This don't make me queer?"

"No," Forrest panted. "Never has. Never will. Don't mean nothin'. Not a damn thing. It's all right. You're a man's man. Let me concentrate."

Forrest had to concentrate. He hated this business, but it was part of the job. And, of course, unknown to Beems, he was putting the meat to Beems's wife. So, if he wanted to keep doing that, he had to stay in with the boss. And Mrs. Beems, of course, had no idea he was reaming her husband's dirty ditch, or that her husband had about as much interest in women as a pig does a silver tea service.

What a joke. He was fucking Beems's old lady, doing the dog work for Beems, for a good price, and was reaming Beems's asshole and assuring Beems he wasn't what he was, a fairy. And as an added benefit, he didn't have to fight the nigger tomorrow night. That was a big plus. That sonofabitch hit like a mule kicked. He hoped this McBride would tap him good. The nigger died, he'd make a point of shitting on his grave. Right at the head of it.

Well, maybe, Forrest decided, as he drove his hips forward hard enough to make Beems scream a little, he didn't hate this business after all. Not completely. He took so much crap from Beems, this was kinda nice, having the bastard bent over a couch, dicking him so hard his head slammed the wall. Goddamn nutless queer, insulting him in public, trying to act tough.

Forrest took the bottle of baby oil off the end table and poured it onto Beems's ass. He put the bottle back and realized he was going soft. He tried to imagine he was plunging into Mrs. Beems, who had the smoothest ass and the brightest blonde pubic hair he had ever seen. "I'm almost there," Forrest said.

"Stroke, Forrest! Stroke, man. Stroke!"

In the moment of orgasm, Beems imagined that the dick plunging into his hairy ass belonged to the big nigger, "Lil" Arthur. He thought about "Lil" Arthur all the time. Ever since he had seen him fight naked in a Battle Royale while wearing a Sambo mask for the enjoyment of the crowd.

And the way "Lil" Arthur had whipped Forrest. Oh, God. So thoroughly. So expertly. Forrest had been the man until then, and that made him want Forrest, but now, he wanted the nigger.

Oh God, Beems thought, to have him in me, wearing that mask, that would do it for all time. Just once. Or twice. Jesus, I want it so bad I got to be sure the nigger gets killed. I got to be sure I don't try to pay the nigger money to do this, because he lives after the fight with McBride, I know I'll break down and try. And I break down and he doesn't do it, and word gets around, or he does it, and word gets around, or I get caught... I couldn't bear that. This is bad enough. But a nigger...?

Then there was McBride. He thought about him. He had touched McBride's balls and feigned disgust, but he hadn't washed that hand yet, just as McBride suggested.

McBride won the fight with the nigger, better yet, killed him, maybe McBride would do it with him. McBride was a gent that liked money, and he liked to hurt whoever he was fucking. Beems could tell that from the way the redhead was battered. That would be good. That would be all right. McBride was the type who'd fuck anyone or anything, Beems could tell.

He imagined it was McBride at work instead of Forrest. McBride, naked, except for the bowler.

Forrest, in his moment of orgasm, grunted, said, "Oh yeah," and almost called Mrs. Beems's name. He lifted his head as he finished, saw the hard, glass eyes of the stuffed wild boar. The eyes were full of sunlight. Then the curtains fluttered and the eyes were full of darkness.

4:45 P.M.

The steamship *Pensacola,* outbound from Galveston, reached the Gulf, and a wind reached the *Pensacola.* Captain Slater felt his heart clinch. The sea came high and savage from the east, and the ship rose up and dived back down, and the waves, dark green and shadowed by the thick clouds overhead, reared up on either side of the steamship, hissed, plunged back down, and the *Pensacola* rode up.

Jake Bernard, the pilot commissioner, came onto the bridge looking green as the waves. He was Slater's guest on this voyage, and now he wished he were back home. He couldn't believe how ill he felt. Never, in all his years, had he encountered seas like this, and he had thought himself immune to seasickness.

"I don't know about you, Slater," Bernard said, "but I ain't had this much fun since a bulldog gutted my daddy."

Slater tried to smile, but couldn't make it. He saw that Bernard, in spite of his joshing, didn't look particularly jovial. Slater said, "Look at the glass."

Bernard checked the barometer. It was falling fast.

"Never seen it that low," Bernard said.

"Me either," Slater said. He ordered his crew then. Told them to take in the awning, to batten the hatches, and to prepare for water.

Bernard, who had not left the barometer, said, "God. Look at this, man!"

Slater looked. The barometer read 28.55.

Bernard said, "Way I heard it, ever gets that low, you're supposed to bend forward, kiss your root, and tell it good-bye."

6:30 P.M.

The Coopers, Bill and Angelique and their eighteen-month-old baby, Teddy, were on their way to dinner at a restaurant by buggy, when their horse, Bess, a beautiful, chocolate-colored mare, made a run at the crashing sea.

It was the sea that frightened the horse, but in its moment of fear, it had tried to plunge headlong toward the source of its fright, assuring Bill that horses were, in fact, the most stupid animals in God's creation.

Bill jerked the reins and cussed the horse. Bess wheeled, lurched the buggy so hard Bill thought they might tip, but the buggy bounced on line, and he maneuvered Bess back on track.

Angelique, dark-haired and pretty, said, "I think I soiled my bloomers... I smell it... No, that's Teddy. Thank goodness."

Bill stopped the buggy outside the restaurant, which was situated on high posts near the beach, and Angelique changed the baby's diaper, put the soiled cloth in the back of the buggy.

When she was finished, they tied up the reins and went in for a steak dinner. They sat by a window where they could see the buggy. The horse bucked and reared and tugged so much, Bill feared she might break the reins and bolt. Above them, they could hear the rocks that covered the flat roof rolling and tumbling about like mice battling over morsels. Teddy sat in a high chair provided by the restaurant; whammed a spoon in a plate of applesauce.

"Had I known the weather was this bad," Angelique said, "we'd have stayed home. I'm sorry, Bill."

"We stay home too much," Bill said, realizing the crash of the surf was causing him to raise his voice. "Building that upper deck on the house isn't doing much for my nerves either. I'm beginning to realize I'm not much of a carpenter."

Angelique widened her dark brown eyes. "No? You, not a carpenter?"

Bill smiled at her.

"I could have told you that, just by listening to all the cussing you were doing. How many times did you hit your thumb, dear?"

"Too many to count."

Angelique grew serious. "Bill. Look."

Many of the restaurant's patrons had abandoned their meals and were standing at the large windows, watching the sea. The tide was high and it was washing up to the restaurant's pilings, splashing against them hard, throwing spray against the glass.

"Goodness," Bill said. "It wasn't this bad just minutes ago."

"Hurricane?" Angelique asked.

"Yeah. It's a hurricane all right. The flags are up. I saw them."

"Why so nervous? We've had hurricanes before."

"I don't know. This feels different, I guess... It's all right. I'm just jittery is all."

They ate quickly and drove the buggy home, Bess pulling briskly all the way. The sea crashed behind them and the clouds raced above them like apparitions.

8:00 P.M.

Captain Slater figured the wind was easily eighty knots. A hurricane. The *Pensacola* was jumping like a frog. Crockery was crashing below. A medicine chest so heavy two men couldn't move it leaped up and struck the window of the bridge, went through onto the deck, slid across it, hit the railing, bounced high, and dropped into the boiling sea.

Slater and Bernard bumped heads so hard they nearly knocked each other out. When Slater got off the floor, he got a thick rope out from under a shelf and tossed it around a support post, made a couple of wraps, then used the loose ends to tie bowlines around his and Bernard's waists. That way, he and Bernard could move about the bridge if they had to, but they wouldn't end up following the path of the medicine chest.

Slater tried to think of something to do, but all he knew to do he had done. He'd had the crew drop anchor in the open Gulf; down to a hundred fathoms, and he'd instructed them to find the best shelter possible close to their posts, and to pray.

The *Pensacola* swung to the anchor, struggled like a bull on a leash. Slater could hear the bolts and plates that held the ship together screaming in agony. Those bolts broke, the plates cracked, he didn't need Captain Ahab to tell him they'd go down to Davy Jones's locker so fast they wouldn't have time to take in a lungful of air.

Using the wall for support, Slater edged along to where the bridge glass had been broken by the flying chest. Sea spray slammed against him like needles shot from a cannon. He was concentrating on the foredeck, watching it dip, when he heard Bernard make a noise that was not quite a word, yet more expressive than a grunt.

Slater turned, saw Bernard clutching the latch on one of the bridge windows so tightly he thought he would surely twist it off. Then he saw what Bernard saw.

The sea had turned black as a Dutch oven, the sky the color of gangrene, and between sea and sky there appeared to be something rising out of the water, something huge and oddly shaped, and then Slater realized what it was. It was a great wall of water, many times taller than the ship, and it was moving directly toward and over them.

SATURDAY, SEPTEMBER 8, 3:30 A.M.

Bill Cooper opened his eyes. He had been overwhelmed by a feeling of dread. He rose carefully, so as not to wake Angelique, went into the bedroom across the hall and checked on Teddy. The boy slept soundly, his thumb in his mouth.

Bill smiled at the child, reached down, and gently touched him. The boy was sweaty, and Bill noted that the air in the room smelled foul. He opened a window, stuck his head out, and looked up. The sky had cleared and the moon was bright. Suddenly, he felt silly. Perhaps this storm business, the deck he was building on the upper floor of the house, had made him restless and worried. Certainly, it looked as if the storm had passed them by.

Then his feeling of satisfaction passed. For when he examined the yard, he saw it had turned to molten silver. And then he realized it was moonlight on water. The Gulf had crept all the way up to the house. A small rowboat, loose from its moorings, floated by.

8:06 A.M.

Issac Cline had driven his buggy down the beach, warning residents near the water to evacuate. Some had. Some had not. Most had weathered many storms and felt they could weather another.

Still, many residents and tourists made for the long, wooden trestle bridge to mainland Texas. Already, the water was leaping to the bottom of the bridge, slapping at it, testing its strength.

Wagons, buggies, horses, pedestrians were as thick on the bridge as ants on gingerbread. The sky, which had been oddly clear and bright and full of moon early that morning, had now grown gray and it was raining. Of the three railway bridges that led to the mainland, one was already underwater.

3:45 P.M.

Henry Johnson, aided by "Lil" Arthur, climbed up on the wagon beside his wife. Tina held an umbrella over their heads. In the back of the wagon was the rest of the family, protected by upright posts planted in the corners, covered with the tarp that had formerly been on the roof of the house.

All day Henry had debated whether they should leave. But by 2:00, he realized this wasn't going to be just another storm. This was going to be a goddamn, wet-assed humdinger. He had organized his family, and now, by hook or crook, he was leaving. He glanced at his shack, the water pouring through the roof like the falls of Niagara. It wasn't much, but it was all he had. He doubted it could stand much of this storm, but he tried not to think about that. He had greater concerns. He said to "Lil" Arthur, "You come on with us."

"I got to fight," "Lil" Arthur said.

"You got to do nothin'. This storm'll wash your ass to sea."

"I got to, Papa."

Tina said, "Maybe yo papa's right, baby. You ought to come."

"You know I can't. Soon as the fight's over, I'll head on out. I promise. In fact, weather's so bad, I'll knock this McBride out early."

"You do that," Tina said.

"Lil" Arthur climbed on the wagon and hugged his mama and shook his father's hand. Henry spoke quickly without looking at "Lil" Arthur, said, "Good luck, son. Knock him out."

"Lil" Arthur nodded. "Thanks, Papa." He climbed down and went around to the back of the wagon and threw up the tarp and hugged his sisters one at a time and shook hands with his brother-in-law, Clement. He pulled Clement close to him, said, "You stay out of my sister, hear?"

"Yeah, Arthur. Sure. But I think maybe we done got a problem. She's already swole up."

"Ah, shit," "Lil" Arthur said.

4:03 P.M.

As Henry Johnson drove the horses onto the wooden bridge that connected Galveston to the mainland, he felt ill. The water was washing over the sides, against the wagon wheels. The horses were nervous, and the line of would-be escapees on the bridge was tremendous. It would take them a long time to cross, maybe hours, and from the look of things, the way the water was rising, wouldn't be long before the bridge was underwater.

He said a private prayer: "Lord, take care of my family. And especially that fool son of mine, 'Lil' Arthur."

It didn't occur to him to include himself in the prayer.

4:37 P.M.

Bill and Angelique Cooper moved everything of value they could carry to the second floor of the house. Already the water was sloshing in the doorway. Rain splattered against the windows violently enough to shake them, and shingles flapped boisterously on the roof.

Bill paused in his work and shuffled through ankle-deep water to a window and looked out. He said, "Angelique, I think we can stop carrying."

"But I haven't carried up the —"

"We're leaving."

"Leaving? It's that bad?"

"Not yet."

Bess was difficult to hook to the buggy. She was wild-eyed and skittish. The barn was leaking badly. Angelique held an umbrella over her head, waiting for the buggy to be fastened. She could feel water rising above her high button shoes.

Bill paused for a moment to calm the horse, glanced at Angelique, thought she looked oddly beautiful, the water running off the umbrella in streams. She held Teddy close to her. Teddy was asleep, totally unaware of what was going on around him. Any other time, the baby would be squalling, annoyed. The rain and the wind were actually helping him to sleep. At least, thought Bill, I am grateful for that.

By the time the buggy was hooked, they were standing in calf-deep water. Bill opened the barn door with great difficulty, saw that the yard was gone, and so was the street. He would have to guess at directions. Worse yet, it wasn't rain water running through the street. It was definitely seawater; the water of the Gulf had risen up as if to swallow Galveston the way the ocean was said to have swallowed Atlantis.

Bill helped Angelique and Teddy into the buggy, took hold of the reins, clucked to Bess. Bess jerked and reared, and finally, by reins and voice, Bill calmed her. She began to plod forward through the dark, powerful water.

5:00 P.M.

McBride awoke. The wind was howling. The window glass was rattling violently, even though the windows were raised. The air was cool for a change, but damp. It was dark in the room.

The madam, wrapped in a blanket, sat in a chair pulled up against the far wall. She turned and looked at McBride. She said, "All hell's broken loose."

"Say it has?" McBride got up, walked naked to the windows. The wind was so furious it pushed him. "Damn," he said. "It's dark as midnight. This looks bad."

"Bad?" The madam laughed. "Worst hurricane I've ever seen, and I don't even think it's cranked up good yet."

"You don't think they'll call off the fight do you?"

"Can you fight in a boat?"

"Hell, honey, I can fight and fuck at the same time on a boat. Come to think of it, I can fight and fuck on a rolling log, I have to. I used to be a lumberjack up north."

"I was you, I'd find a log, and get to crackin'."

A bolt of lightning, white as eternity, split the sky, and when it did, the darkness outside subsided, and in that instant, McBride saw the street was covered in waist-deep water.

"Reckon I better start on over there," he said. "It may take me a while."

The madam thought: *Well, honey, go right ahead, and I hope you drown.*

5:20 P.M.

"Lil" Arthur was standing on the porch, trying to decide if he should brave the water, which was now up to the lip of the porch, when he saw a loose rowboat drift by.

Suddenly he was in the water, swimming, and the force of the water carried him after the boat, and soon he had hold of it. When he climbed inside, he found the boat was a third filled with water.

He found a paddle and a pail half-filled with dirt. The dirt had turned to mud and was beginning to flow over the top of the bucket. A few dead worms swirled in the mess. The world was atumble with wind, water, and darkness.

"Lil" Arthur took the bucket and poured out the mud and the worms and started to bail. Now and then he put the bucket aside and used the boat paddle. Not that he needed it much. The water was carrying him where he wanted to go. Uptown.

5:46 P.M.

Uptown the water was not so deep, but it took McBride almost an hour to get to the Sporting Club. He waded through waist-deep water for a block, then knee-deep, and finally ankle-deep. His bowler hat had lost all its shape when he arrived, and his clothes were ruined. The water hadn't done his revolver or his razor any good either.

When he arrived at the building, he was surprised to find a crowd of men had gathered on the steps. Most stood under umbrellas, but many were bareheaded. There were a few women among them. Whores mostly. Decent women didn't go to prizefights.

McBride went up the steps, and the crowd blocked him. He said, "Look here. I'm McBride. I'm to fight the nigger."

The crowd parted, and McBride, with words of encouragement and pats on the back, was allowed indoors. Inside, the wind could still be heard, but it sounded distant. The rain was just a hum.

Beems, Forrest, and the two oldsters were standing in the foyer, looking tense as fat hens at noontime. As soon as they saw McBride, their faces relaxed, and the elderly gentlemen went away. Beems said, "We were afraid you wouldn't make it."

"Worried about your investment?"

"I suppose."

"I'd have come if I had to swim."

"The nigger doesn't show, the title and the money's yours."

"I don't want it like that," McBride said. "I want to hit him. Course, he don't show, I'll take the money. You seen it this bad before?"

"No," Beems said.

"I didn't expect nobody to be here."

"Gamblers always show," Forrest said. "They gamble their money, they gamble their lives."

"Go find something to do, Forrest," Beems said. "I'll show Mr. McBride the dressing room."

Forrest looked at Beems, grinned a little, showed Beems he knew what he had in mind. Beems fumed. Forrest went away. Beems took hold of McBride's elbow and began to guide him.

"I ain't no dog got to be led," McBride said.

"Very well," Beems said, and McBride followed him through a side door and down into a locker room. The room had two inches of water in it.

"My God," Beems said. "We've sprung a leak somewhere."

"Water like this," McBride said. "The force…it's washing out the mortar in the bricks, seeping through the chinks in the wall… Hell, it's all right for what I got to do."

"There's shorts and boots in the locker there," Beems said. "You could go ahead and change."

McBride sloshed water, sat on a bench and pulled off his shoes and socks with his feet resting on the bench. Beems stood where he was, watching the water rise.

McBride took the razor out of the side of one of the shoes, held it up for Beems to see, said, "Mexican boxing glove."

Beems grinned. He watched as McBride removed his bowler, coat, and shirt. He watched carefully as he removed his pants and shorts. McBride reached into the locker Beems had recommended, paused, turned, stared at Beems.

"You're liking what you're seein', ain't you, buddy?"

Beems didn't say anything. His heart was in his throat.

McBride grinned at him. "I knew first time I seen you, you was an Alice."

"No," Beems said. "Nothing like that. It's not like that at all."

McBride smiled. He looked very gentle in that moment. He said, "It's all right. Come here. I don't mind that."

"Well…"

"Naw. Really. It's just, you know, you got to be careful. Not let everyone know. Not everyone understands, see."

Beems, almost licking his lips, went over to McBride. When he was close, McBride's smile widened, and he unloaded a right uppercut into Beems's stomach. He hit him so hard Beems dropped to his knees in the water, nodded forward, and banged his head on the bench. His top hat came off, hit the water, sailed along the row of lockers, made a right turn near the wall, flowed out of sight behind a bench.

McBride picked Beems up by the hair and pulled his head close to his dick, said, "Look at it a minute, 'cause that's all you're gonna do."

Then McBride pulled Beems to his feet by his pretty hair and went to work on him. Lefts and rights. Nothing too hard. But more than Beems had ever gotten. When he finished, he left Beems lying in the water next to the bench, coughing.

McBride said, "Next time you piss, you'll piss blood, Alice." McBride got a towel out of the locker and sat on the bench and put his feet up and dried them. He put on the boxing shorts. There was a mirror on the inside of the locker, and McBride was upset to see his hair. It was a mess. He spent several minutes putting it in place. When he finished, he glanced down at Beems, who was pretending to be dead.

McBride said, "Get up, fairy-ass. Show me where I'm gonna fight."

"Don't tell anybody," Beems said. "I got a wife. A reputation. Don't tell anybody."

"I'll make you a promise," McBride said, closing the locker door. "That goddamn nigger beats me, I'll fuck you. Shit, I'll let you fuck me. But don't get your butthole all apucker. I ain't losin' nothin'. Tonight, way I feel, I could knock John L. Sullivan on his ass."

McBride started out of the locker room, carrying his socks and the boxing shoes with him. Beems lay in the water, giving him plenty of head start.

6:00 P.M.

Henry couldn't believe how slow the line was moving. Hundreds of people, crawling for hours. When the Johnsons were near the end of the bridge, almost to the mainland, the water rushed in a dark brown wave and washed the buggy in front of them off the bridge. The Johnsons' wagon felt the wave, too, but only slid to the railing. But the buggy hit the railing, bounced, went over, pulling the horse into the railing after it. For a moment the horse hung there, its back legs slipping through, pulling with its front legs, then the railing cracked and the whole kit and caboodle went over.

"Oh Jesus," Tina said.

"Hang on," Henry said. He knew he had to hurry, before another wave washed in, because if it was bigger, or caught them near the gap the buggy had made, they, too, were gone.

Behind them the Johnsons could hear screams of people fleeing the storm. The water was rising rapidly over the bridge, and those to the middle and the rear realized that if they didn't get across quickly, they weren't going to make it. As they fought to move forward, the bridge cracked and moaned as if with a human voice.

The wind ripped at the tarp over the wagon and tore it away. "Shit," said Clement. "Ain't that something?"

A horse bearing a man and a woman, the woman wearing a great straw hat that drooped down on each side of her head, raced by the Johnsons. The bridge was too slick and the horse was moving too fast. Its legs splayed and it went down and started sliding. Slid right through the opening the buggy had made. Disappeared immediately beneath the water. When Henry ventured a look in that direction, he saw the woman's straw hat come up once, then blend with the water.

When Henry's wagon was even with the gap, a fresh, brown wave came over the bridge, higher and harder this time. It hit his horses and the wagon broadside. The sound of it, the impact of it, reminded Henry of when he was in the Civil War and a wagon he was riding in was hit by Yankee cannon fire. The impact had knocked him spinning, and when he tried to get up, his leg had been ruined. He thought he would never be that frightened again. But now, he was even more afraid.

The wagon drifted sideways, hit the gap, but was too wide for it. It hung on the ragged railing, the sideboards cracking with the impact. Henry's family screamed and lay down flat in the wagon as the water came down on them like a heavy hand. The pressure of the water snapped the wagon's wheels off the axle, slammed the bottom of the wagon against the bridge, but the sideboards held together.

"Everybody out!" Henry said.

Henry, his weak leg failing to respond, tumbled out of the wagon onto the bridge, which was now under a foot of water. He got hold of a sideboard and pulled himself up, helped Tina down, reached up, and snatched his cane off the seat.

Clement and the others jumped down, started hustling toward the end of the bridge on foot. As they came even with Henry, he said, "Go on, hurry. Don't worry none about me."

Tina clutched his arm. "Go on, woman," he said. "You got young'uns to care about. I got to free these horses." He patted her hand. She moved on with the others.

Henry pulled out his pocketknife and set to cutting the horses free of the harness. As soon as they were loose, both fool animals bolted directly into the railing. One of them bounced off of it, pivoted, made for the end of the bridge at a splashing gallop, but the other horse hit with such impact it flipped over, turning its feet to the sky. It pierced the water and was gone.

Henry turned to look for his family. They were no longer visible. Surely, they had made the mainland by now.

Others had come along to fill their place; people in wagons, and buggies, on horseback and on foot. People who seemed to be scrambling on top of water, since the bridge was now completely below sea level.

Then Henry heard a roar. He turned to the east side of the bridge. There was a heavy sheet of water cocked high above him, and it was coming down, like a monstrous, wet flyswatter. And when it struck Henry and the bridge, and all those on it, it smashed them flat and drove them into the churning belly of the sea.

6:14 P.M.

Bill and Angelique Cooper, their buggy half-submerged in water, saw the bridge through the driving rain, then suddenly they saw it no more. The bridge and the people were wadded together and washed down.

The bridge rose up on the waves a moment later, like a writhing spinal column. People still clung to it. It leaped forward into the water, the end of it lashing the air, then it was gone and the people with it.

"God have mercy on their souls," Angelique said.

Bill said, "That's it then."

He turned the buggy around in the water with difficulty, headed home. All around him, shingles and rocks from the roofs of structures flew like shrapnel.

7:39 P.M.

"Lil" Arthur, as he floated toward town, realized it was less deep here. It was just as well, the rain was pounding his boat and filling it with water. He couldn't bail and paddle as fast as it went in. He climbed over the side and let the current carry the boat away.

The water surprised him with its force. He was almost swept away, but it was shallow enough to get a foothold and push against the flow. He waded to the Sporting Club, went around back to the colored entrance. When he got there, an elderly black man known as Uncle Cooter let him in, said, "Man, I'd been you, I'd stayed home."

"What," "Lil" Arthur said, "and missed a boat ride?"

"A boat ride?"

"Lil" Arthur told him how he had gotten this far.

"Damnation," Uncle Cooter said. "God gonna put this island underwater 'cause it's so evil. Like that Sodom and Gomorrah place."

"What have you and me done to God?"

Uncle Cooter smiled. "Why, we is the only good children God's got. He gonna watch after us. Well, me anyway. You done gonna get in with this Mr. McBride, and he's some bad stuff, 'Lil' Arthur. God ain't gonna help you there. And this Mr. McBride, he ain't got no sense neither. He done beat up Mr. Beems, and Mr. Beems the one settin' this up, gonna pay him money."

"Why'd he beat him up?"

"Hell, you can't figure white people. They all fucked up. But Mr. Beems damn sure look like a raccoon now. Both his eyes all black, his lip pouched out."

"Where do I change?"

"Janitor's closet. They done put your shorts and shoes in there. And there's some gauze for your hands."

"Lil" Arthur found the shorts. They were old and faded. The boxing shoes weren't too good either. He found some soiled rags and used those to dry himself. He used the gauze to wrap his hands, then his dick. He figured, once you start a custom, you stick with it.

7:45 P.M.

When Bill and Angelique and Teddy arrived at their house, they saw that the water had pushed against the front door so violently, it had come open. Water was flowing into the hall and onto the bottom step of the stairs. Bill looked up and saw a lamp burning upstairs. They had left so quickly, they had forgotten to extinguish it.

With a snort, Bess bolted. The buggy jerked forward, hit a curb, and the harness snapped so abruptly Bill and his family were not thrown from their seat, but merely whipped forward and back against the seat. The reins popped through Bill's hands so swiftly, the leather cut his palms.

Bess rushed across the yard and through the open doorway of the house, and slowly and carefully, began to climb the stairs.

Angelique said, "My lands."

Bill, a little stunned, climbed down, went around, and helped Angelique and the baby out of the buggy. The baby was wet and crying, and Angelique tried to cover him with the umbrella, but now the wind and rain seemed to come from all directions. The umbrella was little more than a wad of cloth.

They waded inside the house, tried to close the door, but the water was too much for them. They gave it up.

Bess had reached the top landing and disappeared. They followed her up. The bedroom door was open and the horse had gone in there. She stood near the table bearing the kerosene lamp. Shaking.

"Poor thing," Angelique said, gathering some towels from a chifforobe. "She's more terrified than we are."

Bill removed the harness that remained on Bess, stroked her, tried to soothe her. When he went to the window and looked out, the horse went with him. The world had not miraculously dried up. The water was obviously rising.

"Maybe we'll be all right here," Angelique said. She was drying Teddy, who was crying violently because he was cold and wet. "Water can't get this high, can it?"

Bill idly stroked Bess's mane, thought of the bridge. The way it had snapped like a wooden toy. He said, "Of course not."

8:15 P.M.

The fight had started late, right after two one-legged colored boys had gone a couple of rounds, hopping about, trying to club each other senseless with oversized boxing gloves.

The crowd was sparse but vocal. Loud enough that "Lil" Arthur forgot the raging storm outside. The crowd kept yelling, "Kill the nigger," and had struck up a chorus of "All coons look alike to me" — a catchy little number that "Lil" Arthur liked in spite of himself.

The yelling, the song, was meant to drop his spirits, but he found it fired him up. He liked being the underdog. He liked to make assholes eat their words. Besides, he was the Galveston Champion, not McBride, no matter what the crowd wanted. He was the one who would step through the ropes tonight the victor. And he had made a change. He would no longer allow himself to be introduced as "Lil" Arthur. When his name had been called, and he had been reluctantly named Galveston Sporting Club Champion by the announcer, the announcer had done as he had asked. He had called him by the name he preferred from here on. Not "Lil" Arthur Johnson. Not Arthur John Johnson, but the name he called him, the name he called himself. Jack Johnson.

So far, however, the fight wasn't going either way, and he had to hand it to McBride, the fella could hit. He had a way of throwing short, sharp punches to the ribs, punches that felt like knife stabs.

Before the fight, Jack, as McBride had surely done, had used his thumbs to rearrange as much of the cotton in his gloves as possible. Arrange it so that his knuckles would be against the leather and would make good contact with McBride's flesh. But so far McBride had avoided most of his blows. The man was a master of slipping and sliding the punches. Jack had never seen anything like that before. McBride could also pick off shots with a flick of his forearms. It was very professional and enlightening.

Even so, Jack found he was managing to take the punches pretty well, and he'd discovered something astonishing. The few times he'd hit McBride was when he got excited, leaned forward, went flat-footed, and threw the uppercut. This was not a thing he had trained for much, and when he had, he usually threw the uppercut by coming up on his toes, twisting his body, the prescribed way to throw it. But he found, against all logic, he could throw it flat-footed and leaning forward, and he could throw it hard.

He thought he had seen a bit of surprise on McBride's face when he'd hit him with it. He knew that he'd certainly surprised himself.

It went like that until the beginning of the fourth round, then when McBride came out, he said, "I've carried you enough, nigger. Now you got to fight."

Then Jack saw stuff he'd never seen before. The way this guy moved, it was something. Bounced around like a cat, like the way he'd heard Gentleman Jim fought, and the guy was fast with those hands. Tossed bullets, and the bullets stunned a whole lot worse than before. Jack realized McBride had been holding back, trying to make the fight interesting. And he realized something else. Something important about himself. He didn't know as much about boxing as he thought.

He tried hooking McBride, but McBride turned the hooks away with his arms, and Jack tried his surprise weapon, the uppercut, found he could catch McBride a little with that, in the stomach, but not enough to send McBride to the canvas. When the fifth round came up, Jack was scared. And hurt. And the referee — a skinny bastard with a handlebar moustache — wasn't helping. Anytime he tied McBride up, the referee separated them. McBride tied him up, thumbed him in the eye, butted him, the referee grinned like he was eating jelly.

Jack was thinking maybe of taking a dive. Just going down and lying there, getting himself out of this misery next time McBride threw one of those short ones that connected solid, but then the bell rang and he sat on his bench, and Uncle Cooter, who was the only man in his corner, sprayed water in his mouth and let him spit blood in a bucket.

Uncle Cooter said, "I was you, son, I'd play possum. Just hit that goddamn canvas and lay there like you axed. You don't, this shithead gonna cut you to pieces. This way, you get a little payday and you don't die. Paydays is all right. Dyin' ain't nothin' to rush."

"Jesus, he's good. How can I beat him?"

Uncle Cooter rubbed Jack's shoulders. "You can't. Play dead."

"There's got to be a way."

"Yeah," Uncle Cooter said. "He might die on you. That's the only way you gonna beat him. He got to just die."

"Thanks, Cooter. You're a lot of help."

"You welcome."

Jack feared the sound of the bell. He looked in McBride's corner, and McBride was sitting on his stool as if he were lounging, drinking from a bottle of beer, chatting with a man in the audience. He was asking the man to go get him a sandwich.

Forrest Thomas was in McBride's corner, holding a folded towel over his arm, in case McBride might need it, which, considering he needed to break a good sweat first, wasn't likely.

Forrest looked at Jack, pointed a finger, and lowered his thumb like it was the hammer of a revolver. Jack could see a word on Forrest's lips. The word was: POW!

The referee wandered over to McBride's corner, leaned on the ring post, had a laugh with McBride over something.

The bell rang. McBride gave the bottle of beer to Forrest and came out. Jack rose, saw Beems, eyes blacked, looking rough, sitting in the front row. Rough or not, Beems seemed happy. He looked at Jack and smiled like a gravedigger.

This time out, Jack took a severe pounding. He just couldn't stop those short, little hooks of McBride's, and he couldn't seem to hit McBride any kind of blow but the uppercut, and that not hard enough. McBride was getting better as he went along, getting warmed up. If he had another beer and a sandwich, hell, he might go ahead and knock Jack out so he could have coffee and pie.

Jack decided to quit trying to hit the head and the ribs, and just go in and pound McBride on the arms. That way, he could at least hit something. He did, and was amazed at the end of the round to find McBride lowering his guard.

Jack went back to his corner and Uncle Cooter said, "Keep hittin' him on the arms. That's gettin' to him. You wreckin' his tools."

"I figured that much. Thanks a lot."

"You welcome."

Jack examined the crowd in the Sporting Club bleachers. They were not watching the ring. They had turned their heads toward the east wall, and for good reason. It was vibrating. Water was seeping in, and it had filled the floor beneath the ring six inches deep. The people occupying the bottom row of bleachers, all around the ring, had been forced to lift their feet. Above him, Jack heard a noise that sounded like something big and mean peeling skin off an elephant's head.

By the time the bell rang and Jack shuffled out, he noticed that the water had gone up another two inches.

8:46 P.M.

Bill held the lantern in front of him at arm's length as he crouched at the top of the stairs. The water was halfway up the steps. The house was shaking like a fat man's ass on a bucking bronco. He could hear shingles ripping loose, blowing away.

He went back to the bedroom. The wind was screaming. The windows were vibrating; panes had blown out of a couple of them. The baby was crying. Angelique sat in the middle of the bed, trying to nurse the child, but Teddy wouldn't have any of that. Bess was facing a corner of the room, had her head pushed against the wall. The horse lashed her tail back and forth nervously, made nickering noises.

Bill went around and opened all the windows to help take away some of the force of the wind. Something he knew he should have done long ago, but he was trying to spare the baby the howl of the wind, the dampness.

The wind charged through the open windows and the rain charged with it. Bill could hardly stand before them, they were so powerful.

Fifteen minutes later, he heard the furniture below thumping on the ceiling, floating against the floor on which he stood.

9:00 P.M.

My God, thought Jack, how many rounds this thing gonna go? His head ached and his ribs ached worse and his insides felt as if he had swallowed hot tacks and was trying to regurgitate them. His legs, though strong, were beginning to feel the wear. He had thought this was a fifteen-round affair, but realized now it was twenty, and if he wasn't losing by then, he might get word it would go twenty-five.

Jack slammed a glove against McBride's left elbow, saw McBride grimace, drop the arm. Jack followed with the uppercut, and this time he not only hit McBride, he hit him solid. McBride took the shot so hard, he farted. The sandwich he'd eaten between rounds probably didn't seem like such a good idea now.

Next time Jack threw the combination, he connected with the uppercut again. McBride moved back, and Jack followed, hitting him on the arms, slipping in the uppercut now and then, even starting to make contact with hooks and straight rights.

Then every light in the building went out as the walls came apart and the bleachers soared up on a great surge of water and dumped the boxing patrons into the wet darkness. The ring itself began to move, to rise to the ceiling, but before it tilted out from under Jack, McBride hit him a blow so hard Jack thought he felt past lives cease to exist; ancestors fresh from the slime rocked from that blow, and the reverberations of it rippled back to the present and into the future, and back again. The ceiling went away on a torrent of wind, Jack reached out and got hold of something and clung for dear life.

"You stupid sonofabitch," Uncle Cooter said, "you got me by the goddamn head."

9:05 P.M.

Captain Slater thought they would be at the bottom of the Gulf by now, and was greatly surprised they were not. A great wave of water had hit them so hard the night before it had snapped the anchor chain. The ship was driven down, way down, and then all the water in the world washed over them and there was total darkness and horror, and then, what seemed like hours later but could only have been seconds, the water broke and the *Pensacola* flew high up as if shot from a cannon, came down again, leaned starboard so far it took water, then, miraculously, corrected itself. The sea had been choppy and wild ever since.

Slater shook shit and seawater out of his pants legs and followed the rope around his waist to the support post. He got hold of the post, felt for the rest of the rope. In the darkness, he cried out, "Bernard. You there?"

"I think so," came Bernard's voice from the darkness. And then they heard a couple of bolts pop free, fire off like rifle blasts. Then: "Oh, Jesus," Bernard said. "Feel that swell? Here it comes again."

Slater turned his head and looked out. There was nothing but a great wall of blackness moving toward them. It made the first great wave seem like a mere rise; this one was bigger than the Great Wall of China.

10:00 P.M.

Bill and Angelique lay on the bed with Teddy. The water was washing over the edges of the feather mattress, blowing wet, cold wind over them. They had started the Edison and a gospel record had been playing, but the wind and rain had finally gotten into the mechanism and killed it.

As it went dead, the far wall cracked and leaned in and a ripple of cracking lumber went across the floor and the ceiling sagged and so did the bed. Bess suddenly disappeared through a hole in the floor. One moment she was there, the next she was gone, beneath the water.

Bill grabbed Angelique by the arm, pulled her to her feet in the knee-deep water. She held Teddy close to her. He pulled them across the room as the floor shifted, pulled them through the door that led onto the unfinished deck, stumbled over a hammer that lay beneath the water, but managed to keep his feet.

Bill couldn't help but think of all the work he had put in on this deck. Now it would never be finished. He hated to leave anything unfinished. He hated worse that it was starting to lean.

There was one central post that seemed to stand well enough, and they took position behind that. The post was one of several that the house was built around; a support post to lift the house above the normal rise of water. It connected bedroom to deck.

Bill tried to look through the driving rain. All he could see was water. Galveston was covered by the sea. It had risen up and swallowed the city and the island.

The house began to shake violently. They heard lumber splintering, felt it

The Best of Joe R. Lansdale

shimmying. The deck swayed more dynamically.

"We're not going to make it, are we, Bill?" Angelique said.

"No, darling. We aren't."

"I love you."

"I love you."

He held her and kissed her. She said, "It doesn't matter, you and I. But Teddy. He doesn't know. He doesn't understand. God, why Teddy? He's only a baby... How do I drown, darling?"

"One deep breath and it's over. Just one deep pull of the water, and don't fight it."

Angelique started to cry. Bill squatted, ran his hand under the water and over the deck. He found the hammer. It was lodged in its spot because it was caught in a gap in the unfinished deck. Bill brought the hammer out. There was a big nail sticking out of the main support post. He had driven it there the day before, to find it easily enough. It was his last big nail and it was his intent to save it.

He used the claw of the hammer to pull it out. He looked at Angelique. "We can give Teddy a chance."

Angelique couldn't see Bill well in the darkness, but she somehow felt what his face was saying. "Oh, Bill."

"It's a chance."

"But..."

"We can't stand against this, but the support post —"

"Oh Lord, Bill," and Angelique sagged, holding Teddy close to her chest. Bill grabbed her shoulders, said, "Give me my son."

Angelique sobbed, then the house slouched far to the right — except for the support post. All the other supports were washing loose, but so far, this one hadn't budged.

Angelique gave Teddy to Bill. Bill kissed the child, lifted him as high on the post as he could, pushed the child's back against the wood, and lifted its arm. Angelique was suddenly there, supporting the baby. Bill kissed her. He took the hammer and the nail, and placing the nail squarely against Teddy's little wrist, drove it through the child's flesh with one swift blow.

Then the storm blew more furious and the deck turned to gelatin. Bill clutched Angelique, and Angelique almost managed to say, "Teddy," then all the powers of nature took them and the flimsy house away.

High above it all, water lapping around the post, Teddy, wet and cold, squalled with pain.

Bess surfaced among lumber and junk. She began to paddle her legs furiously, snorting water. A nail on a board cut across her muzzle, opening a deep gash. The horse nickered, thrashed its legs violently, lifted its head, trying to stay afloat.

SUNDAY, SEPTEMBER 9, 4:00 A.M.

The mechanism that revolved the Bolivar lighthouse beam had stopped working. The stairs that led up to the lighthouse had gradually filled with people fleeing the storm, and as the water rose, so did the people. One man with a young boy had come in last, and therefore was on the constantly rising bottom rung. He kept saying, "Move up. Move up, lessen' you want to see a man and his boy drown." And everyone would move up. And then the man would soon repeat his refrain as the water rose.

The lighthouse was becoming congested. The lighthouse tower had begun to sway. The lighthouse operator, Jim Marlin, and his wife, Elizabeth, lit the kerosene lamp and placed it in the center of the circular magnifying lens, and tried to turn the beam by hand. They wanted someone to know there was shelter here, even though it was overcrowded, and might soon cease to exist. The best thing to do was to douse the light and hope they could save those who were already there, and save themselves. But Jim and Elizabeth couldn't do that. Elizabeth said, "Way I see it, Jim. It's all or nothing, and the good Lord would want it that way. I want it that way."

All night long they had heard screams and cries for help, and once, when the lighthouse beam was operating, they had seen a young man clinging to a timber. When the light swung back to where the young man had been, he had vanished.

Now, as they tried to turn the light by hand, they found it was too much of a chore. Finally, they let it shine in one direction, and there in the light they saw a couple of bodies being dragged by a large patch of canvas from which dangled ropes, like jellyfish tentacles. The ropes had grouped and twisted around the pair, and the canvas seemed to operate with design, folded and opened like a pair of great wings, as if it were an exotic sea creature bearing them off to a secret lair where they could be eaten in privacy.

Neither Jim nor Elizabeth Marlin knew the bloated men tangled in the ropes together, had no idea they were named Ronald Beems and Forrest Thomas.

5:00 A.M.

A crack of light. Dawn. Jim and Elizabeth had fallen asleep leaning against the base of the great light, and at the first ray of sunshine, they awoke, saw a ship's bow at the lighthouse window, and standing at the bow, looking in at them, was a bedraggled man in uniform, and he was crying savagely.

Jim went to the window. The ship had been lifted up on piles of sand and lumber. Across the bow he could see the letters *PENSACOLA*. The man was leaning against the glass. He wore a captain's hat. He held out his hand, palm first. Jim put his hand to the glass, trying to match the span of the crying captain's hand.

Behind the captain a number of wet men appeared. When they saw the lighthouse they fell to their knees and lifted their heads to the heavens in prayer, having forgotten that it was in fact the heavens that had devastated them.

6:00 A.M.

The day broke above the shining water, and the water began to go down, rapidly, and John McBride sat comfortably on the great hour hand of what was left of the City Hall clock. He sat there with his arms wrapped around debris that dangled from the clock. In the night, a huge spring mechanism had jumped from the face of the clock and hit him a glancing blow in the head, and for a moment, McBride had thought he was still battling the nigger. He wasn't sure which was worse to fight. The hurricane or the nigger. But through the night he had become grateful for the spring to hold on to.

Below him he saw much of what was left of the Sporting Club, including the lockers where he had put his belongings. The whole damn place had washed up beneath the clock tower.

McBride used his teeth to work off the binds of his boxing gloves and slip his hands free. All through the night the gloves had been a burden. He feared his lack of grip would cause him to fall. It felt good to have his hands out of the tight, wet leather.

McBride ventured to take hold of the minute hand of the clock, swing on it a little, and cause it to lower him onto a pile of rubble. He climbed over lumber and junk and found a mass of bloated bodies, men, women, and children, most of them sporting shingles that had cut into their heads and bodies. He searched their pockets for money and found none, but one of the women — he could tell it was a woman by her hair and dress only, her features were lost in the fleshy swelling of her face — had a ring. He tried to pull it off her finger, but it wouldn't come off. The water had swollen her flesh all around it.

He sloshed his way to the pile of lockers. He searched through them until he found the one where he had put his clothes. They were so filthy with mud, he left them. But he got the razor and the revolver. The revolver was full of grit. He took out the shells and shook them and put them back. He stuck the gun in his soaked boxing trunks. He opened the razor and shook out the silt and went over to the woman and used the razor to cut off her finger. The blade cut easily through the flesh, and he whacked through the bone. He pushed the ring on his little finger, closed the razor, and slipped it into the waistband of his trunks, next to his revolver.

This was a hell of a thing to happen. He had hidden his money back at the whorehouse, and he figured it and the plump madam were probably far at sea, the madam possibly full of harpoon wounds.

And the shitasses who were to pay him were now all choked, including the main one, the queer Beems. And if they weren't, they were certainly no longer men of means.

This had been one shitty trip. No clothes. No money. No whipped nigger. And no more pussy. He'd come with more than he was leaving with.

What the hell else could go wrong?

He decided to wade toward the whorehouse, see if it was possibly standing, maybe find some bodies along the way to loot — something to make up for his losses.

As he started in that direction, he saw a dog on top of a doghouse float by. The dog was chained to the house and the chain had gotten tangled around some floating rubble and it had pulled the dog flat against the roof. It lifted its eyes and saw McBride, barked wearily for help. McBride determined it was well within pistol shot.

McBride lifted the revolver and pulled the trigger. It clicked, but nothing happened. He tried again, hoping against hope. It fired this time and the dog took a blast in the skull and rolled off the house, and hung by the chain, then sailed out of sight.

McBride said, "Poor thing."

7:03 A.M.

The water was falling away rapidly, returning to the sea, leaving in its wake thousands of bodies and the debris that had once been Galveston. The stench was awful. Jack and Cooter, who had spent the night in a child's tree house, awoke, amazed they were alive.

The huge oak tree they were in was stripped of leaves and limbs, but the tree house was unharmed. It was remarkable. They had washed right up to it, just climbed off the lumber to which they had been clinging, and went inside. It was dry in there, and they found three hard biscuits in a tin and three hot bottles of that good ole Waco, Texas, drink, Dr Pepper. There was a phone on the wall, but it was a fake, made of lumber and tin cans. Jack had the urge to try it, as if it might be a line to God, for surely, it was God who had brought them here.

Cooter had helped Jack remove his gloves, then they ate the biscuits, drank a bottle of Dr Pepper apiece, then split the last bottle and slept.

When it was good and light, they decided to climb down. The ladder, a series of boards nailed to the tree, had washed away, but they made it to the ground by sliding down like firemen on a pole.

When they reached the earth, they started walking, sloshing through the mud and water that had rolled back to ankle-deep. The world they had known was gone. Galveston was a wet mulch of bloated bodies — humans, dogs, mules, and horses — and mashed lumber. In the distance they saw a bedraggled family walking along like ducks in a row. Jack recognized them. He had seen them around town. They were Issac Cline, his brother Joseph, Issac's wife and children. He wondered if they knew where they were going, or were they like him and Cooter, just out there? He decided on the latter.

Jack and Cooter decided to head for higher ground, back uptown. Soon they could see the tower of City Hall, in sad shape but still standing, the clock having sprung a great spring. It poked from the face of the mechanism like a twisted, metal tongue.

They hadn't gone too far toward the tower when they encountered a man coming toward them. He was wearing shorts and shoes like Jack and was riding a chocolate brown mare bareback. He had looped a piece of frayed rope around the horse's muzzle and was using that as a primitive bridle. His hair was combed to perfection. It was McBride.

"Shit," Cooter said. "Ain't this somethin'? Well, Jack, you take care, I gonna be seein' you."

"Asshole," Jack said.

Cooter put his hands in his pockets and turned right, headed over piles of junk and bodies on his way to who knew where.

McBride spotted Jack, yelled, "You somethin', nigger. A hurricane can't even drown you."

"You neither," Jack said. They were within twenty feet of one another now. Jack could see the revolver and the razor in McBride's waistband. The horse, a beautiful animal with a deep cut on its muzzle, suddenly buckled and lay down with its legs folded beneath it, dropped its head into the mud.

McBride stepped off the animal, said, "Can you believe that? Goddamn horse survived all this and it can't carry me no ways at all."

McBride pulled his pistol and shot the horse through the head. It rolled over gently, lay on its side without so much as one last heave of its belly. McBride turned back to Jack. The revolver lay loose in his hand. He said, "Had it misfired, I'd have had to beat that horse to death with a board. I don't believe in animals suffering. Gun's been underwater, and it's worked two out of three. Can you believe that?"

"That horse would have been all right," Jack said.

"Naw, it wouldn't," McBride said. "Why don't you shake it, see if it'll come around?" McBride pushed the revolver into the waistband of his shorts. "How's about you and me? Want to finish where we left off?"

"You got to be jokin'," Jack said.

"You hear me laughin'?"

"I don't know about you, peckerwood, but I feel like I been in a hurricane, then swam a few miles in boxing gloves, then slept all night in a tree house and had biscuits and Dr Pepper for breakfast."

"I ain't even had no breakfast, nigger. Listen here. I can't go home not knowing I can whip you or not. Hell, I might never get home. I want to know I can take you. You want to know."

"Yeah. I do. But I don't want to fight no pistol and razor."

McBride removed the pistol and razor from his trunks, found a dry spot and put them there. He said, "Come on."

"Where?"

"Here's all we got."

Jack turned and looked. He could see a slight rise of dirt beyond the piles of wreckage. A house had stood there. One of its great support poles was still visible.

"Over there," Jack said.

They went over there and found a spot about the size of a boxing ring. Down below them on each side were heaps of bodies and heaps of gulls on the bodies, scrambling for soft flesh and eyeballs. McBride studied the bodies, what was left of Galveston, turned to Jack, said, "Fuck the rules."

They waded into each other, bare knuckle. It was obvious after only moments that they were exhausted. They were throwing hammers, not punches, and the sounds of their strikes mixed with the caws and cries of the gulls. McBride ducked his head beneath Jack's chin, drove it up. Jack locked his hands behind McBride's neck, kneed him in the groin.

They rolled on the ground and in the mud, then came apart. They regained their feet and went at it again. Then the sounds of their blows and the shrieks of the gulls were overwhelmed by a cry so unique and savage, they ceased punching.

"Time," Jack said.

"What in hell is that?" McBride said.

They walked toward the sound of the cry, leaned on the great support post. Once a fine house had stood here, and now, there was only this. McBride said, "I don't know about you, nigger, but I'm one tired sonofabitch."

The cry came again. Above him. He looked up. A baby was nailed near the top of the support. Its upraised, nailed arm was covered in caked blood. Gulls were flapping around its head, making a kind of halo.

"I'll be goddamned," Jack said. "Boost me, McBride."

"What?"

"Boost me."

"You got to be kidding."

Jack lifted his leg. McBride sighed, made a stirrup with his cupped hands, and Jack stood, got hold of the post and worked his way painfully up. At the bottom, McBride picked up garbage and hurled it at the gulls.

"You gonna hit the baby, you jackass," Jack said.

When he got up there, Jack found the nail was sticking out of the baby's wrist by an inch or so. He wrapped his legs tight around the post, held on with one arm while he took hold of the nail and tried to work it free with his fingers. It wouldn't budge.

"Can't get it loose," Jack yelled down. He was about to drop; his legs and arms had turned to butter.

"Hang on," McBride said, and went away.

It seemed like forever before he came back. He had the revolver with him. He looked up at Jack and the baby. He looked at them for a long moment. Jack watched him, didn't move. McBride said, "Listen up, nigger. Catch this, use it to work out the nail."

McBride emptied the remaining cartridges from the revolver and tossed it up. Jack caught it on the third try. He used the trigger guard to snag the nail, but mostly mashed the baby's wrist. The baby had stopped crying. It was making a kind of mewing sound, like a dying goat.

The nail came loose, and Jack nearly didn't grab the baby in time and when he did, he got hold of its nailed arm and he felt and heard its shoulder snap out of place. He was weakening, and he knew he was about to fall.

"McBride," he said, "catch."

The baby dropped and so did the revolver. McBride reached out and grabbed the child. It screamed when he caught it, and McBride raised it over his head and laughed. He laid the baby on top of a pile of wide lumber and looked at it.

Jack was about halfway down the post when he fell, landing on his back, knocking the wind out of him. By the time he got it together enough to get up and find the revolver and wobble over to McBride, McBride had worked the child's shoulder back into place and was cooing to him.

Jack said, "He ain't gonna make it. He's lost lots of blood."

McBride stood up with the baby on his shoulder. He said, "Naw. He's tough as a warthog. Worse this little shit will have is a scar. Elastic as he is, there ain't no real damage. And he didn't bleed out bad neither. He gets some milk in him, fifteen, sixteen years from now, he'll be chasin' pussy. Course, best thing is, come around when he's about two and go on and kill him. He'll just grow up to be men like us."

McBride held the child out and away from him, looked him over. The baby's penis lifted and the child peed all over him. McBride laughed uproariously.

"Well, shit, nigger. I reckon today ain't my day, and it ain't the day you and me gonna find out who's the best. Here. I don't know no one here. Take 'em."

Jack took the child, gave McBride his revolver, said, "I don't know there's anyone I know anymore."

"I tell you, you're one lucky nigger," McBride said. "I'm gonna forgo you a beating, maybe a killing."

"That right?"

"Uh-huh. Someone's got to tote this kid to safety, and if'n I kept him, I might get tired of him in an hour. Put his little head underwater."

"You would, wouldn't you?"

"I might. And you know, you're a fool to give me back my gun."

"Naw. I broke it gettin' that nail loose."

McBride grinned, tossed the gun in the mud, shaded his eyes, and looked at the sky. "Can you beat that? Looks like it's gonna be a nice day."

Jack nodded. The baby sucked on his shoulder. He decided McBride was right. This was one tough kid. It was snuggled against him as if nothing had happened, trying to get milk. Jack wondered about the child's family. Wondered about his own. Where were they? Were they alive?

McBride grinned, said, "Nigger, you got a hell of an uppercut." Then he turned and walked away.

Jack patted the baby's back, watched McBride find his razor, then walk on. Jack watched him until he disappeared behind a swell of lumber and bodies, and he never saw him again.

Duck Hunt

THERE WERE THREE hunters and three dogs. The hunters had shiny shotguns, warm clothes, and plenty of ammo. The dogs were each covered in big, blue spots and were sleek and glossy and ready to run. No duck was safe.

The hunters were Clyde Barrow, James Clover, and little Freddie Clover, who was only fifteen and very excited to be asked along. However, Freddie did not really want to see a duck, let alone shoot one. He had never killed anything but a sparrow with his BB gun and that had made him sick. But he was nine then. Now he was ready to be a man. His father told him so.

With this hunt he felt he had become part of a secret organization. One that smelled of tobacco smoke and whiskey breath; sounded of swear words, talk about how good certain women were, the range and velocity of rifles and shotguns, the edges of hunting knives, the best caps and earflaps for winter hunting.

In Mud Creek the hunt made the man.

Since Freddie was nine he had watched with more than casual interest, how when a boy turned fifteen in Mud Creek, he would be invited to The Hunting Club for a talk with the men. Next step was a hunt, and when the boy returned he was a boy no longer. He talked deep, walked sure, had whiskers bristling on his chin, and could take up with the assurance of not being laughed at, cussing, smoking, and watching women's butts as a matter of course.

Freddie wanted to be a man too. He had pimples, no pubic hair to speak of (he always showered quickly at school to escape derisive remarks about the size of his equipment and the thickness of his foliage), scrawny legs, and little, gray, watery eyes that looked like ugly planets spinning in white space.

And truth was, Freddie preferred a book to a gun.

But came the day when Freddie turned fifteen and his father came home from the Club, smoke and whiskey smell clinging to him like a hungry tick, his face slightly dark with beard and tired-looking from all-night poker.

He came into Freddie's room, marched over to the bed where Freddie was reading THOR, clutched the comic from his son's hands, sent it fluttering across the room with a rainbow of comic panels.

"Nose out of a book," his father said. "Time to join the Club."

Freddie went to the Club, heard the men talk ducks, guns, the way the smoke and blood smelled on cool morning breezes. They told him the kill was the measure of a man. They showed him heads on the wall. They told him to go home with his father and come back tomorrow bright and early, ready for his first hunt.

His father took Freddie downtown and bought him a flannel shirt (black and red), a thick jacket (fleece lined), a cap (with earflaps), and boots (waterproof). He took Freddie home and took a shotgun down from the rack, gave him a box of ammo, walked him out back to the firing range, and made him practice while he told his son about hunts and the war and about how men and ducks died much the same.

Next morning before the sun was up, Freddie and his father had breakfast. Freddie's mother did not eat with them. Freddie did not ask why. They met Clyde over at the Club and rode in his jeep down dirt roads, clay roads, and trails, through brush and briars until they came to a mass of reeds and cattails that grew thick and tall as Japanese bamboo.

They got out and walked. As they walked, pushing aside the reeds and cattails, the ground beneath their feet turned marshy. The dogs ran ahead.

When the sun was two hours up, they came to a bit of a clearing in the reeds, and beyond them Freddie could see the break-your-heart blue of a shiny lake. Above the lake, coasting down, he saw a duck. He watched it sail out of sight.

"Well boy?" Freddie's father said.

"It's beautiful," Freddie said.

"Beautiful, hell, are you ready?"

"Yes, sir."

On they walked, the dogs way ahead now, and finally they stood within ten feet of the lake. Freddie was about to squat down into hiding as he had heard of others doing, when a flock of ducks burst up from a mass of reeds in the lake and Freddie, fighting off the sinking feeling in his stomach, tracked them with the barrel of the shotgun, knowing what he must do to be a man.

His father's hand clamped over the barrel and pushed it down. "Not yet," he said.

"Huh?" said Freddie.

"It's not the ducks that do it," Clyde said.

Freddie watched as Clyde and his father turned their heads to the right, to where the dogs were pointing noses, forward, paws upraised — to a thatch of underbrush. Clyde and his father made quick commands to the dogs to stay, then they led Freddie into the brush, through a twisting maze of briars and out into a clearing where all the members of The Hunting Club were waiting.

In the center of the clearing was a gigantic duck decoy. It looked ancient and there were symbols carved all over it. Freddie could not tell if it were made of clay, iron, or wood. The back of it was scooped out, gravy bowl-like, and there was a pole in the center of the indention; tied to the pole was a skinny man. His head had been caked over with red mud and there were duck feathers sticking in it, making it look like some kind of funny cap. There was a ridiculous, wooden duck bill held to his head by thick elastic straps. Stuck to his butt was a duster of duck feathers. There was a sign around his neck that read DUCK.

The man's eyes were wide with fright and he was trying to say or scream something, but the bill had been fastened in such a way he couldn't make any more than a mumble.

Freddie felt his father's hand on his shoulder. "Do it," he said. "He ain't nobody to anybody we know. Be a man."

"Do it! Do it! Do it!" came the cry from The Hunting Club.

Freddie felt the cold air turn into a hard ball in his throat. His scrawny legs shook. He looked at his father and The Hunting Club. They all looked tough, hard, and masculine.

"Want to be a titty baby all your life?" his father said.

That put steel in Freddie's bones. He cleared his eyes with the back of his sleeve and steadied the barrel on the derelict's duck's head.

"Do it!" came the cry. "Do it! Do it! Do it!"

At that instant he pulled the trigger. A cheer went up from The Hunting Club, and out of the clear, cold sky, a dark blue norther blew in and with it came a flock of ducks. The ducks lit on the great idol and on the derelict. Some of them dipped their bills in the derelict's wetness.

When the decoy and the derelict were covered in ducks, all of The Hunting Club lifted their guns and began to fire.

The air became full of smoke, pellets, blood, and floating feathers.

When the gunfire died down and the ducks died out, The Hunting Club went forward and bent over the decoy, did what they had to do. Their smiles were red when they lifted their heads. They wiped their mouths gruffly on the backs of their sleeves and gathered ducks into hunting bags until they bulged. There were still many carcasses lying about.

Fred's father gave him a cigarette. Clyde lit it.

"Good shooting, son," Fred's father said and clapped him manfully on the back.

"Yeah," said Fred, scratching his crotch, "got that sonofabitch right between the eyes, pretty as a picture."

They all laughed.

The sky went lighter, and the blue norther that was rustling the reeds and whipping feathers about blew up and out and away in an instant. As the men walked away from there, talking deep, walking sure, whiskers bristling on all their chins, they promised that tonight they would get Fred a woman.

Incident On and Off a Mountain Road

WHEN ELLEN CAME to the moonlit mountain curve, her thoughts, which had been adrift with her problems, grounded, and she was suddenly aware that she was driving much too fast. The sign said CURVE: 30 MPH, and she was doing fifty.

She knew too that slamming on the brakes was the wrong move, so she optioned to keep her speed and fight the curve and make it, and she thought she could.

The moonlight was strong, so visibility was high, and she knew her Chevy was in good shape, easy to handle, and she was a good driver.

But as she negotiated the curve a blue Buick seemed to grow out of the ground in front of her. It was parked on the shoulder of the road, at the peak of the curve, its nose sticking out a foot too far, its rear end against the moon-wet, silver railing that separated the curve from a mountainous plunge.

Had she been going an appropriate speed, missing the Buick wouldn't have been a problem, but at her speed she was swinging too far right, directly in line with it, and was forced, after all, to use her brakes. When she did, the back wheels slid and the brakes groaned and the front of the Chevy hit the Buick, and there was a sound like an explosion and then for a dizzy instant she felt as if she were in the tumblers of a dryer.

Through the windshield came: Moonlight. Blackness. Moonlight.

One high bounce and a tight roll, and the Chevy came to rest upright with the engine dead, the right side flush against the railing. Another inch of jump or greater impact against the rail, and the Chevy would have gone over.

Ellen felt a sharp pain in her leg and reached down to discover that during the tumble she had banged it against something, probably the gear shift, and had ripped her stocking and her flesh. Blood was trickling into her shoe. Probing her leg cautiously with the tips of her fingers, she determined the wound wasn't bad and that all other body parts were operative.

She unfastened her seat belt, and as a matter of habit, located her purse and slipped its strap over her shoulder. She got out of the Chevy feeling wobbly, eased around front of it and saw the hood and bumper and roof were crumpled. A wisp of radiator steam hissed from beneath the wadded hood, rose into the moonlight and dissolved.

She turned her attentions to the Buick. Its tail end was now turned to her, and as she edged alongside it, she saw the front left side had been badly damaged. Fearful of what she might see, she glanced inside.

The moonlight shone through the rear windshield bright as a spotlight and revealed no one, but the back seat was slick with something dark and wet and there was plenty of it. A foul scent seeped out of a partially rolled down back window. It was a hot coppery smell that gnawed at her nostrils and ached her stomach.

God, someone had been hurt. Maybe thrown free of the car, or perhaps they had gotten out and crawled off. But when? She and the Chevy had been airborne for only a moment, and she had gotten out of the vehicle instants after it ceased to roll. Surely she would have seen someone get out of the Buick, and if they had been thrown free by the collision, wouldn't at least one of the Buick's doors be open? If it had whipped back and closed, it seemed unlikely that it would be locked, and all the doors of the Buick were locked, and all the glass was intact, and only on her side was it rolled down, and only a crack. Enough for the smell of the blood to escape, not enough for a person to slip through unless they were thin and flexible as a feather.

On the other side of the Buick, on the ground, between the back door and the railing, there were drag marks and a thick swath of blood, and another swath on the top of the railing; it glowed there in the moonlight as if it were molasses laced with radioactivity.

Ellen moved cautiously to the railing and peered over.

No one lay mangled and bleeding and oozing their guts. The ground was not as precarious there as she expected it. It was pebbly and sloped out gradually and there was a trail going down it. The trail twisted slightly and as it deepened the foliage grew denser on either side of it. Finally it curlicued its way into the dark thicket of a forest below, and from the forest, hot on the wind, came the strong turpentine tang of pines and something less fresh and not as easily identifiable.

Now she saw someone moving down there, floating up from the forest like an apparition; a white face split by silver — braces, perhaps. She could tell from the way this someone moved that it was a man. She watched as he climbed the trail and came within examination range. He seemed to be surveying her as carefully as she was surveying him.

Could this be the driver of the Buick?

As he came nearer Ellen discovered she could not identify the expression he wore. It was neither joy or anger or fear or exhaustion or pain. It was somehow all and none of these.

When he was ten feet away, still looking up, that same odd expression on his face, she could hear him breathing. He was breathing with exertion, but not to the extent she thought him tired or injured. It was the sound of someone who had been about busy work.

She yelled down, "Are you injured?"

He turned his head quizzically, like a dog trying to make sense of a command, and it occurred to Ellen that he might be knocked about in the head enough to be disoriented.

"I'm the one who ran into your car," she said. "Are you all right?"

His expression changed then, and it was most certainly identifiable this time. He was surprised and angry. He came up the trail quickly, took hold of the top railing, his fingers going into the blood there, and vaulted over and onto the gravel.

Ellen stepped back out of his way and watched him from a distance. The guy made her nervous. Even close up, he looked like some kind of spook.

He eyed her briefly, glanced at the Chevy, turned to look at the Buick.

"It was my fault," Ellen said.

He didn't reply, but returned his attention to her and continued to cock his head in that curious dog sort of way.

Ellen noticed that one of his shirt sleeves was stained with blood, and that there was blood on the knees of his pants, but he didn't act as if he were hurt in any way. He reached into his pants pocket and pulled out something and made a move with his wrist. Out flicked a lock-blade knife. The thin edge of it sucked up the moonlight and spat it out in a silver spray that fanned wide when he held it before him and jiggled it like a man working a stubborn key into a lock. He advanced toward her, and as he came, his lips split and pulled back at the corners, exposing, not braces, but metal-capped teeth that matched the sparkle of his blade.

It occurred to her that she could bolt for the Chevy, but in the same mental flash of lightning, it occurred to her she wouldn't make it.

Ellen threw herself over the railing, and as she leapt, she saw out of the corner of her eye, the knife slashing the place she had occupied, catching moonbeams and throwing them away. Then the blade was out of her view and she hit on her stomach and skidded onto the narrow trail, slid downward, feet first. The gravel and roots tore at the front of her dress and ripped through her nylons and gouged her flesh. She cried out in pain and her sliding gained speed. Lifting her chin, she saw that the man was climbing over the railing and coming after her at a stumbling run, the knife held before him like a wand.

Her sliding stopped, and she pushed off with her hands to make it start again, not knowing if this was the thing to do or not, since the trail inclined sharply on her right side, and should she skid only slightly in that direction, she could hurtle off into blackness. But somehow she kept slithering along the trail and even spun around a corner and stopped with her head facing downward, her purse practically in her teeth.

She got up then, without looking back, and began to run into the woods, the purse beating at her side. She moved as far away from the trail as she could, fighting limbs that conspired to hit her across the face or hold her, vines and bushes that tried to tie her feet or trip her.

Behind her, she could hear the man coming after her, breathing heavily now, not really winded, but hurrying. For the first time in months, she was grateful for Bruce and his survivalist insanity. His passion to be in shape and for her to be in shape with him was paying off. All that jogging had given her the lungs of an ox and strengthened her legs and ankles. A line from one of Bruce's survivalist books came to her: *Do the unexpected.*

She found a trail amongst the pines, and followed it, then, abruptly broke from it and went back into the thicket. It was harder going, but she assumed her pursuer would expect her to follow a trail.

The pines became so thick she got down on her hands and knees and began to crawl. It was easier to get through that way. After a moment, she stopped scuttling and eased her back against one of the pines and sat and listened. She felt reasonably well hidden, as the boughs of the pines grew low and drooped to the ground. She took several deep breaths, holding each for a long moment. Gradually, she began breathing normally. Above her, from the direction of the trail, she could hear the man running, coming nearer. She held her breath.

The running paused a couple of times, and she could imagine the man, his strange, pale face turning from side to side, as he tried to determine what had happened to her. The sound of running started again and the man moved on down the trail.

Ellen considered easing out and starting back up the trail, making her way to her car and driving off. Damaged as it was, she felt it would still run, but she was reluctant to leave her hiding place and step into the moonlight. Still, it seemed a better plan than waiting. If she didn't do something, the man could always go back topside himself and wait for her. The woods, covering acres and acres of land below and beyond, would take her days to get through, and without food and water and knowledge of the geography, she might never make it, could end up going in circles for days.

Bruce and his survivalist credos came back to her. She remembered something he had said to one of his self-defense classes, a bunch of rednecks hoping and praying for a commie take-over so they could show their stuff. He had told them: "Utilize what's at hand. Size up what you have with you and how it can be put to use."

All right, she thought. All right, Brucey, you sonofabitch. I'll see what's at hand.

One thing she knew she had for sure was a little flashlight. It wasn't much, but it would serve for her to check out the contents of her purse. She located it easily, and without withdrawing it from her purse, turned it on and held the open purse close to her face to see what was inside. Before she actually found it, she thought of her nail file kit. Besides the little bottle of nail polish remover, there was an emery board and two metal files. The files were the ticket. They might serve as weapons; they weren't much, but they were something.

She also carried a very small pair of nail scissors, independent of the kit, the points of the scissors being less than a quarter inch. That wouldn't be worth much, but she took note of it and mentally catalogued it.

She found the nail kit, turned off the flash and removed one of the files and returned the rest of the kit to her purse. She held the file tightly, made a little jabbing motion with it. It seemed so light and thin and insignificant.

She had been absently carrying her purse on one shoulder, and now to make sure she didn't lose it, she placed the strap over her neck and slid her arm through.

Clenching the nail file, she moved on hands and knees beneath the pine boughs and poked her head out into the clearing of the trail. She glanced down it first, and there, not ten yards from her, looking up the trail, holding his knife by his side, was the man. The moonlight lay cold on his face and the shadows of the wind-blown boughs fell across him and wavered. It seemed as if she were leaning over a pool and staring down into the water and seeing him at the bottom of it, or perhaps his reflection on the face of the pool.

She realized instantly that he had gone down the trail a ways, became suspicious of her ability to disappear so quickly, and had turned to judge where she might have gone. And, as if in answer to the question, she had poked her head into view.

They remained frozen for a moment, then the man took a step up the trail, and just as he began to run, Ellen went backwards into the pines on her hands and knees.

She had gone less than ten feet when she ran up against a thick limb that lay close to the ground and was preventing her passage. She got down on her belly and squirmed beneath it, and as she was pulling her head under, she saw Moon Face crawling into the thicket, making good time; time made better, when he lunged suddenly and covered half the space between them, the knife missing her by fractions.

Ellen jerked back and felt her feet falling away from her. She let go of the file and grabbed out for the limb and it bent way back and down with her weight. It lowered her enough for her feet to touch ground. Relieved, she realized she had fallen into a wash made by erosion, not off the edge of the mountain.

Above her, gathered in shadows and stray strands of moonlight that showed through the pine boughs, was the man. His metal-tipped teeth caught a moonbeam and twinkled. He placed a hand on the limb she held, as if to lower himself, and she let go of it.

The limb whispered away from her and hit him full in the face and knocked him back.

Ellen didn't bother to scrutinize the damage. Turning, she saw that the wash ended in a slope and that the slope was thick with trees growing out like great, feathered spears thrown into the side of the mountain.

She started down, letting the slant carry her, grasping limbs and tree trunks to slow her descent and keep her balance. She could hear the man climbing down and pursuing her, but she didn't bother to turn and look. Below she could see the incline was becoming steeper, and if she continued, it would be almost straight up and down with nothing but the trees for support, and to move from one to the other, she would have to drop, chimpanzee-like, from limb to limb. Not a pleasant thought.

Her only consolation was that the trees to her right, veering back up the mountain, were thick as cancer cells. She took off in that direction, going wide, and began plodding upwards again, trying to regain the concealment of the forest.

She chanced a look behind her before entering the pines, and saw that the man, who she had come to think of as Moon Face, was some distance away.

Weaving through a mass of trees, she integrated herself into the forest, and as she went the limbs began to grow closer to the ground and the trees became so thick they twisted together like pipe cleaners. She got down on her hands and knees and crawled between limbs and around tree trunks and tried to lose herself among them.

To follow her, Moon Face had to do the same thing, and at first she heard him behind her, but after a while, there were only the sounds she was making.

She paused and listened.

Nothing.

Glancing the way she had come, she saw the intertwining limbs she had crawled under mixed with penetrating moonbeams, heard the short bursts of her breath and the beating of her heart, but detected no evidence of Moon Face. She decided the head start she had, all the weaving she had done, the cover of the pines, had confused him, at least temporarily.

It occurred to her that if she had stopped to listen, he might have done the same, and she wondered if he could hear the pounding of her heart. She took a deep breath and held it and let it out slowly through her nose, did it again. She was breathing more normally now, and her heart, though still hammering furiously, felt as if it were back inside her chest where it belonged.

Easing her back against a tree trunk, she sat and listened, watching for that strange face, fearing it might abruptly burst through the limbs and brush, grinning its horrible teeth, or worse, that he might come up behind her, reach around the tree trunk with his knife and finish her in a bloody instant.

She checked and saw that she still had her purse. She opened it and got hold of the file kit by feel and removed the last file, determined to make better use of it than the first. She had no qualms about using it, knew she would, but what good would it do? The man was obviously stronger than she, and crazy as the pattern in a scratch quilt.

Once again, she thought of Bruce. What would he have done in this situation? He would certainly have been the man for the job. He would have relished it. Would probably have challenged old Moon Face to a one on one at the edge of the mountain, and even with a nail file, would have been confident that he could take him.

Ellen thought about how much she hated Bruce, and even now, shed of him, that hatred burned bright. How had she gotten mixed up with that dumb, macho bastard in the first place? He had seemed enticing at first. So powerful. Confident. Capable. The survivalist stuff had always seemed a little nutty, but at first no more nutty than an obsession with golf or a strong belief in astrology. Perhaps had she known how serious he was about it, she wouldn't have been attracted to him in the first place.

No. It wouldn't have mattered. She had been captivated by him, by his looks and build and power. She had nothing but her own libido and stupidity to blame. And worse yet, when things turned sour, she had stayed and let them sour even more. There had been good moments, but they were quickly eclipsed by Bruce's determination to be ready for the Big Day, as he referred to it. He knew it was coming, if he was somewhat vague on who was bringing it. But someone would start a war of some sort, a nuclear war, a war in the streets, and only the rugged individualist, well-armed and well-trained and strong of body and will, would survive beyond the initial attack. Those survivors would then carry out guerrilla warfare, hit and run operations, and eventually win back the country from…whoever. And if not win it back, at least have some kind of life free of dictatorship.

It was silly. It was every little boy's fantasy. Living by your wits with gun and knife. And owning a woman. She had been the woman. At first Bruce had been kind enough, treated her with respect. He was obviously on the male chauvinist side, but originally it had seemed harmless enough, kind of Old World charming. But when he moved them to the mountains, that charm had turned to domination, and the small crack in his mental state widened until it was a deep, dark gulf.

She was there to keep house and to warm his bed, and any opinions she had contrary to his own were stupid. He read survivalist books constantly and quoted passages to her and suggested she look the books over, be ready to stand tall against the oncoming aggressors.

By the time he had gone completely over the edge, living like a mountain man, ordering her about, his eyes roving from side to side, suspicious of her every move, expecting to hear on his shortwave at any moment World War Three had started, or that race riots were overrunning the U.S., or that a shiny probe packed with extraterrestrial invaders brandishing ray guns had landed on the White House lawn, she was trapped in his cabin in the mountains, with him holding the keys to her Chevy and his jeep.

For a time she feared he would become paranoid enough to imagine she was one of the "bad guys" and put a .357 round through her chest. But now she was free of him, escaped from all that…only to be threatened by another man: a moon-faced, silver-toothed monster with a knife.

She returned once again to the question, what would Bruce do, outside of challenging Moon Face in hand-to-hand combat? Sneaking past him would be the best bet, making it back to the Chevy. To do that Bruce would have used guerrilla techniques. "Take advantage of what's at hand," he always said.

Well, she had looked to see what was at hand, and that turned out to be a couple of fingernail files, one of them lost up the mountain.

Then maybe she wasn't thinking about this in the right way. She might not be able to outfight Moon Face, but perhaps she could outthink him. She had outthought Bruce, and he had considered himself a master of strategy and preparation.

She tried to put herself in Moon Face's head. What was he thinking? For the moment he saw her as his prey, a frightened animal on the run. He might be more cautious because of that trick with the limb, but he'd most likely chalk that one up to accident — which it was for the most part…but what if the prey turned on him?

There was a sudden cracking sound, and Ellen crawled a few feet in the direction of the noise, gently moved aside a limb. Some distance away, discerned faintly through a tangle of limbs, she saw light and detected movement, and knew it was Moon Face. The cracking sound must have been him stepping on a limb.

He was standing with his head bent, looking at the ground, flashing a little pocket flashlight, obviously examining the drag path she had made with her hands and knees when she entered into the pine thicket.

She watched as his shape and the light bobbed and twisted through the limbs and tree trunks, coming nearer. She wanted to run, but didn't know where to.

All right, she thought. All right. Take it easy. Think.

She made a quick decision. Removed the scissors from her purse, took off her shoes and slipped off her pantyhose and put her shoes on again.

She quickly snipped three long strips of nylon from her damaged pantyhose and knotted them together, using the sailor knots Bruce had taught her. She cut more thin strips from the hose — all the while listening for Moon Face's approach — and used all but one of them to fasten her fingernail file, point out, securely to the tapered end of one of the small, flexible pine limbs, then she tied one end of the long nylon strip she had made around the limb, just below the file, and crawled backwards, pulling the limb with her, bending it deep. When she had it back as far as she could manage, she took a death grip on the nylon strip, and using it to keep the limb's position taut, crawled around the trunk of a small pine and curved the nylon strip about it and made a loop knot at the base of a sapling that crossed her knee-drag trail. She used her last strip of nylon to fasten to the loop of the knot, and carefully stretched the remaining length across the trail and tied it to another sapling. If it worked correctly, when he came crawling through the thicket, following her, his hands or knees would hit the strip, pull the loop free, and the limb would fly forward, the file stabbing him, in an eye if she were lucky.

Pausing to look through the boughs again, she saw that Moon Face was on his hands and knees, moving through the thick foliage toward her. Only moments were left.

She shoved pine needles over the strip and moved away on her belly, sliding under the cocked sapling, no longer concerned that she might make noise, in fact hoping noise would bring Moon Face quickly.

Following the upward slope of the hill, she crawled until the trees became thin again and she could stand. She cut two long strips of nylon from her hose with the scissors, and stretched them between two trees about ankle high.

That one would make him mad if it caught him, but the next one would be the corker.

She went up the path, used the rest of the nylon to tie between two saplings, then grabbed hold of a thin, short limb and yanked at it until it cracked, worked it free so there was a point made from the break. She snapped that over her knee to form a point at the opposite end. She made a quick mental measurement, jammed one end of the stick into the soft ground, leaving a point facing up.

At that moment came evidence her first snare had worked — a loud swishing sound as the limb popped forward and a cry of pain. This was followed by a howl as Moon Face crawled out of the thicket and onto the trail. He stood slowly, one hand to his face. He glared up at her, removed his hand. The file had struck him in the cheek; it was covered with blood. Moon Face pointed his blood-covered hand at her and let out an accusing shriek so horrible she retreated rapidly up the trail. Behind her, she could hear Moon Face running.

The trail curved upward and turned abruptly. She followed the curve a ways, looked back as Moon Face tripped over her first strip and hit the ground, came up madder, charged even more violently up the path. But the second strip got him and he fell forward, throwing his hands out. The spike in the trail hit him low in the throat.

She stood transfixed at the top of the trail as he did a pushup and came to one knee and put a hand to his throat. Even from a distance, and with only the moonlight to show it to her, she could see that the wound was dreadful.

Good.

Moon Face looked up, stabbed her with a look, started to rise. Ellen turned and ran. As she made the turns in the trail, the going improved and she theorized that she was rushing up the trail she had originally come down.

This hopeful notion was dispelled when the pines thinned and the trail dropped, then leveled off, then tapered into nothing. Before she could slow up, she discovered she was on a sort of peninsula that jutted out from the mountain and resembled an irregular-shaped diving board from which you could leap off into night-black eternity.

In place of the pines on the sides of the trail were numerous scarecrows on poles, and out on the very tip of the peninsula, somewhat dispelling the diving board image, was a shack made of sticks and mud and brambles.

After pausing to suck in some deep breaths, Ellen discovered on closer examination that it wasn't scarecrows bordering her path after all. It was people.

Dead people. She could smell them.

There were at least a dozen on either side, placed upright on poles, their feet touching the ground, their knees slightly bent. They were all fully clothed, and in various states of deterioration. Holes had been poked through the backs of their heads to correspond with the hollow sockets of their eyes, and the moonlight came through the holes and shined through the sockets, and Ellen noted, with a warm sort of horror, that one wore a white sun dress and...plastic shoes, and through its head she could see stars. On the corpse's finger was a wedding ring, and the finger had grown thin and withered and the ring was trapped there by knuckle bone alone.

The man next to her was fresher. He too was eyeless and holes had been drilled through the back of his skull, but he still wore glasses and was fleshy. There was a pen and pencil set in his coat pocket. He wore only one shoe.

There was a skeleton in overalls, a wilting cigar stuck between his teeth. A fresh UPS man with his cap at a jaunty angle, the moon through his head, and a clipboard tied to his hand with string. His legs had been positioned in such a way it seemed as if he was walking. A housewife with a crumpled, nearly disintegrated grocery bag under her arm, the contents having long fallen through the worn, wet bottom to heap at her feet in a mass of colorless boxes and broken glass. A withered corpse in a ballerina's tutu and slippers, rotting grapefruits tied to her chest with cord to simulate breasts, her legs arranged in such a way she seemed in mid-dance, up on her toes, about to leap or whirl.

The real horror was the children. One pathetic little boy's corpse, still full of flesh and with only his drilled eyes to show death, had been arranged in such a way that a teddy bear drooped from the crook of his elbow. A toy metal tractor and a plastic truck were at his feet.

There was a little girl wearing a red rubber clown nose and a propeller beanie. A green plastic purse hung from her shoulder by a strap and a doll's legs had been taped to her palm with black electrician's tape. The doll hung upside down, holes drilled through its plastic head so that it matched its owner.

Things began to click. Ellen understood what Moon Face had been doing down here in the first place. He hadn't been in the Buick when she struck it. He was disposing of a body. He was a murderer who brought his victims here and set them up on either side of the pathway, parodying the way they were in life, cutting out their eyes and punching through the backs of their heads to let the world in.

Ellen realized numbly that time was slipping away, and Moon Face was coming, and she had to find the trail up to her car. But when she turned to run, she froze.

Thirty feet away, where the trail met the last of the pines, squatting dead center in it, arms on his knees, one hand loosely holding the knife, was Moon Face. He looked calm, almost happy, in spite of the fact a large swath of dried blood was on his cheek and the wound in his throat was making a faint whistling sound as air escaped it.

He appeared to be gloating, savoring the moment when he would set his knife to work on her eyes, the gray matter behind them, the bone of her skull.

A vision of her corpse propped up next to the child with the teddy bear, or perhaps the skeletal ballerina, came to mind; she could see herself hanging there, the light of the moon falling through her empty head, melting into the path.

Then she felt anger. It boiled inside her. She determined she was not going to allow Moon Face his prize easily. He'd earn it.

Another line from Bruce's books came to her.

Consider your alternatives.

She did, in a flash. And they were grim. She could try charging past Moon Face, or pretend to, then dart into the pines. But it seemed unlikely she could make the trees before he overtook her. She could try going over the side of the trail and climbing down, but it was much too steep there, and she'd fall immediately. She could make for the shack and try and find something she could fight with. The last idea struck her as the correct one, the one Bruce would have pursued. What was his quote? "If you can't effect an escape, fall back and fight with what's available to you."

She hurried to the hut, glancing behind her from time to time to check on Moon Face. He hadn't moved. He was observing her calmly, as if he had all the time in the world.

When she was about to go through the doorless entryway, she looked back at him one last time. He was in the same spot, watching, the knife held limply against his leg. She knew he thought he had her right where he wanted her, and that's exactly what she wanted him to think. A surprise attack was the only chance she had. She just hoped she could find something to surprise him with.

She hastened inside and let out an involuntary rasp of breath.

The place stank, and for good reason. In the center of the little hut was a folding card table and some chairs, and seated in one of the chairs was a woman, the flesh rotting and dripping off her skull like candle wax, her eyes empty and holes in the back of her head. Her arm was resting on the table and her hand was clamped around an open bottle of whiskey. Beside her, also without eyes, suspended in a standing position by wires connected to the roof, was a man. He was a fresh kill. Big, dressed in khaki pants and shirt and work shoes. In one hand a doubled belt was taped, and wires were attached in such a way that his arm was drawn back as if ready to strike. Wires were secured to his lips and pulled tight behind his head so that he was smiling in a ghoulish way. Foil gum wrappers were fixed to his teeth, and the moonlight gleaming through the opening at the top of the hut fell on them and made them resemble Moon Face's metal-tipped choppers.

Ellen felt queasy, but fought the sensation down. She had more to worry about than corpses. She had to prevent herself from becoming one.

She gave the place a quick pan. To her left was a rust-framed rollaway bed with a thin, dirty mattress, and against the far wall, was a baby crib, and next to that a camper stove with a small frying pan on it.

She glanced quickly out the door of the hut and saw that Moon Face had moved onto the stretch of trail bordered by the bodies. He was walking very slowly, looking up now and then as if to appreciate the stars.

Her heart pumped another beat.

She moved about the hut, looking for a weapon.

The frying pan.

She grabbed it, and as she did, she saw what was in the crib. What belonged there. A baby. But dead. A few months old. Its skin thin as plastic and stretched tight over pathetic, little rib bones. Eyes gone, holes through its head. Burnt match stubs between blackened toes. It wore a diaper and the stink of feces wafted from it and into her nostrils. A rattle lay at the foot of the crib.

A horrible realization rushed through her. The baby had been alive when taken by this madman, and it had died here, starved and tortured. She gripped the frying pan with such intensity her hand cramped.

Her foot touched something.

She looked down. Large bones were heaped there — discarded mommies and daddies, for it now occurred to her that was who the corpses represented.

Something gleamed amongst the bones. A gold cigarette lighter.

Through the doorway of the hut she saw Moon Face was halfway down the trail. He had paused to nonchalantly adjust the UPS man's clipboard. The geek had made his own community here, his own family, people he could deal with — dead people — and it was obvious he intended for her to be part of his creation.

Ellen considered attacking straight-on with the frying pan when Moon Face came through the doorway, but so far he had proven strong enough to take a file in the cheek and a stick in the throat, and despite the severity of the latter wound, he had kept on coming. Chances were he was strong enough to handle her and her frying pan.

A back-up plan was necessary. Another one of Bruce's pronouncements. She recalled a college friend, Carol, who used to use her bikini panties to launch projectiles at a teddy bear propped on a chair. This graduated to an apple on the bear's head. Eventually, Ellen and her dorm sisters got into the act. Fresh panties with tight elastic and marbles for ammunition were ever ready in a box by the door; the bear and an apple were in constant position. In time, Ellen became the best shot of all. But that was ten years ago. Expertise was long gone, even the occasional shot now and then was no longer taken…still…

Ellen replaced the frying pan on the stove, hiked up her dress and pulled her bikini panties down and stepped out of them and picked up the lighter.

She put the lighter in the crotch of the panties and stuck her fingers into the leg loops to form a fork and took hold of the lighter through the panties and pulled it back, assured herself the elastic was strong enough to launch the projectile.

All right. That was a start.

She removed her purse, so Moon Face couldn't grab it and snare her, and tossed it aside. She grabbed the whiskey bottle from the corpse's hand and turned and smashed the bottom of it against the cook stove. Whiskey and glass flew. The result was a jagged weapon she could lunge with. She placed the broken bottle on the stove next to the frying pan.

Outside, Moon Face was strolling toward the hut, like a shy teenager about to call on his date.

There were only moments left. She glanced around the room, hoping insanely at the last second she would find some escape route, but there was none.

Sweat dripped from her forehead and ran into her eye and she blinked it out and half-drew back the panty sling with its golden projectile. She knew her makeshift weapon wasn't powerful enough to do much damage, but it might give her a moment of distraction, a chance to attack him with the bottle. If she went at him straight on with it, she felt certain he would disarm her and make short work of her, but if she could get him off guard...

She lowered her arms, kept her makeshift slingshot in front of her, ready to be cocked and shot.

Moon Face came through the door, ducking as he did, a sour sweat smell entering with him. His neck wound whistled at her like a teapot about to boil. She saw then that he was bigger than she first thought. Tall and broad-shouldered and strong.

He looked at her and there was that peculiar expression again. The moonlight from the hole in the roof hit his eyes and teeth, and it was as if that light was his source of energy. He filled his chest with air and seemed to stand a full two inches taller. He looked at the woman's corpse in the chair, the man's corpse supported on wires, glanced at the playpen.

He smiled at Ellen, squeaked more than spoke, "Bubba's home, Sissie."

I'm not Sissie yet, thought Ellen. Not yet.

Moon Face started to move around the card table and Ellen let out a blood-curdling scream that caused him to bob his head high like a rabbit surprised by headlights. Ellen jerked up the panties and pulled them back and let loose the lighter. It shot out of the panties and fell to the center of the card table with a clunk.

Moon Face looked down at it.

Ellen was temporarily gripped with paralysis, then she stepped forward and kicked the card table as hard as she could. It went into Moon Face, hitting him waist high, startling, but not hurting him.

Now! thought Ellen, grabbing her weapons. Now!

She rushed him, the broken bottle in one hand, the frying pan in the other. She slashed out with the bottle and it struck him in the center of the face and he let out a scream and the glass fractured and a splash of blood burst from him and in that same instant Ellen saw that his nose was cut half in two and she felt a tremendous throb in her hand. The bottle had broken in her palm and cut her.

She ignored the pain and as Moon Face bellowed and lashed out with the knife, cutting the front of her dress but not her flesh, she brought the frying pan around and caught him on the elbow, and the knife went soaring across the room and behind the rollaway bed.

Moon Face froze, glanced in the direction the knife had taken. He seemed empty and confused without it.

Ellen swung the pan again. Moon Face caught her wrist and jerked her around and she lost the pan and was sent hurtling toward the bed, where she collapsed on the mattress. The bed slid down and smashed through the thin wall of sticks and a foot of the bed stuck out into blackness and the great drop below. The bed tottered slightly, and Ellen rolled off of it, directly into the legs of Moon Face. As his knees bent, and he reached for her, she rolled backwards and went under the bed and her hand came to rest on the knife. She grabbed it, rolled back toward Moon Face's feet, reached out quickly and brought the knife down on one of his shoes and drove it in as hard as she could.

A bellow from Moon Face. His foot leaped back and it took the knife with it. Moon Face screamed, "Sissie! You're hurting me!"

Moon Face reached down and pulled the knife out, and Ellen saw his foot come forward, and then he was grabbing the bed and effortlessly jerking it off of her and back, smashing it into the crib, causing the child to topple out of it and roll across the floor, the rattle clattering behind it. He grabbed Ellen by the back of her dress and jerked her up and spun her around to face him, clutched her throat in one hand and held the knife close to her face with the other, as if for inspection; the blade caught the moonlight and winked.

Beyond the knife, she saw his face, pathetic and pained and white. His breath, sharp as the knife, practically wilted her. His neck wound whistled softly. The remnants of his nose dangled wet and red against his upper lip and cheek and his teeth grinned a moonlit, metal good-bye.

It was all over, and she knew it, but then Bruce's words came back to her in a rush. "When it looks as if you're defeated, and there's nothing left, try anything."

She twisted and jabbed out at his eyes with her fingers and caught him solid enough that he thrust her away and stumbled backwards. But only for an instant. He bolted forward, and Ellen stooped and grabbed the dead child by the ankle and struck Moon Face with it as if it were a club. Once in the face, once in the midsection. The rotting child burst into a spray of desiccated flesh and innards and she hurled the leg at Moon Face and then she was circling around the rollaway bed, trying to make the door. Moon Face, at the other end of the bed, saw this, and when she moved for the door, he lunged in that direction, causing her to jump back to the end of the bed. Smiling, he returned to his end, waited for her next attempt.

She lurched for the door again, and Moon Face deep-stepped that way, and when she jerked back, Moon Face jerked back too, but this time Ellen bent and grabbed the end of the bed and hurled herself against it. The bed hit Moon Face in the knees, and as he fell, the bed rolled over him and he let go of the knife and tried to put out his hands to stop the bed's momentum. The impetus of the rollaway carried him across the short length of the dirt floor and his head hit the far wall and the sticks cracked and hurtled out into blackness, and Moon Face followed and the bed followed him, then caught on the edge of the drop and the wheels buried up in the dirt and hung there.

Ellen had shoved so hard she fell face down, and when she looked up, she saw the bed was dangling, shaking, the mattress slipping loose, about to glide off into nothingness.

Moon Face's hands flicked into sight, clawing at the sides of the bed's frame. Ellen gasped. He was going to make it up. The bed's wheels were going to hold.

She pulled a knee under her, cocking herself, then sprang forward, thrusting both palms savagely against the bed. The wheels popped free and the rollaway shot out into the dark emptiness.

Ellen scooted forward on her knees and looked over the edge. There was blackness, a glimpse of the mattress falling free, and a pale object, like a white-washed planet with a great vein of silver in it, jetting through the cold expanse of space. Then the mattress and the face were gone and there was just the darkness and a distant sound like a water balloon exploding.

Ellen sat back and took a breather. When she felt strong again and felt certain her heart wouldn't tear through her chest, she stood up and looked around the room. She thought a long time about what she saw.

She found her purse and panties, went out of the hut and up the trail, and after a few wrong turns, she found the proper trail that wound its way up the mountainside to where her car was parked. When she climbed over the railing, she was exhausted.

Everything was as it was. She wondered if anyone had seen the cars, if anyone had stopped, then decided it didn't matter. There was no one here now, and that's what was important.

She took the keys from her purse and tried the engine. It turned over. That was a relief.

She killed the engine, got out and went around and opened the trunk of the Chevy and looked down at Bruce's body. His face looked like one big bruise, his lips were as large as sausages. It made her happy to look at him.

A new energy came to her. She got him under the arms and pulled him out and managed him over to the rail and grabbed his legs and flipped him over the railing and onto the trail. She got one of his hands and started pulling him down the path, letting the momentum help her. She felt good. She felt strong. First Bruce had tried to dominate her, had threatened her, had thought she was weak because she was a woman, and one night, after slapping her, after raping her, while he slept a drunken sleep, she had pulled the blankets up tight around him and looped rope over and under the bed and used the knots he had taught her, and secured him.

Then she took a stick of stove wood and had beat him until she was so weak she fell to her knees. She hadn't meant to kill him, just punish him for slapping her around, but when she got started she couldn't stop until she was too worn out to go on, and when she was finished, she discovered he was dead.

That didn't disturb her much. The thing then was to get rid of the body somewhere, drive on back to the city and say he had abandoned her and not come back. It was weak, but all she had. Until now.

After several stops for breath, a chance to lie on her back and look up at the stars, Ellen managed Bruce to the hut and got her arms under his and got him seated in one of the empty chairs. She straightened things up as best as she could. She put the larger pieces of the baby back in the crib. She picked Moon Face's knife up off the floor and looked at it and looked at Bruce, his eyes wide open, the moonlight from the roof striking them, showing them to be dull as scratched glass.

Bending over his face, she went to work on his eyes. When she finished with them, she pushed his head forward and used the blade like a drill. She worked until the holes satisfied her. Now if the police found the Buick up there and came down the trail to investigate, and found the trail leading here, saw what was in the shack, Bruce would fit in with the rest of Moon Face's victims. The police would probably conclude Moon Face, sleeping here with his "family," had put his bed too close to the cliff and it had broken through the thin wall and he had tumbled to his death.

She liked it.

She held Bruce's chin, lifted it, examined her work.

"You can be Uncle Brucey," she said, and gave Bruce a pat on the shoulder. "Thanks for all your advice and help, Uncle Brucey. It's what got me through." She gave him another pat.

She found a shirt — possibly Moon Face's, possibly a victim's — on the opposite side of the shack, next to a little box of Harlequin Romances, and she used it to wipe the knife, pan, all she had touched, clean of her prints, then she went out of there, back up to her car.

The Events Concerning a Nude Fold-Out Found in a Harlequin Romance

LOOKING BACK ON it, I wouldn't have thought something as strange as all this, full of the real coincidence of life, would have begun with a bad circus, but that's how it started, at least for me.

My luck had gone from bad to worse, then over the lip of worse, and into whatever lower level it can descend into. My job at the aluminum chair plant had played out and no rich relatives had died and left me any money. Fact was, I don't think the Cooks, least any that are kin to me, have any money, outside of a few quarters to put in a jukebox come Saturday night, maybe a few bucks to waste on something like pretzels and beer.

Me, I didn't even have money for beer or jukeboxes. I was collecting a little money on unemployment, and I was out beating the bushes for a job, but there didn't seem to be much in the way of work in Mud Creek. I couldn't even get on at the feed store carrying out bags of fertilizer and seed. All the sixteen-year-olds had that job.

It looked like I was going to have to move out of Mud Creek to find work, and though the idea of that didn't hurt my feelings any, there was Jasmine, my teenage daughter, and she still had a year of high school to finish before she went off to Nacogdoches to start her degree in anthropology at Stephen F. Austin State University, and I planned to follow her over there and find a place of my own where we could be near, and improve our relationship, which overall was all right to begin with. I just wanted more time with her.

Right then Jasmine lived with her mother, and her mother doesn't care a damn for me. She wanted to marry a guy that was going to be a high roller, and believe me, I wanted to be a high roller, but what she got was a guy who each time at the mark throws craps. No matter what I do, it turns to shit. Last break I felt I'd had in life was when I was ten and fell down and cracked my ankle. Well, maybe there was one good break after all. One that wasn't a bone. Jasmine. She's smart and pretty and ambitious and the love of my life.

But my marital problems and life's woes are not what this is about. I was saying about the circus.

It was mid-June, and I'd tried a couple places, looking for work, and hadn't gotten any, and I'd gone over to the employment office to talk to the people there and embarrass myself about not finding any work yet. They told me they didn't have anything for me either, but they didn't look embarrassed at all. When it's you and the employment office, better known as the unemployment office, feeling embarrassed is a one-way street and you're the one driving on it. They seem almost proud to tell you how many unemployment checks you got left, so it can kind of hang over your head like an anvil or something.

So, I thanked them like I meant it and went home, and believe me, that's no treat.

Home is a little apartment about the size of a washroom at a Fina Station, only not as nice and without the air conditioning. The window looks out over Main Street, and when a car drives by the window shakes, which is one of the reasons I leave it open most of the time. That and the fact I can hope for some sort of breeze to stir the dead, hot air around. The place is over a used bookstore called MARTHA'S BOOKS, and Martha is an all right lady if you like them mean. She's grumpy, about five hundred years old, weighs two-fifty when she's at her wrestling weight, wears men's clothing and has a bad leg and a faint black mustache to match the black wool ski cap she wears summer or winter, on account of her head is as bald as a river stone. I figure the cap is a funny sort of vanity, considering she doesn't do anything to get rid of that mustache. Still, she always does her nails in pink polish and she smokes those long feminine cigarettes that some women like, maybe thinking if the weeds look elegant enough they won't give them cancer.

Another thing about Martha, is with that bad leg she has a limp, and she helps that along with a golf putter she uses as a cane, putter-side up for a handle. See her coming down the street, which isn't often, you got to think there's not much you could add to make her any more gaudy, unless it's an assful of bright tail feathers and maybe some guys to follow her playing percussion instruments.

I liked to go down to Martha's from time to time and browse the books, and if I had a little spare change, I'd try to actually buy something now and then, or get something for Jasmine. I was especially fond of detective books, and Jasmine, bless her little heart, liked Harlequin Romances. She'd read them four or five a weekend when she wasn't dating boys, and since she was dating quite regularly now, she'd cut back mostly to one or two Harlequins a weekend.

Still, that was too many. I kept hoping she'd outgrow it. The romance novels and the dates. I was scared to death she'd fall in love with some cowboy with a cheek full of snuff and end up ironing Western shirts and wiping baby asses before she was old enough to vote.

Anyway, after I didn't find any jobs and nobody died and left me any money, I went home and brooded, then went downstairs to Martha's to look for a book.

Jasmine had made out a list of the titles she was looking to collect, and I took the list with me just in case I came across something she needed. I thought if I did, I might buy it and get her a detective book too, or something like that, give it to her with the romance and maybe she'd read it. I'd done that several times, and so far, to the best of my knowledge, she hadn't read any of the non-romance novels. The others might as well have been used to level a vibrating refrigerator, but I kept on trying.

The stairs went down from my place and out into the street, and at the bottom, to the left of them, was Martha's. The store was in front and she lived in back. During business hours in the summer the door was always open since Martha wouldn't have put air conditioning in there if half the store had been a meat locker hung with prize beef. She was too cheap for that. She liked her mustache sweat-beaded, her bald head pink beneath her cap. The place smelled of books and faintly of boiled cabbage, or maybe that was some soured clothing somewhere. The two smells have always seemed a lot alike to me. It's the only place I know hotter and filthier than my apartment, but it does have the books. Lots of them.

I went in, and there on the wall was a flyer for a circus at three o'clock that day. Martha had this old post board just inside the door, and she'd let people pin up flyers if they wanted, and sometimes she'd leave them there a whole day before she tore them down and wrote out the day's receipts on the back of them with a stubby, tongue-licked pencil. I think that's the only reason she had the post board and let people put up flyers, so she'd have scratch paper.

The flyer was for a circus called THE JIM DANDY THREE RING CIRCUS, and that should have clued me, but it didn't. Truth is, I've never liked circuses. They depress me. Something about the animals and the people who work there strike me as desperate, as if they're living on the edge of a cliff and the cliff is about to break off. But I saw this flyer and I thought of Jasmine.

When she was little she loved circuses. Her mother and I used to take her, and I remembered the whole thing rather fondly. Jasmine would laugh so hard at the clowns you had to tell her to shut up, and she'd put her hands over her eyes and peek through her fingers at the wild animal acts.

Back then, things were pretty good, and I think her mother even liked me, and truth to tell, I thought I was a pretty good guy myself. I thought I had the world by the tail. It took me a few years to realize the closest I was to having the world by the tail was being a dingle berry on one of its ass hairs. These days, I felt like the most worthless sonofabitch that had ever squatted to shit over a pair of shoes. I guess it isn't hip or politically correct, but to me, a man without a job is like a man without balls.

Thinking about my problems also added to me wanting to go to the circus. Not only would I get a chance to be with Jasmine, it would help me get my mind off my troubles.

I got out my wallet and opened it and saw a few sad bills in there, but it looked to me that I had enough for the circus, and maybe I could even spring for dinner afterwards, if Jasmine was in the mood for a hot dog and a soda pop. She wanted anything more than that, she had to buy me dinner, and I'd let her, since the money came from her mother, my darling ex-wife, Connie — may she grow like an onion with her head in the ground.

Mommy Dearest didn't seem to be shy of the bucks these days on account of she was letting old Gerald the Oil Man drop his drill down her oil shaft on a nightly basis.

Not that I'm bitter about it or anything. Him banging my ex-wife and being built like Tarzan and not losing any of his hair at the age of forty didn't bother me a bit.

I put my wallet away and turned and saw Martha behind the counter looking at me. She twisted on the stool and said, "Got a job yet?"

I just love a small town. You fart and everyone looks in your direction and starts fanning.

"No, not yet," I said.

"You looking for some kind of a career?"

"I'm looking for work."

"Any kind of work?"

"Right now, yes. You got something for me?"

"Naw. Can't pay my rent as it is."

"You're just curious, then?"

"Yeah. You want to go to that circus?"

"I don't know. Maybe. Is this a trick question too?"

"Guy put up the flyer gave me a couple tickets for letting him have the space on the board there. I'd give them to you for stacking some books. I don't really want to do it."

"Stack the books or give me the tickets?"

"Neither one. But you stack them Harlequins for me, I'll give you the tickets."

I looked at my wrist where my watch used to be before I pawned it. "You got the time?"

She looked at her watch. "Two o'clock."

"I like the deal," I said, "but the circus starts at three and I wanted to take my daughter."

Martha shook out one of her delicate little cigarettes and lit it, studied me. It made me feel funny. Like I was a shit smear on a laboratory slide. Most I'd ever talked to her before was when I asked where the new detective novels were and she grumped around and finally told me, as if it was a secret she'd rather have kept.

"Tell you what," Martha said, "I'll give you the tickets now, and you come back tomorrow morning and put up the books for me."

"That's nice of you," I said.

"Not really. I know where you live, and you don't come put up my romance novels tomorrow, I'll hunt you down and kill you."

I looked for a smile, but I didn't see any.

"That's one way to do business," I said.

"The only way. Here." She opened a drawer and pulled out the tickets and I went over and took them. "By the way, what's your name, boy? See you in here all the time, but don't know your name."

Boy? Was she talking to me?

"Plebin Cook," I said. "And I've always assumed you're Martha."

"Martha ain't much of a name, but it beats Plebin. Plebin's awful. I was named that I'd get it changed. Call yourself most anything and it'd be better than Plebin."

"I'll tell my poor, old, gray-haired mother what you said."

"You must have been an accident and that's why she named you that. You got an older brother or sister?"

"A brother."

"How much older?"

Earning these tickets was getting to be painful. "Sixteen years."

"What's his name?"

"Jim."

"There you are. You were an accident. Jim's a normal name. Her naming you Plebin is unconscious revenge. I read about stuff like that in one of those psychology books came in. Called *Know Why Things Happen to You*. You ought to read it. Thing it'd tell you is to get your name changed to something normal. Right name will give you a whole nuther outlook about yourself."

I had a vision of shoving those circus tickets down her throat, but I restrained myself for Jasmine's sake. "No joke? Well, I'll see you tomorrow."

"Eight o'clock sharp. Go stacking 'em after nine, gets so hot in here you'll faint. A Yankee visiting some relatives came in here and did just that. Found him about closing time over there by the historicals and the Gothic Romances. Had to call an ambulance to come get him. Got out of here with one of my Gothics clutched in his hand. Didn't pay me a cent for it."

"And people think a job like this is pretty easy."

"They just don't know," Martha said.

I said thanks and goodbye and started to turn away.

"Hey," Martha said. "You decide to get your name changed, they'll do stuff like that for you over at the court house."

"I'll keep that in mind," I said.

I didn't want any more of Martha, so I went over to the drug store and used the payphone there and called Jasmine. Her mother answered.

"Hi, Connie," I said.

"Get a job yet?"

"No," I said. "But I'm closing in on some prospects."

"Bet you are. What do you want?"

"Jasmine in?"

"You want to talk to her?"

No, I thought. Just ask for the hell of it. But I said, "If I may."

The phone clattered on something hard, a little more violently than necessary, I thought. A moment later Jasmine came on the line. "Daddy."

"Hi, Baby Darling. Want to go to the circus?"

"The circus?"

"The Jim Dandy Circus is in town, and I've got tickets."

"Yeah. Really." She sounded as if I'd asked her if she wanted to have her teeth cleaned.

"You used to like the circuses."

"When I was ten."

"That was just seven years ago."

"That's a long time."

"Only when you're seventeen. Want to go or not? I'll even spring for a hot dog."

"You know what they make hot dogs out of?"

"I try not to think about it. I figure I get some chili on it, whatever's in the dog dies."

"Guess you want me to come by and get you?"

"That would be nice. Circus starts at three. That's less than an hour away."

"All right, but Daddy?"

"Yeah."

"Don't call me Baby Darling in public. Someone could hear."

"We can't have that."

"Really, Daddy. I'm getting to be a woman now. It's… I don't know…kind of…"

"Hokey?"

"That's it."

"Gottcha."

The circus was not under the big top, but was inside the Mud Creek Exhibition center, which Mud Creek needs about as much as I need a second dick. I don't use the first one as it is. Oh, I pee out of it, but you know what I mean.

The circus was weak from the start, but Jasmine seemed to have a pretty good time, even if the performing bears were so goddamned old I thought we were going to have to go down there and help them out of their cages. The tiger act was scary, because it looked as if the tigers were definitely in control, but the overweight Ringmaster got out alive, and the elephants came on, so old and wrinkled they looked like drunks in baggy pants. That was the best of it. After that, the dog act, conducted by Waldo the Great, got out of hand, and his performing poodles went X-rated, and the real doo-doo hit the fan.

Idiot trainer had apparently put one of the bitches to work while she was in heat, and in response, the male dogs jumped her and started poking, the biggest male finally winning the honors and the other five running about as if their brains had rolled out of their ears.

Waldo the Great went a little nuts and started kicking the fornicating dogs, but they wouldn't let up. The male dog kept his goober in the slot even when Waldo's kicks made his hind legs leave the ground. He didn't even yip.

I heard a kid behind us say, "Mommy, what are the puppies doing?"

And Mommy, not missing a beat, said, "They're doing a trick, dear."

Children were screaming. Waldo began kicking at the remaining dogs indiscriminately, and they darted for cover. Members of the circus rushed Waldo the

Great. There were disappointed and injured dogs hunching and yipping all over the place. Waldo went back to the horny male and tried once more to discourage him. He really put the boot to him, but the ole boy really hung in there. I was kind of proud of him. One of the other dogs, innocent, except for confusion, and a gyrating ass and a dick like a rolled-back lipstick tube, made an error in geography and humped air past Waldo and got a kick in the ass for it.

He sailed way up and into the bleachers, went so high his fleas should have served cocktails and dinner on him. Came down like a bomb, hit between a crack in the bleachers with a yip. I didn't see him come out from under there. He didn't yip again.

The little boy behind me, said, "Is that a trick too?"

"Yes," Mommy said. "It doesn't hurt him. He knows how to land."

I certainly hoped so.

Not everyone took it as casually as Mommy. Some dog lovers came out of the bleachers and there was a fight. Couple of cowboys started trying to do to Waldo what he had done to the poodles.

Meanwhile, back at the ranch, so to speak, the two amorous mutts were still at it, the male laying pipe like there was no tomorrow.

Yes sir, a pleasant afternoon trip to the circus with my daughter. Another debacle. It was merely typical of the luck I had been experiencing. Even a free ticket to the circus could turn to shit.

Jasmine and I left while a cowboy down from the bleachers was using Waldo the Great as a punching bag. One of the ungrateful poodles was biting the cowboy on the boot.

Me and Jasmine didn't have hot dogs. We ended up at a Mexican place, and Jasmine paid for it. Halfway through the meal Jasmine looked up at me and frowned.

"Daddy, I can always count on you for a good time."

"Hey," I said, "what were you expecting for free tickets? Goddamn Ringling Brothers?"

"Really, Daddy. I enjoyed it. Weirdness follows you around. At Mom's there isn't anything to do but watch television, and Mom and Gerald always go to bed about nine o'clock, so they're no fun."

"I guess not," I said, thinking nine o'clock was awful early to be sleepy. I hoped the sonofabitch gave her the clap.

After dinner, Jasmine dropped me off and next morning I went down to Martha's and she grunted at me and showed me the Harlequins and where they needed to go, in alphabetical order, so I started in placing them. After about an hour of that, it got hot and I had to stop and talk Martha into letting me go over to the drugstore and buy a Coke.

When I came back with it, there was a guy in there with a box of Harlequin Romances. He was tall and lean and not bad-looking, except that he had one of those little pencil-line mustaches that looked as if he'd missed a spot shaving or had a stain line from sipping chocolate milk. Except for a black eye, his face was oddly unlined, as if little that happened to him in life found representation there. I thought he looked familiar. A moment later, it came to me. He was the guy at the circus with the performing dogs. I hadn't recognized him without his gold lamé tights. I could picture him clearly now, his foot up in the air, a poodle being launched from it. Waldo the Great.

He had a box of books on the desk in front of Martha. All Harlequin Romances. He reached out and ran his fingers over the spines. "I really hate to get rid of these," he was saying to Martha, and his voice was as sweet as a cooing turtle dove. "Really hate it, but see, I'm currently unemployed and extra finances, even of a small nature, are needed, and considering all the books I read, well, they're outgrowing my trailer. I tell you, it hurts me to dispense with these. Just seeing them on my shelves cheers me… Oh, I take these books so to heart. If life could be like these, oh what a life that would be. But somebody always messes it up." He touched the books. "True love. Romance. Happy endings. Oh, it should be that way, you know. We live such a miserable existence. We —"

"Hey," Martha said. "Actually, I don't give a shit why you want to get rid of them. And if life was like a Harlequin Romance, I'd put a gun in my mouth. You want to sell this crap, or not?"

Martha always tries to endear herself to her customers. I reckon she's got a trust fund somewhere and her mission on earth is to make as many people miserable as possible. Still, that seemed blunt even for her.

"Well, now," Waldo said. "I was merely expressing a heartfelt opinion. Nothing more. I could take my trade elsewhere."

"No skin off my rosy red ass," Martha said. "You want, that man over there will help you carry this shit back out to the car."

He looked at me. I blushed, nodded, drank more of my Coke.

He looked back at Martha. "Very well. I'll sell them to you, but only because I'm pressed to rid myself of them. Otherwise, I wouldn't take twice what you want to give for them."

"For you, Mister Asshole," Martha said, "just for you, I'll give you half of what I normally offer. Take it or leave it."

Waldo, Mr. Asshole, paused for a moment, studying Martha. I could see the side of his face, and just below his blackened eye there was a twitch, just once, then his face was smooth again.

"All right, let's conduct our business and get it over with," he said.

Martha counted the books, opened the cash register and gave Waldo a handful of bills. "Against my better judgment, there's the whole price."

"What in the world did I ever do to you?" Waldo the Great, alias, Mr. Asshole, said. He almost looked really hurt. It was hard to tell. I'd never seen a face like that. So smooth. So expressionless. It was disconcerting.

"You breathe," Martha said, "that's enough of an offense." With that, Waldo, Mr. Asshole, went out of the store, head up, back straight.

"Friend of yours?" I asked.

"Yeah," Martha said. "Me and him are fuckin'."

"I thought the two of you were pretty warm."

"I don't know. I really can't believe it happened like that."

"You weren't as sweet as usual."

"Can't explain it. One of those things. Ever had that happen? Meet someone right off, and you just don't like them, and you don't know why."

"I always just shoot them. Saves a lot of breath."

She ignored me. "Like it's chemistry or something. That guy came in here, it was like someone drove by and tossed a rattlesnake through the door. I didn't like him on sight. Sometimes I think that there's certain people that are predators, and the rest of us, we pick up on it, even if it isn't obvious through their actions, and we react to it. And maybe I'm an asshole."

"That's a possibility," I said. "You being an asshole, I mean. But I got to tell you, I don't like him much either. Kind of makes my skin crawl, that unlined face and all."

I told her about the circus and the dogs.

"That doesn't surprise me any," Martha said. "I mean, anyone can lose their cool. I've kicked a dog in my time —"

"I find that hard to believe."

"— but I tell you, that guy hasn't got all the corn on his cob. I can sense it. Here, put these up. Earn your goddamn circus tickets."

I finished off the Coke, got the box of Harlequins Waldo had brought in, took them over to the romance section and put them on the floor.

I pulled one out to look at the author's name, and something fell out of the book. It was a folded piece of paper. I picked it up and unfolded it. It was a magazine fold-out of a naked woman, sort you see in the cheaper tits and ass magazines. She had breasts just a little smaller than watermelons and she was grabbing her ankles, holding her legs in a spread eagle position, as if waiting for some unsuspecting traveler to fall in. There were thick black paint lines slashed at the neck, torso, elbows, wrist, waist, knees and ankles. The eyes had been blackened with the marker so that they looked like nothing more than enormous skull sockets. A circle had been drawn around her vagina and there was a big black dot dead center of it, like a bull's-eye. I turned it over. On the back over the printing there was written in black with a firm hand: Nothing really hooks together. Life lacks romance.

Looking at the photograph and those lines made me feel peculiar. I refolded the fold-out and started to replace it inside the book, then I thought maybe I'd throw it in the trash, but finally decided to keep it out of curiosity.

I shoved it into my back pocket and finished putting up the books, then got ready to leave. As I was going, Martha said, "You want a job here putting up books I'll take you on half a day five days a week. Monday through Friday. Saves some wear on my bad leg. I can pay you a little. Won't be much, but I don't figure you're worth much to me."

"That's a sweet offer, Martha, but I don't know."

"You say you want work."

"I do, but half a day isn't enough."

"More than you're working now, and I'll pay in cash. No taxes, no bullshit with the employment office."

"All right," I said. "You got a deal."

"Start tomorrow."

I was lying naked on the bed with just the nightlight on reading a hard-boiled mystery novel. The window was open as always and there was actually a pretty nice breeze blowing in. I felt like I used to when I was twelve and staying up late and reading with a flashlight under the covers and a cool spring wind was blowing in through the window screen, and Mom and Dad were in the next room and I was loved and protected and was going to live forever. Pleasant.

There was a knock at the door.

That figured.

I got up and pulled on my pajama bottoms and put on a robe and went to the door. It was Jasmine. She had her long, dark hair tied back in a pony tail and she was wearing jeans and a shirt buttoned up wrong. She had a suitcase in her hand.

"Connie again?"

"Her and that man," Jasmine said as she came inside. "I hate them."

"You don't hate your mother. She's an asshole, but you don't hate her."

"You hate her."

"That's different."

"Can I stay here for a while?"

"Sure. There's almost enough room for me, so I'm sure you'll find it cozy."

"You're not glad to see me?"

"I'm glad to see you. I'm always glad to see you. But this won't work out. Look how small this place is. Besides, you've done this before. Couple times. You come here, eat all my cereal, start missing your comforts, and then you go home."

"Not this time."

"All right. Not this time. Hungry?"

"I really don't want any cereal."

"I actually have some lunch meat this time. It's not quite green."

"Sounds yummy."

I made a couple of sandwiches and poured us some slightly tainted milk and we talked a moment, then Jasmine saw the fold-out on the dresser and picked it up. I had pulled it from my pocket when I got home and tossed it there.

She opened it up and looked at it, then smiled at me. It was the same smile her mother used when she was turning on the charm, or was about to make me feel small enough to wear doll clothes.

"Daddy, dear!"

"I found it."

"Say you did?"

"Cut it out. It was in one of the books I was putting up today. I thought it was weird and I stuck it in my back pocket. I should have thrown it away."

Jasmine smiled at me, examined the fold-out closely. "Daddy, do men like women like this? That big, I mean?"

"Some do. Yes."

"Do you?"

"Of course not."

"What are these lines?"

"I don't know exactly, but that's what I thought was weird. It got my mind working overtime."

"You mean like the 'What If' game?"

The "What If" game was something Jasmine and I had made up when she was little, and had never really quit playing, though our opportunities to play it had decreased sharply over the last couple of years. It grew out of my thinking

I was going to be a writer. I'd see something and I'd extrapolate. An example was an old car I saw once where someone had finger-written in the dust on the trunk lid: THERE'S A BODY IN THE TRUNK.

Well, I thought about that and tried to make a story of it. Say there was a body in the trunk. How did it get there? Is the woman driving the car aware it's there? Did she commit the murder? That sort of thing. Then I'd try to write a story. After fifty or so stories, and three times that many rejects, I gave up writing them, and Jasmine and I started kicking ideas like that back and forth, for fun. That way I could still feed my imagination, but I could quit kidding myself that I could write. Also, Jasmine got a kick out of it.

"Let's play, Daddy?"

"All right. I'll start. I saw those slashes on that fold-out, and I got to thinking, why are these lines drawn?"

"Because they look like cuts," Jasmine said. "You know, like a chart for how to butcher meat."

"That's what I thought. Then I thought, it's just a picture, and it could have been marked up without any real motive. Absentminded doodling. Or it could have been done by someone who didn't like women, and this was sort of an imaginary revenge. Turning women into meat in his mind. Dehumanizing them."

"Or it could be representative of what he's actually done or plans to do. Wow! Maybe we've got a real mystery here."

"My last real mystery was what finished your mom and I off."

That was the body in the trunk business. I didn't tell it all before. I got so into that scenario I called a friend of mine, Sam, down at the cop shop and got him geared up about there being a body in the trunk of a car. I told it good, with details I'd made up and didn't even know I'd made up. I really get into this stuff. The real and the unreal get a little hard for me to tell apart. Or it used to be that way. Not anymore.

Bottom line is Sam pursued the matter, and the only thing in the trunk was a spare tire. Sam was a little unhappy with me. The cop shop was a little unhappy with him. My wife, finally tired of my make-believe, kicked me out and went for the oil man. He didn't make up stories. He made money and had all his hair and was probably hung like a water buffalo.

"But say we knew the guy who marked this picture, Daddy. And say we started watching him, just to see —"

"We do know him. Kind of."

I told her about Waldo the Great and his books and Martha's reaction.

"That's even weirder," Jasmine said. "This bookstore lady —"

"Martha."

"— does she seem like a good judge of character?"

"She hates just about everybody, I think."

"Well, for 'What If's' sake, say she is a good judge of character. And this guy really is nuts. And he's done this kind of thing to a fold-out because… say…say…"

"He wants life to be like a Harlequin Romance. Only it isn't. Women don't always fit his image of what they should be — like the women in the books he reads."

"Oh, that's good, Daddy. Really. He's gone nuts, not because of violent films and movies, but because of a misguided view about romance. I love it."

"Makes as much sense as a guy saying he axed a family because he saw a horror movie or read a horror novel. There's got to be more to it than that, of course. Rotten childhood, genetic makeup. Most people who see or read horror novels, romance novels, whatever, get their thrills vicariously. It's a catharsis. But in the same way a horror movie or book might set someone off who's already messed up, someone wound-up and ready to spring, the Harlequins do it for our man. He has so little idea what real life is like, he expects it to be like the Harlequins, or desperately wants it to be that way, and when it isn't, his frustrations build, and —"

"He kills women, cuts them up, disposes of their bodies. It's delicious. Really delicious."

"It's silly. There's a sleeping bag in the closet. Get it out when you get sleepy. Me, I'm going to go to bed. I got a part-time job downstairs at Martha's, and I start tomorrow."

"That's great, Daddy. Mom said you'd never find a job."

On that note, I went to bed.

Next morning I went down to Martha's and started to work. She had a storeroom full of books. Some of them were stuck together with age, and some were full of worms. Being a fanatic book-lover, it hurt me, but I got rid of the bad ones in the dumpster out back, then loaded some boxes of good-condition books on a hand truck and wheeled them out and began putting them up in alphabetical order in their proper sections.

About nine that morning, Jasmine came down and I heard her say something to Martha, then she came around the corner of the detective section and smiled at me. She looked so much like her mother it hurt me. She had her hair pulled back and tied at her neck and she was starting to sweat. She wore white shorts, cut a little too short if you ask me, and a loose red T-shirt and sandals. She was carrying a yellow pad with a pencil.

"What you doing?" I asked.

"Figuring out what Waldo the Great's up to. I been working on it ever since I got up. I got lots of notes here."

"What'd you have for breakfast?"

"Same as you, I bet. A Coke."

"Right. It's important we pay attention to nutrition, Baby Darling."

"You want to hear about Waldo or not?"

"Yeah, tell me, what's he up to?"

"He's looking for a job."

"Because he got fired for the dog-kicking business?"

"Yeah. So, he's staying in the trailer park here, and he's looking for a job. Or maybe he's got some savings and he's just hanging out for a while before he moves on. Let's just say all that for 'What If's' sake."

"All right, now what?"

"Just for fun, to play the game all the way, let's go out to the trailer park and see if he's living there. If he is, we ought to be able to find him. He's got all these dogs, so there should be some signs of them, don't you think?"

"Wait a minute. You're not planning on checking?"

"Just for the 'What If' game."

"Like I said, he could have moved on."

"That's what we'll find out. Later, we can go over to the trailer park and look around, play detective."

"That's carrying it too far."

"Why? It's just a game. We don't have to bother him."

"I don't know. I don't think so."

"Why not?" It was Martha. She came around the corner of the bookshelves leaning on her golf putter. "It's just a game."

"Aren't you supposed to be counting your money, or something?" I said to Martha. "Kill some of those roaches in your storeroom. That club would be just the tool for it."

"I couldn't help but overhear you because I was leaning against the other side of the bookshelf listening," Martha said.

"That'll do it," I said, and shelved a Mickey Spillane.

"We've spoke, but I don't think we've actually met," Jasmine said to Martha. "I'm his daughter."

"Tough to admit, I'm sure," Martha said.

Jasmine and Martha smiled at each other and shook hands.

"Why don't we go over there tonight?" Martha said. "I need something to do."

"To the trailer park?" I asked.

"Of course," Martha said.

"Not likely," I said. "I've had it with the detective business, imaginary or otherwise. It'll be a cold day in hell when I have anything else to do with it, in any manner, shape or form. And you can take that to the bank."

That night, presumably an example of a cold day in hell, around nine-thirty, we drove over to the only trailer park in Mud Creek and looked around.

Waldo hadn't moved on. Being astute detectives, we found his trailer right away. It was bright blue and there was red lettering on the side that read: WALDO THE GREAT AND HIS MAGNIFICENT CANINES. The trailer was next to a big pickup with a trailer hitch and there were lights on in the trailer.

We were in Martha's old Dodge van, and we drove by Waldo's and around the loop in the park and out of there. Martha went a short distance, turned down a hard clay road that wound along the side of the creek and through a patch of woods and ended up at the rear of the trailer park, about even with Waldo's trailer. It was a bit of distance away, but you could see his trailer through the branches of the trees that surrounded the park. Martha parked to the side of the road and spoke to Jasmine. "Honey, hand me them binoculars out of the glove box."

Jasmine did just that.

"These suckers are infra-red," Martha said. "You can see a mole on a gnat's ass with one of these dead of night during a blizzard."

"And why in the world would you have a pair?" I asked.

"I used to do a little surveillance for a private investigation agency in Houston. I sort of borrowed these when I left. You know, boss I had hadn't been such a dick, I'd have stayed with that job. I was born to it."

"Sounds exciting," Jasmine said.

"It beat smelling book dust, I'll tell you that." Martha rolled down her window and put the glasses to her face and pointed them at Waldo's trailer.

"He's at the window," she said.

"This has gone far enough," I said. "We're not supposed to be doing this. It's an invasion of privacy."

"Settle down. He ain't got his pecker out or nothing" Martha said. "Wish he did, though. He's an asshole, but he ain't bad-looking. I wonder what kind of rod he's got on him?"

I looked at Jasmine. She looked a little stunned. "Listen here," I said. "My daughter's here."

"No shit," Martha said. "Listen, you stuffy old fart. She's grown up enough to know a man's got a hooter on him and what it looks like."

Jasmine's face was split by a weak smile. "Well, I know what they are, of course."

"All right, we're all versed in biology," I said. "Let's go. I've got a good book waiting at home."

"Hold the goddamn phone," Martha said. "He's coming out of the trailer."

I looked, and I could see Waldo's shape framed in the trailer's doorway. One of the poodles ran up behind him and he back-kicked it inside without even looking, went down the metal steps and closed and locked the trailer, got in his pickup and drove away.

"He's off," Martha said.

"Yeah. Probably to a fried chicken place," I said.

Martha lowered the binoculars and looked over her seat at me. "Would you quit fucking up the game? 'What If' is going on here."

"Yeah, Daddy," Jasmine said. "We're playing 'What If'."

Martha cranked the van and followed the clay road as it curved around the park and out into the street. She went right. A moment later, we saw the back of Waldo's pickup. He had an arm hanging out the window and a cigarette was between his fingers and sparks were flaring off of it and flickering into the night.

"Smokey Bear'd come down on his ass like a ton of bricks, he seen that," Martha said.

We followed him to the end of the street and out onto the main drag, such as it is in Mud Creek. He pulled into a fried chicken joint.

"See," I said.

"Even murderers have to eat," Martha said, and she drove on by.

My plan was to end the business there, but it didn't work that way. I pulled out of it and let them stay with it. All that week Martha and Jasmine played "What If." They pinned up the fold-out in my apartment and they wrote out scenarios for who Waldo was and what he'd done, and so on. They drove out to his place at night and discovered he kept weird hours, went out at all times of the night. They discovered he let the poodles out for bathroom breaks twice a night and that there was one less than there had been during the circus act. I guess Mommy had been wrong when she told her kid the poodle knew how to land.

It was kind of odd seeing Jasmine and Martha become friends like that. Martha had struck me as having all the imagination of a fencepost, but under that rough exterior and that loud mouth was a rough exterior and a loud mouth with an imagination.

I also suspicioned that she had lied about not being able to pay her rent. The store didn't make that much, but she always seemed to have money. As far as the store went, it got so I was running it by myself, fulltime, not only putting up books, but waiting on customers and closing up at night. Martha paid me well enough for it, however, so I didn't complain, but when she and Jasmine would come down from my place talking about their "killer," etc., I felt a little jealous. Jasmine had moved in with me, and now that I had my daughter back, she spent all her time with a bald-headed, mustached lady who was her father's boss.

Worse, Connie had been on my case about Jasmine and how my only daughter was living in a shithole and being exposed to bad elements. The worst being me, of course. She came by the apartment a couple of times to tell me about it and to try and get Jasmine to go home.

I told her Jasmine was free to go home anytime she chose, and Jasmine explained that she had no intention of going home. She liked her sleeping bag and Daddy let her have Coke for breakfast. I sort of wish she hadn't mentioned the Coke part. She'd only had that for breakfast one morning, but she knew it'd get her mother's goat, and it had. Only thing was, now Connie could hang another sword over my head. Failure to provide proper nutrition for my only child.

Anyway, I was working in the store one day — well, working on reading a detective novel — when Martha and Jasmine came in.

"Get your goddamn feet off my desk," Martha said.

"Glad to see you," I said, lowering my feet and putting a marker in the book.

"Get off my stool," Martha said. "Quit reading that damn book and put some up."

I got off the stool. "You two have a pleasant day, Massah Martha?"

"Eat shit, Plebin," Martha said, leaning her golf club against the counter and mounting her stool.

"Daddy, Martha and I have been snooping. Listen what we got. Martha had this idea to go over to the newspaper office in LaBorde and look at back issues —"

"LaBorde?" I said.

"Bigger town. Bigger paper," Martha said, sticking one of her dainty cigarettes into her mouth and lighting it.

"We went through some older papers," Jasmine said, "and since LaBorde covers a lot of the small towns around here, we found ads for the Jim Dandy Circus in several of them, and we were able to pinpoint on a map the route of the circus up to Mud Creek, and the latest paper showed Marvel Creek to be the next stop, and —"

"Slow down," I said. "What's the circus got to do with your so-called investigation?"

"You look at the papers and read about the towns where the circus showed up," Martha said, "and there's in every one of them something about a missing woman, or young girl. In a couple cases, bodies have been found. Sometimes they were found a week or so after the circus came to town, but most of the news articles indicate the missing women disappeared at the time of the circus."

"Of course, we determined this, not the papers," Jasmine said. "We made the connection between the circus and the bodies."

"In the case of the bodies, both were found after the circus passed through," Martha said, "but from the estimated times of death the papers gave, we've been able to figure they were killed about the time the circus was in town. And my guess is those missing women are dead too, and by the same hand."

"Waldo's?" I said.

"That's right," Martha said.

I considered all that.

Jasmine said, "Pretty coincidental, don't you think?"

"Well, yeah," I said, "but that doesn't mean —"

"And the two bodies had been mutilated," Martha said. She leaned against the counter and reached into her shirt pocket and pulled out the fold-out I had found. She smoothed it out on the counter top. "Body parts were missing. And I bet they were cut up, just like this fold-out is marked. As for the missing body parts, eyes and pussies, I figure. Those are the parts he has circled and blacked out."

"Watch your language," I said to Martha.

No one seemed to take much note of me.

"The bodies were found in the town's local dump," Jasmine said.

"It's curious," I admitted, "but still, to accuse a man of murder on the basis of circumstantial evidence."

"One more thing," Martha said. "Both bodies had traces of black paint on them. Like it had been used to mark the areas the killer wanted to cut, and I presume, did cut. That's certainly a lot of goddamn circumstantial evidence, isn't it?"

"Enough that we're going to keep an eye on Waldo," Jasmine said.

I must admit right now that I didn't think even then, after what I had been told, there was anything to this Waldo the Great as murderer. It struck me that murders and disappearances happen all the time, and that if one were to look through the LaBorde paper carefully, it would be possible to discover there had been many of both, especially disappearances, before and after the arrival of the circus. I mean that paper covered a lot of small towns and communities, and LaBorde was a fairly large town itself. A small city actually. Most of the disappearances would turn out to be nothing more than someone leaving on a trip for a few days without telling anyone, and most of the murders would be committed by a friend or relative of the victim and would have nothing to do with the circus or marked-up fold-outs.

Of course, the fact that the two discovered bodies had been mutilated gave me pause, but not enough to go to the law about it. That was just the sort of half-baked idea that had gotten my ass in a crack earlier.

Still, that night, I went with Martha and Jasmine out to the trailer park.

It was cloudy that night and jags of lightning made occasional cuts through the cloud cover and thunder rumbled and light drops of rain fell on the windshield of Martha's van.

We drove out to the road behind the park about dark, peeked out the windows and through the gaps in the trees. The handful of pole lights in the park were gauzy in the wet night and sad as dying fireflies. Their poor, damp rays fell against some of the trees — their branches waving in the wind like the fluttering hands of distressed lunatics — and forced the beads of rain on the branches to give up tiny rainbows. The rainbows rose up, misted outward a small distance, then once beyond the small circumference of light, their beauty was consumed by the night.

Martha got out her binoculars and Jasmine sat on the front passenger side with a notepad and pen, ready to record anything Martha told her to. They felt that the more documentation they had, the easier it would be to convince the police that Waldo was a murderer.

I was in the seat behind theirs, my legs stretched out and my back against the van, looking away from the trailer most of the time, wondering how I had let myself in on this. About midnight I began to feel both sleepy and silly. I unwrapped a candy bar and ate it.

"Would you quit that goddamn smacking back there," Martha said. "It makes me nervous."

"Pardon me all to hell," I said, and wadded up the wrapper noisily and tossed it on the floorboard.

"Daddy, would you quit?" Jasmine said.

"Now we got something," Martha said.

I sat up and turned around. There were no lights on in the trailers in the park except for Waldo's trailer; a dirty, orange glow shone behind one of his windows, like a fresh slice of smoked cheese. Other than that, there was only the pole lights, and they didn't offer much. Just those little rainbows made of bad light and rain. Without the binoculars there was little to observe in detail, because it was a pretty good distance from where we were to Waldo's trailer, but I could see him coming out of the door, holding it open, the whole pack of poodles following after.

Waldo bent down by the trailer and pulled a small shovel out from beneath it. The poodles wandered around and started doing their bathroom business. Waldo cupped his hands over a cigarette and lit it with a lighter and smoked while he noted the dog's delivery spots. After a while he went about scooping up their messes with his shovel and making several trips to the dumpster to get rid of it.

Finished, he pushed the shovel beneath the trailer and smoked another cigarette and ground it hard beneath his heel and opened the trailer door and called to the dogs. They bounded up the steps and into the trailer like it was one of their circus tricks. No poodle tried to fuck another poodle. Waldo didn't kick anybody. He went inside, and a moment later came out again, this time minus the poodles. He was carrying something. A box. He looked about carefully, then placed the box in the back of his pickup. He went back inside the trailer.

"Goddamn," Martha said. "There's a woman's leg in that box."

"Let me see," I said.

"You can't see it now," she said. "It's down in the bed of the truck."

She gave me the binoculars anyway, and I looked. She was right. I couldn't see what was in the bed of the truck. "He wouldn't just put a woman's leg in the back of his pickup," I said.

"Well, he did," Martha said.

"Oh God," Jasmine said, and she flicked on her pen light and glanced at her watch and started writing on her notepad, talking aloud as she did. "Twelve-o-five, Waldo put woman's leg in the bed of his truck. Oh, shit, who do you think it could be?"

"One could hope it's that goddamn bitch down at the county clerk's office,"

Martha said. "I been waiting for something to happen to her."

"Martha!" Jasmine said.

"Just kidding," Martha said. "Kinda."

I had the binoculars tight against my face as the trailer door opened again. I could see very well with the infra-red business. Waldo came out with another box. As he came down the steps, the box tilted slightly. It was open at the top and I could see very clearly what was in it.

"A woman's head," I said. My voice sounded small and childish.

"Jesus Christ," Martha said. "I didn't really, really, believe he was a murderer."

Waldo was back inside the trailer. A moment later he reappeared. Smaller boxes under each arm.

"Let me see," Jasmine said.

"No," I said. "You don't need to."

"But…" Jasmine began.

"Listen to your father," Martha said.

I handed the binoculars back to Martha. She didn't look through them. We didn't need to try and see what was in the other boxes. We knew. The rest of Waldo's victim.

Waldo unfolded a tarp in the back of his pickup and stretched it across the truck bed and fastened it at all corners, then got inside the cab and cranked the engine.

"Do we go to the police now?" Jasmine said.

"After we find out where he's taking the body," Martha said.

"You're right," I said. "Otherwise, if he's disposed of all the evidence, we've got nothing." I was thinking too of my record at the police station. Meaning, of course, more than my word would be needed to start an investigation.

Martha cranked the van and put on the park lights and began to ease along, giving Waldo the time he needed to get out of the trailer park and ahead of us.

"I've got a pretty good idea where he's going," Martha said. "Bet he scoped the place out first day he got to town."

"The dump," Jasmine said. "Place they found those other bodies."

We got to the street and saw Waldo was headed in the direction of the dump. Martha turned on the van's headlights after the pickup was down the road a bit, then eased out in pursuit. We laid back and let him get way ahead, and when we got out of town and he took the turnoff to the dump, we passed on by and turned down a farm-to-market road and parked as close as we could to a barbed wire fence. We got out and climbed the fence and crossed a pasture and came to a rise and went up that and poked our heads over carefully and looked down on the dump.

There was smoke rising up in spots, where signs of burning refuse had been covered at some point, and it filled the air with stink. The dump had been like that forever. As a little boy, my father would bring me out to the dump to toss our family garbage, and even in broad daylight, I thought the place spooky, a sort of poor-boy, blue-collar hell. My dad said there were fires out here that had never been put out, not by the weight of garbage and dirt, or by winter ice or spring's rain storms. Said no matter what was done to those fires, they still burned. Methane maybe. All the stuff in the dump heating up like compost, creating some kind of combustible chemical reaction.

Within the dump, bordered off by a wide layer of scraped earth, were two great oil derricks. They were working derricks too, and the great rocking horse pumps dipped down and rose up constantly, night or day, and it always struck me that this was a foolish place for a dump full of never-dying fires to exist, next to two working oil wells. But the dump still stood and the derricks still worked oil. The city council had tried to have the old dump shut down, moved, but so far nothing had happened. They couldn't get those fires out completely for one thing. I felt time was against the dump and the wells. Eventually, the piper, or in this case, the pipeline, had to be paid. Some day the fires in the dump would get out of hand and set the oil wells on fire and the explosion that would occur would send Mud Creek and its surrounding rivers and woodlands to some place north of Pluto.

At night, the place was even more eerie. Flames licking out from under the debris like tongues, the rain seeping to its source, making it hiss white smoke like dragon breath. The two old derricks stood tall against the night and lightning wove a flickering crown of light around one of them and went away. In that instant, the electrified top of the derrick looked like Martian machinery. Inside the derricks, the still-working well pumps throbbed and kerchunked and dipped their dark, metal hammerheads then lifted them again. Down and up. Down and up. Taking with them on the drop and the rise, rain-wet shadows and flickers of garbage fire.

Waldo's truck was parked beside the road, next to a mound of garbage the height of a first-story roof. He had peeled off the tarp and put it away and was unloading his boxes from the truck, carrying them to a spot near one of the oil derricks, arranging them neatly, as if he were being graded on his work. When the boxes were all out, Waldo stood with his back to us and watched one of the derrick's pumps nod for a long time, as if the action of it amazed or offended him.

After a time, he turned suddenly and kicked at one of the boxes. The head in it popped up like a Mexican jumping bean and fell back down inside. Waldo took a deep breath, as if he were preparing to run a race, then got in his truck, turned it around, and drove away.

"He didn't even bother to bury the pieces," Jasmine said, and even in the bad light, I could see she was as white as Frosty the Snowman.

"Probably wants it to be found," Martha said. "We know where the corpse is now. We have evidence, and we saw him dispose of the body ourselves. I think we can go to the law now."

We drove back to town and called Sam from Martha's bookstore. He answered the phone on the fifth ring. He sounded like he had a sock in his mouth.

"What?"

"Plebin, Sam. I need your help."

"You in a ditch? Call a wrecker, man. I'm bushed."

"Not exactly. It's about murder."

"Ah, shit, Plebin. You some kind of fool, or what? We been through this. Call some nuthouse doctor or something. I need sleep. Day I put in today was bad enough, but I don't need you now and some story about murder. Lack of sleep gives me domestic problems."

"This one's different. I've got two witnesses. A body out at the dump. We saw it disposed of. A woman cut up in pieces, I kid you not. Guy named Waldo did it. He used to be with the circus. Directed a dog act."

"The circus?"

"That's right."

"And he has a dog act."

"Had. He cut up a woman and took her to the dump."

"Plebin?"

"Yes."

"I go out there, and there's no dead body, I could change that, supply one, mood I'm in. Understand?"

"Just meet us at the dump."

"Who's us?"

I told him, gave him some background on Waldo, explained what Martha and Jasmine found in the LaBorde newspapers, hung up, and me and my fellow sleuths drove back to the dump.

We waited outside the dump in Martha's van until Sam showed in his blue

Ford. We waved at him and started the van and led him into the dump. We drove up to the spot near the derrick and got out. None of us went over to the boxes for a look. We didn't speak. We listened to the pumps doing their work inside the derricks. Kerchunk, kerchunk, kerchunk.

Sam pulled up behind us and got out. He was wearing blue jeans and tennis shoes and his pajama top. He looked at me and Jasmine and Martha. Fact is, he looked at Martha quite a while.

"You want maybe I should send you a picture, or something?" Martha said.

Sam didn't say anything. He looked away from Martha and said to me, "All right. Where's the body?"

"It's kind of here and there," I said, and pointed. "In those boxes. Start with the little one, there. That's her head."

Sam looked in the box, and I saw him jump a little. Then he went still, bent forward and pulled the woman's head out by the hair, held it up in front of him and looked at it. He spun and tossed it to me. Reflexively, I caught it, then dropped it. By the time it hit the ground I felt like a number one horse's ass.

It wasn't a human head. It was a mannequin head with a black paint mark covering the stump of the neck, which had been neatly sawed in two.

"Here, Jasmine," Sam said. "You take a leg," and he hoisted a mannequin leg out of another box and tossed it at her. She shrieked and dodged and it landed on the ground. "And you that's gonna send me a picture. You take an arm." He pulled a mannequin arm out of another box and tossed it at Martha, who swatted it out of the air with her putter cane.

He turned and kicked another of the boxes and sent a leg and an arm sailing into a heap of brush and old paint cans.

"Goddamn it, Plebin," he said. "You've done it again." He came over and stood in front of me. "Man, you're nuts. Absolutely nuts."

"Wasn't just Plebin," Martha said. "We all thought it. The guy brought this stuff out here is a weirdo. We've been watching him."

"You have?" Sam said. "Playing detective, huh? That's sweet. That's real sweet. Plebin, come here, will you?"

I went over and stood by him. He put an arm around my shoulders and walked me off from Jasmine and Martha. He whispered to me.

"Plebin. You're not learning, man. Not a bit. Not only are you fucking up your life, you're fucking up mine. Listen here. Me and the old lady, we're not doing so good, see."

"I'm sorry to hear it. Toni has always been so great."

"Yeah, well, you see, she's jealous. You know that."

"Oh yeah. Always has been."

"There you are. She's gotten worse too. And you see, I spend a lot of time away from the home. Out of the bed. Bad hours. You getting what I'm saying here?"

"Yeah."

He pulled me closer and patted my chest with his other hand. "Good. Not only is that bad, me spending those hours away from home and out of the bed at bedtime, but hey, I'm so bushed these days, I get ready to lay a little pipe, well, I got no lead in the pencil. Like a goddamn spaghetti, that's how it is. Know what I'm saying?"

"Least when you do get it hard, you get to lay pipe," I said.

"But I'm not laying it enough. It's because I don't get rest. But Toni, you know what she thinks? She thinks it's because I'm having a little extracurricular activity. You know what I mean? Thinks I'm out banging hole like there's no tomorrow."

"Hey, I'm sorry, Sam, but…"

"So now I've got the rest problem again. I'm tired right now. I don't recover like I used to. I don't get eight hours of sack time, hey, I can't get it up. I have a bad day, which I do when I'm tired, I can't get it up. My shit comes out different, I can't get it up. I've gotten sensitive in my old age. Everything goes straight to my dick. Toni, she gets ready for me to do my duty, guess what?"

"You're too tired. You can't get it up."

"Bingo. The ole Johnson is like an empty sock. And when I can't get it up, what does Toni think?"

"You're fucking around?"

"That's right. And it's not bad enough I gotta be tired for legitimate reasons, but now I got to be tired because you and your daughter and Ma Frankenstein over there are seeing heads in boxes. Trailing some innocent bystander and trying to tie him in with murder when there's nobody been murdered. Know what I'm saying?"

"Sam, the guy looks the part. Acts it. There's been murders everywhere the circus goes…"

"Plebin, ole buddy. Hush your mouth, okay? Listen up tight. I'm going home now. I'm going back to bed. You wake me up again, I'll run over you with a truck. I don't have a truck, but I'll borrow one for the purpose. Got me?"

"Yeah."

"All right. Good night." He took his arm off my shoulders, walked back to his car and opened the door. He started to get inside, then straightened. He looked over the roof at me. "Come by and have dinner next week. Toni still makes a good chicken-fried steak. Been a while since she's seen you."

"I'll keep it in mind. Give her my love."

"Yeah. And Plebin, don't call with any more murders, all right? You got a good imagination, but as a detective, you're the worst." He looked at Jasmine. "Jasmine, you stick with your mother." He got in his car, backed around and drove away.

I went over and stood with my fellow sleuths and looked down at the mannequin head. I picked it up by the hair and looked at it. "I think I'll have this mounted," I said. "Just to remind me what a jackass I am."

Back at the apartment I sat on the bed with the window open, the mannequin head on the pillow beside me. Jasmine sat in the dresser chair and Martha had one of my rickety kitchen chairs turned around backwards and she sat with her arms crossed on the back of it, sweat running out from under her wool cap, collecting in her mustache.

"I still think something funny is going on there," Jasmine said.

"Oh, shut up," I said.

"We know something funny is going on," Martha said.

"We means you two," I said. "Don't include me. I don't know anything except I've made a fool out of myself and Sam is having trouble with his sex life, or maybe what he told me was some kind of parable."

"Sex life," Jasmine said. "What did he tell you?"

"Forget," I said.

"That Sam is some sorry cop," Martha said. "He should have at least investigated Waldo. Guy who paints and cuts up mannequins isn't your everyday fella, I'd think. I bet he's painting and sawing them up because he hasn't picked a victim yet. It's his way of appeasing himself until he's chosen someone. Akin to masturbation instead of real sex."

"If we could see inside his trailer," Jasmine said, "I bet we'd find evidence of something more than mannequins. Evidence of past crimes maybe."

"I've had enough" I said. "And Jasmine, so have you. And Martha, if you're smart, so have you."

Martha got out one of her little cigarettes.

"Don't light that in here," I said.

She got out a small box of kitchen matches.

"I can't stand smoke," I said.

She pulled a match from the box and struck it on her pants leg and lit up, puffed, studied the ceiling.

"Put it out, Martha. This is my place."

She blew smoke at the ceiling. "I think Jasmine's right," she said. "If we could divert him. Get him out of the trailer so we could have a look inside, find some evidence, then maybe that small town idiot cop friend of yours would even be convinced."

"Waldo's not going to keep a human head in there," I said.

"He might," Martha said. "It's been known to happen. Or maybe something a victim owned. Guys like that keep souvenirs of their murders. That way they can fantasize, relive it all."

"We could watch his place tomorrow," Jasmine said, "then if he goes out, we could slip in and look around. We find something incriminating, something definite, there's a way to cue the police in on it, even one as stubborn and stupid as Sam."

"I'm sure Waldo locks his doors," I said.

"That's no trouble," Martha said. "I can pick the lock on Heaven's door."

"You're just a basket of fine skills," I said.

"I used to work for a repo company, years back," Martha said. "I learned to use lock jocks and keys and picks on car doors and garage doors. You name it, I can get in it, and in a matter of moments."

"Listen, you two," I said, "leave it be. We don't know this guy's done anything, and if he is a murderer, you damn sure don't need to be snooping around there, or you may end up on the victim list. Let's get on with our lives."

"Such as yours and mine is," Martha said. "What have I got to look forward to? Selling a few books? Meeting the right man? Me, a gargoyle with a golf club?"

"Martha, don't say that," Jasmine said.

"No, let's call a spade a spade here," Martha said. She snatched off her wool cap and showed us her bald head. I had seen a glimpse of it a time or two before I went to work there, when she was taking off and adjusting her cap or scratching her head, but this was the first time I'd seen it in all its sweaty, pink glory for more than a few moments. "What's gonna pull a mate in for me? My glorious head of hair. I started losing it when I was in my twenties. No man would look twice at me. Besides that, I'm ugly and have a mustache."

"A mate isn't everything," I said.

"It's something," Martha said. "And I think about it. I won't kid you. But I know it isn't possible. I've been around, seen some things, had some interesting jobs. But I haven't really made any life for myself. Not so it feels like one. And you know what? After all these years, Jasmine and you are my only real friends, and in your case, Plebin, I don't know that amounts to much."

"Thanks," I said.

"You could get a wig," Jasmine said.

"I could have these whiskers removed," Martha said. "But I'd still be a blimp with a bum leg. No. There's nothing for me in the looks department. Not unless I could change bodies with some blonde bimbo. Since that isn't going to happen, all I got is what I make out of life. Like this mystery. A real mystery, I think. And if Waldo is a murderer, do we let him go on to the next town and find a victim? Or for that matter, a victim here, before he leaves?

"We catch this guy. Prove he's responsible for murders, then we've actually done something important with our lives. There's more to my life than the bookstore. More to yours, Plebin, than a bad name and unemployment checks. And…well, in your case Jasmine, there is more to your life. You're beautiful, smart, and you're going places. But for all of us, wouldn't it be worthwhile to catch a killer?"

"If he is a killer," I said. "Maybe he just hates mannequins because they look better in their clothes than he does."

"Women's clothes?" Jasmine said.

"Maybe it's women's clothes he likes to wear," I said. "Thing is, we could end up making fools of ourselves, spend some time in jail, even."

"I'll chance it," Jasmine said.

"No you won't," I said. "It's over for you, Jasmine. Martha can do what she wants. But you and me, we're out of it."

Martha left.

Jasmine got out her sleeping bag and unrolled it, went to the bathroom to brush her teeth. I tried to stay awake and await my turn in there, but couldn't. Too tired. I lay down on the bed, noted vaguely that rain had stopped pounding on the apartment roof, and I fell immediately asleep.

I awoke later that night, early morning really, to the smell of more oncoming rain, and when I rolled over I could see flashes of lightning in the west.

The west. The direction of the dump. It was as if a storm was originating there, moving toward the town.

Melodrama. I loved it.

I rolled over and turned my head to the end table beside the bed, and when the lightning flashed I could see the mannequin head setting there, its face turned toward me, its strange, false eyes alight with the fire of the western lightning. The paint around the mannequin's neck appeared very damp in that light, like blood.

I threw my legs from beneath the covers and took hold of the head. The paint on its neck was wet in my hands. The humidity had caused it to run. I sat the head on the floor where I wouldn't have to look at it, got up to go to the bathroom and wash my hands.

Jasmine's sleeping bag was on the floor, but Jasmine wasn't in it. I went on to the bathroom, but she wasn't in there either. I turned on the light and washed my hands and felt a little weak. There was no place else to be in the apartment. I looked to see if she had taken her stuff and gone home, but she hadn't. The door that led out to the stairway was closed, but unlocked.

No question now. She had gone out.

I had an idea where, and the thought of it gave me a chill. I got dressed and went downstairs and beat on the bookstore, pressed my face against the windows, but there was no light or movement. I went around to the rear of the building to beat on the backdoor, to try and wake Martha up in her living quarters, but when I got there I didn't bother. I saw that Martha's van was gone from the carport and Jasmine's car was still in place.

I went back to my apartment and found Jasmine's car keys on the dresser and thought about calling the police, then thought better of it. Their memory of my body in the trunk stunt was a long one, and they might delay. Blow off the whole thing, in fact, mark it up to another aggravation from the boy who cried wolf. If I called Sam it wouldn't be any better. Twice in one night he'd be more likely to kill me than to help me. He was more worried about his pecker than a would-be killer, and he might not do anything at all.

Then I reminded myself it was a game of "What If" and that there wasn't anything to do, nothing to fear. I told myself the worst that could happen would be that Jasmine and Martha would annoy Waldo and make fools of themselves, and then it would all be over for good.

But those thoughts didn't help much, no matter how hard I tried to be convinced. I realized then that it hadn't been just the rain and the humidity that had awakened me. I had been thinking about what Martha said. About Waldo picking a victim later on if we didn't stop him. About the mannequins being a sort of warm-up for what he really wanted to do and would do.

It wasn't just a game anymore. Though I had no real evidence for it, I believed then what Jasmine and Martha believed.

Waldo the Great was a murderer.

I drove Jasmine's car out to the trailer park and pulled around where we had parked before, and sure enough, there was Martha's van. I pulled in behind it and parked.

I got out, mad as hell, went over to the van and pulled the driver's door open. There wasn't anyone inside. I turned then and looked through the bushes toward the trailer park. Lightning moved to the west and flicked and flared as if it were fireworks on a vibrating string. It lit up the trailer park, made what was obvious momentarily bright and harsh.

Waldo's truck and trailer were gone. There was nothing in its spot but tire tracks.

I tore through the bushes, fought back some blackberry vines, and made the long run over to the spot where Waldo's trailer had been.

I walked around in circles like an idiot. I tried to think, tried to figure what had happened.

I made up a possible scenario: Martha and Jasmine had come out here to spy on Waldo, and maybe Waldo, who kept weird hours, had gone out, and Jasmine and Martha had seen their chance and gone in.

Perhaps Waldo turned around and came back suddenly. Realized he'd forgotten his cigarettes, his money, something like that, and he found Jasmine and Martha snooping.

And if he was a murderer, and he found them, and they had discovered incriminating evidence…

Then what?

What would he have done with them?

It struck me then.

The dump. To dispose of the bodies.

God, the bodies.

My stomach soured and my knees shook. I raced back through the tangled growth, back to Jasmine's car. I pulled around the van and made the circle and whipped onto the road in front of the trailer park and headed for the dump at high speed. If a cop saw me, good. Let him chase me, on out to the dump.

Drops of rain had begun to fall as I turned on the road to the dump. Lightning was crisscrossing more rapidly and more heatedly than before. Thunder rumbled.

I killed the lights and eased into the dump, using the lightning flashes as my guide, and there, stretched across the dump road, blocking passage, was Waldo's trailer. The truck the trailer was fastened to was off the road and slightly turned in my direction, ready to leave the dump. I didn't see any movement. The only sounds were from the throbbing thunder and the hissing lightning. Raindrops were falling faster.

I jerked the car into park in front of the trailer and got out and ran over there, then hesitated. I looked around and spotted a hunk of wood lying in some garbage. I yanked it out and ran back to the trailer and jerked open the door. The smell of dogs was thick in the air.

Lightning flashed in the open doorway and through the thin curtains at the windows. I saw Martha lying on the floor, face down, a meat cleaver in the small of her back. I saw that the bookshelves on the wall were filled with Harlequin Romances, and below them nailed onto the shelves, were strange hunks of what in the lightning flashes looked like hairy leather.

Darkness.

A beat.

Lighting flash.

I looked around, didn't see Waldo hiding in the shadows with another meat cleaver.

Darkness again.

I went over to Martha and knelt beside her, touched her shoulder. She raised her head, tried to jerk around and grab me, but was too weak. "Sonofabitch," she said.

"It's me," I said.

"Plebin," she said. "Waldo nailed me a few times... Thinks I'm dead... He's got Jasmine. Tried to stop him... Couldn't... You got to. They're out...there."

I took hold of the cleaver and jerked it out of her back and tossed it on the floor.

"Goddamn," Martha said, and almost did a push up, but lay back down. "Could have gone all day without that... Jasmine. The nut's got her. Go on!"

Martha closed her eyes and lay still. I touched her neck. Still a pulse. But I couldn't do anything now. I had to find Jasmine. Had to hope the bastard hadn't done his work.

I went out of the trailer, around to the other side, looked out over the dump. The light wasn't good, but it was good enough that I could see them immediately. Jasmine, her back to me, upside down, nude, was tied to the inside of the nearest derrick, hung up like a goat for the slaughter. Waldo stood at an angle, facing her, holding something in his hand.

Lightning strobed, thunder rumbled. The poodles were running about, barking and leaping. Two of the dogs were fucking out next to the derrick, flopping tongues. The great black hammerhead of the oil pump rose up and went down. Fires glowed from beneath debris and reflected on the metal bars of the derrick and the well pump, and when the rain hit the fires beneath the garbage they gave up white smoke and the smoke rolled in the wind like great balls of cotton, tumbled over Jasmine and Waldo and away.

Waldo swung what he had in his hand at Jasmine. Caught her across the neck with it. Her body twitched. I let out a yell that was absorbed by a sudden peal of thunder and a slash of lightning.

I started running, yelling as I went.

Waldo slashed at Jasmine again, and then he heard me yelling. He stepped to the side and stared at me, surprised. I ran up the little rise that led to the derrick before he could get it together, and as I ducked under a bar on the derrick, he dropped what he was holding.

A long paint brush.

It fell next to a can of dark paint. Rain plopped in the paint and black balls of paint flew up in response and fell down again. One of the dogs jumped the can of paint for no reason I could determine and ran off into the rain.

Jasmine made a noise like a smothered cough. Out of the corner of my eye I could see a strip of thick, gray tape across her mouth, and where Waldo had slashed her neck with the brush was a band of paint, dissolving in the rain, running down her neck, over her cheeks and into her eyes and finally her hair, like blood in a black-and-white movie.

Waldo reached behind his back and came back with a knife. The edge of the blade caught a flash of lightning and gave a wicked wink. Waldo's face was full of expression this time, as if he had saved all his passion for this moment.

"Come on, asshole," I said. "Come on. Cut me."

He leapt forward, very fast. The knife went out and caught me across the chest as I jumped back and hit my head on a metal runner of the derrick. I felt something warm on my chest. Shit. I hadn't really wanted him to cut me. He was a fast little bastard.

I didn't invite him to do that again.

I cocked my piece of wood and let him get as close as I could allow without fear taking over, then I ducked under the metal runner and he ducked under it after me, poking straight out with the knife.

I swung at him, and the wood, rotten, possibly termite ridden, came apart close to my hand and went sailing and crumbling across the dump.

Waldo and I watched the chunk of wood until it hit the dirt by the derrick and exploded into a half dozen fragments.

Waldo turned his attention to me again, smiled, and came fast. I jumped backwards and my feet went out from under me and dogs yelped.

The lover mutts. I had backed over them while they were screwing. I looked up between my knees and saw the dogs turned butt to butt, hung up, and then

I looked higher, and there was Waldo and his knife. I rolled and came up and grabbed a wet cardboard box of something and threw it. It struck Waldo in the chest and what was in the box flew out and spun along the wet ground. It was half a mannequin torso.

"You're ruining everything," Waldo said.

I glanced down and saw one of the mannequin legs Sam had pulled from a box and tossed. I grabbed the leg and cocked it on my shoulder like a baseball bat.

"Come on, asshole," I said. "Come on. Let's see if I can put one over the fence with you."

He went nuts then, dove for me. The knife jabbed out, fast and blurry.

I swatted. My swing hit his arm and his knife hand went wide and opened up and the knife flew into a pile of garbage and out of sight.

Waldo and I both looked at where it had disappeared.

We looked at one another. It was my turn to smile.

He staggered back and I followed, rotating the leg, trying to pick my shot.

He darted to his right, dipped, came up clutching one of the mannequin's arms. He held it by the wrist and smiled. He rotated it the way I had the leg.

We came together, leg and arm swinging. He swung at my head. I blocked with the leg and swung at his knees. He jumped the swing, kicked beautifully while airborne, hit me in the chin and knocked my head back, but I didn't go down.

Four of the poodles came out of nowhere, bouncing and barking beside us, and one of them got hold of my pants leg and started tugging. I hit at him. He yelped. Waldo hit me with the arm across the shoulder. I hit him back with the leg and kicked out and shook the poodle free.

Waldo laughed.

Another of the poodles got hold of his pants legs.

Waldo quit laughing. "Not me, you dumb ingrate!"

Waldo whacked the poodle hard with the arm. It let go, ran off a distance, whirled, took a defiant stance and barked.

I hit Waldo then. It was a good shot, clean and clear and sweet with the sound of the wind, but he got his shoulder up and blocked the blow and he only lost a bit of shirt sleeve, which popped open like a flower blossoming.

"Man, I just bought this shirt," he said.

I swung high to his head and let my body go completely around with the swing, twisting on the balls of my feet, and as I came back around, I lowered the blow and hit him in the ribs. He bellowed and tripped over something, went down and dropped his mannequin arm. Three poodles leapt on his chest and one grabbed at his ankle. Behind him, the other two were still hung up, tongues dangling happily. They were waiting for the seasons to change. The next ice age. It didn't matter. They were in no hurry.

I went after Waldo, closing for the kill. He wiped the poodles off his chest with a sweep of his arm and grabbed the mannequin arm beside him, took it by the thick end and stuck it at me as I was about to lower the boom on him. The tips of the mannequin's fingers caught me in the family jewels and a moment later a pain went through me that wasn't quite as bad as being hit by a truck. But it didn't keep me from whacking him over the head with everything I had. The mannequin leg fragmented in my hands and Waldo screamed and rolled and came up and charged me, his forehead streaked with blood, a poodle dangling from one pants leg by the teeth. The poodle stayed with him as he leaped and grabbed my legs at the knees and drove his head into my abdomen and knocked me back into a heap of smoking garbage. The smoke rose up around us and closed over us like a pod and with it came a stink that brought bile to my throat and I felt heat on my back and something sharp like glass and I yelled and rolled with Waldo and the growling poodle and out of the corner of my eye, in mid-roll, I saw another of the poodles had caught on fire in the garbage and was running about like a low-flying comet. We tumbled over some more junk, and over again. Next thing I knew Waldo had rolled away and was up and over me, had hold of six feet of two-by-four with a couple of nails hanging out of the end.

"Goodnight," Waldo said.

The board came around and the tips of the nails caught some light from the garbage fires, made them shine like animal eyes in the dark. The same light made Waldo look like the Devil. Then the side of my neck exploded. The pain and shock were like things that had burrowed inside me to live. They owned me. I lay where I was, unable to move, the board hung up in my neck. Waldo tugged, but the board wouldn't come free. He put a foot on my chest and worked the board back and forth. The nails in my neck made a noise like someone trying to whistle through gapped teeth. I tried to lift a hand and grab at the board, but I was too weak. My hands fluttered at my sides as if I were petting the ground. My head wobbled back and forth with Waldo's efforts. I could see him through a blur. His teeth were clenched and spittle was foaming across his lips.

I found my eyes drifting to the top of the oil derrick, perhaps in search of a heavenly choir. Lightning flashed rose-red and sweat-stain yellow in the distance. My eyes fell back to Waldo. I watched him work. My body started trembling as if electrically charged.

Eventually Waldo worked the nails out of my neck. He stood back and took a breath. Getting that board loose was hard work. I noted in an absent kind of way that the poodle had finally let go of his ankle and had wandered off. I felt blood gushing out of my neck, maybe as much as the oil well was pumping. I thought sadly of what was going to happen to Jasmine.

My eyelids were heavy and I could hardly keep them open. A poodle came up and sniffed my face. Waldo finally got his breath. He straddled me and cocked the board and positioned his features for the strike; his face showed plenty of expression now. I wanted to kick up between his legs and hit him in the balls, but I might as well have wanted to be in Las Vegas.

"You're dog food," Waldo said, and just before he swung, my eyes started going out of focus like a movie camera on the fade, but I caught fuzzy movement behind him and there was a silver snake leaping through the air and the snake bit Waldo in the side of the head and he went away from me as if jerked aside by ropes.

My eyes focused again, slowly, and there was Martha, wobbling, holding the golf club properly, end of the swing position. She might have been posing for a photo. The striking end of the club was framed beautifully against the dark sky. I hadn't realized just how pretty her mustache was, all beaded up there in the firelight and the occasional bright throb of the storm.

Martha lowered the club and leaned on it. All of us were pretty tuckered out tonight.

Martha looked at Waldo who lay face down in the trash, not moving, his hand slowly letting loose of the two-by-four, like a dying octopus relaxing its grip on a sunken ship timber.

"Fore, motherfucker," she said, then she slid down the golf club to her knees. Blood ran out from beneath her wool cap. Things went fuzzy for me again. I closed my eyes as a red glow bloomed to my left, where Waldo's trailer was. It began to rain harder. A poodle licked my bleeding neck.

When I awoke in the hospital I felt very stiff, and I could feel that my shoulders were slightly burned. No flesh missing back there, though, just a feeling akin to mild sunburn. I weakly raised an arm to the bandage on my neck and put it down again. That nearly wore me out.

Jasmine and Martha and Sam came in shortly thereafter. Martha was on crutches and minus her wool cap. Her head was bandaged. Her mustache was clean and well groomed, as if with a toothbrush.

"How's the boy?" Sam said.

"You'd listened, could have been a lot better." I said.

"Yeah, well, the boy that cried wolf and all that," Sam said.

"Jasmine, baby," I said, "how are you?"

"I'm all right. No traumatic scars. Martha got us both out of there."

"I had to rest awhile," Martha said, "but all's well that ends well. You did nearly bleed to death."

"What about you?" I said. "You look pretty good after all that."

"Hey," Martha said, "I've got enough fat and muscle on me to take a few meat cleaver blows. He'd have done better to drive a truck over me. When he caught us sneaking around his trailer, he came up behind me and clubbed me in the head with a meat cleaver before I knew he was there, or I'd have kicked his ass into next Tuesday. After he hit me in the head he worked on me some more when I went down. He should have stuck to my head instead of pounding me in the back. That just tired me out for a while."

"Daddy, there were all kinds of horrid things in his trailer. Photographs, and...there were some pieces of women."

"Pussies," Martha said. "He'd tanned them. Had one on a belt. I figure he put it on and wore it now and then. One of those pervert types."

"What about old Waldo?" I asked.

"I made a hole-in-one on that sonofabitch," Martha said, "but looks like he'll recover. And though the trailer burned down, enough evidence survived to hang him. If we're lucky they'll give his ass the hot needle. Right, Sam?"

"That's right," Sam said.

"Whoa," I said. "How'd the trailer burn down?"

"One of the poodles caught on fire in the garbage," Jasmine said. "Poor thing. It ran back to the trailer and the door was open and it ran inside and jumped up in the bed, burned that end of the trailer up."

"Ruined a bunch of Harlequin Romances," Martha said. "Wish the little fuck had traded those in too. Might have made us a few dollars. Thing is, most of the photographs and the leather pussies survived, so we got the little shit by the balls."

I looked at Jasmine and smiled.

She smiled back, reached out and patted my shoulder. "Oh, yeah," she said, and opened her purse and took out an envelope. "This is for you. From Mama."

"Open it," I said.

Jasmine opened it and handed it to me. I took it. It was a get well card that had been sent to Connie at some time by one of her friends. She had blatantly marked out her name, and the senders name, had written under the canned sentiment printed there, "Get well, SLOWLY."

"I'm beginning to think me and your Mom aren't going to patch things up," I said.

"Afraid not," Jasmine said.

"Good reason to move then," Martha said. "I'm getting out of this one-dog town. I'll level with you. I got a little inheritance I live off of. An uncle left it to me. Said in the will, since I was the ugliest one in the family, I'd need it."

"That's awful," Jasmine said. "Don't you believe that."

"The hell it's awful," Martha said. "I didn't have that money put back to live on, me and those damn books would be on the street. Ugly has its compensations. I've decided to start a bookstore in LaBorde, and I'm gonna open me a private investigations agency with it. Nice combo, huh? Read a little. Snoop a little. And you two, you want, can be my operatives. You full time, Plebin, and Jasmine, you can work part time while you go to college. What do you think?"

"Do we get a discount on paperbacks?" I asked.

Martha considered that. "I don't think so," she said.

"Air conditioning?"

"I don't think so."

"Let me consider it," I said.

Suddenly, I couldn't keep my eyes open.

Jasmine gently placed her hand on my arm. "Rest now," she said.

And I did.

White Mule, Spotted Pig

FRANK'S PAPA, THE summer of nineteen hundred and nine, told him right before he died that he had a good chance to win the annual Camp Rapture mule race. He told Frank this 'cause he needed money to keep getting drunk, and he wasn't about to ride no mule himself, fat as he was. If the old man had known he was about to die, Frank figured he would have saved his breath on the race talk and asked for whisky instead, maybe a chaw. But as it was, he said it, and it planted in Frank's head the desire to ride and win.

Frank hated that about himself. Once a thing got into his head he couldn't derail it. He was on the track then, and had to see it to the end. Course, that could be a good trait, but problem was, and Frank knew it, the only things that normally caught up in his head like that and pushed him were bad ideas. Even if he could sense their badness, he couldn't seem to stop their running forward and dragging him with them. He also thought his mama had been right when she told him once that their family was like shit on shoes, the stink of it followed them wherever they went.

But this idea. Winning a mule race. Well, that had some good sides to it. Mainly money.

He thought about what his papa said, and how he said it, and then how, within a few moments, the old man grabbed the bed sheets, moaned once, dribbled some drool, and was gone to where ever it was he was supposed to go, probably a stool next to the devil at fireside.

He didn't leave Frank nothing but an old run down place with a bit of dried out corn crop, a mule, a horse with one foot in the grave and the other on a slick spot. And his very own shit to clean out of the sheets, 'cause when the old man let go and departed, he left Frank that present, which was the only kind he had ever given. Something dirty. Something painful. Something shitty.

Frank had to burn the mattress and set fire to the bed clothes, so there really wasn't any really cleaning about it. Then he dug a big hole, and cut roots to do it. Next he had to wrap the old man's naked body in a dirty canvas and put him down and cover him up. It took some work, 'cause the old man must have weighed three hundred pounds, and he wasn't one inch taller than five three if he was wearing boots with dried cow shit on the heels and paper tucked inside them to jack his height. Dragging him along on his dead ass from the house had damn near caused one of Frank's balls to swell up and pop out.

Finished with the burying, Frank leaned against a sickly sweet gum tree and rolled himself a smoke, and thought: Shit, I should have dragged the old man over here on the tarp. Or maybe hitched him up to the mule and dragged his naked ass face down through the dirt. That would have been the way to go, not pulling his guts out.

But, it was done now, and as always, he had used his brain late in the game.

Frank scratched a match on a thumbnail and leaned on a sick sweet gum and smoked and considered. It wasn't that he was all that fond of his old man, but damn if he still didn't in some way want to make him proud, or rather be proud to his memory. He thought: Funny, him not being worth a damn, and me still wanting to please him. Funnier yet, considering the old man used to beat him like a tom-tom. Frank had seen him knock Mama down once and put his foot on the back of her neck and use his belt to beat her ass while he cussed her for having burned the cornbread. It wasn't the only beating she got, but it was damn sure the champion.

It was shortly after that she decamped with the good horse, a bag of corn meal, some dried meat and a butcher knife. She also managed, with what Frank thought must have been incredible aim, to piss in one of his old man's liquor jugs. This was discovered by the old man after he took a good strong jolt of refreshment.

Papa had ridden out after her on the mule but hadn't found her, which wasn't a surprise, because the only thing Papa had been good at tracking was a whisky bottle or some whore, provided she was practically tied down and didn't cost much. He probably tracked the whores he messed with by their stench.

Back from the hunt, drunk and pissed and empty handed, Papa had said it was bad enough Frank's mama was a horse and meal thief, but at least she hadn't taken the mule, and frankly, she wasn't that good a cook anyhow.

The mule's name was Rupert, and he could run like his tail was on fire. Papa had actually thought about the mule as a contender for a while, and had put out a little money to have him trained by Leroy, who though short in many departments, and known for having been caught fucking a goat by a half-dozen hunters, was pretty good with mules and horses.

The night after Frank buried his pa, he got in some corn squeezings, and got drunk enough to imagine weasels crawling out from under the floorboards. To clear his head and to relieve his bladder, he went out to do something on his father's grave that would never pass for prayers. He stood there watering, thinking about the prize money and what he would do with it. He looked at the house and the barn and the lot, out to where he could see the dead corn standing in rows like dehydrated soldiers. The house leaned to the left, and one of the windowsills was near on the ground. When he slept at night, he slept on a bed with one side jacked up with flat rocks so that it was high enough and even enough he wouldn't roll out of bed. The barn had one side missing and the land was all rutted from run off.

With the exception of the hill where they grazed their bit of stock, the place was void of grass, and all it brought to mind was brown things and dead things, though there were a few bedraggled chickens who wandered the yard like wild Indians, taking what they could find, even eating one another should one of them keel over dead from starvation or exhaustion. Frank, on more than one occasion, had seen a half-dozen chickens go at a weak one lying on the ground, tearing him apart like a dozen miners at a free lunch table.

Frank smoked his cigarette and thought if he could win that race, he would move away from this shit pile. Sell it to some fool. Move into town and get a job that would keep him. Never again would he look up a mule's ass or fit his hands around the handles on a plow. He was thinking on this while looking up the hill at his mule, Rupert.

The hill was surrounded by a rickety rail fence within which the mule resided primarily on the honor system. At the top of the hill was a bunch of oaks and pines and assorted survivor trees. As Frank watched the sun fall down behind the hill, it seemed as if the limbs of the trees wadded together into a crawling shadow, way the wind blew them and mixed them up. Rupert was clearly outlined near a pathetic persimmon tree from which the mule had stripped the persimmons and much of the leaves.

Frank thought Rupert looked quite noble up there, his mule ears standing high in outline against the redness of the sun behind the dark trees. The world seemed strange and beautiful, as if just created. In that moment Frank felt much older than his years and not so fresh as the world seemed, but ancient and worn like the old Indian pottery he had found while plowing through what had once been great Indian mounds. And now, even as he watched, he noted the sun seemed to darken, as if it were a hot wound turning black from infection. The wind cooled and began to whistle. Frank turned his head to the north and watched as clouds pushed across the fading sky. In an instant, all the light was gone and there were just shadows, spitting and twisting in the heavens and filling the hard-blowing wind with the aroma of wet dirt.

When Frank turned again to note Rupert, the mule was still there, but was now little more than a peculiar shape next to the ragged persimmon tree. Had Frank not known it was the mule, he might well have mistaken it for a peculiar rise in the terrain, or a fallen tree lying at an odd angle.

The storm was from the north and blowing west. Thunder boomed and lightning cracked in the dirty sky like snap beans, popped and fizzled like a doused campfire. In that moment, the shadow Frank knew to be Rupert, lifted its head, and pointed its dark muzzle toward the sky, as if in defiance. A bolt of lightning, crooked as a dog's hind leg, jumped from the heavens and dove for the mule, striking him a perfect white-hot blow on the tip of his nose, making him glow, causing Frank to think that he had in fact seen the inside of the mule light up with all its bones in a row. Then Rupert's head exploded, his body blazed, the persimmon leaped to flames, and the mule fell over in a swirl of heavenly fire and a cannon shot of flying mule shit. The corpse caught a patch of dried grass a blaze. The flames burned in a perfect circle around the corpse and blinked out, leaving a circle of smoke rising skyward.

"Goddamn," Frank said. "Shit."

The clouds split open, and pissed all over the hillside, and not a drop, not one goddamn drop, was thrown away from the hill. The rain just covered that spot, put out the mule and the persimmon tree with a sizzling sound, then passed on, taking darkness, rain, and cool wind with it.

Frank stood there for a long time, looking up the hill, watching his hundred dollars crackle and smoke. Pretty soon the smell from the grilled mule floated down the hill and filled his nostrils.

"Shit," Frank said. "Shit. Shit. Shit."

Late morning, when Frank could finally drag himself out of bed, he went out and caught the horse, Dobbin, hitched him to a single tree and fastened on some chains, and drove him out to where the mule lay. He hooked one of the mule's hind legs to the rigging and Dobbin dragged the corpse up the hill, between the trees, to the other side. Frank figured he'd just let the body rot there, on the other side of the hill where there was less chance of the wind carrying the smell.

After that, Frank moped around for a few days, drank enough to see weasels again, and then had an idea. His idea was to seek out Leroy, who had been

Rupert's trainer. See if he could work a deal with him.

Frank rode Dobbin over to Leroy's place, which was even nastier than his own due to the yard being full not only of chickens and goats, but children. Leroy had five of them, and when Frank rode up, he saw them right away, running about, raising hell in the yard, one of them minus pants, his little johnson flopping about like a grub worm on a hot griddle. Leroy's old lady was on the porch, fat and greasy with her hair tied up. She was yelling at the kids and telling them how she was going to kill them and feed them to the chickens. One of the boys, the ten-year-old, ran by the porch whooping, and the Mrs., moving deftly for such a big woman, scrambled to the edge of the porch, stuck her foot out, caught him one just above the waist and sent him tumbling. He went down hard. She laughed like a lunatic. The boy got up with a bloody nose and ran off across the yard and into the woods, screaming.

Frank climbed down from Dobbin and went over to Leroy who was sitting on a bucket in the front yard whittling a green limb with a knife big enough to sword fight. Leroy was watching his son retreat into the greenery. As Frank came up, leading Dobbin, Leroy said, "Does that all the time. Sometimes, though, she'll throw something at him. Good thing wasn't nothing lying about. She's got a pretty good throwin' arm on her. Seen her hit a seed salesman with a tossed frying pan from the porch there to about where the road meets the property. Knocked him down and knocked his hat off. Scattered his seed samples, which the chickens ate. Must have laid there for an hour afore he got up and wandered off. Forgot his hat. Got it on my head right now, though I had to put me some newspaper in the band to make it fit."

Wasn't nothing Frank could say to that, so he said, "Leroy, Rupert got hit by lightning. Right in the head."

"The head?"

"Wouldn't have mattered had it been the ass. It killed him deader than a post and burned him up."

"Damn. That there is a shame," Leroy said, and stopped whittling. He pushed the seed salesman's hat up on his forehead to reveal some forks of greasy brown hair. Leroy studied Frank. "Is there something I can do for you? Or you come around to visit?"

"I'm thinking you might could help me get a mule and get back in the race."

"Mules cost."

"I know. Thought we might could come up with something. And if we could, and we won, I'd give you a quarter of the prize money."

"I get a quarter for grooming folks' critters in town."

"I mean a quarter of a hundred. Twenty-five dollars."

"I see. Well, I am your man for animals. I got a knack. I can talk to them like I was one of them. Except for chickens. Ain't no one can talk to chickens."

"They're birds."

"That there is the problem. They ain't animal enough."

"I know you run in the circles of them that own or know about mules." Frank said. "Why I thought you maybe could help me."

Leroy took off the seed salesman's hat, put it on his knee, threw his knife in the dirt, let the whittling stick fall from his hand. "I could sneak up on an idea or two. Old Man Torrence, he's got a mule he's looking to sale. And by his claim, it's a runner. He ain't never ridden it himself, but he's had it ridden. Says it can run."

"There's that buying stuff again. I ain't got no real money."

"Takes money to make money."

"Takes money to have money."

Leroy put the seed salesman's hat back on. "You know, we might could ask him if he'd rent out his mule. Race is a ways off yet, so we could get some good practice in. You being about a hundred and twenty-five pounds, you're light enough to make a good rider."

"I've ridden a lot. I was ready on Rupert, reckon I can get ready on another mule."

"Deal we might have to make is, we won the race, we bought the mule afterwards. That might be the way he'd do it."

"Buy the mule?"

"At a fair price."

"How fair?"

"Say twenty-five dollars."

"That's a big slice of the prize money. And a mule for twenty-five, that's cheap."

"I know Torrence got the mule cheap. Fella that owed him made a deal. Besides, times is hard. So they're selling cheap. Cost more, we can make extra money on side bets. Bet on ourselves. Or if we don't think we got a chance, we bet against ourselves."

"I don't know. We lose, it could be said we did it on purpose."

"I can get someone to bet for us."

"Only if we bet to win. I ain't never won nothing or done nothing right in my life, and I figure this here might be my chance."

"You gettin' Jesus?"

"I'm gettin' tired," Frank said.

There are no real mountains in East Texas, and only a few hills of consequence, but Old Man Torrence lived at the top of a big hill that was called with a kind of braggarts lie, Barrow Dog Mountain. Frank had no idea who Barrow or Dog were, but that was what the big hill had been called for as long as he remembered, probably well before he was born. There was a ridge at the top of it that overlooked the road below. Frank found it an impressive sight as he and Leroy rode in on Dobbin, he at the reins, Leroy riding double behind him.

It was pretty on top of the hill too. The air smelled good, and flowers grew all about in red, blue and yellow blooms and the cloudless sky was so blue you felt as if a great lake were falling down from the heavens. Trees fanned out bright green on either side of the path, and near the top, on a flat section, was Old Man Torrence's place. It was made of cured logs, and he had a fine chicken coop that was built straight and true. There were hog pens and a nice barn of thick, cured logs with a roof that had all of its roofing slats. There was a sizable garden that rolled along the top of the hill, full of tall bright green corn stalks, so tall they shaded the rows between them. There was no grass between the rows, and the dirt there looked freshly laid by. Squash and all manner of vegetables exploded out of the ground alongside the corn, and there were little clumps of beans and peas growing in long pretty rows.

In a large pen next to the barn was a fifteen-hands-high chocolate-colored mule, prettiest thing Frank had ever seen in the mule flesh department. Its ears stood up straight, and it gave Frank and Leroy a snort as they rode in.

"He's a big one," Leroy said.

"Won't he be slow, being that big?" Frank asked.

"Big mule's also got big muscles, he's worked right. And he looks to have been worked right. Got enough muscles, he can haul some freight. Might be fast as Rupert."

"Sure faster right now," Frank said.

As they rode up, they saw Old Man Torrence on the front porch with his wife and three kids, two boys and a girl. Torrence was a fat, ruddy-faced man. His wife was a little plump, but pretty. His kids were all nice looking and they, unlike Leroy's kids, had their hair combed, and looked clean. Coming closer, Frank could see that none of the kids looked whacked on. They were laughing at something the mother was saying. It certainly was different than from his own upbringing, different from Leroy's place. Wasn't anyone tripping anyone, cussing, tossing frying pans, threatening to cripple one another or put out an eye. Thinking on this, Frank felt something twist around inside of him like some kind of serpent looking for a rock to slide under.

He and Leroy got off Dobbin and tied him to a little hitching post that was built out front of the house, took off their hats, and walked up to the steps.

After being offered lemonade, which they turned down, Old Man Torrence came off the porch, ruffling one of his kid's hair as he did. He smiled back at his wife, and then walked with Frank and Leroy out toward the mule pen, Leroy explaining what they had in mind.

"You want to rent my mule? What if I wanted to run him?"

"Well, I don't know," Leroy said. "It hadn't occurred to me you might. You ain't never before, though I heard tell he was a mule could be run."

"It's a good mule," Torrence said. "Real fast."

"You've ridden him?" Frank asked.

"No. I haven't had the pleasure. But my brother and his boys have. They borrow him from time to time, and they thought on running him this year. Nothing serious. Just a thought. They say he can really cover ground."

"Frank here," Leroy said, "plans on entering the mule race, and we would like to rent your mule. If we win, we could give you a bit of the prize money. What say we rent him for ten, and if he wins, we give you another fifteen. That way you pick up twenty-five dollars."

Frank was listening to all this, thinking this purse I haven't won yet is getting smaller and smaller.

"And if he don't win?" Torrence asked.

"You've made ten dollars," Leroy said.

"And I got to take the chance my mule might go lame or get hurt or some such. I don't know. Ten dollars, that's not a lot of money for what you're asking. It ain't even your mule."

"Which is why we're offering the ten dollars," Leroy said.

They went over and leaned on the fence and looked at the great mule, watched his muscles roll beneath his chocolate flesh as he trotted nervously about the pen.

"He looks excitable," Frank said.

"Robert E. Lee has just got a lot of energy is all," Torrence said.

"He's named Robert E. Lee?" Frank asked.

"Best damn general ever lived. Tell you boys what. You give me twenty-five, and another twenty-five if he wins, and you got a deal."

"But I give you that, and Leroy his share, I don't have nothing hardly left."

"You ain't got nothing at all right now," Torrence said.

"How's about," Leroy said, "we do it this way. We give you fifteen, and another fifteen if he wins. That's thirty. Now that's fair for a rented mule. Hell, we might could go shopping, buy a mule for twenty-five, and even if he don't win, we got a mule. He don't race worth a damn, we could put him to plow."

Old Man Torrence pursed his lips. "That sounds good. All right," he said sticking out his hand, "deal."

"Well, now," Frank said, not taking the hand. "Before I shake on that, I'd like to make sure he can run. Let me ride him."

Old Man Torrence withdrew his hand and wiped it on his pants as if something had gotten on his palm. "I reckon I could do that, but seeing how we don't have a deal yet, and ain't no fifteen dollars has changed hands, how's about I ride him for you. So you can see."

Frank and Leroy agreed, and watched from the fence as Torrence got the equipment and saddled up Robert E. Lee. Torrence walked Robert E. Lee out of the lot, and onto a pasture atop the hill, where the overhang was. The pasture was huge and the grass was as green as Ireland. It was all fenced in with barb wire strung tight between deeply planted posts.

"I'll ride him around in a loop. Once slow, and then real fast toward the edge of the overhang there, then cut back before we get there. I ain't got a pocket watch, so you'll have to be your own judge."

Torrence swung into the saddle. "You boys ready?"

"Let'er rip," Leroy said.

Old Man Torrence gave Robert E. Lee his heels. The mule shot off so fast that Old Man Torrence's hat flew off, and Leroy, in sympathy, took hold of the brim of the seed salesman's hat, as if Robert E. Lee's lunge might blow it off his head.

"Goddamn," Leroy said. "Look how low that mule is to the ground. He's goin' have the grass touching his belly."

And so the mule ran, and as it neared the barb wire fence, Old Man Torrence gave the mule a tug, to turn him. But, Robert E. Lee wasn't having any. The critter's speed picked up, and the barb wire fence came closer.

Leroy said, "Uh oh."

Robert E. Lee hit the fence hard. So hard it caused his head to dip over the top wire and his ass to rise up as if he might be planning a head stand. Over the mule flipped, tearing loose the fence, causing a strand of wire to snap and strike Old Man Torrence just as he was thrown ahead of the tumbling mule. Over the overhang. Out of sight. The mule did in fact do a headstand, landed hard that way, its hind legs high in the air, wiggling. For a moment, it seemed as if he might hang there, and then, Robert E. Lee lost his headstand and went over after his owner.

"Damn," Leroy said.

"Damn," Frank said.

They both ran toward the broken fence. When they got there Frank hesitated, not able to look. He glanced away, back across the bright green field.

Leroy scooted up to the cliff's edge and took a gander, studied what he saw for a long time.

"Well?" Frank said, finally turning his head back to Leroy.

"Robert E. Lee just met his Gettysburg. And Old Man Torrence is somewhere between Gettysburg and Robert E. Lee… Actually, you can't tell which is which. Mule, Gettysburg, or Old Man Torrence. It's all kind of bunched up."

When Frank and Leroy got down there, which took some considerable time, as they worked their way down a little trail on foot, they discovered that Old Man Torrence had been lucky in a fashion. He had landed in sand, and the force of Robert E. Lee's body had driven him down deep into it, his nose poking up and out enough to take in air. Robert E. Lee was as dead as a three-penny nail, and his tail was stuck up in the air and bent over like a flag that had been broken at the staff. The wind moved the hairs on it a little.

Frank and Leroy went about digging Old Man Torrence out, starting first with his head so he could breathe better. When Torrence had spat enough sand out of his mouth, he looked up and said, "You sonsabitches. This is your fault."

"Our fault?" Leroy said. "You was riding him."

"You goat fucking bastard-child, get me out of here."

Leroy's body sagged a little. "I knew that was gonna get around good. Ain't nobody keeps a secret. There was only that one time too, and them hunters had to come up on me."

They dug Torrence out from under the mule, and Frank went up the trail and got Old Dobbin and rode to the doctor. When Frank got back with the sawbones, Torrence was none the happier to see him. Leroy had gone off to the side to sit by himself, which made Frank think maybe the business about the goat had come up.

Old Man Torrence was mostly all right, but he blamed Frank and Leroy, especially Leroy, from then on. And he walked in a way that when he stepped with his right leg, it always looked as if he were about to bend over and tie his shoe. Even in later years, when Frank saw him, he went out of his way to avoid him, and Leroy dodged him like the small pox, not wanting to hear reference to the goat.

But in that moment in time, the important thing to Frank was simply that he was still without a mule. And the race was coming closer.

That night, as Frank lay in his sagging bed, looking out from it at the slanted wall of the room, listening to the crickets saw their fiddles both outside and inside the house, he closed his eyes and remembered how Old Man Torrence's place had looked. He saw himself sitting with the pretty plump wife and the clean, polite kids. Then he saw himself with the wife inside that pretty house, on the bed, and he imagined that for a long time.

It was a pleasant thought, the wife and the bed, but even more pleasant was imagining Torrence's place as his. All that greenery and high growing corn and blooming squash and thick pea and bean vines dripping with vegetables. The house and the barn and the pasture. And in his dream, the big mule, alive, not yet a confusion of bones and flesh and fur, the tail a broken flag.

He thought then of his mother, and the only way he could remember her was with her hair tied back and her face sweaty and both of her eyes blacked. That was how she had looked the last time he had seen her, right before she run off with a horse and some corn meal and a butcher knife. He wondered where she was, and if she now lived in a place where the buildings were straight and the grass was green and the corn was tall.

After a while he got up and peed out the window, and smelled the aroma of other nights drifting up from the ground he had poisoned with his water, and thought: I am better than Papa. He just peed in the corner of the room and shit out the window, splattering it all down the side of the house. I don't do that. I pee out the window, but I don't shit, and I don't pee in the corner. That's a step up. I go outside for the messy business. And if I had a good house I'd use the slop jar. I'd go to the privy.

Thinking on all this didn't stop him from finishing his pee. Peeing was the one thing he was really good at. He could piss like a horse and from a goodly distance. He had even won money on his ability. It was the one thing his father had been proud of. "My son, Frank. He can piss like a goddamn horse. Get it out, Frank. Show them."

And he would.

But, compared to what he wanted out of life, his ability to throw water from his johnson didn't seem all that wonderful right then.

Frank thought he ought to call a halt to his racing plans, but like so many of his ideas, he couldn't let it go. It blossomed inside of him until he was filled with it. Then he was obsessed with an even wilder plan. A story he had heard came back to him, and ran round inside his head like a greased pig.

He would find the White Mule and capture it and run it. It was a mule he could have for free, and it was known to be fast, if wild. And, of course, he would have to capture its companion, The Spotted Pig. Though, he figured, by now, the pig was no longer a pig, but a hog, and the mule would be three, maybe four years old.

If they really existed.

It was a story he had heard for the last three years or so, and it was told for the truth by them who told him, his papa among them. But if drinking made him see weasels oozing out of the floorboards, it might have made Papa see white mules and spotted pigs on parade. But the story wasn't just Papa's story. He had heard it from others and it went like this:

Once upon a time, there was this pretty white mule with pink eyes, and the mule was fine and strong and set to the plow early on, but he didn't take to it. Not at all. But the odder part of the story was that the mule took up with a farm pig, and they became friends. There was no explaining it. It happened now and then, a horse or mule adopting their own pet, and that was what had happened with the white mule and the spotted pig.

When Frank had asked his papa, why would a mule take up with a pig, his father had said: "Ain't no explaining. Why the hell did I take up with your mother?"

Frank thought the question went the other way, but the tale fascinated him, and that night his papa was just drunk enough to be in a good mood. Another pint swallowed, he'd be kicking Frank's ass or his mama's. But he pushed while he could, trying to get the goods on the tale, since outside of worrying about dying corn and sagging barns, there wasn't that much in life that excited him.

The story his papa told him was the farmer who owned the mule, and no one could ever put a name to who that farmer was, had supposedly found the mule wouldn't work if the pig wasn't around, leading him between the rows. The pig was in front, the mule plowed fine. The pig wasn't there, the mule wouldn't plow.

This caused the farmer to come up with an even better idea. What would the mule do if the pig was made to run? The farmer got the mule all tacked up, then had one of his boys put the pig out front of the mule and swat it with a knotted plow line, and away went the pig and away went the white mule. The pig pretty soon veered off, but the mule, once set to run, couldn't stop, and would race so fast that the only way it halted was when it was tuckered out.

Then it would go back to the start, and look for its pig. Never failed.

One night the mule broke loose, kicked the pig's pen down, and he and the pig, like they was Jesse and Frank James, headed for the hills. Went into the East Texas greenery and wound in amongst the trees, and were lost to the farmer. Only to be seen after that in glimpses and in stories that might or might not be true. Stories about how they raided corn fields and ate the corn and how the mule kicked down pens and let hogs and goats and cattle go free.

The White Mule and The Spotted Pig. Out there. On the run. Doing whatever it was that white mules and spotted pigs did when they weren't raiding crops and freeing critters.

Frank thought on this for a long time, saddled up Dobbin and rode over to Leroy's place. When Frank arrived, Leroy was out in the yard on his back, unconscious, the seed salesman hat spun off to the side and was being moved around by a curious chicken. Finding Leroy like this didn't frighten Frank any. He often found Leroy that way, cold as a wedge from drink, or unconscious from the missus having snuck up behind him with a stick of stove wood. They were rowdy, Leroy's bunch.

The missus came out on the porch and shook her fist at Frank, and not knowing anything else to do, he waved. She spat a stream of brown tobacco off the porch in his direction and went inside. A moment later one of the kids bellowed from being whapped, and there was a sound like someone slamming a big fish on flat ground. Then silence.

Frank bent down and shook Leroy awake. Leroy cursed, and Frank dragged him over to an overturned bucket and sat him up on it, asked him, "What happened?"

"Missus come up behind me. I've got so I don't watch my back enough."

"Why'd she do it?"

"Just her way. She has spells."

"You all right?"

"I got a headache."

Frank went straight to business. "I come to say maybe we ain't out of the mule business."

"What you mean?"

Frank told him about the mule and the pig, about his idea.

"Oh, yeah. Mule and pig are real. I've seen 'em once myself. Out hunting. I looked up, and there they were at the end of a trail, just watching. I was so startled, just stood there looking at them."

"What did they do?"

"Well, Frank, they ran off. What do you think? But it was kind of funny. They didn't get in no hurry, just turned and went around the trail, showing me their ass, the pig's tail curled up and a little swishy, and the mule swatting his like at flies. They just went around that curve in the trail, behind some oaks and blackberry vines, and they was gone. I tracked them a bit, but they got down in a stream and walked it. I could find their tracks in the stream with my hands, but pretty soon the whole stream was brown with mud, and they come out of it somewhere I didn't find, and they was gone like a swamp fog come noon."

"Was the mule really white?"

"Dirty a bit, but white. Even from where I was standing, just bits of light coming in through the trees, I could see he had pink eyes. Story is, that's why he don't like to come out in day much, likes to stay in the trees, and do his crop raiding at night. Say the sun hurts his skin."

"That could be a drawback."

"You act like you got him in a pen somewhere."

"I'd like to see if I could get hold of him. Story is, he can run, and he needs the pig to do it."

"That's the story. But stories ain't always true. I even heard stories about how the pig rides the mule. I've heard all manner of tale, and ain't maybe none of it got so much as a nut of truth in it. Still, it's one of them ideas that kind of appeals to me. Course, you know, we might catch that mule and he might not can run at all. Maybe all he can do is sneak around in the woods and eat corn crops."

"Well, it's all the idea I got," Frank said, and the thought of that worried Frank more than a little. He considered on his knack for clinging to bad notions like a rutting dog hanging onto a fella's leg. But, like the dog, he was determined to finish what he started.

"So what you're saying here," Leroy said, "is you want to capture the mule, and the pig, so the mule has got his help mate. And you want to ride the mule in the race?"

"That's what I said."

Leroy paused for a moment, rubbed the knot on the back of his noggin. "I think we should get Nigger Joe to help us track him. We want that mule, that's the way we do it. Nigger Joe catches him, and we'll break him, and you can ride him."

Nigger Joe was part Indian and part Irish and part Negro. His skin was somewhere between brown and red and he had a red cast to his kinky hair and strawberry freckles and bright green eyes. But the black blood named him, and he himself went by the name, Nigger Joe.

He was supposed to be able to track a bird across the sky, a fart across the yard. He had two women that lived with him and he called them his wives. One of them was a Negro, and the other one was part Negro and Cherokee. He called the black one Sweetie, the red and black one Pie.

When Frank and Leroy rode up double on Dobbin, and stopped in Nigger Joe's yard, a rooster was fucking one of the hens. It was a quick matter, and a moment later the rooster was strutting across the yard like he was ten foot tall and bullet proof.

They got off Dobbin, and no sooner had they hit the ground, than Nigger Joe was beside them, tall and broad-shouldered with his freckled face.

"Damn, man," Frank said, "where did you come from?"

Nigger Joe pointed in an easterly direction.

"Shit," Leroy said, "coming up on a man like that could make him bust a heart."

"Want something?" Nigger Joe asked.

"Yeah," Leroy said. "We want you to help track the White Mule and the Spotted Pig, 'cause Frank here, he's going to race him."

"Pig or mule?" Nigger Joe asked.

"The mule," Leroy said. "He's gonna ride the mule."

"Eat the pig?"

"Well," Leroy said, continuing his role as spokesman, "not right away. But there could come a point."

"He eats the pig, I get half of pig," Nigger Joe said.

"If he eats it, yeah," Leroy said. "Shit, he eats the mule, he'll give you half of that."

"My women like mule meat," Nigger Joe said. "I've eat it, but it don't agree with me. Horse is better," and to strengthen his statement, he gave Dobbin a look over.

"We was thinking," Leroy said, "we could hire you to find the mule and the pig, capture them with us."

"What was you thinking of giving me, besides half the critters if you eat them?"

"How about ten dollars?"

"How about twelve?"

"Eleven."

"Eleven-fifty."

Leroy looked at Frank. Frank sighed and nodded, stuck out his hand. Nigger Joe shook it, then shook Leroy's hand.

Nigger Joe said, "Now, mule runs like the rock, ain't my fault. I get the eleven-fifty anyway."

Frank nodded.

"Okay, tomorrow morning," Nigger Joe said, "just before light, we'll go look for him real serious and then some."

"Thing does come to me," Frank said, "is haven't other folks tried to get hold of this mule and pig before? Why are you so confident."

Nigger Joe nodded. "They weren't Nigger Joe."

"You could have tracked them before on your own," Frank said. "Why now?"

Nigger Joe looked at Frank. "Eleven-fifty."

In the pre-dawn light, down in the swamp, the fog moved through the trees like someone slow-pulling strands of cotton from cotton boles. It wound its way amongst the limbs that were low down, along the ground. There were wisps of it on the water, right near the bank, and as Frank and Leroy and Nigger Joe stood there, they saw what looked like dozens of sticks rise up in the swamp water and move along briskly.

Nigger Jim said, "Cottonmouth snakes. They going with they heads up, looking for anything foolish enough to get out there. You swimming out there now, pretty quick you be bit good and plenty and swole up like old tick. Only you burst all over and spill green poison, and die. Seen it happen."

"Ain't planning on swimming," Frank said.

"Watch your feet," Nigger Joe said. "Them snakes is thick this year. Them cottons and them copperheads. Cottons, they always mad."

"We've seen snakes," Leroy said.

"I know it," Nigger Joe said, "but where we go, they are more than a few, that's what I'm trying to tell you. Back there where mule and pig hides, it's thick in snakes and blackberry vines. And the trees thick like the wool on a sheep. It a goat or a sheep you fucked?"

"For Christ sakes," Leroy said. "You heard that too?"

"Wives talk about it when they see you yesterday. There the man who fuck a sheep, or a goat, or some such. Say you ain't a man can get pussy."

"Oh, hell," Leroy said.

"So, tell me some," Nigger Joe said. "Which was it, now."

"Goat," Leroy said.

"That is big nasty," Nigger Joe said, and started walking, leading them along a narrow trail along by the water. Frank watched the cottonmouth snakes swim on ahead, their evil heads sticking up like some sort of water devil erections.

The day grew hot and the trees held the hot and made it hotter and made it hard to breathe, like sucking down wool and chunks of flannel. Frank and Leroy sweated their clothes through and their hair turned to wet strings. Nigger Joe, though sweaty, appeared as fresh as a virgin in spring.

"Where you get your hat?" Nigger Joe asked Leroy suddenly, when they stopped for a swig from canteens.

"Seed salesman. My wife knocked him out and I kept the hat."

"Huh, no shit?" Nigger Joe took off his big old hat and waved around. "Bible salesman. He told me I was gonna go to hell, so I beat him up, kept his hat. I shit in his Bible case."

"Wow, that's mean," Frank said.

"Him telling me I'm going to hell, that make me real mad. I tell you that to tell you not to forget my eleven-fifty. I'm big on payment."

"You can count on us, we win," Frank said.

"No. You owe me eleven-fifty win or lose." Nigger Joe said this, putting his hat back carefully on his head, looking at the two smaller men like a man about to pick a hen for neck wringing and Sunday dinner.

"Sure," Frank said. "Eleven-fifty, win or lose. Eleven-fifty when we get the pig and the mule."

"Now that's the deal as I see it," Nigger Joe said. "I tell women it's eight dollars, that way I make some whisky money. Nigger Joe didn't get up yesterday. No he didn't. And when he gets up, he's got Bible salesman's hat on."

Frank thought: What? What the hell does that mean?

They waded through the swamp and through the woods for some time, and just before dark, Nigger Joe picked up on the mule's unshod tracks. He bent down and looked at them. He said, "We catch him, he's gonna need trimming and shoes. Not enough rock to wear them down. Soft sand and swamp. And here's the pig's tracks. Hell, he's big. Tracks say, three hundred pounds. Maybe more."

"That's no pig," Leroy said. "That's a full blown hog."

"Damn," Frank said. "They're real."

"But can he race?" Leroy said. "And will the pig co-operate?"

They followed the tracks until it turned dark. They threw up a camp, made a fire, and made it big so the smoke was strong, as the mosquitoes were everywhere and hungry and the smoke kept them off a little. They sat there in the night before the fire, the smoke making them cough, watching it churn up above them, through the trees. And up there, as if resting on a limb, was a piece of the moon.

They built the fire up big one last time, turned into their covers, and tried to sleep. Finally, they did, but before morning, Frank awoke, his bladder full, his mind as sharp as if he had slept well. He got up and stoked up the fire, and walked out a few paces in the dark and let it fly. When he looked up to button his pants, he saw through the trees, across a stretch of swamp water, something moving.

He looked carefully, because whatever it was had stopped. He stood very still for a long time, and finally what he had seen moved again. He thought at first it was a deer, but no. There was enough light from the early rising sun shining through the trees that he could now see clearly what it was.

The White Mule. It stood between two large trees, just looking at him, its head held high, its tall ears alert. The mule was big. Fifteen hands high, like Robert E. Lee, and it was big chested, and its legs were long. Something moved beside it.

The Spotted Pig. It was big and ugly, with one ear turned up and one ear turned down. It grunted once, and the mule snorted, but neither moved.

Frank wasn't sure what to do. He couldn't go tearing across the stretch of swamp after them, since he didn't know how deep it was, and what might be waiting for him. Gators, snakes and sink holes. And by the time he woke up the others, the mule and hog would be gone. He just stood there instead, staring at them. This went on for a long time, and finally the hog turned and started moving away, behind some thicket. The mule tossed its head, turned and followed.

My God, thought Frank. The mule is beautiful. And the hog, he's a pistol. He could tell that from the way it had grunted at him. He had some strange feelings inside of him that he couldn't explain. Some sensation of having had a moment that was greater than any moment he had had before.

He walked back to the fire and lay down on his blankets, tried to figure the reason behind the feeling, but only came up with a headache and more mosquito bites. He closed his eyes and slept a little while longer, thinking of the mule and the hog, and the way they were free and beautiful. Then he was awakened by the toe of Nigger Joe's boot in his ribs.

"Time to do it," Nigger Joe said.

Frank sat up. "I saw them."

"What?" Leroy said, stirring out of his blankets.

Frank told them what he had seen, and how there was nothing he could do then. Told them all this, but didn't tell them how the mule and the hog had made him feel.

"Shit," Leroy said. "You should have woke us."

Nigger Joe shook his head. "No matter. We see over there where they stood. See what tracks they leave us. Then we do the sneak on them."

They worked their way to the other side of the swamp, swatting mosquitoes and killing a cottonmouth in the process, and when they got to where the mule and the hog stood, they found tracks and mule droppings.

"You not full of shit, like Nigger Joe thinking," Nigger Joe said. "You really see them."

"Yep," Frank said.

Nigger Joe bent down and rubbed some of the mule shit between his fingers, and smelled it. "Not more than a couple hours old."

"Should have got us up," Leroy said.

"Easier to track in the day," Nigger Joe said. "They got their place they stay. They got some hideout."

The mosquitoes were not so bad now, and finally they came to some clear areas, marshy, but clear, and they lost the tracks there, but Nigger Joe said, "The two of them, they probably cross here. It's a good spot. Pick their tracks up in the trees over there, on the soft ground."

When the crossed the marshy stretch, they came to a batch of willows and looked around there. Nigger Joe was the one who found their tracks.

"Here they go," he said. "Here they go."

They traveled through woods and more swamp, and from time to time they lost the tracks, but Nigger Joe always found them again. Sometimes Frank couldn't even see what Nigger Joe saw. But Nigger Joe saw something, because he kept looking at the ground, stopping to stretch out on the earth, his face close to it. Sometimes he would pinch the earth between finger and thumb, rub it about. Frank wasn't sure why he did that, and he didn't ask. Like Leroy, he just followed.

Midday, they came to a place that amazed Frank. Out there in the middle of what should have been swamp, there was a great clear area, at least a hundred acres. They found it when they came out of a stretch of shady oaks. The air was sweeter there, in the trees, and the shadows were cooling, and at the far edge was a drop of about fifty feet. Down below was the great and natural pasture. A fire, brought on by heat or lightning, might have cleared the place at some point in time. It had grown back without trees, just tall green grass amongst a few rotting, ant-infested stumps. It was surrounded by the oaks, high up on their side, and low down on the other. The oaks on the far side stretched out and blended with sweet gums and black jack and hickory and bursts of pines. From their vantage point they could see all of this, and see the cool shadow on the other side amongst the trees.

A hawk sailed over it all, and Frank saw there was a snake in its beak. Something stirred again inside of Frank, and he was sure it wasn't his last meal. "You're part Indian," Frank said to Nigger Joe. "That hawk and that snake, does it mean something?"

"Means that snake is gonna get et," Nigger Joe said. "Damn trees. Don't you know that make a lot of good hard lumber... Go quiet. Look there."

Coming out of the trees into the great pasture was the mule and the hog. The hog lead the way, and the mule followed close behind. They came out into the sunlight, and pretty soon the hog began to root and the mule began to graze.

"Got their own paradise," Frank said.

"We'll fix that," Leroy said.

They waited there, sitting amongst the oaks, watching, and late in the day the hog and the mule wandered off into the trees across the way.

"Ain't we gonna do something besides watch?" Leroy said.

"They leave, tomorrow they come back," Nigger Joe said. "Got their spot. Be back tomorrow. We'll be ready for them."

Just before dark they came down from their hiding place on a little trail, crossed the pasture and walked over to where the mule and the hog had come out of the trees. Nigger Joe looked around for some time, said, "Got a path. Worked it out. Always the same. Same spot. Come through here, out into the pasture. What we do is we get up in a tree. Or I get in tree with my rope. I rope the mule and tie him off and let him wear himself down."

"He could kill himself, thrashing," Frank said.

"Could kill myself, him thrashing. I think it best tie him to a tree, folks."

Frank translated Nigger Joe's strange way of talking in his head, said, "He dies, you don't get the eleven-fifty."

"Not how I understand it," Nigger Joe said.

"That's how it is," Frank said, feeling as if he might be asking for a knife in his belly, his guts spilled. Out here, no one would ever know. Nigger Joe might think he could do that, kill Leroy too, take their money. Course, they didn't have any money. Not here. There was fifteen dollars buried in a jar out back of the house, eleven-fifty of which would go to Nigger Joe, if he didn't kill them.

Nigger Joe studied Frank for a long moment. Frank shifted from one foot to the other, trying not to do it, but unable to stop. "Okay," Nigger Joe said. "That will work up good enough."

"What about Mr. Porky?" Leroy asked.

"That gonna be you two's job. I rope damn mule, and you two, you gonna rope damn pig. First, we got to smell like dirt."

"What?" Frank said.

Nigger Joe rubbed himself down with dark soil. He had Frank and Leroy rub themselves down with it. Leroy hated it and complained, but Frank found the earth smelled like incoming rain, and he thought it pleasant. It felt good on his skin, and he had a sudden strange thought, that when he died, he would become one and the same as the earth, and he wondered how many dead animals, maybe people, made up the dirt he had rubbed onto himself. He felt odd thinking that way. He felt odd thinking in any way.

They slept for a while, then Nigger Joe kicked him and Leroy awake. It was still dark when they rolled dirty out of their bed clothes.

"Couldn't we have waited on the dirt," Leroy said, climbing out of his blankets. "It's all in my bed roll."

"Need time for dirt to like you good, so you smell like it," Nigger Joe said. "We put some more on now, rub in the hair good, then get ready."

"It's still dark," Frank said. "They gonna come in the dark? How you know when they're gonna come?"

"They come. But we gotta be ready. They have a good night in farmer's corn fields, they might come real soon, full bellies. Way ground reads, they come here to stand and to wallow. Hog wallows all time, way ground looks. And they shit all over. This their spot. They don't get corn and peas and such, they'll be back here. Water not far from spot, and they got good grass. Under the trees, hog has some acorns. Hogs like acorns. Wife, Sweetie, makes sometimes coffee from acorns."

"How about I make some regular coffee, made from coffee?" Leroy said.

"Nope. We don't want a smoke smell. Don't want our smell. Need to piss or shit, don't let free here. Go across pasture there. Far side. Dump over there. Piss over there. Use the heel of your shoe to cover it all. Give it lots of dirt."

"Walk all the way across?" Leroy said.

"Want hog and mule," Nigger Joe said. "Walk all the way across. Now, eat some jerky, do your shit over on other side. Put more dirt on. And wait."

The sun rose up and it got hot, and the dirt on their skins itched, or at least Frank itched, and he could tell Leroy itched, but Nigger Joe, he didn't seem to. Sat silent. And when the early morning was eaten up by the heat, Nigger Joe showed them places to be. He had them lie down in trenches they scooped in the dirt, and Nigger Joe covered them with leaves and dirt and bits of hog and mule's shit. It was terrible. They lay their with their ropes and waited. Nigger Joe, with his lasso, climbed up into an oak and sat on a fat limb, his feet stretched along it, his back against the trunk, the rope in his lap.

The day crawled forward and so did the worms. They were all around Frank, and it was all he could do not to jump up screaming. It wasn't that he was afraid of them. He had put a many of them on hooks for fishing. But to just lay there and have them squirm against your arm, your neck. And there was something that bit. Something in the hog shit was Frank's thought.

Frank heard a sound. A different sound. Being close to the ground it seemed to move the earth. It was the slow careful plodding of the mule's hooves, and another sound. The hog, maybe.

They listened and waited and the sounds came closer, and then Frank, lying there, trying not to tremble with anticipation, heard a whizzing sound. The rope. And then there was a bray, and a scuffle sound.

Frank lifted his head slightly.

Not ten feet from him was the great white mule, the rope around its neck, the length of it stretching up into the tree. Frank could see Nigger Joe. He had wrapped the rope around the limb and was holding onto it, tugging, waiting for the mule to wear itself out.

The hog was bounding about near the mule, as if it might jump up and grab the rope and chew it in two. It actually went up on its hind legs once.

Frank knew it was time. He burst out of his hiding place, and Leroy came out of his. The hog went straight for Leroy. Frank darted in front of the leaping mule and threw his rope and caught the hog around the neck. It turned instantly and went for him.

Leroy dove and grabbed the hog's hind leg. The hog kicked him in the face, but Leroy hung on. The hog dragged Leroy across the ground, going for Frank, and as his rope became more slack, Frank darted for a tree.

By the time Frank arrived at the tree trunk, Leroy had managed to put his rope around the hog's hind leg, and now Frank and Leroy had the hog in a kind of tug of war.

"Don't hurt him now some," Nigger Joe yelled from the tree. "Got to keep him up for it. He's the mule leader. Makes him run."

"What the hell did he say?" Frank said.

"Don't hurt the goddamn pig," Leroy said.

"Ha," Frank said, tying off his end of the rope to a tree trunk. Leroy stretched his end, giving the hog a little slack, and tied off to another tree. Nearby the mule bucked and kicked.

Leroy made a move to try and grab the rope on the mule up short, but the mule whipped as if on a Yankee dollar, and kicked Leroy smooth in the chest, launching him over the hog and into the brush. The hog would have had him then, but the rope around its neck and back leg held it just short of Leroy, but close enough a string of hog spittle and snot was flung across Leroy's face.

"Goddamn," Leroy said, as he inched farther away from the hog.

For a long while, they watched the mule kick and buck and snort and snap its large teeth.

It was near nightfall when the mule, exhausted, settled down on its front knees first, then rolled over on its side. The hog scooted across the dirt and came to rest near the great mule, its snout resting on the mule's flank.

"I'll be damned," Leroy said. "The hog's girlie or something."

It took three days to get back, because the mule wasn't co-operating, and the hog was no pushover either. They had to tie logs on either side of the hog, so that he had to drag them. It wore the hog down, but it wore the men down too, because the logs would tangle in vines and roughs, and constantly had to be untangled. The mule was hobbled loosely, so that it could walk, but couldn't bolt. The mule was lead by Nigger Joe, and fastened around the mule's waist was a rope with two rope lines leading off to the rear. They were in turn fastened to a heavy log that kept the mule from bolting forward to have a taste of Nigger Joe, and to keep him, like the hog, worn down.

At night they left the logs on the critters, and built make-do corrals of vines and limbs and bits of leather straps.

By the time they were out of the woods and the swamp, the mule and the hog were covered in dirt and mud and such. The animals heaved as they walked, and Frank feared they might keel over and die.

They made it though, and they took the mule up to Nigger Joe's. He had a corral there. It wasn't much, but it was solid and it held the mule in. The hog they put in a small pen. There was hardly room for the hog to turn around. Now that the hog was well placed, Frank stood by the pen and studied the animal. The beast looked at him with a feral eye. This wasn't a hog who had been slopped and watered. This was an animal who early on had escaped into the wild, as a pig, and had made his way to adulthood. The hog's spotted hide was covered in scars, and though he had a coating of fat on him, his body was long and muscular, and when the critter flexed its shoulders to startle a fly, muscles rolled beneath its skin like snakes beneath a tight-stretched blanket.

The mule, after the first day, began to perk up. But he didn't do much. Stood around mostly, and when they walked away for a distance, it began to trot the corral, stopping often to look out at his friend in the hog pen. The mule made a sound, and the hog made a sound back.

"Damn, if I don't think they're talking to one another," Leroy said.

"Oh yeah. You can bet. They do that all right," Nigger Joe said.

The race was coming closer, and within the week, Leroy and Nigger Joe had the mule's hooves trimmed, but no shoes. Decided he didn't need them, as the ground was soft this time of year. They got him saddled. Leroy got bucked off and kicked and bitten once, a big plug was out of his right elbow.

"Mean one," Nigger Joe said. "Real bastard, this mule. Strong. He got the time, he eat Leroy."

"Do you think he can run?" Frank asked.

"Time to see soon," Nigger Joe said.

That night, when the saddling and bucking was done, the mule began to wear down, let Nigger Joe stay on his back. As a reward, Nigger Joe fed the mule well on grain, but gave him only a little water. He fed the hog some pulled-up weeds, a bit of corn, watered him.

"Want mule strong, but hog weak," Nigger Joe said. "Don't want hog strong enough to do digging out of pen that's for some sure."

Frank listened to this, wondering where Nigger Joe had learned his American.

Nigger Joe went in for the night, his two wives calling him to supper. Leroy walked home. Frank saddled up Dobbin, but before he left, he led the horse out to the corral and stared at the mule. There in the starlight, the beams settled around the mule's head, and made it very white. The mud was gone now and the mule had been groomed, cleaned of briars and burrs from the woods, and the beast looked magnificent. Once Frank had seen a book. It was the only book he had ever seen other than the Bible, which his mother owned. But he had seen this one in the window of the General Store downtown. He hadn't opened the book, just looked at it through the window. There on the cover was a white horse with wings on its back. Well, the mule didn't look like a horse, and it didn't have wings on its back, but it certainly had the bearing of the beast on the book's cover. Like maybe it was from somewhere else other than here; like the sky had ripped open and the mule had ridden into this world through the tear.

Frank led Dobbin over to the hog pen. There was nothing beautiful about the spotted hog. It stared up at him, and the starlight filled its eyes and made them sharp and bright as shrapnel.

As Frank was riding away, he heard the mule make a sound, then the hog. They did it more than once, and were still doing it when he rode out of earshot.

It took some doing, and it took some time, and Frank, though he did little but watch, felt as if he were going to work every day. It was a new feeling for him. His Old Man often made him work, but as he grew older he had quit, just like his father. The fields rarely got attention, and being drunk became more important than hoeing corn and digging taters. But here he was not only showing up early, but staying all day, handing harness and such to Nigger Joe and Leroy, bringing out feed and pouring water.

In time Nigger Joe was able to saddle up the mule with no more than a snort from the beast, and he could ride about the pen without the mule turning to try and bite him or buck him. He even stopped kicking at Nigger Joe and Leroy, who he hated, when they first entered the pen.

The hog watched all of this through the slats of his pen, his beady eyes slanting tight, its battle-torn ears flicking at flies, its curly tail curled even tighter. Frank wondered what the hog was thinking. He was certain, whatever it was, was not good.

Soon enough, Nigger Joe had Frank enter the pen, climb up in the saddle. Sensing a new rider, the mule threw him. But the second time he was on board, the mule trotted him around the corral, running lightly with that kind of rolling barrel run mules have.

"He's about ready for a run, he is," Nigger Joe said.

Frank led the mule out of the pen and out to the road, Leroy following. Nigger Joe led Dobbin. "See he'll run that way. Not so fast at first," Nigger Joe said. "Me and this almost dead horse, we follow and find you, you ain't neck broke in some ditch somewheres."

Cautiously, Frank climbed on the white mule's back. He took a deep breath, then settling himself in the saddle, he gave the mule a kick.

The mule didn't move.

He kicked again.

The mule trotted down the road about twenty feet, then turned, dipped its head into the grass that grew alongside the red clay road, and took a mouthful.

Frank kicked at the mule some more, but the mule wasn't having any. He only moved a few feet down the road, then across the road and into the grass, amongst the trees, biting leaves off of them with a sharp snap of his head, a smack of his teeth.

Nigger Joe trotted up on Dobbin.

"You ain't going so fast."

"Way I see it too," Frank said. "He ain't worth a shit."

"We not bring the hog in on some business yet."

"How's that gonna work? I mean, how's he gonna stay around and not run off."

"Maybe hog run off in goddamn woods and not see again, how it may work. But, nothing else, hitch mule to plow or sell. You done paid me eleven-fifty."

"Your job isn't done," Frank said.

"You say, and may be right, but we got the one card, the hog, you see. He don't deal out with an ace, we got to call him a joker, and call us assholes, and the mule, we got to make what we can. We have to, shoot and eat the hog. Best, keep him up a few more days, put some corn in him, make him better than what he is. Fatter. The mule, I told you ideas. Hell, eat mule too if nothing other works out."

They let the hog out of the pen.

Or rather Leroy did. Just picked up the gate, and out came the hog. The hog didn't bolt. It bounded over to the mule, on which Frank was mounted. The mule dipped its head, touched noses with the hog.

"I'll be damn," Frank said, thinking he had never had a friend like that. Leroy was as close as it got, and he had to watch Leroy. He'd cheat you. And if you had a goat, he might fuck it. Leroy was no real friend. Frank thought Leroy was like most things in his life, just something to make do till the real thing came along, and so far, he was still waiting. It made Frank feel lonesome.

Nigger Joe took the bridle on the mule away from Frank, and led them out to the road. The hog trotted beside the mule.

"Now, story is, hog likes to run," Nigger Joe said. "And when he run, mule follows. And then hog, he falls off, not keeping up, and mule, he got the arrow-sight then, run like someone put turpentine on his nut sack. Or that the story as I hear it. You?"

"Pretty close," Frank said.

Frank took the reins back, and the hog stood beside the mule. Nothing happened.

"Gonna say go, is what I'm to do here now. And when I say, you kick mule real goddamn hard. Me, I'm gonna stick boot in hog's big ass. Hear me now, Frank?"

"I do."

"Signal will be me shouting when kick the hog's ass, okay?"

"Okay."

"Ready some."

"Ready."

Nigger Joe yelled, "Git, hog," and kicked the hog in the ass with all his might. The hog did a kind of hop, and bolted. A hog can move quick for its size for a short distance, haul some serious freight, and the old spotted hog, he was really fast, hauling the whole freight line. Frank expected the hog to dart into the woods, and be long gone. But it didn't. The hog bounded down the road running for all it was worth, and before Frank could put his heels to the mule, the mule leaped. That was the only way to describe it. The mule did not seem cocked to fire, but suddenly it was a white bullet, shooting forward so fast Frank nearly flew out of the saddle. But he clung, and the mule ran, and the hog ran, and after a bit, the mule ducked its head and the hog began to fade. But the mule was no longer following the hog. Not even close. It snorted, and its nose appeared to get long and the ears laid back flat. The mule jetted by the fat porker and stretched its legs longer, and Frank could feel the wind whipping cool on his face. The body of the mule rolled like a barrel, but man, my God, thought Frank, this sonofabitch can run.

There was one problem. Frank couldn't turn him. When he felt the mule had gone far enough, it just kept running, and no amount of tugging led to response. That booger was gone. Frank just leaned forward over the mule's neck, hung on, and let him run.

Eventually the mule quit, just stopped, dipped its head to the ground, then looked left and right. Trying to find the hog, Frank figured. It was like the mule had gone into a kind of spell, and now he was out of it and wanted his friend.

He could turn the mule then. He trotted it back down the road, not trying to get it to run anymore, just letting it trot, and when it came upon Nigger Joe and Leroy, standing in the road, the hog came out of the woods and moseyed up beside the mule.

As Nigger Joe reached up and took the mule's reins, he said, "See that there. Hog and him are buddies. He stays around. He don't want to run off. Wants to be with mule. Hog a goddamn fool. Could be long gone, out in the woods. Find some other wild hog and fuck it. Eat acorns. Die of old age. Now he gonna get et sometime."

"Dumb shit hog," Leroy said.

The mule tugged at the reins, dipped its head. The hog and the mule's noses came together. The mule snorted. The hog made a kind of squealing sound.

They trained for several days the same way. The hog would start, and then the mule would run. Fast. They put the mule up at night in the corral, hobbled, and the hog, they didn't have to pen him anymore. He stayed with the mule by choice.

One day, after practice, Frank said, "He seems pretty fast."

"Never have seen so fast," Nigger Joe said. "He's moving way good."

"Do you think he can win?" Leroy said.

"He can win, they let us bring hog in. No hog. Not much on the run. Got to have hog. But there's one mule give him trouble. Dynamite. He runs fast too. Might can run faster."

"You think?"

"Could be. I hear he can go lickity split. Tomorrow, we find out, hey?"

The world was made of men and mules and dogs and one hog. There were women too, most of them with parasols. Some sitting in the rows of chairs at the starting line, their legs tucked together primly, their dresses pulled down tight to the ankles.. The air smelled of early summer morning and hot mule shit and sweat and perfume, cigar smoke, beer and farts. Down from it all, in tents, were other women who smelled different and wore fewer clothes. The women with parasols would not catch their eyes, but some of the men would, many when their wives or girls were not looking.

Frank was not interested. He couldn't think of anything but the race. Leroy was with him, and of course, Nigger Joe. They brought the mule in, Nigger Joe leading him. Frank on Old Dobbin, Leroy riding double. And the hog, loose, on its own, strutting as if he were the one throwing the whole damn shindig.

The mules at the gathering were not getting along. There were bites and snorts and kicks. The mules could kick backwards, and they could kick out sideways like cattle. You had to watch them.

The White Mule was surprisingly docile. It was as if his balls had been clipped. He walked with his head down, the pig trotting beside him.

As they neared the forming line of mules, Frank looked at them. Most were smaller than the white mule, but there was one that was bigger, jet black, and had a roaming eye, as if he might be searching for victims. He had a big hard-on and it was throbbing in the sunlight like a fat cottonmouth.

"That mule there, big dicked one, " Nigger Joe said. "He the kind get a hard-on he gonna race or fight, maybe quicker than the fuck, you see. He's the one to watch. Anything that like the running or fighting better than pussy, him the one you got to keep the eye on."

"That's Dynamite," Leroy said. "Got all kinds of mule muscle, that's for sure."

White Mule saw Dynamite, lifted his head high, threw back his ears and snorted.

"Oh, yeah," said Leroy. "There's some shit between them already."

"Somebody gonna outrun somebody or fuck other in ass, that's what I tell you for sure. Maybe they fight some too. Whole big blanket of business here."

White Mule wanted to trot, and Nigger Joe had to run a little to keep up with him. They went right through a clutch of mules about to be lined up, and moved quickly so that White Mule was standing beside Dynamite. The two mules looked at one another and snorted. In that moment, the owner of Dynamite slipped blinders and a bridle onto Dynamite's head, tossing off the old bridal to a partner.

The spotted hog slid in between the feet of his mule, stood with his head poking out beneath his buddy's legs, looking up with his ugly face, flaring his nostrils, narrowing his cave-dark eyes.

Dynamite's owner was Levi Crone, one big gent in a dirty white shirt with the sleeves ripped out. He had a big red face and big fat muscles and a belly like a big iron wash pot. He wore a hat you could have bathed in. He was as tall as Nigger Joe, six foot two or more. Hands like hams, feet like boats. He looked at the White Mule, said, "That ain't the story mule is it?"

"One and the same," Frank said, as if he had raised the white mule from a colt.

"I heard someone had him. That he had been caught. Catch and train him?"

"Me and my partners."

"You mean Leroy and the nigger?"

"Yeah."

"That the hog in the stories, too, I guess?"

"Yep," Frank said.

"What's he for? A step stool?"

"He runs with the mule. For a ways."

"That ain't allowed."

"Where say can't do it, huh?" Nigger Joe asked.

Crone thought. "Nowhere, but it stands to reason."

"What about rule can't run with the dick hard," Nigger Joe said, pointing at Dynamite's member.

"Ain't no rule like that," Crone said. "Mule can't help that."

"Ain't no rule about goddamn hog none either," Nigger Joe said.

"It don't matter," Crone said. "You got this mule from hell, given to you by the goddamn red-assed Devil his own self, and you got the pork chop there too from the same place, it ain't gonna matter. Dynamite here, he's gonna outrun him. Gets finished, he'll fuck your mule in the ass and shit a turd on him."

"Care to make a bet on the side some?" Nigger Joe said.

"Sure," Crone said. "I'll bet you all till my money runs out. That ain't good enough, I'll arm wrestle you or body wrestle you or see which of us can shoot jack-off the farthest. You name it speckled nigger."

Nigger Joe studied Crone as if he might be thinking about where to make all the prime cuts, but he finally just grinned, got out ten of the eleven-fifty he had been paid. "There mine. You got some holders?"

"Ten dollars. I got sight of it, and I got your word, which better be good," Crone said.

"Where's your money?" Leroy said.

Crone pulled out a wad from his front pocket, presented it with open palm as if he might be giving a teacher an apple. He looked at Leroy, said, "You gonna trade a goat? I hear you like goats."

"Okay," Leroy said. "Okay. I fucked a goddamn goat. What of it?"

Crone laughed at him. He shook the money at Nigger Joe. "Good enough?"

"Okay," Nigger Joe said.

"Here's three dollars," Frank said, dug in his pocket, held it so Crone could see.

Crone nodded.

Frank slipped the money back in his pocket.

"Well," Leroy said. "I ain't got shit, so I just throw out my best wishes."

"You boys could bet the mule," Crone said.

"That could be an idea," Leroy said.

"No," Frank said. "We won't do that."

"Ain't we partners?" Leroy said, taking off his seed salesman's hat.

"We got a deal," Frank said, "but I'm the one paid Nigger Joe for catching and training. So, I decide. And that's about as partner as we get."

Leroy shrugged, put the seed salesman's hat back on.

The mules lined up and it was difficult to make them stay the line. Dynamite, still toting serious business on the undercarriage, lined up by White Mule, stood at least a shoulder above him. Both wore blinders now, but they turned their heads and looked at one another. Dynamite snapped at the white mule, who moved quickly, nearly throwing Frank from the saddle. White Mule snapped back at Dynamite's nose, grazing him. He threw a little kick sideways that made Dynamite shuffle to his right.

There was yelling from the judges, threats of disqualification, though no one expected that. The crowd had already figured this race out. White Mule, the forest legend, and Dynamite, of the swinging big dick, they were the two to watch.

Leroy and Nigger Joe had pulled the hog back with a rope, but now they brought him out and let him stand in front of his mule. They had to talk to the judges on the matter, explain. There wasn't any rule for or against it. One judge said he didn't like the idea. One said the hog would get trampled to death anyway. Another said, shit, why not. Final decision, they let the hog stay in the race.

So the mules and the hog and the riders lined up, the hog just slightly to the side of the white mule. The hog looked over its shoulder at Nigger Joe standing behind him. By now the hog knew what was coming. A swift kick in the ass.

Frank climbed up on the white mule, and a little guy with a face like a timber axe, climbed up on Crone's mule, Dynamite.

Out front of the line was a little bald man in a loose shirt and suspenders holding up his high-water pants, showing his scuffed and broken-laced boots. He had a pistol in his hand. He has a voice loud as Nester on the Greek line.

"Now, we got us a mule race today, ladies and gentleman. And there will be no cheatin', or there will be disqualification, and a butt-beating you can count on to be remembered by everyone, 'specially the cheater. What I want now, line of mules and riders, is a clean race. This here path is wide enough for all twenty of you, and you can't fan too much to the right or left, as we got folks all along the run watching. You got to keep up pretty tight. Now, there might be some biting and kicking, and that's to be expected. From the mules. You riders got to be civil. Or mostly. A little out of line is all right, but no knives or guns or such. Everyone understand and ain't got no questions, let up a shout."

A shout came from the line. The mules stirred, stepped back, stepped forward.

"Anybody don't understand what I just said? Anyone not speak Texan or Meskin here that's gonna race?"

No response.

"All right, then. Watch women and children, and try not to run over the men or the whores neither. I'm gonna step over there to the side, and I'm gonna raise this pistol, and when you hear the shot, there you go. May the best mule and the best rider win. Oh, yeah. We got a hog in the race too. He ain't supposed to stay long. Just kind of lead. No problems with that from anybody, is there?"

There were no complaints.

"All right, then."

The judge stepped briskly to the side of the road and raised his old worn .36 Navy at the sky and got an important look on his face. Nigger Joe removed the rope from the pig's neck and found a solid position between mules and behind the hog. He cocked his foot back.

The judge fired his pistol. Nigger Joe kicked the hog in the ass. The mule line charged forward.

The hog, running for all it was worth surged forward as well, taking the lead even. White Mule and Dynamite ran dead even. The mules ran so hard a cloud of dust was thrown up. The mules and the men and the hog were swallowed by it. Frank, seeing nothing but dust, coughed and cursed and lay tight against the white mule's neck, and squinted his eyes. He feared, without the white mule being able to see the hog, he might bolt. Maybe run into another mule, throw him into a stampede, get him stomped flat. But as they ran the cloud moved behind them, and when Frank came coughing out of the cloud, he was amazed to see the hog was well out in front, running as if he could go like that all the way to Mexico.

To his right, Frank saw Dynamite and his little axe-faced rider. The rider looked at him and smiled with gritty teeth. "You gonna get run into a hole, shit breath."

"Shitass," Frank said. It was the best he could come up with, but he threw it out with meaning.

Dynamite was leading the pack now, leaving the white mule and the others behind, throwing dust in their face. White Mule saw Dynamite start to straighten out in front of him, and he moved left, nearly knocking against a mule on that side. Frank figured it was so he could see the hog. The hog was moving his spotted ass on down the line.

"Git him, White Mule," Frank said, leaning close to the mule's left ear, resting his head against the mule's mane. The white mule focused on the hog and started hauling some ass. He went lower and his strides got longer and the barrel back and belly rolled. When Frank looked up, the hog was bolting left, across the path of a dozen mules, just making it off the trail before taking a tumble under hooves. He fell, rolled over and over in the grass.

Frank thought: Shit, White Mule, he's gonna bolt, gonna go after the hog. But, nope, he was true to the trail, and closing on Dynamite. The spell was on. And now the other mules were moving up too, taking a whipping, getting their sides slapped hard enough Frank could hear it, thing it sounded like Papa's belt on his back.

"Come on, White Mule. You don't need no hittin', don't need no hard heels. You got to outrun that hard dick for your own sake."

It was as if White Mule understood him. White Mule dropped lower and his strides got longer yet. Frank clung for all he was worth, fearing the saddle might twist and lose him.

But no, Leroy, for all his goat-fucking and seed salesman's hat stealing, could fasten harness and belly bands better than anyone that walked.

The trail became shady as they moved into a line of oaks on either side of the road. For a long moment the shadows were so thick they ran in near darkness. Then there were patches of lights through the leaves and the dust was lying closer to the ground and the road was sun-baked and harder and showing clay the color of a poison-ivy rash.

Scattered here and there along the road were viewers. A few in chairs. Most standing.

Frank ventured a look over his shoulder. The other mules and riders were way back, and some of them were already starting to falter. He noticed a couple of the mules were riderless, and one had broken rank with its rider and was off trail, cutting across the grass, heading toward the creek that twisted down amongst a line of willow trees.

As White Mule closed on Dynamite, the mule took a snapping bite at Dynamite's tail, jerking its head back with teeth full of tail hair.

Dynamite tried to turn and look, but his rider pulled his head back into line. White Mule lunged forward, going even lower than before. Lower than Frank had ever seen him go. Lower than he thought he could go. Now White Mule was pulling up on Dynamite's left. Dynamite's rider jerked Dynamite back into the path in front of White Mule. Frank wheeled his mount to the right side of Dynamite. In mid-run, Dynamite wheeled and kicked, hit White Mule in the side hard enough there was an explosion of breath that made Frank think his mule would go down.

Dynamite pulled ahead.

White Mule was not so low now. He was even staggering a little as he ran.

"Easy, boy," Frank said. "You can do it. You're the best goddamn mule ever ran a road."

White Mule began to run evenly again, or as even as a mule can run. He began to stretch out again, going low. Frank was surprised to see they were closing on Dynamite again.

Frank looked back.

No one was in sight. Just a few twists of dust, a ripple of heat waves. It was White Mule and Dynamite, all the way.

As Frank and White Mule passed Dynamite, Frank noted Dynamite didn't run with a hard-on anymore. Dynamite's rider let the mule turn its head and snap at White Mule. Frank, without really thinking about it, slipped his foot from the saddle and kicked the mule in the jaw.

"Hey," yelled Dynamite's rider. "Stop that."

"Hey, shitass," Frank said. "You better watch…that limb."

Dynamite and his rider had let White Mule push them to the right side of the road, near the trees, and a low hanging hickory limb was right in line with them. The rider ducked it by a half-inch, losing only his cap.

Shouldn't have told him, thought Frank. What he was hoping was to say something smart just as the limb caught the bastard. That would have made it choice, seeing the little axe-faced shit take it in the teeth. But he had outsmarted his own self.

"Fuck," Frank said.

Now they were thundering around a bend, and there were lots of people there, along both sides. There had been a spot of people here and there, along the way, but now they were everywhere.

Must be getting to the end of it, thought Frank.

Dynamite had lost a step for a moment, allowing White Mule to move ahead, but now he was closing again. Frank looked up. He could see that a long red ribbon was stretched across in front of them. It was almost the end.

Dynamite lit a fuse.

He came up hard on the left, and began to pass. The axe-faced rider slapped out with the long reins and caught Frank across the face.

"You goddamn turd," Frank said, and slashed out with his own reins, missing by six inches. Dynamite and axe-face pulled ahead.

Frank turned his attention back to the finish line. Thought: this is it. White Mule was any lower to the ground he'd have a belly full of gravel, stretched out any farther, he'd come apart. He's gonna be second. And no prize.

"You done what you could," Frank said, putting his mouth close to the bobbing head of the mule, rubbing the side of his neck with the tips of his fingers.

White Mule brought out the reinforcements. He was low and he was stretched, but now his legs were moving even faster, and for a long, strange moment, Frank thought the mule had sprung wings, like that horse he had seen on that book so long ago. It was as if he and White Mule were floating on air.

Frank couldn't believe it. Dynamite was falling behind, snorting and blowing, his body lathering up as if he were soaped.

White Mule leaped through the red ribbon a full three lengths ahead to win.

Frank let White Mule run past the watchers, on until he slowed and began to trot, and then walk. He let the mule go on like that for some time, then he gently pulled the reins and got out of the saddle. He walked the mule a while. Then he stopped and unbuttoned the belly band. He slid the saddle into the dirt. He pulled the bridle off of the mule's head.

The mule turned and looked at him.

"You done your part," Frank said, and swung the bridle gently against the mule's ass. "Go on."

White Mule sort of skipped forward and began running down the road, then turned into the trees. And was gone.

Frank walked all the way back to the beginning of the race, the viewers amazed he was without his mule.

But he was still the winner.

"You let him go?" Leroy said. "After all we went through, you let him go?"

"Yep," Frank said.

Nigger Joe shook his head. "Could have run him again. Plowed him. Ate him."

Frank took his prize money from the judges and side bet from Crone, paid Leroy his money, watched Nigger Joe follow Crone away from the race's starting line, on out to Crone's horse and wagon. Dynamite, his head down, was being led to the wagon by axe-face.

Frank knew what was coming. Nigger Joe had not been paid, and on top of that, he was ill tempered and grudge-minded. As Frank watched, Nigger Joe hit Crone and knocked him flat. No one did anything.

Black man or not, you didn't mess with Nigger Joe.

Nigger Joe took his money from Crone's wallet, punched the axe-faced rider in the nose for the hell of it, and walked back in their direction.

Frank didn't wait. He went over to where the hog lay on the grass. His front and back legs had been tied and a kid about thirteen was poking him with a stick. Frank slapped the kid in the back of the head, knocking his hat off. The kid bolted like a deer.

Frank got Dobbin and called Nigger Joe over. "Help me."

Nigger Joe and Frank loaded the hog across the back of Dobbin as if he were a sack of potatoes. Heavy as the porker was, it was accomplished with some difficulty, the hog's head hanging down on one side, his feet on the other. The hog seemed defeated. He hardly even squirmed.

"Misses that mule," Nigger Joe said.

"You and me got our business done, Joe," Frank asked.

Nigger Joe nodded.

Frank took Dobbin's reins and started leading him away.

"Wait," Leroy said.

Frank turned on him. "No. I'm through with you. You and me. We're quits."

"What?" Leroy said.

Frank pulled at the reins and kept walking. He glanced back once to see Leroy standing where they had last spoke, standing in the road looking at him, wearing the seed salesman's hat.

Frank put the hog in the old hog pen at his place and fed him good. Then he ate and poured out all the liquor he had, and waited until dark. When it came he sat on a large rock out back of the house. The wind carried the urine smell of all those out-the-window pees to his nostrils. He kept his place.

The moon was near full that night and it had risen high above the world and its light was bright and silver. Even the old ugly place looked good under that light.

Frank sat there for a long time, finally dozed. He was awakened by the sound of wood cracking. He snapped his head up and looked out at the hog pen. The mule was there. He was kicking at the slats of the pen, trying to free his friend.

Frank got up and walked out there. The mule saw him, ran back a few paces, stared at him.

"Knew you'd show," Frank said. "Just wanted to see you one more time. Today, buddy, you had wings."

The mule turned its head and snorted.

Frank lifted the gate to the pen and the hog ran out. The hog stopped beside the mule and they both looked at Frank.

"It's all right," Frank said. "I ain't gonna try and stop you."

The mule dipped its nose to the hog's snout and they pressed them together. Frank smiled. The mule and the hog wheeled suddenly, as if by agreed signal, and raced toward the rickety rail fence near the hill.

The mule, with one beautiful leap, jumped the fence, seemed pinned in the air for a long time, held there by the rays of the moon. The way the rays fell, for a strange short instant, it seemed as if he were sprouting gossamer wings.

The hog wiggled under the bottom rail and the two of them ran across the pasture, between the trees and out of sight. Frank didn't have to go look to know that the mule had jumped the other side of the fence as well, that the hog had worked his way under. And that they were gone.

When the sun came up and Frank was sure there was no wind, he put a match to a broom's straw and used it to start the house afire, then the barn and the rotten out-buildings. He kicked the slats on the hog pen until one side of it fell down.

He went out to where Dobbin was tied to a tree, saddled and ready to go. He mounted him and turned his head toward the rail fence and the hill. He looked at it for a long time. He gave a gentle nudge to Dobbin with his heels and started out of there, on down toward the road and town.

On The Far Side of the Cadillac Desert with Dead Folks

I

AFTER A MONTH'S chase, Wayne caught up with Calhoun one night at a little honky-tonk called Rosalita's. It wasn't that Calhoun had finally gotten careless, it was just that he wasn't worried. He'd killed four bounty hunters so far, and Wayne knew a fifth didn't concern him.

The last bounty hunter had been the famous Pink Lady McGuire — one mean mama — three hundred pounds of rolling, ugly meat that carried a twelve-gauge Remington pump and a bad attitude. Story was, Calhoun jumped her from behind, cut her throat, and as a joke, fucked her before she bled to death. This not only proved to Wayne that Calhoun was a dangerous sonofabitch, it also proved he had bad taste.

Wayne stepped out of his '57 Chevy reproduction, pushed his hat back on his forehead, opened the trunk, and got the sawed-off double barrel and some shells out of there. He already had a .38 revolver in the holster at his side and a bowie knife in each boot, but when you went into a place like Rosalita's it was best to have plenty of backup.

Wayne put a handful of shotgun shells in his shirt pocket, snapped the flap over them, looked up at the red-and-blue neon sign that flashed ROSALITA'S: COLD BEER AND DEAD DANCING, found his center, as they say in Zen, and went on in.

He held the shotgun against his leg, and as it was dark in there and folks were busy with talk or drinks or dancing, no one noticed him or his artillery right off.

He spotted Calhoun's stocky, black-hatted self immediately. He was inside the dance cage with a dead buck-naked Mexican girl of about twelve. He was holding her tight around the waist with one hand and massaging her rubbery ass with the other like it was a pillow he was trying to shape. The dead girl's handless arms flailed on either side of Calhoun, and her little tits pressed to his thick chest. Her wire-muzzled face knocked repeatedly at his shoulder and drool whipped out of her mouth in thick spermy ropes, stuck to his shin, faded and left a patch of wetness.

For all Wayne knew, the girl was Calhoun's sister or daughter. It was that kind of place. The kind that had sprung up immediately after that stuff had gotten out of a lab upstate and filled the air with bacteria that brought dead humans back to life, made their basic motor functions work and made them hungry for human flesh; made it so if a man's wife, daughter, sister, or mother went belly up and he wanted to turn a few bucks, he might think: "Damn, that's tough about ole Betty Sue, but she's dead as hoot-owl shit and ain't gonna be needing nothing from here on out, and with them germs working around in her, she's just gonna pull herself out of the ground and cause me a problem. And the ground out back of the house is harder to dig than a calculus problem is to work, so I'll just toss her cold ass in the back of the pickup next to the chain saw and the barbed-wire roll, haul her across the border to sell her to the Meat Boys to sell to the tonics for dancing.

"It's a sad thing to sell one of your own, but shit, them's the breaks. I'll just stay out of the tonics until all the meat rots off her bones and they have to throw her away. That way I won't go in some place for a drink and see her up there shaking her dead tits and end up going sentimental and dewy-eyed in front of one of my buddies or some ole two-dollar gal."

This kind of thinking supplied the dancers. In other parts of the country, the dancers might be men or children, but here it was mostly women. Men were used for hunting and target practice.

The Meat Boys took the bodies, cut off the hands so they couldn't grab, ran screws through their jaws to fasten on wire muzzles so they couldn't bite, sold them to the honky-tonks about the time the germ started stirring.

Bar owners put them inside wire enclosures up front of their joints, staffed music, and men paid five dollars to get in there and grab them and make like they were dancing when all the women wanted to do was grab and bite, which, muzzled and handless, they could not do.

If a man liked his partner enough, he could pay more money and have her tied to a cot in the back and he could get on her and at some business. Didn't have to hear no arguments or buy presents or make promises or make them come. Just fuck and hike.

As long as the establishment sprayed the dead for maggots and kept them perfumed and didn't keep them so long hunks of meat came off on a man's dick, the customers were happy as flies on shit.

Wayne looked to see who might give him trouble, and figured everyone was a potential customer. The six foot two, two-hundred-fifty-pound bouncer being the most immediate concern.

But, there wasn't anything to do but to get on with things and handle problems when they came up. He went into the cage where Calhoun was dancing, shouldered through the other dancers and went for him.

Calhoun had his back to Wayne, and as the music was loud, Wayne didn't worry about going quietly. But Calhoun sensed him and turned with his hand full of a little .38.

Wayne clubbed Calhoun's arm with the barrel of the shotgun. The little gun flew out of Calhoun's hand and went skidding across the floor and clanked against the metal cage.

Calhoun wasn't outdone. He spun the dead girl in front of him and pulled a big pigsticker out of his boot and held it under the girl's armpit in a threatening manner, which with a knife that big was no feat.

Wayne shot the dead girl's left kneecap out from under her and she went down. Her armpit trapped Calhoun's knife. The other men deserted their partners and went over the wire netting like squirrels.

Before Calhoun could shake the girl loose, Wayne stepped in and hit him over the head with the barrel of the shotgun. Calhoun crumpled and the girl began to crawl about on the floor as if looking for lost contacts.

The bouncer came in behind Wayne, grabbed him under the arms and tried to slip a full nelson on him.

Wayne kicked back on the bouncer's shin and raked his boot down the man's instep and stomped his foot. The bouncer let go. Wayne turned and kicked him in the balls and hit him across the face with the shotgun.

The bouncer went down and didn't even look like he wanted up.

Wayne couldn't help but note he liked the music that was playing. When he turned he had someone to dance with.

Calhoun.

Calhoun charged him, hit Wayne in the belly with his head, knocked him over the bouncer. They tumbled to the floor and the shotgun went out of Wayne's hands and scraped across the floor and hit the crawling girl in the head. She didn't even notice, just kept snaking in circles, dragging her blasted leg behind her like a skin she was trying to shed.

The other women, partnerless, wandered about the cage. The music changed. Wayne didn't like this tune as well. Too slow. He bit Calhoun's earlobe off.

Calhoun screamed and they grappled around on the floor. Calhoun got his arm around Wayne's throat and tried to choke him to death.

Wayne coughed out the earlobe, lifted his leg and took the knife out of his boot. He brought it around and back and hit Calhoun in the temple with the hilt.

Calhoun let go of Wayne and rocked on his knees, then collapsed on top of him.

Wayne got out from under him and got up and kicked him in the head a few times. When he was finished, he put the bowie in its place, got Calhoun's .38 and the shotgun. To hell with the pigsticker.

A dead woman tried to grab him, and he shoved her away with a thrust of his palm. He got Calhoun by the collar, started pulling him toward the gate.

Faces were pressed against the wire, watching. It had been quite a show. A friendly cowboy type opened the gate for Wayne and the crowd parted as he pulled Calhoun by. One man felt helpful and chased after them and said, "Here's his hat, Mister," and dropped it on Calhoun's knee and it stayed there.

Outside, a professional drunk was standing between two cars taking a leak on the ground. As Wayne pulled Calhoun past, the drunk said, "Your buddy don't look so good."

"Look worse than that when I get him to Law Town," Wayne said.

Wayne stopped by the '57, emptied Calhoun's pistol and tossed it as far as he could, then took a few minutes to kick Calhoun in the ribs and ass. Calhoun grunted and farted, but didn't come to.

When Wayne's leg got tired, he put Calhoun in the passenger seat and handcuffed him to the door.

He went over to Calhoun's '62 Impala replica with the plastic bull horns mounted on the hood — which was how he had located him in the first place, by his well known car — and kicked the glass out of the window on the driver's side and used the shotgun to shoot the bull horns off. He took out his pistol and shot all the tires flat, pissed on the driver's door, and kicked a dent in it.

By then he was too tired to shit in the back seat, so he took some deep breaths and went back to the '57 and climbed in behind the wheel.

Reaching across Calhoun, he opened the glove box and got out one of his thin, black cigars and put it in his mouth.

He pushed the lighter in, and while he waited for it to heat up, he took the shotgun out of his lap and reloaded it.

A couple of men poked their heads outside of the tonk's door, and Wayne stuck the shotgun out the window and fired above their heads. They disappeared inside so fast they might have been an optical illusion.

Wayne put the lighter to his cigar, picked up the wanted poster he had on the seat, and set fire to it. He thought about putting it in Calhoun's lap as a joke, but didn't. He tossed the flaming poster out of the window.

He drove over close to the tonk and used the remaining shotgun load to shoot at the neon Rosalita's sign. Glass tinkled onto the tonk's roof and onto the gravel drive.

Now if he only had a dog to kick.

He drove away from there, bound for the Cadillac Desert, and finally Law Town on the other side.

2

The Cadillacs stretched for miles, providing the only shade in the desert. They were buried nose down at a slant, almost to the windshields, and Wayne could see skeletons of some of the drivers in the cars, either lodged behind the steering wheels or lying on the dashboards against the glass. The roof and hood guns had long since been removed and all the windows on the cars were rolled up, except for those that had been knocked out and vandalized by travelers, or dead folks looking for goodies.

The thought of being in one of those cars with the windows rolled up in all this heat made Wayne feel even more uncomfortable than he already was. Hot as it was, he was certain even the skeletons were sweating.

He finished pissing on the tire of the Chevy, saw the piss had almost dried. He shook the drops off, watched them fall and evaporate against the burning sand. Zipping up, he thought about Calhoun, and how when he'd pulled over earlier to let the sonofabitch take a leak, he'd seen there was a little metal ring through the head of his dick and a Texas emblem dangling from that. He could understand the Texas emblem, being from there himself, but he couldn't for the life of him imagine why a fella would do that to his general. Any idiot who would put a ring through the head of his pecker deserved to die, innocent or not.

Wayne took off his cowboy hat and rubbed the back of his neck and ran his hand over the top of his head and back again. The sweat on his fingers was thick as lube oil, and the thinning part of his hairline was tender; the heat was cooking the hell out of his scalp, even through the brown felt of his hat.

Before he put his hat on, the sweat on his fingers was dry. He broke open the shotgun, put the shells in his pocket, opened the Chevy's back door and tossed the shotgun on the floorboard.

He got in the front behind the wheel and the seat was hot as a griddle on his back and ass. The sun shone through the slightly tinted windows like a polished chrome hubcap; it forced him to squint.

Glancing over at Calhoun, he studied him. The fucker was asleep with his head thrown back and his black wilted hat hung precariously on his head — it looked jaunty almost. Sweat oozed down Calhoun's red face, flowed over his eyelids and around his neck, running in rivulets down the white seat covers, drying quickly. He had his left hand between his legs, clutching his balls, and his right was on the arm rest, which was the only place it could be since he was handcuffed to the door.

Wayne thought he ought to blow the bastard's brains out and tell God he died. The shithead certainly needed shooting, but Wayne didn't want to lose a thousand dollars off his reward. He needed every penny if he was going to get that wrecking yard he wanted. The yard was the dream that went before him like a carrot before a donkey, and he didn't want any more delays. If he never made another trip across this goddamn desert, that would suit him fine.

Pop would let him buy the place with the money he had now, and he could pay the rest out later. But that wasn't what he wanted to do. The bounty business had finally gone sour, and he wanted to do different. It wasn't any goddamn fun anymore. Just met the dick cheese of the earth. And when you ran the sonofabitches to ground and put the cuffs on them, you had to watch your ass 'til you got them turned in. Had to sleep with one eye open and a hand on your gun. It wasn't any way to live.

And he wanted a chance to do right by Pop. Pop had been like a father to him. When he was a kid and his mama was screwing the Mexicans across the border for the rent money, Pop would let him hang out in the yard and climb on the rusted cars and watch him fix the better ones, tune those babies so fine they purred like dick-whipped women.

When he was older, Pop would haul him to Galveston for the whores and out to the beach to take potshots at all the ugly, fucked-up critters swimming around in the Gulf. Sometimes he'd take him to Oklahoma for the Dead Roundup. It sure seemed to do the old fart good to whack those dead fuckers with a tire iron, smash their diseased brains so they'd lay down for good. And it was a challenge. 'Cause if one of those dead buddies bit you, you could put your head between your legs and kiss your rosy ass goodbye.

Wayne pulled out of his thoughts of Pop and the wrecking yard and turned on the stereo system. One of his favorite country-and-western tunes whispered at him. It was Billy Conteegas singing, and Wayne hummed along with the music as he drove into the welcome, if mostly ineffectual, shadows provided by the Cadillacs.

"My baby left me,
She left me for a cow,
But I don't give a flying fuck,
She's gone radioactive now,
Yeah, my baby left me,
Left me for a six-tittied cow."

Just when Conteegas was getting to the good part, doing the trilling sound in his throat he was famous for, Calhoun opened his eyes and spoke up.

"Ain't it bad enough I got to put up with the fucking heat and your fucking humming without having to listen to that shit? Ain't you got no Hank Williams stuff, or maybe some of that nigger music they used to make? You know, where the coons harmonize and one of 'em sings like his nuts are cut off."

"You just don't know good music when you hear it, Calhoun."

Calhoun moved his free hand to his hatband, found one of his few remaining cigarettes and a match there. He struck the match on his knee, lit the smoke and coughed a few rounds. Wayne couldn't imagine how Calhoun could smoke in all this heat.

"Well, I may not know good music when I hear it, capon, but I damn sure know bad music when I hear it. And that's some bad music."

"You ain't got any kind of culture, Calhoun. You been too busy raping kids."

"Reckon a man has to have a hobby," Calhoun said, blowing smoke at Wayne. "Young pussy is mine. Besides, she wasn't in diapers. Couldn't find one that young. She was thirteen. You know what they say. If they're old enough to bleed, they're old enough to breed."

"How old they have to be for you to kill them?"

"She got loud."

"Change channels, Calhoun."

"Just passing the time of day, capon. Better watch yourself, bounty hunter, when you least expect it, I'll bash your head."

"You're gonna run your mouth one time too many, Calhoun, and when you do, you're gonna finish this ride in the trunk with ants crawling on you. You ain't so priceless I won't blow you away."

"You lucked out at the tonk, boy. But there's always tomorrow, and every day can't be like at Rosalita's."

Wayne smiled. "Trouble is, Calhoun, you're running out of tomorrows."

3

As they drove between the Cadillacs, the sky fading like a bad bulb, Wayne looked at the cars and tried to imagine what the Chevy-Cadillac Wars had been like, and why they had been fought in this miserable desert. He had heard it was a hell of a fight, and close, but the outcome had been Chevy's and now they were the only cars Detroit made. And as far as he was concerned, that was the only thing about Detroit that was worth a damn. Cars.

He felt that way about all cities. He'd just as soon lie down and let a diseased dog shit in his face than drive through one, let alone live in one.

Law Town being an exception. He'd go there. Not to live, but to give Calhoun to the authorities and pick up his reward. People in Law Town were always glad to see a criminal brought in. The public executions were popular and varied and supplied a steady income.

Last time he'd been to Law Town he'd bought a front-row ticket to one of the executions and watched a chronic shoplifter, a redheaded rat of a man, get pulled apart by being chained between two souped-up tractors. The execution itself was pretty brief, but there had been plenty of buildup with clowns and balloons and a big-tittied stripper who could swing her tits in either direction to boom-boom music.

Wayne had been put off by the whole thing. It wasn't organized enough and the drinks and food were expensive and the front-row seats were too close to the tractors. He had gotten to see that the redhead's insides were brighter than his hair, but some of the insides got sprinkled on his new shirt, and cold water or not, the spots hadn't come out. He had suggested to one of the management that they put up a big plastic shield so the front row wouldn't get splattered, but he doubted anything had come of it.

They drove until it was solid dark. Wayne stopped and fed Calhoun a stick of jerky and some water from his canteen. Then he handcuffed him to the front bumper of the Chevy.

"See any snakes, Gila monsters, scorpions, stuff like that," Wayne said, "yell out. Maybe I can get around here in time."

"I'd let the fuckers run up my asshole before I'd call you," Calhoun said.

Leaving Calhoun with his head resting on the bumper, Wayne climbed in the back seat of the Chevy and slept with one ear cocked and one eye open.

Before dawn Wayne got Calhoun loaded in the '57 and they started out. After a few minutes of sluicing through the early morning grayness, a wind started up. One of those weird desert winds that come out of nowhere. It carried grit through the air at the speed of bullets, hit the '57 with a sound like rabid cats scratching.

The sand tires crunched on through, and Wayne turned on the windshield blower, the sand wipers, and the head-beams, and kept on keeping on.

When it was time for the sun to come up, they couldn't see it. Too much sand. It was blowing harder than ever and the blowers and wipers couldn't handle it. It was piling up. Wayne couldn't even make out the Cadillacs anymore.

He was about to stop when a shadowy, whale-like shape crossed in front of him and he slammed on the brakes, giving the sand tires a workout. But it wasn't enough.

The '57 spun around and rammed the shape on Calhoun's side. Wayne heard Calhoun yell, then felt himself thrown against the door and his head smacked metal and the outside darkness was nothing compared to the darkness into which he descended.

4

Wayne rose out of it as quickly as he had gone down. Blood was trickling into his eyes from a slight forehead wound. He used his sleeve to wipe it away.

His first clear sight was of a face at the window on his side; a sallow, moon-terrain face with bulging eyes and an expression like an idiot contemplating Sanskrit. On the man's head was a strange, black hat with big round ears, and in the center of the hat, like a silver tumor, was the head of a large screw. Sand lashed at the face, imbedded in it, struck the unblinking eyes and made the round-eared hat flap. The man paid no attention. Though still dazed, Wayne knew why. The man was one of the dead folks.

Wayne looked in Calhoun's direction. Calhoun's door had been mashed in and the bending metal had pinched the handcuff attached to the arm rest in two. The blow had knocked Calhoun to the center of the seat. He was holding his hand in front of him, looking at the dangling cuff and chain as if it were a silver bracelet and a line of pearls.

Leaning over the hood, cleaning the sand away from the windshield with his hands, was another of the dead folks. He too was wearing one of the round-eared hats. He pressed a wrecked face to the clean spot and looked in at Calhoun. A string of snot-green saliva ran out of his mouth and onto the glass.

More sand was wiped away by others. Soon all the car's glass showed the pallid and rotting faces of the dead folks. They stared at Wayne and Calhoun as if they were two rare fish in an aquarium.

Wayne cocked back the hammer of the .38.

"What about me," Calhoun said. "What am I supposed to use?"

"Your charm," Wayne said, and at that moment, as if by signal, the dead folk faded away from the glass, leaving one man standing on the hood holding a baseball bat. He hit the glass and it went into a thousand little stars. The bat came again and the heavens fell and the stars rained down and the sand storm screamed in on Wayne and Calhoun.

The dead folks reappeared in full force. The one with the bat started though the hole in the windshield, heedless of the jags of glass that ripped his ragged clothes and tore his flesh like damp cardboard.

Wayne shot the batter through the head, and the man, finished, fell through, pinning Wayne's arm with his body.

Before Wayne could pull his gun free, a woman's hand reached through the hole and got hold of Wayne's collar. Other dead folks took to the glass and hammered it out with their feet and fist. Hands were all over Wayne; they felt dry and cool like leather seat covers. They pulled him over the steering wheel and dash and outside. The sand worked at his flesh like a cheese grater. He could hear Calhoun yelling, "Eat me, motherfuckers, eat me and choke."

They tossed Wayne on the hood of the '57. Faces leaned over him. Yellow teeth and toothless gums were very near. A road-kill odor washed through his nostrils. He thought: now the feeding frenzy begins. His only consolation was that there were so many dead folks, there wouldn't be enough of him left to come back from the dead. They'd probably have his brain for dessert.

But no. They picked him up and carried him off. Next thing he knew was a clearer view of the whale-shape the '57 had hit, and its color. It was a yellow school bus.

The door to the bus hissed open. The dead folks dumped Wayne inside on his belly and tossed his hat after him. They stepped back and the door closed, just missing Wayne's foot.

Wayne looked up and saw a man in the driver's seat smiling at him. It wasn't a dead man. Just fat and ugly. He was probably five feet tall and bald except for a fringe of hair around his shiny bald head the color of a shit ring in a toilet bowl. He had a nose so long and dark and malignant-looking it appeared as if it might fall off his face at any moment, like an overripe banana. He was wearing what Wayne first thought was a bathrobe, but proved to be a robe like that of a monk. It was old and tattered and moth-eaten and Wayne could see pale flesh through the holes. An odor wafted from the fat man that was somewhere between the smell of stale sweat, cheesy balls and an unwiped asshole.

"Good to see you," the fat man said.

"Charmed," Wayne said.

From the back of the bus came a strange, unidentifiable sound. Wayne poked his head around the seats for a look.

In the middle of the aisle, about halfway back, was a nun. Or sort of a nun. Her back was to him and she wore a black-and-white nun's habit. The part that covered her head was traditional, but from there down was quite a departure from the standard attire. The outfit was cut to the middle of her thigh and she wore black fishnet stockings and thick high heels. She was slim with good legs and a high little ass that, even under the circumstances, Wayne couldn't help but appreciate. She was moving one hand above her head as if sewing the air.

Sitting on the seats on either side of the aisle were dead folks. They all wore the round-eared hats, and they were responsible for the sound.

They were trying to sing.

He had never known dead folks to make any noise outside of grunts and groans, but here they were singing. A toneless sort of singing to be sure, some of the words garbled and some of the dead folks just opening and closing their mouths soundlessly, but, by golly, he recognized the tune. It was "Jesus Loves Me."

Wayne looked back at the fat man, let his hand ease down to the bowie in his right boot. The fat man produced a little .32 automatic from inside his robe and pointed it at Wayne.

"It's small caliber," the fat man said, "but I'm a real fine shot, and it makes a nice, little hole."

Wayne quit reaching in his boot.

"Oh, that's all right," said the fat man. "Take the knife out and put it on the floor in front of you and slide it to me. And while you're at it, I think I see the hilt of one in your other boot."

Wayne looked back. The way he had been thrown inside the bus had caused his pants legs to hike up over his boots, and the hilts of both his bowies were revealed. They might as well have had blinking lights on them.

It was shaping up to be a shitty day.

He slid the bowies to the fat man, who scooped them up nimbly and dumped them on the other side of his seat.

The bus door opened and Calhoun was tossed in on top of Wayne. Calhoun's hat followed after.

Wayne shrugged Calhoun off, recovered his hat, and put it on. Calhoun found his hat and did the same. They were still on their knees.

"Would you gentlemen mind moving to the center of the bus?"

Wayne led the way. Calhoun took note of the nun now, said, "Man, look at that ass."

The fat man called back to them. "Right there will do fine."

Wayne slid into the seat the fat man was indicating with a wave of the .32, and Calhoun slid in beside him. The dead folks entered now, filled the seats up front, leaving only a few stray seats in the middle empty.

Calhoun said, "What are those fuckers back there making that noise for?"

"They're singing," Wayne said. "Ain't you got no churchin'?"

"Say they are?" Calhoun turned to the nun and the dead folks and yelled, "Y'all know any Hank Williams?"

The nun did not turn and the dead folks did not quit their toneless singing.

"Guess not," Calhoun said. "Seems like all the good music's been forgotten."

The noise in the back of the bus ceased and the nun came over to look at Wayne and Calhoun. She was nice in front too. The outfit was cut from throat to crotch, laced with a ribbon, and it showed a lot of tit and some tight, thin, black panties that couldn't quite hold in her escaping pubic hair, which grew as thick and wild as kudzu. When Wayne managed to work his eyes up from that and look at her face, he saw she was dark-complected with eyes the color of coffee and lips made to chew on.

Calhoun never made it to the face. He didn't care about faces. He sniffed, said into her crotch, "Nice snatch."

The nun's left hand came around and smacked Calhoun on the side of the head.

He grabbed her wrist, said, "Nice arm, too."

The nun did a magic act with her right hand; it went behind her back and hiked up her outfit and came back with a double-barreled derringer. She pressed it against Calhoun's head.

Wayne bent forward, hoping she wouldn't shoot. At that range the bullet might go through Calhoun's head and hit him too.

"Can't miss," the nun said.

Calhoun smiled. "No you can't," he said, and let go of her arm.

She sat down across from them, smiled, and crossed her legs high. Wayne felt his Levi's snake swell and crawl against the inside of his thigh.

"Honey," Calhoun said, "you're almost worth taking a bullet for."

The nun didn't quit smiling. The bus cranked up. The sand blowers and wipers went to work, and the windshield turned blue, and a white dot moved on it between a series of smaller white dots.

Radar. Wayne had seen that sort of thing on desert vehicles. If he lived through this and got his car back, maybe he'd rig up something like that. And maybe not, he was sick of the desert.

Whatever, at the moment, future plans seemed a little out of place.

Then something else occurred to him. Radar. That meant these bastards had known they were coming and had pulled out in front of them on purpose.

He leaned over the seat and checked where he figured the '57 hit the bus. He didn't see a single dent. Armored, most likely. Most school buses were these days, and that's what this had been. It probably had bullet-proof glass and puncture-proof sand tires too. School buses had gone that way on account of the race riots and the sending of mutated calves to school just like they were humans. And because of the Codgers — old farts who believed kids ought to be fair game to adults for sexual purposes, or for knocking around when they wanted to let off some tension.

"How about unlocking this cuff?" Calhoun said. "It ain't for shit now anyway."

Wayne looked at the nun. "I'm going for the cuff key in my pants. Don't shoot."

Wayne fished it out, unlocked the cuff, and Calhoun let it slide to the floor. Wayne saw the nun was curious and he said, "I'm a bounty hunter. Help me get this man to Law Town and I could see you earn a little something for your troubles."

The woman shook her head.

"That's the spirit," Calhoun said. "I like a nun that minds her own business... You a real nun?"

She nodded.

"Always talk so much?"

Another nod.

Wayne said, "I've never seen a nun like you. Not dressed like that and with a gun."

"We are a small and special order," she said.

"You some kind of Sunday school teacher for these dead folks?"

"Sort of."

"But with them dead, ain't it kind of pointless? They ain't got no souls now, do they?"

"No, but their work adds to the glory of God."

"Their work?" Wayne looked at the dead folks sitting stiffly in their seats. He noted that one of them was about to lose a rotten ear. He sniffed. "They may be adding to the glory of God, but they don't do much for the air."

The nun reached into a pocket on her habit and took out two round objects. She tossed one to Calhoun, and one to Wayne. "Menthol lozenges. They help you stand the smell."

Wayne unwrapped the lozenge and sucked on it. It did help overpower the smell, but the menthol wasn't all that great either. It reminded him of being sick.

"What order are you?" Wayne asked.

"Jesus Loved Mary," the nun said.

"His mama?"

"Mary Magdalene. We think he fucked her. They were lovers. There's evidence in the scriptures. She was a harlot and we have modeled ourselves on her. She gave up that life and became a harlot for Jesus."

"Hate to break it to you, sister," Calhoun said, "but that do-gooder Jesus is as dead as a post. If you're waiting for him to slap the meat to you, that sweet thing of yours is going to dry up and blow away."

"Thanks for the news," the nun said. "But we don't fuck him in person. We fuck him in spirit. We let the spirit enter into men so they may take us in the fashion Jesus took Mary."

"No shit?"

"No shit."

"You know, I think I feel the old boy moving around inside me now. Why don't you shuck them drawers, honey, throw back in that seat there and let ole Calhoun give you a big load of Jesus."

Calhoun shifted in the nun's direction.

She pointed the derringer at him, said, "Stay where you are. If it were so, if you were full of Jesus, I would let you have me in a moment. But you're full of the Devil, not Jesus."

"Shit, sister, give ole Devil a break. He's a fun kind of guy. Let's you and me mount up... Well, be like that. But if you change your mind, I can get religion at a moment's notice. I dearly love to fuck. I've fucked...anything I could get my hands on but a parakeet, and I'd have fucked that little bitch if I could have found the hole."

"I've never known any dead folks to be trained," Wayne said, trying to get the nun talking in a direction that might help, a direction that would let him know what was going on and what sort of trouble he had fallen into.

"As I said, we are a very special order. Brother Lazarus," she waved a hand at the bus driver, and without looking he lifted a hand in acknowledgement, "is the founder. I don't think he'll mind if I tell his story, explain about us, what we do and why. It's important that we spread the word to the heathens."

"Don't call me no fucking heathen," Calhoun said. "This is heathen, riding 'round in a fucking bus with a bunch of stinking dead folks with funny hats on. Hell, they can't even carry a tune."

The nun ignored him. "Brother Lazarus was once known by another name, but that name no longer matters. He was a research scientist, and he was one of those who worked in the laboratory where the germs escaped into the air and made it so the dead could not truly die as long as they had an undamaged brain in their heads.

"Brother Lazarus was carrying a dish of the experiment, the germs, and as a joke, one of the lab assistants pretended to trip him, and he, not knowing it was a joke, dodged the assistant's leg and dropped the dish. In a moment, the air conditioning system had blown the germs throughout the research center. Someone opened a door, and the germs were loose on the world.

"Brother Lazarus was consumed by guilt. Not only because he dropped the dish, but because he helped create it in the first place. He quit his job at the laboratory, took to wandering the country. He came out here with nothing more than basic food, water and books. Among these books was the Bible, and the lost books of the Bible: the Apocrypha and the many cast-out chapters of the New Testament. As he studied, it occurred to him that these cast-out books actually belonged. He was able to interpret their higher meaning, and an angel came to him in a dream and told him of another book, and Brother Lazarus took up his pen and recorded the angel's words, direct from God, and in this book, all the mysteries were explained."

"Like screwing Jesus," Calhoun said.

"Like screwing Jesus, and not being afraid of words that mean sex. Not being afraid of seeing Jesus as both God and man. Seeing that sex, if meant for Christ and the opening of the mind, can be a thrilling and religious experience, not just the rutting of two savage animals.

"Brother Lazarus roamed the desert, the mountains, thinking of the things the Lord had revealed to him, and lo and behold, the Lord revealed yet another thing to him. Brother Lazarus found a great amusement park."

"Didn't know Jesus went in for rides and such," Calhoun said.

"It was long deserted. It had once been part of a place called Disneyland. Brother Lazarus knew of it. There had been several of these Disneylands built about the country, and this one had been in the midst of the Chevy-Cadillac Wars, and had been destroyed and sand had covered most of it."

The nun held out her arms. "And in this rubble, he saw a new beginning."

"Cool off, baby," Calhoun said, "before you have a stroke."

"He gathered to him men and women of a like mind and taught the gospel to them. The Old Testament. The New Testament. The Lost Books. And his own Book of Lazarus, for he had begun to call himself Lazarus. A symbolic name signifying a new beginning, a rising from the dead and coming to life and seeing things as they really are."

The nun moved her hands rapidly, expressively as she talked. Sweat beaded on her forehead and upper lip.

"So he returned to his skills as a scientist, but applied them to a higher purpose — God's purpose. And as Brother Lazarus, he realized the use of the dead. They could be taught to work and build a great monument to the glory of God. And this monument, this coed institution of monks and nuns would be called Jesus Land."

At the word "Jesus," the nun gave her voice an extra trill, and the dead folks, cued, said together, "Eees num be prased."

"How the hell did you train them dead folks?" Calhoun said. "Dog treats?"

"Science put to the use of our lord Jesus Christ, that's how. Brother Lazarus made a special device he could insert directly into the brains of dead folks, through the tops of their heads, and the device controls certain cravings. Makes them passive and responsive — at least to simple commands. With the regulator, as Brother Lazarus calls the device, we have been able to do much positive work with the dead."

"Where do you find these dead folks?" Wayne asked.

"We buy them from the Meat Boys. We save them from amoral purposes."

"They ought to be shot through the head and put in the goddamn ground," Wayne said.

"If our use of the regulator and the dead folks was merely to better ourselves, I would agree. But it is not. We do the Lord's work."

"Do the monks fuck the sisters?" Calhoun asked.

"When possessed by the Spirit of Christ. Yes."

"And I bet they get possessed a lot. Not a bad setup. Dead folks to do the work on the amusement park —"

"It isn't an amusement park now."

"— and plenty of free pussy. Sounds cozy. I like it. Old shithead up there's smarter than he looks."

"There is nothing selfish about our motives or those of Brother Lazarus. In fact, as penance for loosing the germ on the world in the first place, Brother

Lazarus injected a virus into his nose. It is rotting slowly."

"Thought that was quite a snorkel he had on him," Wayne said.

"I take it back," Calhoun said. "He *is* as dumb as he looks."

"Why do the dead folks wear those silly hats?" Wayne asked.

"Brother Lazarus found a storeroom of them at the site of the old amusement park. They are mouse ears. They represent some cartoon animal that was popular once and part of Disneyland. Mickey Mouse, he was called. This way we know which dead folks are ours, and which ones are not controlled by our regulators. From time to time, stray dead folks wander into our area. Murder victims. Children abandoned in the desert. People crossing the desert who died of heat or illness. We've had some of the sisters and brothers attacked. The hats are a precaution."

"And what's the deal with us?" Wayne asked.

The nun smiled sweetly. "You, my children, are to add to the glory of God."

"Children?" Calhoun said. "You call an alligator a lizard, bitch?"

The nun slid back in the seat and rested the derringer in her lap. She pulled her legs into a cocked position, causing her panties to crease in the valley of her vagina; it looked like a nice place to visit, that valley.

Wayne turned from the beauty of it and put his head back and closed his eyes, pulled his hat down over them. There was nothing he could do at the moment, and since the nun was watching Calhoun for him, he'd sleep, store up and figure what to do next. If anything.

He drifted off to sleep wondering what the nun meant by, "You, my children, are to add to the glory of God."

He had a feeling that when he found out, he wasn't going to like it.

5

He awoke off and on and saw that the sunlight filtering through the storm had given everything a greenish color. Calhoun, seeing he was awake, said, "Ain't that a pretty color? I had a shirt that color once and liked it lots, but I got in a fight with this Mexican whore with a wooden leg over some money and she tore it. I punched that little bean bandit good."

"Thanks for sharing that," Wayne said, and went back to sleep.

Each time he awoke it was brighter, and finally he awoke to the sun going down and the storm having died out. But he didn't stay awake. He forced himself to close his eyes and store up more energy. To help him nod off he listened to the hum of the motor and thought about the wrecking yard and Pop and all the fun they could have, just drinking beer and playing cards and fucking the border women, and maybe some of those mutated cows they had over there for sale.

Nah. Nix the cows, or any of those genetically altered critters. A man had to draw the line somewhere, and he drew it at fucking critters, even if they had been bred so that they had human traits. You had to have some standards.

'Course, those standards had a way of eroding. He remembered when he said he'd only fuck the pretty ones. His last whore had been downright scary looking. If he didn't watch himself he'd be as bad as Calhoun, trying to find the hole in the parakeet.

He awoke to Calhoun's elbow in his ribs and the nun was standing beside their seat with the derringer. Wayne knew she hadn't slept, but she looked bright-eyed and bushy-tailed. She nodded toward their window, said, "Jesus Land."

She had put that special touch in her voice again, and the dead folks responded with, "Eees num be prased."

It was good and dark now, a crisp night with a big moon the color of hammered brass. The bus sailed across the white sand like a mystical schooner with a full wind in its sails. It went up an impossible hill toward what looked like an aurora borealis, then dove into an atomic rainbow of colors that filled the bus with fairy lights.

When Wayne's eyes became accustomed to the lights, and the bus took a right turn along a precarious curve, he glanced down into the valley. An aerial view couldn't have been any better than the view from his window.

Down there was a universe of polished metal and twisted neon. In the center of the valley was a great statue of Jesus crucified that must have been twenty-five stories high. Most of the body was made of bright metals and multicolored neon; and much of the light was coming from that. There was a crown of barbed wire wound several times around a chromium plate of a forehead and some rust-colored strands of neon hair. The savior's eyes were huge, green strobes that swung left and right with the precision of an oscillating fan. There was an ear-to-ear smile on the savior's face and the teeth were slats of sparkling metal with wide cavity-black gaps between them. The statue was equipped with a massive dick of polished, interwoven cables and coils of neon, the dick was thicker and more solid looking than the arthritic steel-tube legs on either side of it; the head of it was made of an enormous spotlight that pulsed the color of irritation.

The bus went around and around the valley, descending like a dead roach going down a slow drain, and finally the road rolled out straight and took them into Jesus Land.

They passed through the legs of Jesus, under the throbbing head of his cock, toward what looked like a small castle of polished gold bricks with an upright drawbridge inlayed with jewels.

The castle was only one of several tall structures that appeared to be made of rare metals and precious stones: gold, silver, emeralds, rubies, and sapphires. But the closer they got to the buildings, the less fine they looked and the more they looked like what they were: stucco, cardboard, phosphorescent paint, colored spotlights, and bands of neon.

Off to the left Wayne could see a long, open shed full of vehicles, most of them old school buses. And there were unlighted hovels made of tin and tar paper; homes for the dead, perhaps. Behind the shacks and the bus barn rose skeletal shapes that stretched tall and bleak against the sky and the candy-gem lights; shapes that looked like the bony remains of beached whales.

On the right, Wayne glimpsed a building with an open front that served as a stage. In front of the stage were chairs filled with monks and nuns. On the stage, six monks — one behind a drum set, one with a saxophone, the others with guitars — were blasting out a loud, rocking rhythm that made the bus shake. A nun with the front of her habit thrown open, her headpiece discarded, sang into a microphone with a voice like a suffering angel. The voice screeched out of the amplifiers and came in through the windows of the bus, crushing the sound of the engine. The nun crowed "Jesus" so long and hard it sounded like a plea from hell. Then she leapt up and came down doing the splits, the impact driving her back to her feet as if her ass had been loaded with springs.

"Bet that bitch can pick up a quarter with that thing," Calhoun said.

Brother Lazarus touched a button, the pseudo-jeweled drawbridge lowered over a narrow moat, and he drove them inside.

It wasn't as well lighted in there. The walls were bleak and gray. Brother Lazarus stopped the bus and got off, and another monk came on board. He was tall and thin and had crooked buck teeth that dented his bottom lip. He also had a twelve-gauge pump shotgun.

"This is Brother Fred," the nun said. "He'll be your tour guide."

Brother Fred forced Wayne and Calhoun off the bus, away from the dead folks in their mouse-ear hats and the nun in her tight, black panties, jabbed them along a dark corridor, up a swirl of stairs and down a longer corridor with open doors on either side and rooms filled with dark and light and spoiled meat and guts on hooks and skulls and bones lying about like discarded walnut shells and broken sticks; rooms full of dead folks (truly dead) stacked neat as firewood, and rooms full of stone shelves stuffed with beakers of fiery-red and sewer-green and sky-blue and piss-yellow liquids, as well as glass coils through which other colored fluids fled as if chased, smoked as if nervous, and ran into big flasks as if relieved; rooms with platforms and tables and boxes and stools and chairs covered with instruments or dead folks or dead-folk pieces or the asses of monks and nuns as they sat and held charts or tubes or body parts and frowned at them with concentration, lips pursed as if about to explode with some earth-shattering pronouncement; and finally they came to a little room with a tall, glassless window that looked out upon the bright, shiny mess that was Jesus Land.

The room was simple. Table, two chairs, two beds — one on either side of the room. The walls were stone and unadorned. To the right was a little bath-room without a door.

Wayne walked to the window and looked out at Jesus Land pulsing and thumping like a desperate heart. He listened to the music a moment, leaned over and stuck his head outside.

They were high up and there was nothing but a straight drop. If you jumped, you'd wind up with the heels of your boots under your tonsils.

Wayne let out a whistle in appreciation of the drop. Brother Fred thought it was a compliment for Jesus Land. He said, "It's a miracle, isn't it?"

"Miracle?" Calhoun said. "This goony light show? This ain't no miracle. This is for shit. Get that nun on the bus back there to bend over and shit a perfectly round turd through a hoop at twenty paces, and I'll call that a miracle, Mr. Fucked-up Teeth. But this Jesus Land crap is the dumbest fucking idea since dog sweaters.

"And look at this place. You could use some knickknacks or something in here. A picture of some ole naked gal doing a donkey, couple of pigs fucking. Anything. And a door on the shitter would be nice. I hate to be straining out a big one and know someone can look in on me. It ain't decent. A man ought to have his fucking grunts in private. This place reminds me of a motel I stayed at in Waco one night, and I made the goddamn manager give me my money back. The roaches in that shit hole were big enough to use the shower."

Brother Fred listened to all this without blinking an eye, as if seeing Calhoun talk was as amazing as seeing a frog sing. He said, "Sleep tight, don't let the bed bugs bite. Tomorrow you start to work."

"I don't want no fucking job," Calhoun said.

"Goodnight, children," Brother Fred said, and with that he closed the door and they heard it lock, loud and final as the clicking of the drop board on a gallows.

6

At dawn, Wayne got up and took a leak, went to the window to look out. The stage where the monks had played and the nun had jumped was empty. The skeletal shapes he had seen last night were tracks and frames from rides long abandoned. He had a sudden vision of Jesus and his disciples riding a roller coaster, their long hair and robes flapping in the wind.

The large crucified Jesus looked unimpressive without its lights and night's mystery, like a whore in harsh sunlight with makeup gone and wig askew.

"Got any ideas how we're gonna get out of here?" Calhoun asked.

Wayne looked at Calhoun. He was sitting on the bed, pulling on his boots.

Wayne shook his head.

"I could use a smoke. You know, I think we ought to work together. Then we can try to kill each other."

Unconsciously, Calhoun touched his ear where Wayne had bitten off the lobe.

"Wouldn't trust you as far as I could kick you," Wayne said.

"I hear that. But I give my word. And my word's something you can count on. I won't twist it."

Wayne studied Calhoun, thought: Well, there wasn't anything to lose. He'd just watch his ass.

"All right," Wayne said. "Give me your word you'll work with me on getting us out of this mess, and when we're good and free, and you say your word has gone far enough, we can settle up."

"Deal," Calhoun said, and offered his hand. Wayne looked at it.

"This seals it," Calhoun said.

Wayne took Calhoun's hand and they shook.

7

Moments later the door unlocked and a smiling monk with hair the color and texture of mold fuzz came in with Brother Fred, who still had his pump shotgun. There were two dead folks with them. A man and a woman. They wore torn clothes and the mouse-ear hats. Neither looked long dead or smelled particularly bad. Actually, the monks smelled worse.

Using the barrel of the shotgun, Brother Fred poked them down the hall to a room with metal tables and medical instruments.

Brother Lazarus was on the far side of one of the tables. He was smiling. His nose looked especially cancerous this morning. A white pustule the size of a thumb tip had taken up residence on the left side of his snout, and it looked like a pearl onion in a turd.

Nearby stood a nun. She was short with good, if skinny, legs, and she wore the same outfit as the nun on the bus. It looked more girlish on her, perhaps because she was thin and small-breasted. She had a nice face, and eyes that were all pupil. Wisps of blond hair crawled out around the edges of her headgear. She looked pale and weak, as if wearied to the bone. There was a birthmark on her right cheek that looked like a distant view of a small bird in flight.

"Good morning," Brother Lazarus said. "I hope you gentlemen slept well."

"What's this about work?" Wayne said.

"Work?" Brother Lazarus said.

"I described it to them that way," Brother Fred said. "Perhaps an impulsive description."

"I'll say," Brother Lazarus said. "No work here, gentlemen. You have my word on that. We do all the work. Lie on these tables and we'll take a sampling of your blood."

"Why?" Wayne said.

"Science," Brother Lazarus said. "I intend to find a cure for this germ that makes the dead come back to life, and to do that, I need living human beings to study. Sounds kind of mad scientist, doesn't it? But I assure you, you've nothing to lose but a few drops of blood. Well, maybe more than a few drops, but nothing serious."

"Use your own goddamn blood," Calhoun said.

"We do. But we're always looking for fresh specimens. Little here, little there. And if you don't do it, we'll kill you."

Calhoun spun and hit Brother Fred on the nose. It was a solid punch and Brother Fred hit the floor on his butt, but he hung onto the shotgun and pointed it up at Calhoun. "Go on," he said, his nose streaming blood. "Try that again."

Wayne flexed to help, but hesitated. He could kick Brother Fred in the head from where he was, but that might not keep him from shooting Calhoun, and there would go the extra reward money. And besides, he'd given his word to the bastard that they'd try to help each other survive until they got out of this.

The other monk clasped his hands and swung them into the side of Calhoun's head, knocking him down. Brother Fred got up, and while Calhoun was trying to rise, he hit him with the stock of the shotgun in the back of the head, hit him so hard it drove Calhoun's forehead into the floor. Calhoun rolled over on his side and lay there, his eyes fluttering like moth wings.

"Brother Fred, you must learn to turn the other cheek," Brother Lazarus said. "Now put this sack of shit on the table."

Brother Fred checked Wayne to see if he looked like trouble. Wayne put his hands in his pockets and smiled.

Brother Fred called the two dead folks over and had them put Calhoun on the table. Brother Lazarus strapped him down.

The nun brought a tray of needles, syringes, cotton and bottles over, put it down on the table next to Calhoun's head. Brother Lazarus rolled up Calhoun's sleeve and fixed up a needle and stuck it in Calhoun's arm, drew it full of blood. He stuck the needle through the rubber top of one of the bottles and shot the blood into that.

He looked at Wayne and said, "I hope you'll be less trouble."

"Do I get some orange juice and a little cracker afterwards?" Wayne said.

"You get to walk out without a knot on your head," Brother Lazarus said.

"Guess that'll have to do."

Wayne got on the table next to Calhoun and Brother Lazarus strapped him down. The nun brought the tray over and Brother Lazarus did to him what he had done to Calhoun. The nun stood over Wayne and looked down at his face. Wayne tried to read something in her features but couldn't find a clue.

When Brother Lazarus was finished he took hold of Wayne's chin and shook it. "My, but you two boys look healthy. But you can never be sure. We'll have to run the blood through some tests. Meantime, Sister Worth will run a few additional tests on you, and," he nodded at the unconscious Calhoun, "I'll see to your friend here."

"He's no friend of mine," Wayne said.

They took Wayne off the table, and Sister Worth and Brother Fred, and his shotgun, directed him down the hall into another room.

The room was lined with shelves that were lined with instruments and bottles. The lighting was poor, most of it coming through a slatted window, though there was an anemic yellow bulb overhead. Dust motes swam in the air.

In the center of the room on its rim was a great, spoked wheel. It had two straps well spaced at the top, and two more at the bottom. Beneath the bottom straps were blocks of wood. The wheel was attached in back to an upright metal bar that had switches and buttons all over it.

Brother Fred made Wayne strip and get on the wheel with his back to the hub and his feet on the blocks. Sister Worth strapped his ankles down tight, then he was made to put his hands up, and she strapped his wrists to the upper part of the wheel.

"I hope this hurts a lot," Brother Fred said.

"Wipe the blood off your face," Wayne said. "It makes you look silly."

Brother Fred made a gesture with his middle finger that wasn't religious and left the room.

8

Sister Worth touched a switch and the wheel began to spin, slowly at first, and the bad light came through the windows and poked through the rungs and the dust swam before his eyes and the wheel and its spokes threw twisting shadows on the wall.

As he went around, Wayne closed his eyes. It kept him from feeling so dizzy, especially on the down swings.

On a turn up, he opened his eyes and caught sight of Sister Worth standing in front of the wheel staring at him. He said, "Why?" and closed his eyes as the wheel dipped.

"Because Brother Lazarus says so," came the answer after such a long time Wayne had almost forgotten the question. Actually, he hadn't expected a response. He was surprised that such a thing had come out of his mouth, and he felt a little diminished for having asked.

He opened his eyes on another swing up, and she was moving behind the wheel, out of his line of vision. He heard a snick like a switch being flipped and lightning jumped through him and he screamed in spite of himself. A little fork of electricity licked out of his mouth like a reptile tongue tasting air.

Faster spun the wheel and the jolts came more often and he screamed less loud, and finally not at all. He was too numb. He was adrift in space wearing only his cowboy hat and boots, moving away from earth very fast. Floating all around him were wrecked cars. He looked and saw that one of them was his '57, and behind the steering wheel was Pop. Sitting beside the old man was a Mexican. Two more were in the back seat. They looked a little drunk.

One of the whores in back pulled up her dress and cocked it high up so he could see her pussy. It looked like that needed a shave.

He smiled and tried to go for it, but the '57 was moving away, swinging wide and turning its tail to him. He could see a face at the back window. Pop's face. He had crawled back there and was waving slowly and sadly. A whore pulled Pop from view.

The wrecked cars moved away too, as if caught in the vacuum of the '57's retreat. Wayne swam with his arms, kicked with his legs, trying to pursue the '57 and the wrecks. But he dangled where he was, like a moth pinned to a board. The cars moved out of sight and left him there with his arms and legs stretched out, spinning amidst an infinity of cold, uncaring stars.

"...how the tests are run...marks everything about you...charts it...EKG, brain waves, liver...everything...it hurts because Brother Lazarus wants it to... thinks I don't know these things...that I'm slow...slow, not stupid...smart really...used to be scientist...before the accident...Brother Lazarus is not holy...he's mad...made the wheel because of the Holy Inquisition...knows a lot about the Inquisition...thinks we need it again...for the likes of men you... the unholy, he says... But he just likes to hurt...I know."

Wayne opened his eyes. The wheel had stopped. Sister Worth was talking in her monotone, explaining the wheel. He remembered asking her, "Why" about three thousand years ago.

Sister Worth was staring at him again. She went away and he expected the wheel to start up, but when she returned, she had a long, narrow mirror under her arm. She put it against the wall across from him. She got on the wheel with him, her little feet on the wooden platforms beside his. She hiked up the bottom of her habit and pulled down her black panties. She put her face close to his, as if searching for something.

"He plans to take your body...piece by piece...blood, cells, brain, your cock...all of it... He wants to live forever."

She had her panties in her hand, and she tossed them. Wayne watched them fly up and flutter to the floor like a dying bat.

She took hold of his dick and pulled on it. Her palm was cold and he didn't feel his best, but he began to get hard. She put him between her legs and rubbed his dick between her thighs. They were as cold as her hands, and dry.

"I know him now...know what he's doing...the dead germ virus...he was trying to make something that would make him live forever...it made the dead come back...didn't keep the living alive, free of old age..."

His dick was throbbing now, in spite of the coolness of her body.

"He cuts up dead folks to learn...experiments on them...but the secret of eternal life is with the living...that's why he wants you...you're an outsider... those who live here he can...test...but he must keep them alive to do his bidding...not let them know how he really is...needs your insides and the other man's...he wants to be a God...flies high above us in a little plane and looks down... Likes to think he is the creator, I bet..."

"Plane?"

"Ultralight."

She pushed his cock inside her, and it was cold and dry in there, like liver left overnight on a drainboard. Still, he found himself ready. At this point, he would have gouged a hole in a turnip.

She kissed him on the ear and alongside the neck; cold little kisses, dry as toast.

"…thinks I don't know… But I know he doesn't love Jesus… He loves himself, and power… He's sad about his nose…"

"I bet."

"Did it in a moment of religious fervor…before he lost the belief… Now he wants to be what he was… A scientist. He wants to grow a new nose…know how…saw him grow a finger in a dish once…grew it from the skin off a knuckle of one of the brothers… He can do all kinds of things."

She was moving her hips now. He could see over her shoulder into the mirror against the wall. Could see her white ass rolling, the black habit hiked up above it, threatening to drop like a curtain. He began to thrust back, slowly, firmly.

She looked over her shoulder into the mirror, watching herself fuck him. There was a look more of study than rapture on her face.

"Want to feel alive," she said. "Feel a good, hard dick… Been too long."

"I'm doing the best I can," Wayne said. "This ain't the most romantic of spots."

"Push so I can feel it."

"Nice," Wayne said. He gave it everything he had. He was beginning to lose his erection. He felt as if he were auditioning for a job and not making the best of impressions. He felt like a knothole would be dissatisfied with him.

She got off of him and climbed down.

"Don't blame you," he said.

She went behind the wheel and touched some things on the upright. She mounted him again, hooked her ankles behind his. The wheel began to turn. Short electrical shocks leaped through him. They weren't as powerful as before. They were invigorating. When he kissed her it was like touching his tongue to a battery. It felt as if electricity was racing through his veins and flying out the head of his dick; he felt as if he might fill her with lightning instead of come.

The wheel creaked to a stop; it must have had a timer on it. They were upside down and Wayne could see their reflection in the mirror; they looked like two lizards fucking on a window pane.

He couldn't tell if she had finished or not, so he went ahead and got it over with. Without the electricity he was losing his desire. It hadn't been an A-one piece of ass, but hell, as Pop always said, "Worse pussy I ever had was good."

"They'll be coming back," she said. "Soon… Don't want them to find us like this… Other tests to do yet."

"Why did you do this?"

"I want out of the order… Want out of this desert… I want to live… And I want you to help me."

"I'm game, but the blood is rushing to my head and I'm getting dizzy. Maybe you ought to get off me."

After an eon she said, "I have a plan."

She untwined from him and went behind the wheel and hit a switch that turned Wayne upright. She touched another switch and he began to spin slowly, and while he spun and while lightning played inside him, she told him her plan.

9

"I think ole Brother Fred wants to fuck me," Calhoun said. "He keeps trying to get his finger up my asshole."

They were back in their room. Brother Fred had brought them back, making them carry their clothes, and now they were alone again, dressing.

"We're getting out of here," Wayne said. "The nun, Sister Worth, she's going to help."

"What's her angle?"

"She hates this place and wants my dick. Mostly, she hates this place."

"What's the plan?"

Wayne told him first what Brother Lazarus had planned. On the morrow he would have them brought to the room with the steel tables, and they would go on the tables, and if the tests had turned out good, they would be pronounced fit as fiddles and Brother Lazarus would strip the skin from their bodies, slowly, because according to Sister Worth he liked to do it that way, and he would drain their blood and percolate it into his formulas like coffee, cut their brains out and put them in vats and store their veins and organs in freezers.

All of this would be done in the name of God and Jesus Christ (Eees num be prased) under the guise of finding a cure for the dead folks germ. But it would all instead be for Brother Lazarus who wanted to have a new nose, fly his ultralight above Jesus Land, and live forever.

Sister Worth's plan was this:

She would be in the dissecting room. She would have guns hidden. She would make the first move, a distraction, then it was up to them.

"This time," Wayne said, "one of us has to get on top of that shotgun."

"You had your finger up your ass in there today, or we'd have had them."

"We're going to have surprise on our side this time. Real surprise. They won't be expecting Sister Worth. We can get up there on the roof and take off in that ultralight. When it runs out of gas we can walk, maybe get back to the '57 and hope it runs."

"We'll settle our score then. Whoever wins keeps the car and the split tail. As for tomorrow, I've got a little ace."

Calhoun pulled on his boots. He twisted the heel of one of them. It swung out and a little knife dropped into his hand. "It's sharp," Calhoun said. "I cut a Chinaman from gut to gill with it. It was easy as sliding a stick through fresh shit."

"Been nice if you'd had that ready today."

"I wanted to scout things out first. And to tell the truth, I thought one pop to Brother Fred's mouth and he'd be out of the picture."

"You hit him in the nose."

"Yeah, goddamn it, but I was aiming for his mouth."

10

Dawn and the room with the metal tables looked the same. No one had brought in a vase of flowers to brighten the place.

Brother Lazarus's nose had changed however; there were two pearl onions nestled in it now.

Sister Worth, looking only a little more animated than yesterday, stood nearby. She was holding the tray with the instruments. This time the tray was full of scalpels. The light caught their edges and made them wink.

Brother Fred was standing behind Calhoun, and Brother Mold Fuzz was behind Wayne. They must have felt pretty confident today. They had dispensed with the dead folks.

Wayne looked at Sister Worth and thought maybe things were not good. Maybe she had lied to him in her slow talking way. Only wanted a little dick and wanted to keep it quiet. To do that, she might have promised anything. She might not care what Brother Lazarus did to them.

If it looked like a double cross, Wayne was going to go for it. If he had to jump right into the mouth of Brother Fred's shotgun. That was a better way to go than having the hide peeled from your body. The idea of Brother Lazarus and his ugly nose leaning over him did not appeal at all.

"It's so nice to see you," Brother Lazarus said. "I hope we'll have none of the unpleasantness of yesterday. Now, on the tables."

Wayne looked at Sister Worth. Her expression showed nothing. The only thing about her that looked alive was the bent wings of the bird birthmark on her cheek.

All right, Wayne thought, I'll go as far as the table, then I'm going to do something. Even if it's wrong.

He took a step forward, and Sister Worth flipped the contents of the tray into Brother Lazarus's face. A scalpel went into his nose and hung there. The tray and the rest of its contents hit the floor.

Before Brother Lazarus could yelp, Calhoun dropped and wheeled. He was under Brother Fred's shotgun and he used his forearm to drive the barrel upwards. The gun went off and peppered the ceiling. Plaster sprinkled down.

Calhoun had concealed the little knife in the palm of his hand and he brought it up and into Brother Fred's groin. The blade went through the robe and buried to the hilt.

The instant Calhoun made his move, Wayne brought his forearm back and around into Brother Mold Fuzz's throat, then turned and caught his head and jerked that down and kneed him a couple of times. He floored him by driving an elbow into the back of his neck.

Calhoun had the shotgun now, and Brother Fred was on the floor trying to pull the knife out of his balls. Calhoun blew Brother Fred's head off, then did the same for Brother Mold Fuzz.

Brother Lazarus, the scalpel hanging from his nose, tried to run for it, but he stepped on the tray and that sent him flying. He landed on his stomach. Calhoun took two deep steps and kicked him in the throat. Brother Lazarus made a sound like he was gargling and tried to get up.

Wayne helped him. He grabbed Brother Lazarus by the back of his robe and pulled him up, slammed him back against a table. The scalpel still dangled from the monk's nose. Wayne grabbed it and jerked, taking away a chunk of nose as he did. Brother Lazarus screamed.

Calhoun put the shotgun in Brother Lazarus's mouth and that made him stop screaming. Calhoun pumped the shotgun. He said, "Eat it," and pulled the trigger. Brother Lazarus's brains went out the back of his head riding on a chunk of skull. The brains and skull hit the table and sailed onto the floor like a plate of scrambled eggs pushed the length of a cafe counter.

Sister Worth had not moved. Wayne figured she had used all of her concentration to hit Brother Lazarus with the tray.

"You said you'd have guns," Wayne said to her.

She turned her back to him and lifted her habit. In a belt above her panties were two .38 revolvers. Wayne pulled them out and held one in each hand. "Two-Gun Wayne," he said.

"What about the ultralight?" Calhoun said. "We've made enough noise for a prison riot. We need to move."

Sister Worth turned to the door at the back of the room, and before she could say anything or lead, Wayne and Calhoun snapped to it and grabbed her and pushed her toward it.

There were stairs on the other side of the door and they took them two at a time. They went through a trap door and onto the roof and there, tied down with bungee straps to metal hoops, was the ultralight. It was blue-and-white canvas and metal rods, and strapped to either side of it was a twelve gauge pump and a bag of food and a canteen of water.

They unsnapped the roof straps and got in the two-seater and used the straps to fasten Sister Worth between them. It wasn't comfortable, but it was a ride.

They sat there. After a moment, Calhoun said, "Well?"

"Shit," Wayne said. "I can't fly this thing."

They looked at Sister Worth. She was staring at the controls.

"Say something, damn it," Wayne said.

"That's the switch," she said. "That stick...forward is up, back brings the nose down...side to side..."

"Got it."

"Well, shoot this bastard over the side," Calhoun said. Wayne cranked it, gave it the throttle. The machine rolled forward, wobbled.

"Too much weight," Wayne said.

"Throw the cunt over the side," Calhoun said.

"It's all or nothing," Wayne said. The ultralight continued to swing its tail left and right, but leveled off as they went over the edge.

They sailed for a hundred yards, made a mean curve Wayne couldn't fight, and fell straight away into the statue of Jesus, striking it in the head, right in the midst of the barbed wire crown. Spot lights shattered, metal groaned, the wire tangled in the nylon wings of the craft and held it. The head of Jesus nodded forward, popped off, and shot out on the electric cables inside like a jack-in-the-box. The cables pulled tight a hundred feet from the ground and worked the head and the craft like a yo-yo. Then the barbed wire crown unraveled and dropped the craft the rest of the way. It hit the ground with a crunch and a rip and a cloud of dust.

The head of Jesus bobbed above the shattered ultralight like a bird preparing to peck a worm.

II

Wayne crawled out of the wreckage and tried his legs. They worked.

Calhoun was on his feet cussing, unstrapping the shotguns and supplies.

Sister Worth lay in the midst of the wreck, the nylon and aluminum supports folded around her like butterfly wings.

Wayne started pulling the mess off of her. He saw that her leg was broken. A bone punched out of her thigh like a sharpened stick. There was no blood.

"Here comes the church social," Calhoun said.

The word was out about Brother Lazarus and the others. A horde of monks, nuns and dead folks were rushing over the drawbridge. Some of the nuns and monks had guns. All of the dead folks had clubs. The clergy was yelling.

Wayne nodded toward the bus barn, "Let's get a bus." Wayne picked up Sister Worth, cradled her in his arms, and made a run for it. Calhoun, carrying the guns and the supplies, passed them. He jumped through the open doorway of a bus and dropped out of sight. Wayne knew he was jerking wires loose, trying to hotwire them a ride. Wayne hoped he was good at it and fast.

When Wayne got to the bus, he laid Sister Worth down beside it and pulled the .38s and stood in front of her. If he was going down he wanted to go like Wild Bill Hickok: A blazing gun in either fist and a woman to protect.

Actually, he'd prefer the bus to start.

It did.

Calhoun jerked it in gear, backed it out and around in front of Wayne and Sister Worth. The monks and nuns had started firing and their rounds bounced off the side of the armored bus.

From inside Calhoun yelled, "Get the hell on."

Wayne stuck the guns in his belt, grabbed up Sister Worth and leapt inside. Calhoun jerked the bus forward and Wayne and Sister Worth went flying over a scat and into another.

"I thought you were leaving," Wayne said.

"I wanted to. But I gave my word."

Wayne stretched Sister Worth out on the seat and looked at her leg. After that tossing Calhoun had given them, the break was sticking out even more.

Calhoun closed the bus door and checked his wing-mirror. Nuns and monks and dead folks had piled into a couple of buses, and now the buses were pursuing them. One of them moved very fast, as if souped up.

"I probably got the granny of the bunch," Calhoun said. They climbed over a ridge of sand, then they were on the narrow road that wound itself upwards. Behind them, one of the buses had fallen back, maybe some kind of mechanical trouble. The other was gaining.

The road widened and Calhoun yelled, "I think this is what the fucker's been waiting for."

Even as Calhoun spoke, their pursuer put on a burst of speed and swung left and came up beside them, tried to swerve over and push them off the road, down into the deepening valley. But Calhoun fought the curves and didn't budge.

The other bus swung its door open and a nun, the very one who had been on the bus that brought them to Jesus Land, stood there with her legs spread wide, showing the black-pantied mound of her crotch. She had one arm bent around a seat post and was holding in both hands the ever-popular clergy tool, the twelve-gauge pump.

As they made a curve, the nun fired a round into the window next to Calhoun. The window made a cracking noise and thin, crooked lines spread in all directions, but the glass held.

She pumped a round into the chamber and fired again. Bulletproof or not, this time the front sheet of glass fell away. Another well-placed round and the rest of the glass would go and Calhoun could wave his head goodbye.

Wayne put his knees in a seat and got the window down. The nun saw him, whirled and fired. The shot was low and hit the bottom part of the window and starred it and pelleted the chassis.

Wayne stuck a .38 out of the window and fired as the nun was jacking another load into position. His shot hit her in the head and her right eye went big and wet, and she swung around on the pole and lost the shotgun. It went out the door. She clung there by the bend of her elbow for a moment, then her arm straightened and she fell outside. The bus ran over her and she popped red and juicy at both ends like a stomped jelly roll.

"Waste of good pussy," Calhoun said. He edged into the other bus, and it pushed back. But Calhoun pushed harder and made it hit the wall with a screech like a panther.

The bus came back and shoved Calhoun to the side of the cliff and honked twice for Jesus.

Calhoun down-shifted, let off the gas, allowed the other bus to soar past by half a length. Then he jerked the wheel so that he caught the rear of it and knocked it across the road. He speared it in the side with the nose of his bus and the other started to spin. It clipped the front of Calhoun's bus and peeled the bumper back. Calhoun braked and the other bus kept spinning. It spun off the road and down into the valley amidst a chorus of cries.

Thirty minutes later they reached the top of the canyon and were in the desert. The bus began to throw up smoke from the front and make a noise like a dog strangling on a chicken bone. Calhoun pulled over.

"Goddamn bumper got twisted under there and it's shredded the tire some," Calhoun said. "I think if we can peel the bumper off, there's enough of that tire to run on."

Wayne and Calhoun got hold of the bumper and pulled but it wouldn't come off. Not completely. Part of it had been creased, and that part finally gave way and broke off from the rest of it.

"That ought to be enough to keep from rubbing the tire," Calhoun said.

Sister Worth called from inside the bus. Wayne went to check on her. "Take me off the bus," she said. "…I want to feel free air and sun."

"There doesn't feel like there's any air out there," Wayne said. "And the sun feels just like it always does. Hot."

"Please."

He picked her up and carried her outside and found a ridge of sand and laid her down so her head was propped against it.

"I…I need batteries," she said.

"Say what?" Wayne said.

She lay looking straight into the sun. "Brother Lazarus's greatest work…a dead folk that can think…has memory of the past… Was a scientist too…" Her hand came up in stages, finally got hold of her head gear and pushed it off.

Gleaming from the center of her tangled blond hair was a silver knob.

"He…was not a good man… I am a good woman. I want to feel alive…like before…batteries going…brought others."

Her hand fumbled at a snap pocket on her habit. Wayne opened it for her and got out what was inside. Four batteries.

"Uses two…simple."

Calhoun was standing over them now. "That explains some things," he said.

"Don't look at me like that…" Sister Worth said, and Wayne realized he had never told her his name and she had never asked. "Unscrew…put the batteries in… Without them I'll be an eater… Can't wait too long."

"All right," Wayne said. He went behind her and propped her up on the sand drift and unscrewed the metal shaft from her skull. He thought about when she had fucked him on the wheel and how desperate she had been to feel something, and how she had been cold as flint and lustless. He remembered how she had looked in the mirror hoping to see something that wasn't there.

He dropped the batteries in the sand and took out one of the revolvers and put it close to the back of her head and pulled the trigger. Her body jerked slightly and fell over, her face turning toward him.

The bullet had come out where the bird had been on her cheek and had taken it completely away, leaving a bloodless hole.

"Best thing," Calhoun said. "There's enough live pussy in the world without you pulling this broken-legged dead thing around after you on a board."

"Shut up," Wayne said.

"When a man gets sentimental over women and kids, he can count himself out."

Wayne stood up.

"Well boy," Calhoun said. "I reckon it's time."

"Reckon so," Wayne said.

"How about we do this with some class? Give me one of your pistols and we'll get back-to-back and I'll count to ten, and when I get there, we'll turn and shoot."

Wayne gave Calhoun one of the pistols. Calhoun checked the chambers, said, "I've got four loads."

Wayne took two out of his pistol and tossed them on the ground. "Even Steven," he said.

They got back-to-back and held the guns by their legs.

"Guess if you kill me you'll take me in," Calhoun said. "So that means you'll put a bullet through my head if I need it. I don't want to come back as one of the dead folks. Got your word on that?"

"Yep."

"I'll do the same for you. Give my word. You know that's worth something."

"We gonna shoot or talk?"

"You know, boy, under different circumstances, I could have liked you. We might have been friends."

"Not likely."

Calhoun started counting, and they started stepping. When he got to ten, they turned.

Calhoun's pistol barked first, and Wayne felt the bullet punch him low in the right side of his chest, spinning him slightly. He lifted his revolver and took his time and shot just as Calhoun fired again.

Calhoun's second bullet whizzed by Wayne's head. Wayne's shot hit Calhoun in the stomach.

Calhoun went to his knees and had trouble drawing a breath. He tried to lift his revolver but couldn't; it was as if it had turned into an anvil.

Wayne shot him again. Hitting him in the middle of the chest this time and knocking him back so that his legs were curled beneath him.

Wayne walked over to Calhoun, dropped to one knee and took the revolver from him.

"Shit," Calhoun said. "I wouldn't have thought that for nothing. You hit?"

"Scratched."

"Shit."

Wayne put the revolver to Calhoun's forehead and Calhoun closed his eyes and Wayne pulled the trigger.

13

The wound wasn't a scratch. Wayne knew he should leave Sister Worth where she was and load Calhoun on the bus and haul him in for bounty. But he didn't care about the bounty anymore.

He used the ragged piece of bumper to dig them a shallow side-by-side grave. When he finished, he stuck the fender fragment up between them and used the sight of one of the revolvers to scratch into it: HERE LIES SISTER WORTH AND CALHOUN WHO KEPT HIS WORD.

You couldn't really read it good and he knew the first real wind would keel it over, but it made him feel better about something, even if he couldn't put his finger on it.

His wound had opened up and the sun was very hot now, and since he had lost his hat he could feel his brain cooking in his skull like meat boiling in a pot.

He got on the bus, started it and drove through the day and the night and it was near morning when he came to the Cadillacs and turned down between them and drove until he came to the '57.

When he stopped and tried to get off the bus, he found he could hardly move. The revolvers in his belt were stuck to his shirt and stomach because of the blood from his wound.

He pulled himself up with the steering wheel, got one of the shotguns and used it for a crutch. He got the food and water and went out to inspect the '57.

It was for shit. It had not only lost its windshield, the front end was mashed way back and one of the big sand tires was twisted at such an angle he knew the axle was shot.

He leaned against the Chevy and tried to think. The bus was okay and there was still some gas in it, and he could get the hose out of the trunk of the '57 and siphon gas out of its tanks and put it in the bus. That would give him a few miles.

Miles.

He didn't feel as if he could walk twenty feet, let alone concentrate on driving.

He let go of the shotgun, the food and water. He scooted onto the hood of the Chevy and managed himself to the roof. He lay there on his back and looked at the sky.

It was a clear night and the stars were sharp with no fuzz around them. He felt cold. In a couple of hours the stars would fade and the sun would come up and the cool would give way to heat.

He turned his head and looked at one of the Cadillacs and a skeleton face pressed to its windshield, forever looking down at the sand.

That was no way to end, looking down.

He crossed his legs and stretched out his arms and studied the sky. It didn't feel so cold now, and the pain had almost stopped. He was more numb than anything else.

He pulled one of the revolvers and cocked it and put it to his temple and continued to look at the stars. Then he closed his eyes and found that he could still see them. He was once again hanging in the void between the stars wearing only his hat and cowboy boots, and floating about him were the junk cars and the '57, undamaged.

The cars were moving toward him this time, not away. The '57 was in the lead, and as it grew closer he saw Pop behind the wheel and beside him was a Mexican puta, and in the back, two more. They were all smiling and Pop honked the horn and waved.

The '57 came alongside him and the back door opened.

Sitting between the whores was Sister Worth. She had not been there a moment ago, but now she was. And he had never noticed how big the back seat of the '57 was.

Sister Worth smiled at him and the bird on her cheek lifted higher. Her hair was combed out long and straight and she looked pink-skinned and happy. On the floorboard at her feet was a chest of iced-beer. Lone Star, by God.

Pop was leaning over the front seat, holding out his hand and Sister Worth and the whores were beckoning him inside.

Wayne worked his hands and feet, found this time that he could move. He swam through the open door, touched Pop's hand, and Pop said, "It's good to see you, son," and at the moment Wayne pulled the trigger, Pop pulled him inside.

Not from Detroit

OUTSIDE IT WAS cold and wet and windy. The storm rattled the shack, slid like razor blades through the window, door and wall cracks, but it wasn't enough to make any difference to the couple. Sitting before the crumbling fireplace in their creaking rocking chairs, shawls across their knees, fingers entwined, they were warm.

A bucket behind them near the kitchen sink collected water dripping from a hole in the roof.

The drops had long since passed the noisy stage of sounding like steel bolts falling on tin, and were now gentle plops.

The old couple were husband and wife; had been for over fifty years. They were comfortable with one another and seldom spoke. Mostly they rocked and looked at the fire as it flickered shadows across the room.

Finally Margie spoke. "Alex," she said, "I hope I die before you."

Alex stopped rocking. "Did you say what I thought you did?"

"I said, I hope I die before you." She wouldn't look at him, just the fire. "It's selfish, I know, but I hope I do. I don't want to live on with you gone. It would be like cutting out my heart and making me walk around. Like one of them zombies."

"There are the children," he said. "If I died, they'd take you in."

"I'd just be in the way. I love them, but I don't want to do that. They got their own lives. I'd just as soon die before you. That would make things simple."

"Not simple for me," Alex said. "I don't want you to die before me. So how about that? We're both selfish, aren't we?"

She smiled. "Well, it ain't a thing to talk about before bedtime, but it's been on my mind, and I had to get it out."

"Been thinking on it too, honey. Only natural we would. We ain't spring chickens anymore."

"You're healthy as a horse, Alex Brooks. Mechanic work you did all your life kept you strong. Me, I got the bursitis and the miseries and I'm tired all the time. Got the old age bad."

Alex started rocking again. They stared into the fire. "We're going to go together, hon," he said. "I feel it. That's the way it ought to be for folks like us."

"I wonder if I'll see him coming. Death, I mean."

"What?"

"My grandma used to tell me she seen him the night her daddy died."

"You've never told me this."

"Ain't a subject I like. But Grandma said this man in a black buggy slowed down out front of their house, cracked his whip three times, and her daddy was gone in instants. And she said she'd heard her grandfather tell how he had seen Death when he was a boy. Told her it was early morning and he was up, about to start his chores, and when he went outside he seen this man dressed in black walk by the house and stop out front. He was carrying a stick over his shoulder with a checkered bundle tied to it, and he looked at the house and snapped his fingers three times. A moment later they found my grandfather's brother, who had been sick with the smallpox, dead in bed."

"Stories, hon. Stories. Don't get yourself worked up over a bunch of old tall tales. Here, I'll heat us some milk."

Alex stood, laid the shawl in the chair, went over to put milk in a pan and heat it. As he did, he turned to watch Margie's back. She was still staring into the fire, only she wasn't rocking. She was just watching the blaze and, Alex knew, thinking about dying.

After the milk they went to bed, and soon Margie was asleep, snoring like a busted chainsaw. Alex found he could not rest. It was partly due to the storm, it had picked up in intensity. But it was mostly because of what Margie had said about dying. It made him feel lonesome.

Like her, he wasn't so much afraid of dying, as he was of being left alone. She had been his heartbeat for fifty years, and without her, he would only be going through motions of life, not living.

God, he prayed silently. When we go, let us go together. He turned to look at Margie. Her face looked unlined and strangely young. He was glad she could turn off most anything with sleep. He, on the other hand, could not.

Maybe I'm just hungry.

He slid out of bed, pulled on his pants, shirt and house shoes; those silly things with the rabbit face and ears his granddaughter had bought him. He padded silently to the kitchen. It was not only the kitchen, it served as a den, living room, and dining room. The house was only three rooms and a closet, and one of the rooms was a small bathroom. It was times like this that Alex thought he could have done better by Margie. Gotten her a bigger house, for one thing. It was the same house where they had raised their kids, the babies sleeping in a crib here in the kitchen.

He sighed. No matter how hard he had worked, he seemed to stay in the same place. A poor place.

He went to the refrigerator and took out a half-gallon of milk, drank directly from the carton.

He put the carton back and watched the water drip into the bucket. It made him mad to see it. He had let the little house turn into a shack since he retired, and there was no real excuse for it. Surely, he wasn't that tired. It was a wonder Margie didn't complain more.

Well, there was nothing to do about it tonight. But he vowed that when dry weather came, he wouldn't forget about it this time. He'd get up there and fix that damn leak.

Quietly, he rummaged a pan from under the cabinet. He'd have to empty the bucket now if he didn't want it to run over before morning. He ran a little water into the pan before substituting it for the bucket so the drops wouldn't sound so loud.

He opened the front door, went out on the porch, carrying the bucket. He looked out at his mud-pie yard and his old, red wrecker, his white logo on the side of the door faded with time: ALEX BROOKS WRECKING AND MECHANIC SERVICE.

Tonight, looking at the old warhorse, he felt sadder than ever. He missed using it the way it was meant to be used. For work. Now it was nothing more than transportation. Before he retired, his tools and hands made a living. Now nothing. Picking up a Social Security check was all that was left.

Leaning over the edge of the porch, he poured the water into the bare and empty flower bed. When he lifted his head and looked at his yard again, and beyond to Highway 59, he saw a light. Headlights, actually, looking fuzzy in the rain, like filmed-over amber eyes. They were way out there on the highway, coming from the south, winding their way toward him, moving fast.

Alex thought that whoever was driving that crate was crazy. Cruising like that on bone-dry highways with plenty of sunshine would have been dangerous, but in this weather, they were asking for a crackup.

As the car neared, he could see it was long, black and strangely shaped. He'd never seen anything like it, and he knew cars fairly well. This didn't look like something off the assembly line from Detroit. It had to be foreign.

Miraculously, the car slowed without so much as a quiver or screech of brakes and tires. In fact, Alex could not even hear its motor, just the faint whispering sound of rubber on wet cement.

The car came even of the house just as lightning flashed, and in that instant, Alex got a good look at the driver, or at least the shape of the driver outlined in the flash, and he saw that it was a man with a cigar in his mouth and a bowler hat on his head. And the head was turning toward the house.

The lightning flash died, and now there was only the dark shape of the car and the red tip of the cigar jutting at the house. Alex felt stalactites of ice dripping down from the roof of his skull, extended through his body and out of the soles of his feet.

The driver hit down on his horn; three sharp blasts that pricked at Alex's mind.

Honk. *(visions of blooming roses, withering going black)*

Honk. *(funerals remembered, loved ones in boxes, going down)*

Honk. *(worms crawling through rotten flesh)*

Then came a silence louder than the horn blasts. The car picked up speed again. Alex watched as its taillights winked away in the blackness. The chill became less chill. The stalactites in his mind melted away.

But as he stood there, Margie's words of earlier that evening came at him in a rush: "Seen Death once…buggy slowed down out front…cracked his whip *three times*…man looked at the house, snapped his fingers *three times*…found dead a moment later…"

Alex's throat felt as if a pine knot had lodged there. The bucket slipped from his fingers, clattered on the porch and rolled into the flowerbed. He turned into the house and walked briskly toward the bedroom,

(Can't be, just a wives' tale)

his hands vibrating with fear,

(Just a crazy coincidence)

Margie wasn't snoring.

Alex grabbed her shoulder, shook her.

Nothing.

He rolled her on her back and screamed her name.

Nothing.

"Oh, baby. No."

He felt for her pulse.

None.

He put an ear to her chest, listening for a heartbeat (the other half of his life bongos), and there was none.

Quiet. Perfectly quiet.

"You can't…" Alex said. "You can't…we're supposed to go together…got to be that way."

And then it came to him. He had *seen* Death drive by, had *seen* him heading on down the highway.

He came to his feet, snatched his coat from the back of the chair, raced toward the front door. "You won't have her," he said aloud. "You won't."

Grabbing the wrecker keys from the nail beside the door, he leaped to the porch and dashed out into the cold and the rain.

A moment later he was heading down the highway, driving fast and crazy in pursuit of the strange car.

The wrecker was old and not built for speed, but since he kept it well-tuned and it had new tires, it ran well over the wet highway. Alex kept pushing the pedal gradually until it met the floor. Faster and faster and faster.

After an hour, he saw Death.

Not the man himself but the license plate. Personalized and clear in his headlights. It read: DEATH/EXEMPT.

The wrecker and the strange black car were the only ones on the road. Alex closed in on him, honked his horn. Death tootled back (not the same horn sound he had given in front of Alex's house), stuck his arm out the window and waved the wrecker around.

Alex went, and when he was alongside the car, he turned his head to look at Death. He could still not see him clearly, but he could make out the shape of his bowler, and when Death turned to look at him, he could see the glowing tip of the cigar, like a bloody bullet wound.

Alex whipped hard right into the car, and Death swerved to the right, then back onto the road. Alex rammed again. The black car's tires hit roadside gravel and Alex swung closer, preventing it from returning to the highway. He rammed yet another time, and the car went into the grass alongside the road, skidded and went sailing down an embankment and into a tree.

Alex braked carefully, backed off the road and got out of the wrecker. He reached a small pipe wrench and a big crescent wrench out from under the seat, slipped the pipe wrench into his coat pocket for insurance, then went charging down the embankment waving the crescent.

Death opened his door and stepped out. The rain had subsided and the moon was peeking through the clouds like a shy child through gossamer curtains. Its light hit Death's round pink face and made it look like a waxed pomegranate. His cigar hung from his mouth by a tobacco strand.

Glancing up the embankment, he saw an old but strong-looking black man brandishing a wrench and wearing bunny slippers, charging down at him.

Spitting out the ruined cigar, Death stepped forward, grabbed Alex's wrist and forearm, twisted. The old man went up and over, the wrench went flying from his hand. Alex came down hard on his back, the breath bursting out of him in spurts.

Death leaned over Alex. Up close, Alex could see that the pink face was slightly pocked and that some of the pinkness was due to makeup. That was rich. Death was vain about his appearance. He was wearing a black T-shirt, pants and sneakers, and of course his derby, which had neither been stirred by the wreck nor by the ju-jitsu maneuver.

"What's with you, man?" Death asked.

Alex wheezed, tried to catch his breath. "You can't…have…her."

"Who? What are you talking about?"

"Don't play…dumb with me." Alex raised up on one elbow, his wind returning. "You're Death and you took my Margie's soul."

Death straightened. "So you know who I am. All right. But what of it? I'm only doing my job."

"It ain't her time."

"My list says it is, and my list is never wrong."

Alex felt something hard pressing against his hip, realized what it was. The pipe wrench. Even the throw Death had put on him had not hurled it from his coat pocket. It had lodged there and the pocket had shifted beneath his hip, making his old bones hurt all the worse.

Alex made as to roll over, freed the pocket beneath him, shot his hand inside and produced the pipe wrench. He hurled it at Death, struck him just below the brim of the bowler and sent him stumbling back. This time the bowler fell off. Death's forehead was bleeding.

Before Death could collect himself, Alex was up and rushing. He used his head as a battering ram and struck Death in the stomach, knocking him to the ground. He put both knees on Death's arms, pinning them, clenched his throat with his strong, old hands.

"I ain't never hurt nobody before," Alex said. "Don't want to now. I didn't want to hit you with that wrench, but you give Margie back."

Death's eyes showed no expression at first, but slowly a light seemed to go on behind them. He easily pulled his arms out from under Alex's knees, reached up, took hold of the old man's wrists and pulled the hands away from his throat.

"You old rascal," Death said. "You outsmarted me."

Death flopped Alex over on his side, then stood up. Grinning, he turned, stooped to recover his bowler, but he never laid a hand on it.

Alex moved like a crab, scissoring his legs, and caught Death from above and behind his knees, twisted, brought him down on his face.

Death raised up on his palms and crawled from behind Alex's legs like a snake, effortlessly. This time he grabbed the hat and put it on his head and stood up. He watched Alex carefully.

"I don't frighten you much, do I?" Death asked.

Alex noted that the wound on Death's forehead had vanished. There wasn't even a drop of blood. "No," Alex said. "You don't frighten me much. I just want my Margie back."

"All right," Death said.

Alex sat bolt upright.

"What?"

"I said, all right. For a time. Not many have outsmarted me, pinned me to the ground. I give you credit, and you've got courage. I like that. I'll give her back. For a time. Come here."

Death walked over to the car that was not from Detroit. Alex got to his feet and followed. Death took the keys out of the ignition, moved to the trunk, worked the key in the lock. It popped up with a hiss.

Inside were stacks and stacks of matchboxes. Death moved his hand over them, like a careful man selecting a special vegetable at the supermarket. His fingers came to rest on a matchbox that looked to Alex no different than the others.

Death handed Alex the matchbox. "Her soul's in here, old man. You stand over her bed, open the box. Okay?"

"That's it?"

"That's it. Now get out of here before I change my mind. And remember, I'm giving her back to you. But just for a while."

Alex started away, holding the matchbox carefully. As he walked past Death's car, he saw the dents he had knocked in the side with his wrecker were popping out. He turned to look at Death, who was closing the trunk.

"Don't suppose you'll need a tow out of here?"

Death smiled thinly. "Not hardly."

Alex stood over their bed; the bed where they had loved, slept, talked and dreamed. He stood there with the matchbox in his hand, his eyes on Margie's cold face. He ever so gently eased the box open. A small flash of blue light, like Peter Pan's friend Tinkerbell, rushed out of it and hit Margie's lips. She made a sharp inhaling sound and her chest rose. Her eyes came open. She turned and looked at Alex and smiled.

"My lands, Alex. What are you doing there, and half-dressed? What have you been up to...is that a matchbox?"

Alex tried to speak, but he found that he could not. All he could do was grin.

"Have you gone nuts?" she asked.

"Maybe a little." He sat down on the bed and took her hand. "I love you, Margie."

"And I love you...you been drinking?"

"No."

Then came the overwhelming sound of Death's horn. One harsh blast that shook the house, and the headbeams shone brightly through the window and the cracks lit up the shack like a cheap nightclub act.

"Who in the world?" Margie asked.

"Him. But he said...stay here."

Alex got his shotgun out of the closet. He went out on the porch. Death's car was pointed toward the house, and the headbeams seemed to hold Alex, like a fly in butter.

Death was standing on the bottom step, waiting.

Alex pointed the shotgun at him. "You git. You gave her back. You gave your word."

"And I kept it. But I said for a while."

"That wasn't any time at all."

"It was all I could give. My present."

"Short time like that's worse than no time at all."

"Be good about it, Alex. Let her go. I got records and they have to be kept. I'm going to take her anyway, you understand that?"

"Not tonight, you ain't." Alex pulled back the hammers on the shotgun. "Not tomorrow night neither. Not anytime soon."

"That gun won't do you any good, Alex. You know that. You can't stop Death. I can stand here and snap my fingers three times, or click my tongue, or go back to the car and honk my horn, and she's as good as mine. But I'm trying to reason with you, Alex. You're a brave man. I did you a favor because you bested me. I didn't want to just take her back without telling you. That's why I came here to talk. But she's got to go. Now."

Alex lowered the shotgun. "Can't…can't you take me in her place? You can do that, can't you?"

"I…I don't know. It's highly irregular."

"Yeah, you can do that. Take me. Leave Margie."

"Well, I suppose."

The screen door creaked open and Margie stood there in her housecoat. "You're forgetting, Alex, I don't want to be left alone."

"Go in the house, Margie," Alex said.

"I know who this is: I heard you talking, Mr. Death. I don't want you taking my Alex. I'm the one you came for. I ought to have the right to go."

There was a pause, no one speaking. Then Alex said, "Take both of us. You can do that, can't you? I know I'm on that list of yours, and pretty high up. Man my age couldn't have too many years left. You can take me a little before my time, can't you? Well, can't you?"

Margie and Alex sat in their rocking chairs, their shawls over their knees. There was no fire in the fireplace. Behind them the bucket collected water and outside the wind whistled. They held hands. Death stood in front of them. He was holding a King Edward cigar box.

"You're sure of this?" Death asked. "You don't both have to go."

Alex looked at Margie, then back at Death.

"We're sure," he said. "Do it."

Death nodded. He opened the cigar box and held it out on one palm. He used his free hand to snap his fingers.

Once. *(the wind picked up, howled)*

Twice. *(the rain beat like drumsticks on the roof)*

Three times. *(lightning ripped and thunder roared)*

"And in you go," Death said.

The bodies of Alex and Margie slumped and their heads fell together between the rocking chairs. Their fingers were still entwined.

Death put the box under his arm and went out to the car. The rain beat on his derby hat and the wind sawed at his bare arms and T-shirt. He didn't seem to mind.

Opening the trunk, he started to put the box inside, then hesitated.

He closed the trunk.

"Damn," he said, "if I'm not getting to be a sentimental old fool."

He opened the box. Two blue lights rose out of it, elongated, touched ground. They took on the shape of Alex and Margie. They glowed against the night.

"Want to ride up front?" Death asked.

"That would be nice," Margie said.

"Yes, nice," Alex said.

Death opened the door and Alex and Margie slid inside. Death climbed in behind the wheel. He checked the clipboard dangling from the dash. There was a woman in a Tyler hospital, dying of brain damage. That would be his next stop.

He put the clipboard down and started the car that was not from Detroit.

"Sounds well-tuned," Alex said.

"I try to keep it that way," Death said.

They drove out of there then, and as they went, Death broke into song. "Row, row, row your boat, gently down the stream," and Margie and Alex chimed in with, "Merrily, merrily, merrily, merrily, life is but a dream."

Off they went down the highway, the taillights fading, the song dying, the black metal of the car melting into the fabric of night, and then there was only the whispery sound of good tires on wet cement and finally not even that. Just the blowing sound of the wind and the rain.

Cowboy

I GOT OFF the plane at Atlanta and caught the shuttle to what I thought was my hotel. But there was some kind of mix-up, and it wasn't my hotel at all. They told me I could go out to the curb and catch this other shuttle and it would take me over to another hotel in their chain, and that it was a short walk from there to where I wanted to go. I thought that was okay, considering I had gotten on the wrong shuttle in the first place.

I sat outside the hotel on a bench and waited for the shuttle. It was October and kind of cool, but not really uncomfortable. The air felt damp.

I had a Western paperback and I got it out of my coat pocket and read a few pages. From time to time I looked up for the shuttle, then at my watch, then back at the paperback. It wasn't a very good Western.

While I was sitting there a little black boy on skates with an empty toy pistol scabbard strapped around his waist went by. He looked at me. His head was practically shaved and his snap-button cowboy shirt was ripped in front. I guess he was about eleven.

I looked back at my book and started reading, then I heard him skate over in front of me. I looked up and saw that he was looking at the picture on the front of the paperback.

"That a cowboy book?" he said.

I told him it was.

"It any good?"

"I don't care much for it. It's a little too much like the last three or four I read."

"I like cowboy books and movies but they don't get some things right."

"I like them too."

"I'm a cowboy," he said, and his tone was a trifle defiant.

"You are?"

"You was thinking niggers can't be cowboys."

"I wasn't thinking that. Don't call yourself that."

"Nigger? It's okay if I'm doing it. I wouldn't want you to say that."

"I wouldn't."

"Anyone says that they got me to fight."

"I don't want to fight. Where's your pistol?"

He didn't answer that. "A black boy can be a cowboy, you know."

"I'm sure of it."

"They weren't all cooks."

"Course not."

"That's way the movies and books got it. There any black cowboys in that book?"

"Not so far."

"There gonna be?"

"I don't know," I said. But I did know. I'd read a lot of cowboy books.

"White boys at school said there weren't any black cowboys. They said no nigger cowboys. They said we couldn't fight Indians and stuff."

"Don't listen to them."

"I'm not going to. I went over to the playground at the school and they took my pistol. There was three of them."

It came clear to me then. His shirt being ripped and the gun missing.

"I'm sorry. That wasn't nice."

"They said a nigger didn't need no cowboy gun. Said I needed me a frying pan or a broom. I used to ride the range and rope steers and stuff. They don't know nothing."

"Is that all you did on the range, rope steers?"

"I did all kinds of things. I did everything cowboys do."

"Was it hard work?"

"It was so hard you wouldn't believe it. I did all kinds of things. Cowboys don't call one another nigger."

"Do your mom and dad work on the range with you?"

"No, my mama has a job. She does clean-up work. My daddy he got killed in Vietnam. He got some medals and stuff. He wasn't a cowboy like me."

I looked up and saw the shuttle. I picked up my suitcase and stood.

"I got to go now," I said. "I hope you get your gun back. Lot of good cowboys lose fights from time to time."

"There was three of them."

"There you are. *Adios.*" As an afterthought I gave him the Western book.

"It hasn't got any black cowboys in it I bet," he said, and gave it back to me.

"I want one with black cowboys in it. I'm not reading any more of 'em unless they got black cowboys in them."

"I'm sure there are some," I said.

"There ought to be."

I got on the shuttle and it carried me to the other hotel. I got off and walked to where I was supposed to be, and on the way over there I put the book in one of those wire trash-baskets that line the streets.

Steppin' Out, Summer, '68

BUDDY DRANK ANOTHER swig of beer and when he brought the bottle down he said to Jake and Wilson, "I could sure use some pussy."

"We could all use some," Wilson said, "problem is we don't never get any."

"That's the way I see it too," Jake said.

"*You* don't get any," Buddy said. "I get plenty, you can count on that."

"Uh huh," Wilson said. "You talk pussy plenty good, but I don't ever see you with a date. I ain't never even seen you walking a dog, let alone a girl. You don't even have a car, so how you gonna get with a girl?"

"That's the way I see it too," Jake said.

"You see what you want," Buddy said. "I'm gonna be getting me a Chevy soon. I got my eye on one."

"Yeah?" Wilson said. "What one?"

"Drew Carrington's old crate."

"Shit," Wilson said, "that motherfucker caught on fire at a streetlight and he run it off in the creek."

"They got it out," Buddy said.

"They say them flames jumped twenty feet out from under the hood before he run it off in there," Jake said.

"Water put the fire out," Buddy said.

"Uh huh," Wilson said, "after the motor blowed up through the hood. They found that motherfucker in a tree out back of Old Maud Page's place. One of the pistons fell out of it and hit her on the head while she was picking up apples. She was in the hospital three days."

"Yeah," Jake said. "And I hear Carrington's in Dallas now, never got better from the accident. Near drowned and some of the engine blew back into the car and hit him in the nuts, castrated him, fucked up his legs. He can't walk. He's on a wheeled board or something, got some retard that pulls him around."

"Them's just stories," Buddy said. "Motor's still in the car. Carrington got him a job in Dallas as a mechanic. He didn't get hurt at all. Old Woman Page didn't get hit by no piston either. It missed her by a foot. Scared her so bad she had a little stroke. That's why she was in the hospital."

"You seen the motor?" Wilson asked. "Tell me you've seen it."

"No," Buddy said, "but I've heard about it from good sources, and they say it can be fixed."

"Jack it up and drive another car under it," Wilson said, "it'll be all right."

"That's the way I see it too," Jake said.

"Listen to you two," Buddy said. "You know it all. You're real operators. I'll tell you morons one thing, I line up a little of the hole that winks and stinks, like I'm doing tonight, you won't get none of it."

Wilson and Jake shuffled and eyed each other. An unspoken but clear message passed between them. They had never known Buddy to actually get any, or anyone else to know of him getting any, but he had a couple of years on them, and he might have gotten some, way he talked about it, and they damn sure knew they weren't getting any, and if there was a chance of it, things had to be patched up.

"Car like that," Wilson said, "if you worked hard enough, you might get it to run. Some new pistons or something... What you got lined up for tonight?"

Buddy's face put on some importance. "I know a gal likes to do the circle, you know what I mean?"

Wilson hated to admit it, but he didn't. "The circle?"

"Pull the train," Buddy said. "Do the team. You know, fuck a bunch of guys, one after the other."

"Oh," Wilson said.

"I knew that," Jake said.

"Yeah," Wilson said. "Yeah sure you did." Then to Buddy: "When you gonna see this gal?"

Buddy, still important, took a swig of beer and pursed his lips and studied the afternoon sky. "Figured I'd walk on over there little after dark. It's a mile or so."

"Say she likes to do more than one guy?" Wilson asked.

"Way I hear it," Buddy said, "she'll do 'em till they ain't able to do. My cousin, Butch, he told me about her."

Butch. The magic word. Wilson and Jake eyed each other again. There could be something in this after all. Butch was twenty, had a fast car, could play a little bit on the harmonica, bought his own beer, cussed in front of adults, and most importantly, he had been seen with women.

Buddy continued. "Her name's Sally. Butch said she cost five dollars. He's done her a few times. Got her name off a bathroom wall."

"She costs?" Wilson asked.

"Think some gal's going to do us all without some money for it?" Buddy said.

Again, an unspoken signal passed between Wilson and Jake. There could be truth in that.

"Butch gave me her address, said her pimp sits on the front porch and you go right up and negotiate with him. Says you talk right, he might take four."

"I don't know," Wilson said. "I ain't never paid for it."

"Me neither," said Jake.

"Ain't neither one of you ever had any at all, let alone paid for it," Buddy said.

Once more, Wilson and Jake were struck with the hard and painful facts.

Buddy looked at their faces and smiled. He took another sip of beer. "Well, you bring your five dollars, and I reckon you can tag along with me. Come by the house about dark and we'll walk over together."

"Yeah, well, all right," Wilson said. "I wish we had a car."

"Keep wishing," Buddy said. "You boys hang with me, we'll all be riding in Carrington's old Chevy before long. I've got some prospects."

It was just about dark when Wilson and Jake got over to Buddy's neighborhood, which was a long street with four houses on it widely spaced. Buddy's house was the ugliest of the four. It looked ready to nod off its concrete blocks at any moment and go crashing into the unkempt yard and die in a heap of rotting lumber and squeaking nails. Great strips of graying Sherwin-Williams flat-white paint hung from it in patches, giving it the appearance of having a skin disease. The roof was tin and loved the sun and pulled it in and held it so that the interior basked in a sort of slow simmer until well after sundown. Even now, late in the day, a rush of heat came off the roof and rippled down the street like the last results of a nuclear wind.

Wilson and Jake came up on the house from the side, not wanting to go to the door. Buddy's mother was a grumpy old bitch in a brown bathrobe and bunny rabbit slippers with an ear missing on the left foot. No one had ever seen her wearing anything else, except now and then she added a shower cap to her uniform, and no one had ever seen her, with or without the shower cap, except through the screenwire door. She wasn't thought to leave the house. She played radio contests and had to be near the radio at strategic times throughout the day so she could phone if she knew the answer to something. She claimed to be listening for household tips, but no one had ever seen her apply any. She also watched her daughter's soap operas, though she never owned up to it. She always pretended to be reading, kept a *Reader's Digest* cracked so she could look over it and see the TV.

She wasn't friendly either. Times Wilson and Jake had come over before, she'd met them at the screen door and wouldn't let them in. She wouldn't even talk to them. She'd call back to Buddy inside, "Hey, those hoodlum friends of yours are here."

Neither Wilson or Jake could see any sort of relationship developing between them and Buddy's mother and they had stopped trying. They hung around outside the house under the open windows until Buddy came out. There were always interesting things to hear while they waited. Wilson told Jake it was educational.

This time, as before, they sidled up close to the house where they could hear. The television was on. A laugh track drifted out to them. That meant Buddy's sister LuWanda was in there watching. If it wasn't on, it meant she was asleep. Like her mother, she was drawing a check. Back problems plagued the family. Except for Buddy's pa. His back was good. He was in prison for sticking up a liquor store. What little check he was getting for making license plates probably didn't amount to much.

Now they could hear Buddy's mother. Her voice had a quality that made you think of someone trying to talk while fatally injured; like she was lying under an overturned refrigerator, or had been thrown free of a car and had hit a tree.

"LuWanda, turn that thing down. You know I got bad feet."

"You don't listen none with your feet, Mama," LuWanda said. Her voice was kind of slow and lazy, faintly squeaky, as if hoisted from her throat by a hand-over pulley.

"No," Buddy's mother said. "But I got to get up on my old tired feet and come in here and tell you to turn it down."

"I can hear you yelling from the bedroom good enough when your radio ain't too high."

"But you still don't turn it down."

"I turn it down anymore, I won't be able to hear it."

"Your tired old mother, she ought to get some respect."

"You get about half my check," LuWanda said, "ain't that enough. I'm gonna get out of here when I have the baby."

"Yeah, and I bet that's some baby, way you lay up with anything's got pants."

"I hardly never leave the house to get the chance," LuWanda said. "It was Pa done it before he tried to knock over that liquor store."

"Watch your mouth, young lady. I know you let them in through the windows. I'll be glad to see you go, way you lie around here an' watch that old TV. You ought to do something educational. Read the *Reader's Digest* like I do. There's tips for living in those, and you could sure profit some."

"Could be something to that all right," LuWanda said. "Pa read the *Reader's Digest* and he's over in Huntsville. I bet he likes there better than here. I bet he has a better time come night."

"Don't you start that again, young lady."

"Way he told me," LuWanda said, "I was always better with him than you was."

"I'm putting my hands right over my ears at those lies. I won't hear them."

"He sure had him a thrust, didn't he Mama?"

"Ooooh, you...you little shit, if I should say such a thing. You'll get yours in hell, sister."

"I been getting plenty of hell here."

Wilson leaned against the house under the window and whispered to Jake. "Where the hell's Buddy?"

This was answered by Buddy's mother's shrill voice. "Buddy, you are *not* going out of this house wearing them nigger shoes."

"Oh, Mama," Buddy said, "these ain't nigger shoes. I bought these over at K-Woolens."

"That's right where the niggers buy their things," she said.

"Ah Mama," Buddy said.

"Don't you Mama me. You march right back in there and take off them shoes and put on something else. And get you a pair of pants that don't fit so tight people can tell which side it's on."

A moment later a window down from Wilson and Jake went up slowly. A hand holding a pair of shoes stuck out. The hand dropped the shoes and disappeared.

Then the screen door slammed and Wilson and Jake edged around to the corner of the house for a peek. It was Buddy coming out, and his mother's voice came after him, "Don't you come back to this house with a disease, you hear?"

"Ah, Mama," Buddy said.

Buddy was dressed in a long-sleeved paisley shirt with the sleeves rolled up so tight over his biceps they bulged as if actually full of muscle. He had on a pair of striped bell-bottoms and tennis shoes. His hair was combed high and hard and it lifted up on one side; it looked as if an oily squirrel were clinging precariously to the side of his head.

When Buddy saw Wilson and Jake peeking around the corner of the house, his chest got full and he walked off the porch with a cool step. His mother yelled from inside the house, "And don't walk like you got a corncob up you."

That cramped Buddy's style a little, but he sneered and went around the corner of the house trying to look like a man who knew things.

"Guess you boys are ready to stretch a little meat," Buddy said. He paused to locate an almost flat half-pack of Camels in his back pocket. He pulled a cigarette out and got a match from his shirt pocket and grinned and held his hand by his cheek and popped the match with his thumb. It sparked and he lit the cigarette and puffed. "Those things with filters, they're for sissies."

"Give us one of those," Wilson said.

"Yeah, well, all right, but this is it," Buddy said. "Only pack I got till I collect some money owed me."

Wilson and Jake stuck smokes in their faces and Buddy snapped another match and lit them up. Wilson and Jake coughed some smoke clouds.

"Sshhh," Buddy said. "The old lady'll hear you."

They went around to the back window where Buddy had dropped the shoes and Buddy picked them up and took off the ones he had on and slipped on the others. They were smooth and dark and made of alligator hide. Their toes were pointed. Buddy wet his thumb and removed a speck of dirt from one of them. He put his tennis shoes under the house, brought a flat little bottle of clear liquid out from there.

"Hooch," Buddy said, and winked "Bought it off Old Man Hoyt."

"Hoyt?" Wilson said. "He sells hooch?"

"Makes it himself," Buddy said. "Get you a quart for five dollars. Got five dollars and he'll sell to bottle babies."

Buddy saw Wilson eyeing his shoes appreciatively.

"Mama don't like me wearing these," he said. "I have to sneak them out."

"They're cool," Jake said. "I wish I had me a pair like 'em."

"You got to know where to shop," Buddy said.

As they walked, the night became rich and cool and the moon went up and it was bright with a fuzzy ring around it. Crickets chirped. The streets they came to were little more than clay, but there were more houses than in Buddy's neighborhood, and they were in better shape.

Some of the yards were mowed. The lights were on in the houses along the street, and the three of them could hear televisions talking from inside houses as they walked.

They finished off the street and turned onto another that was bordered by deep woods. They crossed a narrow wooden bridge that went over Mud Creek. They stopped and leaned on the bridge railing and watched the dark water in the moonlight. Wilson remembered when he was ten and out shooting birds with a BB gun, he had seen a dead squirrel in the water, floating out from under the bridge, face down, as if it were snorkeling. He had watched it sail on down the creek and out of sight. He had popped at it and all around it with his BB gun for as long as the gun had the distance. The memory made him nostalgic for his youth and he tried to remember what he had done with his old Daisy air rifle. Then it came to him that his dad had probably pawned it. He did that sort of thing now and then, when he fell off the wagon. Suddenly a lot of missing items over the years began to come together. He'd have to get him some kind of trunk with a lock on it and nail it to the floor or something. It wasn't nailed down, it and everything in it might end up at the pawn shop for strangers to paw over.

They walked on and finally came to a long street with houses at the end of it and the lights there seemed less bright and the windows the lights came out of much smaller.

"That last house before the street crosses," Buddy said, "that's the one we want."

Wilson and Jake looked where Buddy was pointing. The house was dark except for a smudgy porch light and a sick yellow glow that shone from behind a thick curtain. Someone was sitting on the front porch doing something with their hands. They couldn't tell anything about the person or about what the person was doing. From that distance the figure could have been whittling or masturbating.

"Ain't that niggertown on the other side of the street?" Jake said. "This gal we're after, she a nigger? I don't know I'm ready to fuck a nigger. I heard my old man say to a friend of his that Mammy Clewson will give a hand job for a dollar and a half. I might go that from a nigger, but I don't know about putting it in one."

"House we want is on this side of the street, before niggertown," Buddy said. "That's a full four-foot difference. She ain't a nigger. She's white trash."

"Well...all right," Jake said. "That's different."

"Everybody take a drink," Buddy said, and he unscrewed the lid on the fruit jar and took a jolt. "Wheee. Straight from the horse."

Buddy passed the jar to Wilson and Wilson drank and nearly threw it up. "Goddamn," he said. "Goddamn. He must run that stuff through a radiator hose or something."

Jake took a turn, shivered as if in the early throes of an epileptic fit. He gave the jar back to Buddy. Buddy screwed the lid on and they walked on down the street, stopped opposite the house they wanted and looked at the man on the front porch, for they could clearly see now it was a man. He was old and toothless and he was shelling peas from a big paper sack into a little white wash pan.

"That's the pimp," Buddy whispered. He opened up the jar and took a sip and closed it and gave it to Wilson to hold. "Give me your money."

They gave him their five dollars.

"I'll go across and make the arrangements," Buddy said. "When I signal, come on over. The pimp might prefer we go in the house one at a time. Maybe you can sit on the porch. I don't know yet."

The three smiled at each other. The passion was building.

Buddy straightened his shoulders, pulled his pants up, and went across the street. He called a howdy to the man on the porch.

"Who the hell are you?" the old man said. It sounded as if his tongue got in the way of his words.

Buddy went boldly up to the house and stood at the porch steps. Wilson and Jake could hear him from where they stood, shuffling their feet and sipping from the jar. He said, "We come to buy a little pussy. I hear you're the man to supply it."

"What's that?" the old man said, and he stood up. When he did, it was obvious he had a problem with his balls. The right side of his pants looked to have a baby's head in it.

"I was him," Jake whispered to Wilson, "I'd save up my share of that pussy money and get me a truss."

"What is that now?" the old man was going on. "What is that you're saying, you little shit?"

"Well now," Buddy said, cocking a foot on the bottom step of the porch like someone who meant business, "I'm not asking for free. I've got fifteen dollars here. It's five a piece, ain't it? We're not asking for anything fancy. We just want to lay a little pipe."

A pale light went on inside the house and a plump, blond girl appeared at the screen door. She didn't open it. She stood there looking out.

"Boy, what in hell are you talking about?" the old man said. "You got the wrong house."

"No one here named Sally?" Buddy asked.

The old man turned his head toward the screen and looked at the plump girl.

"I don't know him, Papa," she said. "Honest."

"You sonofabitch," the old man said to Buddy, and he waddled down the step and swung an upward blow that hit Buddy under the chin and flicked his squirrel-looking hairdo out of shape, sent him hurtling into the front yard. The old man got a palm under his oversized balls and went after Buddy, walking like he had something heavy tied to one leg. Buddy twisted around to run and the old man kicked out and caught him one in the seat of the pants, knocked him stumbling into the street.

"You little bastard," the old man yelled, "don't you come sniffing around here after my daughter again, or I'll cut your nuts off."

Then the old man saw Wilson and Jake across the street. Jake, unable to stop himself, nervously lifted a hand and waved.

"Git on out of here, or I'll let Blackie out," the old man said. "He'll tear your asses up."

Buddy came on across the street trying to step casually, but moving briskly just the same. "I'm gonna get that fucking Butch," he said.

The old man found a rock in the yard and threw it at them. It whizzed by Buddy's ear and he and Jake and Wilson stepped away lively.

Behind them they heard a screen door slam and the plump girl whined something and there was a whapping sound, like a fan belt come loose on a big truck, then they heard the plump girl yelling for mercy and the old man cried "Slut" once, and they were out of there, across the street, into the black side of town.

They walked along a while, then Jake said, "I guess we could find Mammy Clewson."

"Oh, shut up," Buddy said. "Here's your five dollars back. Here's both your five dollars back. The both of you can get her to do it for you till your money runs out."

"I was just kidding," Jake said.

"Well don't," Buddy said. "That Butch, I catch him, right in the kisser, man. I don't care how big and mean he is. Right in the kisser."

They walked along the street and turned left up another. "Let's get out of boogie town," Buddy said. "All these niggers around here, it makes me nervous."

When they were well up the street and there were no houses, they turned down a short direct street with a bridge in the middle of it that went over the Sabine River. It wasn't a big bridge because the river was narrow there. Off to the right was a wide pasture. To the left a church. They crossed into the back church yard. There were a couple of wooden pews setting out there under an oak. Buddy went over to one and sat down.

"I thought you wanted to get away from the boogies?" Wilson said.

"Naw," Buddy said. "This is all right. This is fine. I'd like for a nigger to start something. I would. That old man back there hadn't been so old and had his balls fucked up like that, I'd have kicked his ass."

"We wondered what was holding you back," Wilson said.

Buddy looked at Wilson, didn't see any signs of sarcasm.

"Yeah, well, that was it. Give me the jar. There's some other women I know about. We might try something later on, we feel like it."

But a cloud of unspoken resignation, as far as pussy was concerned, had passed over them and they labored beneath its darkness with their fruit jar of hooch. The sat and passed the jar around and the night got better and brighter. Behind them, off in the woods, they could hear the Sabine River running along. Now and then a car would go down or up the street, cross over the bridge with a rumble, and pass out of sight beyond the church, or if heading in the other direction, out of sight behind trees.

Buddy began to see the night's fiasco as funny. He mellowed. "That Butch, he's something, ain't he? Some joke, huh?"

"It was pretty funny," Jake said, "seeing that old man and his balls coming down the porch after you. That thing was any more ruptured, he'd need a wheelbarrow to get from room to room. Shit, I bet he couldn't have turned no dog on us. He'd had one in there, it'd have barked."

"Maybe he called Sally Blackie," Wilson said. "Man, we're better off she didn't take money. You see that face. She could scare crows."

"Shit," Buddy said sniffing at the jar of hooch. "I think Hoyt puts hair oil in this. Don't that smell like Vitalis to you?"

He held it under Wilson's nose, then Jake's.

"It does," Wilson said. "Right now, I wouldn't care if it smelled like sewer. Give me another swig."

"No," Buddy said standing up, wobbling, holding the partially filled jar in front of him. "Could be we've discovered a hair tonic we could sell. Buy it from Hoyt for five, sell it to guys to put on their heads for ten. We could go into business with Old Man Hoyt. Make a fortune."

Buddy poured some hooch into his palm and rubbed it into his hair, fanning his struggling squirrel-do into greater disarray. He gave the jar to Jake, got out his comb and sculptured his hair with it. Hooch ran down from his hairline and along his nose and cheeks. "See that," he said, holding out his arms as if he were styling. "Shit holds like glue."

Buddy seemed an incredible wit suddenly. They all laughed. Buddy got his cigarettes and shook one out for each of them. They lipped them. They smiled at one another. They were great friends. This was a magnificent and important moment in their lives. This night would live in memory forever.

Buddy produced a match, held it close to his cheek like always, smiled and flicked it with his thumb. The flaming head of the match jumped into his hair and lit the alcohol Buddy had combed into it. His hair flared up, and a circle of fire, like a halo for the Devil, wound its way around his scalp and licked at his face and caught the hooch there on fire. Buddy screamed and bolted berserkly into a pew, tumbled over it and came up running. He looked like the Human Torch on a mission.

Wilson and Jake were stunned. They watched him run a goodly distance, circle, run back, hit the turned over pew again and go down.

Wilson yelled, "Put his head out."

Jake reflexively tossed the contents of the fruit jar at Buddy's head, realizing his mistake a moment too late. But it was like when he waved at Sally's pa. He couldn't help himself.

Buddy did a short tumble, came up still burning; in fact, he appeared to be more on fire than before. He ran straight at Wilson and Jake, his tongue out and flapping flames.

Wilson and Jake stepped aside and Buddy went between them, sprinted across the church yard toward the street.

"Throw dirt on his head!" Wilson said. Jake threw down the jar and they went after him, watching for dirt they could toss.

Buddy was fast for someone on fire. He reached the street well ahead of Wilson and Jake and any discovery of available dirt. But he didn't cross the street fast enough to beat the dump truck. Its headlights hit him first, then the left side of the bumper chopped him on the leg and he did a high complete flip, his blazing head resembling some sort of wheeled fireworks display. He landed on the bridge railing on the far side of the street with a crack of bone and a barking noise. With a burst of flames around his head, he fell off the bridge and into the water below.

The dump truck locked up its brakes and skidded.

Wilson and Jake stopped running. They stood looking at the spot where Buddy had gone over, paralyzed with disbelief.

The dump truck driver, a slim white man in overalls and a cap, got out of the truck and stopped at the rear of it, looked at where Buddy had gone over, looked up and down the street. He didn't seem to notice Wilson and Jake. He walked briskly back to the truck, got in, gunned the motor. The truck went away fast, took a right on the next street hard enough the tires protested like a cat with its tail in a crack. It backfired once, then there was only the distant sound of the motor and gears being rapidly shifted.

"Sonofabitch!" Wilson yelled.

He and Jake ran to the street, paused, looked both ways in case of more dump trucks, and crossed. They glanced over the railing.

Buddy lay with his lower body on the bank. His left leg was twisted so that his shoe pointed in the wrong direction. His dark, crisp head was in the water. He was straining his neck to lift his blackened, eyeless face out of the water; white wisps of smoke swirled up from it and carried with it the smell of barbecued meat. His body shifted. He let out a groan.

"Goddamn," Wilson said. "He's alive. Let's get him."

But at that moment there was splashing in the water. A log came sailing down the river, directly at Buddy's head. The log opened its mouth and grabbed Buddy by the head and jerked him off the shore. A noise like walnuts being cracked and a muffled scream drifted up to Wilson and Jake.

"An alligator," Jake said, and noted vaguely how closely its skin and Buddy's shoes matched.

Wilson darted around the railing, slid down the incline to the water's edge. Jake followed. They ran alongside the bank.

The water turned extremely shallow, and they could see the shadowy shape of the gator as it waddled forward, following the path of the river, still holding Buddy by the head. Buddy stuck out of the side of its mouth like a curmudgeon's cigar. His arms were flapping and so was his good leg.

Wilson and Jake paused running and tried to get their breath. After some deep inhalations, Wilson said, "Gets in the deep water, it's all over." He grabbed up an old fence post that had washed onto the bank and began running again, yelling at the gator as he went. Jake looked about, but didn't see anything to hit with. He ran after Wilson.

The gator, panicked by the noisy pursuit, crawled out of the shallows and went into the high grass of a connecting pasture, ducking under the bottom strand of a barbed wire fence. The wire caught one of Buddy's flailing arms and ripped a flap of flesh from it six inches long. Once on the other side of the wire his good leg kicked up and the fine shine on his alligator shoes flashed once in the moonlight and fell down.

Wilson went through the barbed wire and after the gator with his fence post. The gator was making good time, pushing Buddy before it, leaving a trail of mashed grass behind it. Wilson could see its tail weaving in the moonlight. Its stink trailed behind it like fumes from a busted muffler.

Wilson put the fence post on his shoulder and ran as hard as he could, managed to close in. Behind him came Jake, huffing and puffing.

Wilson got alongside the gator and hit him in the tail with the fence post. The gator's tail whipped out and caught Wilson's ankles and knocked his feet from under him. He came down hard on his butt and lost the fence post.

Jake grabbed up the post and broke right as the gator turned in that direction. He caught the beast sideways and brought the post down on its head, and when it hit, Buddy's blood jumped out of the gator's mouth and landed in the grass and on Jake's shoes. In the moonlight it was the color of cough syrup.

Jake went wild. He began to hit the gator brutally, running alongside it, following its every twist and turn. He swung the fence post mechanically, slamming the gator in the head. Behind him Wilson was saying, "You're hurting Buddy, you're hurting Buddy," but Jake couldn't stop, the frenzy was on him. Gator blood was flying, bursting out of the top of the reptile's head. Still, it held to Buddy, not giving up an inch of head. Buddy wasn't thrashing or kicking anymore. His legs slithered along in the grass as the gator ran; he looked like one of those dummies they throw off cliffs in old cowboy movies.

Wilson caught up, started kicking the gator in the side. The gator started rolling and thrashing and Jake and Wilson hopped like rabbits and yelled. Finally the gator quit rolling. It quit crawling. Its sides heaved.

Jake continued to pound it with the post and Wilson continued to kick it. Eventually its sides quit swelling. Jake kept hitting it with the post until he staggered back and fell down in the grass exhausted. He sat there looking at the gator and Buddy. The gator trembled suddenly and spewed gator shit into the grass. It didn't move again.

After a few minutes Wilson said, "I don't think Buddy's alive."

Just then, Buddy's body twitched.

"Hey, hey, you see that?" Jake said.

Wilson was touched with wisdom. "He's alive, the gator might be too."

Wilson got on his knees about six feet from the gator's mouth and bent over to see if he could see Buddy in there. All he could see were the gator's rubbery lips and the sides of its teeth and a little of Buddy's head shredded between them, like gray cheese on a grater. He could smell both the sour smell of the gator and the stink of burnt meat.

"I don't know if he's alive or not," Wilson said. "Maybe if we could get him out of its mouth, we could tell more."

Jake tried to wedge the fence post into the gator's mouth, but that didn't work. It was as if the great jaw was locked with a key.

They watched carefully, but Buddy didn't show any more signs of life.

"I know," Wilson said. "We'll carry him and the gator up to the road, find a house and get some help."

The gator was long and heavy. The best they could do was get hold of its tail and pull it and Buddy along. Jake managed this with the fence post under his arm. He didn't trust the gator and wouldn't give it up.

They went across an acre of grass and came to a barbed wire fence that bordered the street where Buddy had been hit by the dump truck. The bridge was in sight.

They let go of the gator and climbed through the wire. Jake used the fence post to lift up the bottom strand, and Wilson got hold of the gator's tail and tugged the beast under, along with Buddy.

Pulling the gator and Buddy alongside the road, they watched for house lights. They went past the church on the opposite side of the road and turned left where the dump truck had turned right and backfired. They went alongside the street there, occasionally allowing the alligator and Buddy to weave over into the street itself. It was hard work steering a gator and its lunch.

They finally came to a row of houses. The first one had an old Ford pickup parked out beside it and lots of junk piled in the yard. Lawn mowers, oily rope, overturned freezers, wheels, fishing reels and line, bicycle parts, and a busted commode. A tarp had been pulled half-heartedly over a tall stack of old shop creepers. There was a light on behind one window. The rest of the houses were dark.

Jake and Wilson let go of the gator in the front yard, and Wilson went up on the porch, knocked on the door, stepped off the porch and waited.

Briefly thereafter, the door opened a crack and a man called out, "Who's out there? Don't you know it's bed time?"

"We seen your light on," Wilson said.

"I was in the shitter. You trying to sell me a brush or a book or something this time of night, I won't be in no good temper about it. I'm not through shitting either."

"We got a man hurt here," Wilson said. "A gator bit him."

There was a long moment of quiet. "What you want me to do? I don't know nothin' about no gator bites. I don't even know who you are. You might be with the Ku Kluxers."

"He's…he's kind of hung up with the gator," Wilson said.

"Just a minute," said the voice.

Moments later a short, fat black man came out. He was shirtless and barefooted, wearing overalls with the straps off his shoulders, dangling at his waist. He had a ball bat in his hand. He came down the steps and looked at Wilson and Jake carefully, as if expecting them to spring. "You stand away from me with the fence post, hear?" he said. Jake took a step back and this seemed to satisfy the man. He took a look at the gator and Buddy.

He went back up the porch and reached inside the door and turned on the porch light. A child's face stuck through the crack in the door, said, "What's out there, Papa?"

"You get your ass in that house, or I'll kick it," the black man said. The face disappeared.

The black man came off the porch again, looked at the gator and Buddy again, walked around them a couple times, poked the gator with the ball bat, poked Buddy too.

He looked at Jake and Wilson. "Shit," he said. "You peckerwoods is crazy. That motherfucker's dead. He's dead enough for two men. He's deader than I ever seen anybody."

"He caught on fire," Jake offered suddenly, "and we tried to put his head out, and he got hit by a truck, knocked in the river, and the gator got him… We seen him twitch a little a while back… The fella, Buddy, not the gator, I mean."

"Them's nerves," the black man said. "You better dig a hole for this manjack, skin that ole gator out and sell his hide. They bring a right smart price sometimes. You could probably get something for them shoes too, if'n they clean up good."

"We need you to help us load him up into your pickup and take him home," Jake said.

"You ain't putting that motherfucker in my pickup," the black man said. "I don't want no doings with you honkey motherfuckers. They'll be claiming I sicked that gator on him."

"That's silly," Wilson said. "You're acting like a fool."

"Uh-huh," said the black man, "and I'm gonna go on acting like one here in my house."

He went briskly up the porch steps, closed the door and turned out the light. A latch was thrown.

Wilson began to yell. He used the word nigger indiscriminately. He ran up on the porch and pounded on the door. He cussed a lot.

Doors of houses down the way opened up and people moved onto their front porches like shadows, looked at where the noise was coming from.

Jake, standing there in the yard with his fence post, looked like a man with a gun. The gator and Buddy could have been the body of their neighbor. The shadows watched Jake and listened to Wilson yell a moment, then went back inside.

"Goddamn you," Wilson yelled. "Come on out of there so I can whip your ass, you hear me? I'll whip your black ass."

"You come on in here, cocksucker," came the black man's voice from the other side of the door. "Come on in, you think you can. You do, you'll be trying to shit you some twelve gauge shot, that's what you'll be trying to do."

At the mention of the twelve gauge, Wilson felt a certain calm descend on him. He began to acquire perspective. "We're leaving," he said to the door. "Right now." He backed off the porch. He spoke softly so only Jake could hear: "Boogie motherfucker."

"What we gonna do now?" Jake said. He sounded tired. All the juice had gone out of him.

"I reckon," Wilson said, "we got to get Buddy and the gator on over to his house."

"I don't think we can carry him that far," Jake said. "My back is hurting already."

Wilson looked at the junk beside the house. "Wait a minute." He went over to the junk pile and got three shop creepers out from under the tarp and found some hanks of rope. He used the rope to tie the creepers together, end to end. When he looked up, Jake was standing beside him, still holding the fence post. "You go on and stay by Buddy," Wilson said. "Turn your back too long, them niggers will be all over them shoes."

Jake went back to his former position.

Wilson collected several short pieces of rope and a twist of wire and tied them together and hooked the results to one of the creepers and used it as a handle. He pulled his contraption around front by Buddy and the gator. "Help me put 'em on there," he said.

They lifted the gator onto the creeper. He fit with only his tail overlapping. Buddy hung to the side, off the creepers, causing them to tilt.

"That won't work," Jake said.

"Well, here now," Wilson said, and he got Buddy by the legs and turned him. The head and neck were real flexible, like they were made of chewing gum. He was able to lay Buddy straight out in front of the gator. "Now we can pull the gator down a bit, drag all of its tail. That way we got 'em both on there."

When they got the gator and Buddy arranged, Wilson doubled the rope and began pulling. At first it was slow going, but after a moment they got out in the road and the creepers gained momentum and squeaked right along. Jake used his fence post to punch at the edges of the creepers when they swung out of line.

An ancient, one-eyed cocker spaniel with a foot missing, came out and sat at the edge of the road and watched them pass. He barked once when the alligator's tail dragged by in the dirt behind the creepers, then he went and got under a porch.

They squeaked on until they passed the house where Sally lived. They stopped across from it for a breather and to listen. They didn't hear anyone screaming and they didn't hear any beating going on.

They started up again, kept at it until they came to Buddy's street. It was deadly quiet, and the moon had been lost behind a cloud and everything was dark.

At Buddy's house, the silver light of the TV strobed behind the living room curtains. Wilson and Jake stopped on the far side of the street and squatted beside the creepers and considered their situation.

Wilson got in Buddy's back pocket and pulled the smokes out and found that though the package was damp from the water, a couple of cigarettes were dry enough to smoke. He gave one to Jake and took the other for himself. He got a match from Buddy's shirt pocket and struck it on a creeper, but it was too damp to light.

"Here," Jake said, and produced a lighter. "I stole this from my old man in case I ever got any cigarettes. It works most of the time." Jake clicked it repeatedly and finally it sparked well enough to light. They lit up.

"We knock on the door, his mom is gonna be mad," Jake said. "Us bringing home Buddy and an alligator, and Buddy wearing them shoes."

"Yeah," Wilson said. "You know, she don't know he went off with us. We could put him in the yard. Maybe she'll think the gator attacked him there."

"What for," Jake said, "them shoes? He recognized his aunt or something?" He began laughing at his own joke, but if Wilson got it he didn't give a sign. He seemed to be thinking. Jake quit laughing, scratched his head and looked off down the street. He tried to smoke his cigarette in a manful manner.

"Gators come up in yards and eat dogs now and then," Wilson said after a long silence. "We could leave him, and if his mama don't believe a gator jumped him, that'll be all right. The figuring of it will be a town mystery. Nobody would ever know what happened. Those niggers won't be talking. And if they do, they don't know us from anybody else anyway. We all look alike to them."

"I was Buddy," Jake said, "that's the way I'd want it if I had a couple friends involved."

"Yeah, well," Wilson said, "I don't know I really liked him so much."

Jake thought about that. "He was all right. I bet he wasn't going to get that Chevy though."

"If he did," Wilson said, "there wouldn't have been a motor in it, I can promise you that. And I bet he never got any pussy neither."

They pulled the creepers across the road and tipped gator and Buddy onto the ground in front of the porch steps.

"That'll have to do," Wilson whispered.

Wilson crept up on the porch and over to the window, looked through a crack in the curtain and into the living room. Buddy's sister lay on the couch asleep, her mouth open, her huge belly bobbing up and down as she breathed. A half-destroyed bag of Cheetos lay beside the couch. The TV light flickered over her like saintly fire.

Jake came up on the porch and took a look.

"Maybe if she lost some pounds and fixed her hair different," he said.

"Maybe if she was somebody else," Wilson said.

They sat on the porch steps in the dark and finished smoking their cigarettes, watching the faint glow of the television through the curtain, listening to the tinny sound of a late night talk show.

When Jake finished his smoke, he pulled the alligator shoes off Buddy and checked them against the soles of his own shoes. "I think these dudes will fit me. We can't leave 'em on him. His mama sees them, she might not consent to bury him."

He and Wilson left out of there then, pulling the creepers after them.

Not far down the road, they pushed the creepers off in a ditch and continued, Jake carrying the shoes under his arm. "These are all right," he said. "I might can get some pussy wearing these kind of shoes. My mama don't care if I wear things like this."

"Hell, she don't care if you cut your head off," Wilson said.

"That's the way I see it," Jake said.

Fish Night

It was a bleached-bone afternoon with a cloudless sky and a monstrous sun. The air trembled like a mass of gelatinous ectoplasm. No wind blew.

Through the swelter came a worn, black Plymouth, coughing and belching white smoke from beneath its hood. It wheezed twice, backfired loudly, died by the side of the road.

The driver got out and went around to the hood. He was a man in the hard winter years of life, with dead, brown hair and a heavy belly riding his hips. His shirt was open to the navel, the sleeves rolled up past his elbows. The hair on his chest and arms was gray.

A younger man climbed out on the passenger side, went around front too. Yellow sweat-explosions stained the pits of his white shirt. An unfastened, striped tie was draped over his neck like a pet snake that had died in its sleep.

"Well?" the younger man asked.

The old man said nothing. He opened the hood. A calliope note of steam blew out from the radiator in a white puff, rose to the sky, turned clear.

"Damn," the old man said, and he kicked the bumper of the Plymouth as if he were kicking a foe in the teeth. He got little satisfaction out of the action, just a nasty scuff on his brown wingtip and a jar to his ankle that hurt like hell.

"Well?" the young man repeated.

"Well what? What do you think? Dead as the can-opener trade this week. Deader. The radiator's chickenpocked with holes."

"Maybe someone will come by and give us a hand."

"Sure."

"A ride anyway."

"Keep thinking that, college boy."

"Someone is bound to come along," the young man said.

"Maybe. Maybe not. Who else takes these cutoffs? The main highway, that's where everyone is. Not this little no-account shortcut." He finished by glaring at the young man.

"I didn't make you take it," the young man snapped. "It was on the map. I told you about it, that's all. You chose it. You're the one that decided to take it. It's not my fault. Besides, who'd have expected the car to die?"

"I did tell you to check the water in the radiator, didn't I? Wasn't that back as far as El Paso?"

"I checked. It had water then. I tell you, it's not my fault. You're the one that's done all the Arizona driving."

"Yeah, yeah," the old man said, as if this were something he didn't want to hear. He turned to look up the highway.

No cars. No trucks. Just heat waves and miles of empty concrete in sight.

They seated themselves on the hot ground with their backs to the car. That way it provided some shade — but not much. They sipped on a jug of lukewarm water from the Plymouth and spoke little until the sun fell down. By then they had both mellowed a bit. The heat had vacated the sands and the desert chill had settled in. Where the warmth had made the pair snappy, the cold drew them together.

The old man buttoned his shirt and rolled down his sleeves while the young man rummaged a sweater out of the back seat. He put the sweater on, sat back down. "I'm sorry about this," he said suddenly.

"Wasn't your fault. Wasn't anyone's fault. I just get to yelling sometime, taking out the can-opener trade on everything but the can openers and myself. The days of the door-to-door salesman are gone, son."

"And I thought I was going to have an easy summer job," the young man said.

The old man laughed. "Bet you did. They talk a good line, don't they?"

"I'll say!"

"Make it sound like found money, but there ain't no found money, boy. Ain't nothing simple in this world. The company is the only one ever makes any money. We just get tireder and older with more holes in our shoes. If I had any sense I'd have quit years ago. All you got to make is this summer —"

"Maybe not that long."

"Well, this is all I know. Just town after town, motel after motel, house after house, looking at people through screen wire while they shake their heads No. Even the cockroaches at the sleazy motels begin to look like little fellows you've seen before, like maybe they're door-to-door peddlers that have to rent rooms too."

The young man chuckled. "You might have something there."

They sat quietly for a moment, welded in silence. Night had full grip on the desert now. A mammoth gold moon and billions of stars cast a whitish glow from eons away.

The wind picked up. The sand shifted, found new places to lie down. The undulations of it, slow and easy, were reminiscent of the midnight sea. The young man, who had crossed the Atlantic by ship once, said as much.

"The sea?" the old man replied. "Yes, yes, exactly like that. I was thinking the same. That's part of the reason it bothers me. Part of why I was stirred up this afternoon. Wasn't just the heat doing it. There are memories of mine out here," he nodded at the desert, "and they're visiting me again."

The young man made a face. "I don't understand."

"You wouldn't. You shouldn't. You'd think I'm crazy."

"I already think you're crazy. So tell me."

The old man smiled. "All right, but don't you laugh."

"I won't."

A moment of silence moved in between them. Finally the old man said, "It's fish night, boy. Tonight's the full moon and this is the right part of the desert if memory serves me, and the feel is right — I mean, doesn't the night feel like it's made up of some soft fabric, that it's different from other nights, that it's like being inside a big, dark bag, the sides sprinkled with glitter, a spotlight at the top, at the open mouth, to serve as a moon?"

"You lost me."

The old man sighed. "But it feels different. Right? You can feel it too, can't you?"

"I suppose. Sort of thought it was just the desert air. I've never camped out in the desert before, and I guess it is different."

"Different, all right. You see, this is the road I got stranded on twenty years back. I didn't know it at first, least not consciously. But down deep in my gut I must have known all along I was taking this road, tempting fate, offering it, as the football people say, an instant replay."

"I still don't understand about fish night. What do you mean, you were here before?"

"Not this exact spot, somewhere along in here. This was even less of a road back then than it is now. The Navajos were about the only ones who traveled it. My car conked out, like this one today, and I started walking instead of waiting. As I walked the fish came out. Swimming along in the starlight pretty as you please. Lots of them. All the colors of the rainbow. Small ones, big ones, thick ones, thin ones. Swam right up to me...*right through me!* Fish just as far as you could see. High up and low down to the ground.

"Hold on, boy. Don't start looking at me like that. Listen: You're a college boy, you know something about these things. I mean, about what was here before we were, before we crawled out of the sea and changed enough to call ourselves men. Weren't we once just slimy things, brothers to the things that swim?"

"I guess, but —"

"Millions and millions of years ago this desert was a sea bottom. Maybe even the birthplace of man. Who knows? I read that in some science books. And I got to thinking this: If the ghosts of people who have lived can haunt houses, why can't the ghosts of creatures long dead haunt where they once lived, float about in a ghostly sea?"

"Fish with a soul?"

"Don't go small-mind on me, boy. Look here: Some of the Indians I've talked to up north tell me about a thing they call the manitou. That's a spirit. They believe everything has one. Rocks, trees, you name it. Even if the rock wears to dust or the tree gets cut to lumber, the manitou of it is still around."

"Then why can't you see these fish all the time?"

"Why can't we see ghosts all the time? Why do some of us never see them? Time's not right, that's why. It's a precious situation, and I figure it's like some fancy time lock — like the banks use. The lock clicks open at the bank, and there's the money. Here it ticks open and we get the fish of a world long gone."

"Well, it's something to think about," the young man managed.

The old man grinned at him. "I don't blame you for thinking what you're thinking. But this happened to me twenty years ago and I've never forgotten it. I saw those fish for a good hour before they disappeared. A Navajo came along in an old pickup right after and I bummed a ride into town with him. I told him what I'd seen. He just looked at me and grunted. But I could tell he knew what I was talking about. He'd seen it too, and probably not for the first time.

"I've heard that Navajos don't eat fish for some reason or another, and I bet it's the fish in the desert that keep them from it. Maybe they hold them sacred. And why not? It was like being in the presence of the Creator; like crawling back inside your mother and being unborn again, just kicking around in the liquids with no cares in the world."

"I don't know. That sounds sort of..."

"Fishy?" The old man laughed. "It does, it does. So this Navajo drove me to town. Next day I got my car fixed and went on. I've never taken that cutoff again — until today, and I think that was more than accident. My subconscious was driving me. That night scared me, boy, and I don't mind admitting it. But it was wonderful too, and I've never been able to get it out of my mind."

The young man didn't know what to say.

The old man looked at him and smiled. "I don't blame you," he said. "Not even a little bit. Maybe I am crazy."

They sat awhile longer with the desert night, and the old man took his false teeth out and poured some of the warm water on them to clean them of coffee and cigarette residue.

"I hope we don't need that water," the young man said.

"You're right. Stupid of me! We'll sleep awhile, start walking before daylight. It's not too far to the next town. Ten miles at best." He put his teeth back in. "We'll be just fine."

The young man nodded.

No fish came. They did not discuss it. They crawled inside the car, the young man in the front seat, the old man in the back. They used their spare clothes to bundle under, to pad out the cold fingers of the night.

Near midnight the old man came awake suddenly and lay with his hands behind his head and looked up and out the window opposite him, studied the crisp desert sky.

And a fish swam by.

Long and lean and speckled with all the colors of the world, flicking its tail as if in goodbye. Then it was gone.

The old man sat up. Outside, all about, were the fish — all sizes, colors, and shapes.

"Hey, boy, wake up!"

The younger man moaned.

"Wake up!"

The young man, who had been resting face down on his arms, rolled over. "What's the matter? Time to go?"

"The fish."

"Not again."

"Look!"

The young man sat up. His mouth fell open. His eyes bloated. Around and around the car, faster and faster in whirls of dark color, swam all manner of fish.

"Well, I'll be... *How?*"

"I told you, I told you."

The old man reached for the door handle, but before he could pull it a fish swam lazily through the back window glass, swirled about the car, once, twice, passed through the old man's chest, whipped up and went out through the roof.

The old man cackled, jerked open the door. He bounced around beside the road. Leaped up to swat his hands through the spectral fish. "Like soap bubbles," he said. "No. Like smoke!"

The young man, his mouth still agape, opened his door and got out. Even high up he could see the fish. Strange fish, like nothing he'd ever seen pictures of or imagined. They flitted and skirted about like flashes of light.

As he looked up, he saw, nearing the moon, a big dark cloud. The only cloud in the sky. That cloud tied him to reality suddenly, and he thanked the heavens for it. Normal things still happened. The whole world had not gone insane.

After a moment the old man quit hopping among the fish and came out to lean on the car and hold his hand to his fluttering chest.

"Feel it, boy? Feel the presence of the sea? Doesn't it feel like the beating of your own mother's heart while you float inside the womb?"

And the younger man had to admit that he felt it, that inner rolling rhythm that is the tide of life and the pulsating heart of the sea.

"How?" the young man said. "Why?"

"The time lock, boy. The locks clicked open and the fish are free. Fish from a time before man was man. Before civilization started weighing us down. I know it's true. The truth's been in me all the time. It's in us all."

"It's like time travel," the young man said. "From the past to the future, they've come all that way."

"Yes, yes, that's it… Why, if they can come to our world, why can't we go to theirs? Release that spirit inside of us, tune into their time?"

"Now, wait a minute…"

"My God, that's it! They're pure, boy, pure. Clean and free of civilization's trappings. That must be it! They're pure and we're not. We're weighted down with technology. These clothes. That car."

The old man started removing his clothes.

"Hey!" the young man said. "You'll freeze."

"If you're pure, if you're completely pure," the old man mumbled, "that's it… yeah, that's the key."

"You've gone crazy."

"I won't look at the car," the old man yelled, running across the sand, trailing the last of his clothes behind him. He bounced about the desert like a jackrabbit. "God, God, nothing is happening, nothing," he moaned. "This isn't my world.

I'm of that world. I want to float free in the belly of the sea, away from can openers and cars and —"

The young man called the old man's name. The old man did not seem to hear.

"I want to leave here!" the old man yelled. Suddenly he was springing about again. "The teeth!" he yelled. "It's the teeth. Dentist, science, foo!" He punched a hand into his mouth, plucked the teeth free, tossed them over his shoulder.

Even as the teeth fell the old man rose. He began to stroke. To swim up and up and up, moving like a pale, pink seal among the fish.

In the light of the moon the young man could see the pooched jaws of the old man, holding the last of the future's air. Up went the old man, up, up, up, swimming strong in the long-lost waters of a time gone by.

The young man began to strip off his own clothes. Maybe he could nab him, pull him down, put the clothes on him. Something... God, something... But, what if *he* couldn't come back? And there were the fillings in his teeth, the metal rod in his back from a motorcycle accident. No, unlike the old man, this was his world and he was tied to it. There was nothing he could do.

A great shadow weaved in front of the moon, made a wriggling slat of darkness that caused the young man to let go of his shirt buttons and look up.

A black rocket of a shape moved through the invisible sea: a shark, the granddaddy of all sharks, the seed for all of man's fears of the deeps.

And it caught the old man in its mouth, began swimming upward toward the golden light of the moon. The old man dangled from the creature's mouth like a ragged rat from a house cat's jaws. Blood blossomed out of him, coiled darkly in the invisible sea.

The young man trembled. "Oh God," he said once.

Then along came that thick dark cloud, rolling across the face of the moon.

Momentary darkness.

And when the cloud passed there was light once again, and an empty sky.

No fish.

No shark.

And no old man.

Just the night, the moon, and the stars.

Hell Through a Windshield

We are drive-in mutants.
We are not like other people.
We are sick.
We are disgusting.
We believe in blood.
In breasts,
And in beasts.
We believe in Kung Fu City.
If life had a vomit meter,
We'd be off the scale.
As long as one single drive-in remains
On the planet Earth,
We will party like jungle animals.
We will boogie till we puke.
Heads will roll.
The drive-in will never die.
Amen.
—"The Drive-In Oath," by Joe Bob Briggs

THE DRIVE-IN theater may have been born in New Jersey, but it had the good sense to come to Texas to live. Throughout the fifties and sixties it thrived here like a fungus on teenage lusts and families enticed by the legendary Dollar Night or Two Dollars a Carload.

And even now — though some say the drive-in has seen its heyday in the more populated areas, you can drive on in there any night of the week — particularly Special Nights and Saturday — and witness a sight that sometimes makes the one on the screen boring in comparison.

You'll see lawn chairs planted in the backs of pickups, or next to speakers, with cowboys and cowgirls planted in the chairs, beer cans growing out of their fists, and there'll be the sputterings of barbeque pits and the aromas of cooking meats rising up in billows of smoke that slowly melts into the clear Texas sky.

Sometimes there'll be folks with tape decks whining away, even as the movie flickers across the three-story screen and their neighbors struggle to hear the crackling speaker dialogue over ZZ Top doing "Tube Snake Boogie." There'll be lovers sprawled out on blankets spread between two speaker posts, going at it so hot and heavy they ought to just go on and charge admission. And there's plenty of action in the cars too. En route to the concession stand a discerning eye can spot the white moons of un-Levied butts rising and falling to a steady, rocking rhythm just barely contained by well-greased shocks and 4-ply tires.

What you're witnessing is a bizarre subculture in action. One that may in fact be riding the crest of a new wave.

Or to put it another way: Drive-ins are crazy, but they sure are fun.

The drive-in theater is over fifty years old, having been spawned in Camden, New Jersey, June 6, 1933, by a true visionary — Richard Milton Hollingshead.

Camden, as you may know, was the last home of Walt Whitman, and when one considers it was the death place of so prestigious an American poet, it is only fitting that it be the birthplace of such a poetic and All-American institution as the drive-in theater. Or as my dad used to call them, "the outdoor picture show."

Once there were over 4,000 drive-ins in the United States, now there are about 3,000, and according to some experts, they are dropping off fast. However, in Texas there is a re-emergence and new interest in the passion pits of old. They have become nearly as sacred as the armadillo.

The Lone Star State alone has some 209 outdoor theaters in operation, and many of these are multi-screen jobs with different movies running concurrently alongside one another. Not long ago, Gordon McLendon, "The Drive-In Business King," erected the I-45 in Houston, a drive-in capable of holding up to 3,000 automobiles. In fact, it claims to be the biggest drive-in in existence.

Why does the drive-in thrive in Texas when it's falling off elsewhere? Three reasons.

(1) Climate. Generally speaking, Texas has a pretty comfortable climate year round. (2) A car culture. Texas is the champion state for automobile registration,

and Texans have this thing about their cars. The automobile has replaced the horse not only as a mode of transportation, but as a source of mythology. If the Texan of old was supposedly half human and half horse, the modern Texan is half human and half automobile. Try and separate a Texan from his car, or mass transit that sucker against his will, and you're likely to end up kissing grillwork at sixty-five miles an hour. (3) Joe Bob Briggs.

Okay, start the background music. Softly please, a humming version of "The Eyes of Texas." And will all true Texans please remove your hats while we have a short discussion of Joe Bob Briggs, The Patron Saint of Texas Drive-ins, He Who Drives Behind the Speaker Rows, and columnist for the *Dallas Times Herald*. In fact, his column, "Joe Bob Goes to the Drive-in," is the most popular feature in the paper. As it should be, because Joe Bob — who may be the pseudonym for the *Herald*'s regular film critic John Bloom — don't talk no bullcorn, and he don't bother with "hardtop" movie reviews. He's purely a drive-in kind of guy, and boy does he have style.

Here's an example, part of a review for *The Evil Dead:* "Five teenagers become Spam-in-a-cabin when they head for the woods and start turning into flesh-eating zombies. Asks a lot of moral questions, like, 'If your girlfriend turns zombie on you, what do you do? Carve her into itty-bitty pieces or look the other way?' One girl gets raped by the woods. Not in the woods. *By* the woods. The only way to kill zombies: total dismemberment. This one could make *Saw* eligible for the Disney Channel."

Single-handedly, with that wild column of his — which not only reports on movies, but on the good times and bad times of Joe Bob himself — he has given the drive-in a new mystique. Or to be more exact, made the non-drive-in goers aware of it, and reminded the rest of us just how much fun the outdoor picture show can be.

Joe Bob's popularity has even birthed a yearly Drive-in Movie Festival — somewhat sacrilegiously held indoors this year — that has been attended in the past by such guests as Roger Corman, King of the Bs, and this year by "Big Steve," known to some as Stephen King. (If you movie watchers don't recognize the name, he's a writer-feller.) "Big Steve" was given the solemn honor of leading off the 1984 ceremonies with Joe Bob's "drive-in oath" and arrived wearing his JOE BOB BRIGGS IS A PERSONAL FRIEND OF MINE T-shirt.

The festival has also sported such features as the Custom Car Rally, Ralph the Diving Pig (sure hate I missed the boy's act), the stars of *The Texas Chainsaw Massacre*, Miss Custom Body of 1983, "unofficial custom bodies" and Joe Bob his own self. And last, but certainly not least, along with this chic gathering, a number of new movies like *Bloodsuckers from Outer Space* and *Future-Kill* made their world premieres.

What more could you ask from Joe Bob?

Kill the music. Hats on.

The drive-ins I grew up with went by a number of names: The Apache, The Twin Pines, The Riverroad being a few examples. And though they varied somewhat in appearance, basically they were large lots filled with speaker posts — many of which were minus their speakers, due to absent-minded patrons driving off while they were still hooked to their windows, or vandals — a concession stand, a screen at least three stories high (sometimes six), a swing, see-saw and merry-go-round up front for the kiddies, all this surrounded by an ugly six-foot, moon-shimmering tin fence.

They all had the same bad food at the concessions. Hot dogs that tasted like rubber hoses covered in watery mustard, popcorn indistinguishable from the cardboard containers that held it, drinks that were mostly water and ice, and candy so old the worms inside were dead either of old age or sugar diabetes.

And they all came with the *same* restroom. It was as if the Apache, Riverroad, and Twin Pines were equipped with warping devices that activated the moment you stepped behind the wooden "modesty fence." Suddenly, at the speed of thought, you were whisked away to a concrete bunker with floors either so tacky your shoes stuck to it like cat hairs to honey, or so flooded in water you needed skis to make it to the urinals or the john, the latter of which was forever doorless, the hinges hanging like frayed tendons. And both of these public conveniences were invariably stuffed full of floating cigarette butts, candy wrappers and used prophylactics.

Rather than take my life into my own hands in these rather seedy enclosures, I often took my chances battling constipation or urinating into a Coke cup and pouring the prize out the window. The idea of standing over one of those odoriferous urinals — and there was always this item of crayoned wisdom above them: "Remember, crabs can pole vault" — and having something ugly, fuzzy, multilegged and ravenous leap out on me was forever foremost in my mind. Nor did I find those initialed and graffiti carved seats — when there were seats at all — the more inviting. I figured that no matter how precariously I might perch myself, some nameless horror from the pits of sewerdom would find access to that part of my anatomy I most prized.

In spite of these unpleasantries, come Saturday night, a bunch of us guys — the ones who couldn't get dates — would cruise over there, stopping a quarter-mile outside the place to stuff one member of our party in the trunk, this always the fellow who had the least money to pool toward entrance fees, having blown it on beer, *Playboy* magazines and prophylactics that would certainly rot in his wallet. Then we would drive up to the pay booth and promptly be asked, "Got anybody in the trunk?"

Obviously we were a suspicious-looking lot, but we never admitted to a body in the trunk, and for some reason we were never forced to open up. After we had emphatically denied that we would even consider it, and the ticket seller had eyed us over for a while, trying to break our resolve, he would take our money and we would drive inside.

My Plymouth Savoy was rigged so that the man in the trunk could push the back seat from the inside, and it would fold down, allowing our unthrifty, and generally greasy, contortionist to join our party.

That Savoy, what a car, what a drive-in machine. What a death trap. It took a two-man crew to drive it. The gas pedal always stuck to the floor, and when you came whizzing up to a red light you had to jerk your foot off the gas, go for the brake and yell "Pedal!" Then your co-pilot would dive for the floorboards, grab the pedal and yank it up just in time to keep us from plowing broadside into an unsuspecting motorist. However, that folding back seat made the sticking pedal seem like a minor liability, and the Savoy was a popular auto with the drive-in set.

The drive-in gave me many firsts. The first sexual action I ever witnessed was there, and I don't mean on the screen. At the Apache the front-row was somewhat on an incline, and if the car in front of you was parked just right, and you were lying on the roof of your car, any activity going on in the back seat of the front row car was quite visible to you, providing it was a moonlit night and the movie playing was a particularly bright one.

The first sexual activity that included me, also occurred at a drive-in, but that is a personal matter, and enough said.

The first truly vicious fight I ever saw was at the Riverroad. A fellow wearing a cowboy hat got into some kind of a shindig with a hatless fellow right in front of my Savoy. I've no idea what started the fight, but it was a good one, matched only by a live Championship Wrestling match at the Cotton Bowl.

Whatever the beef, the fellow with the hat was the sharper of the two, as he had him a three-foot length of two-by-four, and all the other fellow had was a bag of popcorn. Even as the zombies of *Night of the Living Dead* shuffled across the screen, The Hat laid a lick on Hatless's noggin that sounded like a beaver's tail slapping water. Popcorn flew and the fight was on.

The Hat got Hatless by the lapel and proceeded to knock knots on his head faster than you could count them, and though Hatless was game as all-get-out, he couldn't fight worth a damn. His arms flew over The Hat's shoulders and slapped his back like useless whips of spaghetti, and all the while he just kept making The Hat madder by calling him names and making rude accusations about the man's family tree and what members of it did to one another when the lights were out.

For a while there, The Hat was as busy as the lead in a samurai movie, but finally the rhythm of his blows — originally akin to a Ginger Baker drum solo — died down, and this indicated to me that he was getting tired, and had I been Hatless, this would have been my cue to scream sharply once, then flop at The Hat's feet like a dying fish, and finally pretend to go belly up right there in the lot. But this boy either had the IQ of a can of green beans, or was in such a near-comatose state from the beating, he didn't have the good sense to shut up. In fact his language became so vivid, The Hat found renewed strength and delivered his blows in such close proximity that the sound of wood to skull resembled the angry rattling of a diamondback snake.

Finally, Hatless tried to wrestle The Hat to the ground and then went tumbling over my hood, shamelessly knocking loose my prized hood ornament, a large, in-flight swan that lit up when the lights were on, and ripping off half of The Hat's cowboy shirt in the process.

A bunch of drive-in personnel showed up then and tried to separate the boys. That's when the chili really hit the fan. There were bodies flying all over that lot as relatives and friends of the original brawlers suddenly dealt themselves in. One guy got crazy and ripped a speaker and wire smooth off a post and went at anyone and everybody with it. And he was good too. Way he whipped that baby about made Bruce Lee and his nunchukas look like a third-grade carnival act.

While this went on, a fellow in the car to the right of us, oblivious to the action on the lot, wrapped up in *Night of the Living Dead*, and probably polluted on Thunderbird wine, was yelling in favor of the zombies, "Eat 'em, eat 'em!"

Finally the fight moved on down the lot and eventually dissipated. About half an hour later I looked down the row and saw Hatless crawling out from under a white Cadillac festooned with enough curb feelers to make it look like a centipede. He sort of went on his hands and knees for a few yards, rose to a squatting run, and disappeared into a winding maze of automobiles.

Them drive-in folks, what kidders.

The drive-in is also the source for my darkest fantasy — I refrain from calling it a nightmare, because after all these years it has become quite familiar, a sort of grim friend. For years now I've been waiting for this particular dream to continue, take up a new installment, but it always ends on the same enigmatic note.

Picture this: a crisp summer night in Texas. A line of cars winding from the pay booth of a drive-in out to the highway, then alongside it for a quarter-mile or better. Horns are honking, children are shouting, mosquitoes are buzzing. I'm in a pickup with two friends who we'll call Dave and Bob. Bob is driving. On the rack behind us is a twelve gauge shotgun and a baseball bat, "a bad-ass persuader." A camper is attached to the truck bed, and in the camper we've got lawn chairs, coolers of soft drinks and beer, enough junk food to send a hypoglycemic to the stars.

What a night this is. Dusk to Dawn features, two dollars a carload. Great movies like *The Toolbox Murders*, *Night of the Living Dead*, *Day of the Dead*, *Zombies*, and *I Dismember Mama*.

We finally inch our way past the pay booth and dart inside. It's a magnificent drive-in, like the I-45, big enough for 3,000 cars or better. Empty paper cups, popcorn boxes, chili and mustard-stained hot dog wrappers blow gently across the lot like paper tumbleweeds. And there, standing stark-white against a jet-black sky is a portal into another dimension: the six-story screen.

We settle on a place near the front, about five rows back. Out come the lawn chairs, the coolers and the eats. Before the first flick sputters on and Cameron Mitchell opens that ominous box of tools, we're through an economy-size bag of "tater" chips, a quart of Coke and half a sack of chocolate cookies.

The movie starts, time is lost as we become absorbed in the horrifyingly campy delights of *Toolbox*. We get to the part where Mitchell is about to use the industrial nailer on a young lady he's been watching shower, and suddenly — *there is a light,* so red and bright the images on the screen fade. Looking up, we see a great, crimson comet hurtling towards us. Collision with the drive-in is imminent. Or so it seems; then, abruptly the *comet smiles.* Just splits down the middle to show a mouth full of grinning, jagged teeth not too unlike a power saw blade. It seems that instead of going out of life with a bang, we may go out with a crunch. The mouth gets wider, and the comet surprises us by whipping up, dragging behind it a fiery tail that momentarily blinds us.

When the crimson washes from our eyeballs and we look around, all is as before. At first glance anyway. Because closer observation reveals that everything outside the drive-in, the highway, the trees, the tops of houses and buildings that had been visible above the surrounding tin fence, are gone. There is only blackness, and we're talking BLACKNESS here, the kind of dark that makes fudge pudding look pale. It's as if the drive-in has been ripped up by the roots and miraculously stashed in limbo somewhere. But if so, we are not injured in any way, and the electricity still works. There are lights from the concession stand, and the projector continues to throw the images of *Toolbox* on the screen.

About this time a guy in a station wagon, fat wife beside him, three kids in the back, panics, guns the car to life and darts for the exit. His lights do not penetrate the blackness, and as the car hits it, inch by inch it is consumed by the void. A moment later, nothing.

A cowboy with a hatful of toothpicks and feathers gets out of his pickup and goes over there. He stands on the tire-buster spears, extends his arm... And never in the history of motion pictures or real life have I heard such a scream. He flops back, his arm gone from the hand to elbow. He rolls on the ground. By the time we get over there the rest of his arm is collapsing, as if bone and tissue have gone to mush. His hat settles down on a floppy mess that a moment before was his head. His whole body folds in and oozes out of his clothes in what looks like sloppy vomit. I carefully reach out and take hold of one of his boots, upend it, a loathsome mess pours out and strikes the ground with a plopping sound.

We are trapped in the drive-in.

Time goes by, no one knows how much. It's like the Edgar Rice Burroughs stories about Pellucidar. Without the sun or moon to judge by, time does not exist. Watches don't help either. They've all stopped. We sleep when sleepy, eat when hungry. And the movies flicker on. No one even suggests cutting them off. Their light and those of the concession stand are the only lights, and should we extinguish them, we might be lost forever in a void to match the one outside of the drive-in fence.

At first people are great. The concession folks bring out food. Those of us who have brought food, share it. Everyone is fed.

But as time passes, people are not so great. The concession stand people lock up and post guards. My friends and I are down to our last kernels of popcorn and we're drinking the ice and water slush left in the coolers. The place smells of human waste, as the restrooms have ceased to function altogether. Gangs are forming, even cults based on the movies. There is a Zombie Cult that stumbles and staggers in religious mockery of the "dead" on the screen. And with the lack of food an acute problem, they have taken to human sacrifice and cannibalism. Bob takes down the shotgun. I take down the baseball bat. Dave has taken to wearing a hunting knife he got out of the glove box.

Rape and murder are wholesale, and even if you've a mind to, there's not much you can do about it. You've got to protect your little stretch of ground, your automobile, your universe. But against our will we are forced into the role of saviors when a young girl runs against our truck while fleeing her mother, father and older brother. Bob jerks her inside the truck, holds the family — who are a part of the Zombie Cult and run as if they are cursed with a case of the rickets — at bay with the shotgun. They start to explain that as the youngest member of the family, it's only right that she give herself up to them to provide sustenance. A chill runs up my back. Not so much because it is a horrible thing they suggest, but because I too am hungry, and for a moment they seem to make good sense.

Hunger devours the family's common sense, and the father leaps forward. The shotgun rocks against Bob's shoulder and the man goes down, hit in the head, the way you have to kill zombies. Then the mother is on me, teeth and nails. I swing the bat and down she goes, thrashing at my feet like a headless chicken.

Trembling, I hold the bat before me. It is caked with blood and brains. I fall back against the truck and throw up. On the screen the zombies are feasting on bodies from an exploded pickup.

Rough for the home team. Time creeps by. We are weak. No food. No water. We find ourselves looking at the rotting corpses outside our pickup far too long. We catch the young girl eating their remains, but we do nothing. Somehow, it doesn't seem so bad. In fact, it looks inviting. Food right outside the truck, on the ground, ready for the taking.

But when it seems we are going to join her, there is a red light in the sky. The comet is back, and once again it swoops down, collision looks unavoidable, it smiles with its jagged teeth, peels up and whips its bright tail. And when the glow burns away from our eyes, it is daylight and there is a world outside the drive-in.

A sort of normalcy returns. Engines are tried. Batteries have been unaffected by the wait. Automobiles start up and begin moving toward the exit in single file, as if nothing has ever happened.

Outside, the highway we come to is the same, except the yellow line has faded and the concrete has buckled in spots. But nothing else is the same. On either side of the highway is a great, dank jungle. It looks like something out of a lost world movie.

As we drive along — we're about the fifth automobile in line — we see something move up ahead, to the right. A massive shape steps out of the foliage and onto the highway. It is a Tyrannosaurus Rex covered in bat-like parasites, their wings opening and closing slowly, like contented butterflies sipping nectar from a flower.

The dinosaur does nothing. It gives our line of metal bugs the once over, crosses the highway and is enveloped by the jungle again.

The caravan starts up once more. We drive onward into this prehistoric world split by a highway out of our memories.

I'm riding shotgun and I glance in the wing-mirror on my side. In it I can see the drive-in screen, and though the last movie should still be running, I can't make out any movement there. It looks like nothing more than an oversized slice of Wonder Bread.

Fade out.

That's the dream. And even now when I go to a drive-in, be it the beat up Lumberjack here with its cheap, tin screen, or anywhere else, I find myself occasionally glancing at the night sky, momentarily fearing that out of the depths of space there will come a great, red comet that will smile at me with a mouthful of saw-blade teeth and whip its flaming tail.

Night They Missed the Horror Show

IF THEY'D GONE to the drive-in like they'd planned, none of this would have happened. But Leonard didn't like drive-ins when he didn't have a date, and he'd heard about *Night of the Living Dead,* and he knew a nigger starred in it. He didn't want to see no movie with a nigger star. Niggers chopped cotton, fixed flats, and pimped nigger girls, but he'd never heard of one that killed zombies. And he'd heard too that there was a white girl in the movie that let the nigger touch her, and that peeved him. Any white gal that would let a nigger touch her must be the lowest trash in the world. Probably from Hollywood, New York, or Waco, some godforsaken place like that.

Now Steve McQueen would have been all right for zombie killing and girl handling. He would have been the ticket. But a nigger? No sir.

Boy, that Steve McQueen was one cool head. Way he said stuff in them pictures was so good you couldn't help but think someone had written it down for him. He could sure think fast on his feet to come up with the things he said, and he had that real cool, mean look.

Leonard wished he could be Steve McQueen, or Paul Newman even. Someone like that always knew what to say, and he figured they got plenty of bush too. Certainly they didn't get as bored as he did. He was so bored he felt as if he were going to die from it before the night was out. Bored, bored, bored. Just wasn't nothing exciting about being in the Dairy Queen parking lot leaning on the front of his '64 Impala looking out at the highway. He figured maybe old crazy Harry who janitored at the high school might be right about them flying saucers. Harry was always seeing something. Bigfoot, six-legged weasels, all manner of things. But maybe he was right about the saucers. He'd said he'd seen one a couple nights back hovering over Mud Creek and it was shooting down these rays that looked like wet peppermint sticks. Leonard figured if Harry really had seen the saucers and the rays, then those rays were boredom rays. It would be a way for space critters to get at Earth folks, boring them to death. Getting melted down by heat rays would have been better. That was at least quick, but being bored to death was sort of like being nibbled to death by ducks.

Leonard continued looking at the highway, trying to imagine flying saucers and boredom rays, but he couldn't keep his mind on it. He finally focused on something in the highway. A dead dog.

Not just a dead dog. But a DEAD DOG. The mutt had been hit by a semi at least, maybe several. It looked as if it had rained dog. There were pieces of that pooch all over the concrete and one leg was lying on the curbing on the opposite side, stuck up in such a way that it seemed to be waving hello. Doctor Frankenstein with a grant from Johns Hopkins and assistance from NASA couldn't have put that sucker together again.

Leonard leaned over to his faithful, drunk companion, Billy — known among the gang as Farto, because he was fart-lighting champion of Mud Creek — and said, "See that dog there?"

Farto looked where Leonard was pointing. He hadn't noticed the dog before, and he wasn't nearly as casual about it as Leonard. The puzzle-piece hound brought back memories. It reminded him of a dog he'd had when he was thirteen. A big, fine German shepherd that loved him better than his mama.

Sonofabitch dog tangled its chain through and over a barbed wire fence somehow and hung itself. When Farto found the dog its tongue looked like a stuffed, black sock and he could see where its claws had just been able to scrape the ground, but not quite enough to get a toe hold.

It looked as if the dog had been scratching out some sort of a coded message in the dirt. When Farto told his old man about it later, crying as he did, his old man laughed and said, "Probably a goddamn suicide note."

Now, as he looked out at the highway, and his whiskey-laced Coke collected warmly in his gut, he felt a tear form in his eyes. Last time he'd felt that sappy was when he'd won the fart-lighting championship with a four-inch burner that singed the hairs of his ass and the gang awarded him with a pair of colored boxing shorts. Brown and yellow ones so he could wear them without having to change them too often.

So there they were, Leonard and Farto, parked outside the DQ, leaning on the hood of Leonard's Impala, sipping Coke and whiskey, feeling bored and blue and horny, looking at a dead dog and having nothing to do but go to a show with a nigger starring in it. Which, to be up front, wouldn't have been so bad if they'd had dates. Dates could make up for a lot of sins, or help make a few good ones, depending on one's outlook.

But the night was criminal. Dates they didn't have. Worse yet, wasn't a girl in the entire high school would date them. Not even Marylou Flowers, and she had some kind of disease.

All this nagged Leonard something awful. He could see what the problem was with Farto. He was ugly. Had the kind of face that attracted flies. And though being fart-lighting champion of Mud Creek had a certain prestige among the gang, it lacked a certain something when it came to charming the gals.

But for the life of him, Leonard couldn't figure his own problem. He was handsome, had some good clothes, and his car ran good when he didn't buy that old cheap gas. He even had a few bucks in his jeans from breaking into washaterias. Yet his right arm had damn near grown to the size of his thigh from all the whacking off he did. Last time he'd been out with a girl had been a month ago, and as he'd been out with her along with nine other guys, he wasn't rightly sure he could call that a date. He wondered about it so much, he'd asked Farto if he thought it qualified as a date. Farto, who had been fifth in line, said he didn't think so, but if Leonard wanted to call it one, wasn't no skin off his back.

But Leonard didn't want to call it a date. It just didn't have the feel of one, lacked that something special. There was no romance to it.

True, Big Red had called him Honey when he put the mule in the barn, but she called everyone Honey — except Stoney. Stoney was Possum Sweets, and he was the one who talked her into wearing the grocery bag with the mouth and eye holes. Stoney was like that. He could sweet talk the camel out from under a sand nigger. When he got through chatting Big Red down, she was plumb proud to wear that bag.

When finally it came his turn to do Big Red, Leonard had let her take the bag off as a gesture of goodwill. That was a mistake. He just hadn't known a good thing when he had it. Stoney had had the right idea. The bag coming off spoiled everything. With it on, it was sort of like balling the Lone Hippo or some such thing, but with the bag off, you were absolutely certain what you were getting, and it wasn't pretty.

Even closing his eyes hadn't helped. He found that the ugliness of that face had branded itself on the back of his eyeballs. He couldn't even imagine the sack back over her head. All he could think about was that puffy, too-painted face with the sort of bad complexion that began at the bone.

He'd gotten so disappointed, he'd had to fake an orgasm and get off before his hooter shriveled up and his Trojan fell off and was lost in the vacuum.

Thinking back on it, Leonard sighed. It would certainly be nice for a change to go with a girl that didn't pull the train or have a hole between her legs that looked like a manhole cover ought to be on it. Sometimes he wished he could be like Farto, who was as happy as if he had good sense. Anything thrilled him. Give him a can of Wolf Brand Chili, a big moon pie, Coke and whiskey and he could spend the rest of his life fucking Big Red and lighting the gas out of his asshole.

God, but this was no way to live. No women and no fun. Bored, bored, bored. Leonard found himself looking overhead for spaceships and peppermint-colored boredom rays, but he saw only a few moths fluttering drunkenly through the beams of the DQ's lights.

Lowering his eyes back to the highway and the dog, Leonard had a sudden flash. "Why don't we get the chain out of the back and hook it up to Rex there? Take him for a ride?"

"You mean drag his dead ass around?" Farto asked.

Leonard nodded.

"Beats stepping on a tack," Farto said.

They drove the Impala into the middle of the highway at a safe moment and got out for a look. Up close the mutt was a lot worse. Its innards had been mashed out of its mouth and asshole and it stunk something awful. The dog was wearing a thick, metal-studded collar and they fastened one end of their fifteen-foot chain to that and the other to the rear bumper.

Bob, the Dairy Queen manager, noticed them through the window, came outside and yelled, "What are you fucking morons doing?"

"Taking this doggie to the vet," Leonard said. "We think this sumbitch looks a might peeked. He may have been hit by a car."

"That's so fucking funny I'm about to piss myself," Bob said.

"Old folks have that problem," Leonard said.

Leonard got behind the wheel and Farto climbed in on the passenger side. They maneuvered the car and dog around and out of the path of a tractor-trailer truck just in time. As they drove off, Bob screamed after them, "I hope you two no-dicks wrap that Chevy piece of shit around a goddamn pole."

As they roared along, parts of the dog, like crumbs from a flaky loaf of bread, came off. A tooth here. Some hair there. A string of guts. A dew claw. And some unidentifiable pink stuff. The metal-studded collar and chain threw up sparks now and then like fiery crickets. Finally they hit seventy-five and the dog was swinging wider and wider on the chain, like it was looking for an opportunity to pass.

Farto poured him and Leonard Cokes and whiskey as they drove along. He handed Leonard his paper cup and Leonard knocked it back, a lot happier now than he had been a moment ago. Maybe this night wasn't going to turn out so bad after all.

They drove by a crowd at the side of the road, a tan station wagon and a wreck of a Ford up on a jack. At a glance they could see that there was a nigger in the middle of the crowd and he wasn't witnessing to the white boys. He was hopping around like a pig with a hotshot up his ass, trying to find a break in the white boys so he could make a run for it. But there wasn't any break to be found and there were too many to fight. Nine white boys were knocking him around like he was a pinball and they were a malicious machine.

"Ain't that one of our niggers?" Farto asked. "And ain't that some of the White Tree football players that's trying to kill him?"

"Scott," Leonard said, and the name was dogshit in his mouth. It had been Scott who had outdone him for the position of quarterback on the team. That damn jig could put together a play more tangled than a can of fishing worms, but it damn near always worked. And he could run like a spotted-ass ape.

As they passed, Farto said, "We'll read about him tomorrow in the papers."

But Leonard drove only a short way before slamming on the brakes and whipping the Impala around. Rex swung way out and clipped off some tall, dried sunflowers at the edge of the road like a scythe.

"We gonna go back and watch?" Farto asked. "I don't think them White Tree boys would bother us none if that's all we was gonna do, watch."

"He may be a nigger," Leonard said not liking himself, "but he's our nigger and we can't let them do that. They kill him, they'll beat us in football."

Farto saw the truth of this immediately. "Damn right. They can't do that to our nigger."

Leonard crossed the road again and went straight for the White Tree boys, hit down hard on the horn. The White Tree boys abandoned beating their prey and jumped in all directions. Bullfrogs couldn't have done any better.

Scott stood startled and weak where he was, his knees bent in and touching one another, his eyes as big as pizza pans. He had never noticed how big grillwork was. It looked like teeth there in the night and the headlights looked like eyes. He felt like a stupid fish about to be eaten by a shark.

Leonard braked hard, but off the highway in the dirt it wasn't enough to keep from bumping Scott, sending him flying over the hood and against the glass where his face mashed to it then rolled away, his shirt snagging one of the windshield wipers and pulling it off.

Leonard opened the car door and called to Scott who lay on the ground, "It's now or never."

A White Tree boy made for the car, and Leonard pulled the taped hammer handle out from beneath the seat and stepped out of the car and hit him with it. The White Tree boy went down to his knees and said something that sounded like French but wasn't. Leonard grabbed Scott by the back of the shirt and pulled him up and guided him around and threw him into the open door. Scott scrambled over the front seat and into the back. Leonard threw the hammer handle at one of the White Tree boys and stepped back, whirled into the car behind the wheel. He put the car in gear again and stepped on the gas. The Impala lurched forward, and with one hand on the door Leonard flipped it wider and clipped a White Tree boy with it as if he were flexing a wing. The car bumped back on the highway and the chain swung out and Rex cut the feet out from under two White Tree boys as neatly as he had taken down the dried sunflowers.

Leonard looked in his rear-view mirror and saw two White Tree boys carrying the one he had clubbed with the hammer handle to the station wagon. The others he and the dog had knocked down were getting up. One had kicked the jack out from under Scott's car and was using it to smash the headlights and windshield.

"Hope you got insurance on that thing," Leonard said.

"I borrowed it," Scott said, peeling the windshield wiper out of his T-shirt. "Here, you might want this." He dropped the wiper over the seat and between Leonard and Farto.

"That's a borrowed car?" Farto said. "That's worse."

"Nah," Scott said. "Owner don't know I borrowed it. I'd have had that flat changed if that sucker had had him a spare tire, but I got back there and wasn't nothing but the rim, man. Say, thanks for not letting me get killed, else we couldn't have run that ole pig together no more. Course, you almost run over me. My chest hurts."

Leonard checked the rear-view again. The White Tree boys were coming fast. "You complaining?" Leonard said.

"Nah," Scott said, and turned to look through the back glass. He could see the dog swinging in short arcs and pieces of it going wide and far. "Hope you didn't go off and forget your dog tied to the bumper."

"Goddamn," said Farto, "and him registered too."

"This ain't so funny," Leonard said. "Them White Tree boys are gaining."

"Well speed it up," Scott said.

Leonard gnashed his teeth. "I could always get rid of some excess baggage, you know."

"Throwing that windshield wiper out ain't gonna help," Scott said.

Leonard looked in his mirror and saw the grinning nigger in the back seat. Nothing worse than a comic coon. He didn't even look grateful. Leonard had a sudden horrid vision of being overtaken by the White Tree boys. What if he were killed with the nigger? Getting killed was bad enough, but what if tomorrow they found him in a ditch with Farto and the nigger? Or maybe them White Tree boys would make him do something awful with the nigger before they killed them. Like making him suck the nigger's dick or some such thing. Leonard held his foot all the way to the floor; as they passed the Dairy Queen he took a hard left and the car just made it and Rex swung out and slammed a light pole then popped back in line behind them.

The White Tree boys couldn't make the corner in the station wagon and they didn't even try. They screeched into a car lot down a piece, turned around and came back. By that time the tail lights of the Impala were moving away from them rapidly, looking like two inflamed hemorrhoids in a dark asshole.

"Take the next right coming up," Scott said, "then you'll see a little road off to the left. Kill your lights and take that."

Leonard hated taking orders from Scott on the field, but this was worse. Insulting. Still, Scott called good plays on the field, and the habit of following instructions from the quarterback died hard. Leonard made the right and Rex made it with them after taking a dip in a water-filled bar ditch.

Leonard saw the little road and killed his lights and took it. It carried them down between several rows of large tin storage buildings, and Leonard pulled between two of them and drove down a little alley lined with more. He stopped the car and they waited and listened. After about five minutes, Farto said, "I think we skunked those father rapers."

"Ain't we a team?" Scott said.

In spite of himself, Leonard felt good. It was like when the nigger called a play that worked and they were all patting each other on the ass and not minding what color the other was because they were just creatures in football suits.

"Let's have a drink," Leonard said.

Farto got a paper cup off the floorboard for Scott and poured him up some warm Coke and whiskey. Last time they had gone to Longview, he had peed in that paper cup so they wouldn't have to stop, but that had long since been poured out, and besides, it was for a nigger. He poured Leonard and himself drinks in their same cups.

Scott took a sip and said, "Shit, man, that tastes kind of rank."

"Like piss," Farto said.

Leonard held up his cup. "To the Mud Creek Wildcats and fuck them White Tree boys."

"You fuck 'em," Scott said. They touched their cups, and at that moment the car filled with light.

Cups upraised, the Three Musketeers turned blinking toward it. The light was coming from an open storage-building door and there was a fat man standing in the center of the glow like a bloated fly on a lemon wedge. Behind him was a big screen made of a sheet and there was some kind of movie playing on it. And though the light was bright and fading out the movie, Leonard, who was in the best position to see, got a look at it. What he could make out looked like a gal down on her knees sucking this fat guy's dick (the man was visible only from the belly down) and the guy had a short, black revolver pressed to her forehead. She pulled her mouth off of him for an instant and the man came in her face then fired the revolver. The woman's head snapped out of frame and the sheet seemed to drip blood, like dark condensation on a window pane. Then Leonard couldn't see anymore because another man had appeared in the doorway, and like the first he was fat. Both looked like huge bowling balls that had been set on top of shoes. More men appeared behind these two, but one of the fat men turned and held up his hand and the others moved out of sight. The two fat guys stepped outside and one pulled the door almost shut, except for a thin band of light that fell across the front seat of the Impala.

Fat Man Number One went over to the car and opened Farto's door and said, "You fucks and the nigger get out." It was the voice of doom. They had only thought the White Tree boys were dangerous. They realized now they had been kidding themselves. This was the real article. This guy would have eaten the hammer handle and shit a two-by-four.

They got out of the car and the fat man waved them around and lined them up on Farto's side and looked at them. The boys still had their drinks in their hands, and sparing that, they looked like cons in a lineup.

Fat Man Number Two came over and looked at the trio and smiled. It was obvious the fatties were twins. They had the same bad features in the same fat faces. They wore Hawaiian shirts that varied only in profiles and color of parrots and had on white socks and too-short black slacks and black, shiny, Italian shoes with toes sharp enough to thread needles.

Fat Man Number One took the cup away from Scott and sniffed it. "A nigger with liquor," he said. "That's like a cunt with brains. It don't go together.

Guess you was getting tanked up so you could put the old black snake to some chocolate pudding after a while. Or maybe you was wantin' some vanilla and these boys were gonna set it up."

"I'm not wanting anything but to go home," Scott said. Fat Man Number Two looked at Fat Man Number One and said, "So he can fuck his mother."

The fatties looked at Scott to see what he'd say but he didn't say anything. They could say he screwed dogs and that was all right with him. Hell, bring one on and he'd fuck it now if they'd let him go afterwards.

Fat Man Number One said, "You boys running around with a jungle bunny makes me sick."

"He's just a nigger from school," Farto said. "We don't like him none. We just picked him up because some White Tree boys were beating on him and we didn't want him to get wrecked on account of he's our quarterback."

"Ah," Fat Man Number One said, "I see. Personally, me and Vinnie don't cotton to niggers in sports. They start taking showers with white boys the next thing they want is to take white girls to bed. It's just one step from one to the other."

"We don't have nothing to do with him playing," Leonard said. "We didn't integrate the schools."

"No," Fat Man Number One said, "that was ole Big Ears Johnson, but you're running around with him and drinking with him."

"His cup's been peed in," Farto said. "That was kind of a joke on him, you see. He ain't our friend, I swear it. He's just a nigger that plays football."

"Peed in his cup, huh?" said the one called Vinnie. "I like that, Pork, don't you? Peed in his fucking cup."

Pork dropped Scott's cup on the ground and smiled at him. "Come here, nigger. I got something to tell you."

Scott looked at Farto and Leonard. No help there. They had suddenly become interested in the toes of their shoes; they examined them as if they were true marvels of the world.

Scott moved toward Pork, and Pork, still smiling, put his arm around Scott's shoulders and walked him toward the big storage building. Scott said, "What are we doing?"

Pork turned Scott around so they were facing Leonard and Farto who still stood holding their drinks and contemplating their shoes. "I didn't want to get it on the new gravel drive," Pork said and pulled Scott's head in close to his own and with his free hand reached back and under his Hawaiian shirt and brought out a short, black revolver and put it to Scott's temple and pulled the trigger.

There was a snap like a bad knee going out and Scott's feet lifted in unison and went to the side and something dark squirted from his head and his feet swung back toward Pork and his shoes shuffled, snapped, and twisted on the concrete in front of the building.

"Ain't that somethin'," Pork said as Scott went limp and dangled from the thick crook of his arm. "The rhythm is the last thing to go."

Leonard couldn't make a sound. His guts were in his throat. He wanted to melt and run under the car. Scott was dead and the brains that had made plays twisted as fishing worms and commanded his feet on down the football field were scrambled like breakfast eggs.

Farto said, "Holy shit."

Pork let go of Scott and Scott's legs split and he sat down and his head went forward and clapped on the cement between his knees. A dark pool formed under his face.

"He's better off, boys," Vinnie said. "Nigger was begat by Cain and the ape and he ain't quite monkey and he ain't quite man. He's got no place in this world 'cept as a beast of burden. You start trying to train them to do things like drive cars and run with footballs it ain't nothing but grief to them and the whites too. Get any on your shirt, Pork?"

"Nary a drop."

Vinnie went inside the building and said something to the men there that could be heard but not understood, then he came back with some crumpled newspapers. He went over to Scott and wrapped them around the bloody head and let it drop back on the cement. "You try hosing down that shit when it's dried, Pork, and you wouldn't worry none about that gravel. The gravel ain't nothing."

Then Vinnie said to Farto, "Open the back door of that car." Farto nearly twisted an ankle doing it. Vinnie picked Scott up by the back of the neck and the seat of his pants and threw him onto the floorboard of the Impala.

Pork used the short barrel of his revolver to scratch his nuts, then put the gun behind him, under his Hawaiian shirt. "You boys are gonna go to the river bottoms with us and help us get shed of this nigger."

"Yes, sir," Farto said. "We'll toss his ass in the Sabine for you."

"How about you?" Pork asked Leonard. "You trying to go weak sister?"

"No," Leonard croaked, "I'm with you."

"That's good," Pork said. "Vinnie, you take the truck and lead the way."

Vinnie took a key from his pocket and unlocked the building door next to the one with the light, went inside, and backed out a sharp-looking gold

Dodge pickup. He backed it in front of the Impala and sat there with the motor running.

"You boys keep your place," Pork said. He went inside the lighted building for a moment. They heard him say to the men inside, "Go on and watch the movies. And save some of them beers for us. We'll be back." Then the light went out and Pork came out, shutting the door. He looked at Leonard and Farto and said, "Drink up, boys."

Leonard and Farto tossed off their warm Coke and whiskey and dropped the cups on the ground.

"Now," Pork said, "you get in the back with the nigger, I'll ride with the driver."

Farto got in the back and put his feet on Scott's knees. He tried not to look at the head wrapped in newspaper, but he couldn't help it. When Pork opened the front door and the overhead light came on Farto saw there was a split in the paper and Scott's eye was visible behind it. Across the forehead the wrapping had turned dark. Down by the mouth and chin was an ad for a fish sale.

Leonard got behind the wheel and started the car. Pork reached over and honked the horn. Vinnie rolled the pickup forward and Leonard followed him to the river bottoms. No one spoke. Leonard found himself wishing with all his heart that he had gone to the outdoor picture show to see the movie with the nigger starring in it.

The river bottoms were steamy and hot from the closeness of the trees and the under- and overgrowth. As Leonard wound the Impala down the narrow, red clay roads amidst the dense foliage, he felt as if his car were a crab crawling about in a pubic thatch. He could feel from the way the steering wheel handled that the dog and the chain were catching brush and limbs here and there. He had forgotten all about the dog and now being reminded of it worried him. What if the dog got tangled and he had to stop? He didn't think Pork would take kindly to stopping, not with the dead burrhead on the floorboards and him wanting to get rid of the body.

Finally they came to where the woods cleared out a spell and they drove along the edge of the Sabine River. Leonard hated water and always had. In the moonlight the river looked like poisoned coffee flowing there. Leonard knew there were alligators and gars big as little alligators and water moccasins by the thousands swimming underneath the water, and just the thought of all those slick, darting bodies made him queasy.

They came to what was known as Broken Bridge. It was an old worn-out bridge that had fallen apart in the middle and it was connected to the land on this side only. People sometimes fished off of it. There was no one fishing tonight.

Vinnie stopped the pickup and Leonard pulled up beside it, the nose of the Chevy pointing at the mouth of the bridge. They all got out and Pork made Farto pull Scott out by the feet. Some of the newspapers came loose from Scott's head exposing an ear and part of the face. Farto patted the newspaper back into place.

"Fuck that," Vinnie said. "It don't hurt if he stains the fucking ground. You two idgits find some stuff to weight this coon down so we can sink him."

Farto and Leonard started scurrying about like squirrels, looking for rocks or big, heavy logs. Suddenly they heard Vinnie cry out. "Godamighty, fucking A. Pork. Come look at this."

Leonard looked over and saw that Vinnie had discovered Rex. He was standing looking down with his hands on his hips. Pork went over to stand by him, then Pork turned around and looked at them. "Hey, you fucks, come here."

Leonard and Farto joined them in looking at the dog. There was mostly just a head now, with a little bit of meat and fur hanging off a spine and some broken ribs.

"That's the sickest fucking thing I've ever fucking seen," Pork said.

"Godamighty," Vinnie said.

"Doing a dog like that. Shit, don't you got no heart? A dog. Man's best fucking goddamn friend and you two killed him like this."

"We didn't kill him," Farto said.

"You trying to fucking tell me he done this to himself? Had a bad fucking day and done this."

"Godamighty," Vinnie said.

"No, sir," Leonard said. "We chained him on there after he was dead."

"I believe that," Vinnie said. "That's some rich shit. You guys murdered this dog. Godamighty."

"Just thinking about him trying to keep up and you fucks driving faster and faster makes me mad as a wasp," Pork said.

"No," Farto said. "It wasn't like that. He was dead and we were drunk and we didn't have anything to do, so we —"

"Shut the fuck up," Pork said, sticking a finger hard against Farto's forehead. "You just shut the fuck up. We can see what the fuck you fucks did. You drug this here dog around until all his goddamn hide came off... What kind of mothers you boys got anyhow that they didn't tell you better about animals?"

"Godamighty," Vinnie said.

Everyone grew silent, stood looking at the dog. Finally Farto said, "You want us to go back to getting some stuff to hold the nigger down?"

Pork looked at Farto as if he had just grown up whole from the ground. "You fucks are worse than niggers, doing a dog like that. Get on back over to the car."

Leonard and Farto went over to the Impala and stood looking down at Scott's body in much the same way they had stared at the dog. There, in the dim moonlight shadowed by trees, the paper wrapped around Scott's head made him look like a giant papier-mâché doll. Pork came up and kicked Scott in the face with a swift motion that sent newspapers flying and sent a thonking sound across the water that made frogs jump.

"Forget the nigger," Pork said. "Give me your car keys, ball sweat." Leonard took out his keys and gave them to Pork and Pork went around to the trunk and opened it. "Drag the nigger over here."

Leonard took one of Scott's arms and Farto took the other and they pulled him over to the back of the car.

"Put him in the trunk," Pork said.

"What for?" Leonard asked.

"'Cause I fucking said so," Pork said.

Leonard and Farto heaved Scott into the trunk. He looked pathetic lying there next to the spare tire, his face partially covered with newspaper. Leonard thought, if only the nigger had stolen a car with a spare he might not be here tonight. He could have gotten that flat changed and driven on before the White Tree boys even came along.

"All right, you get in there with him," Pork said, gesturing to Farto.

"Me?" Farto said.

"Nah, not fucking you, the fucking elephant on your fucking shoulder. Yeah, you, get in the trunk. I ain't got all night."

"Jesus, we didn't do anything to that dog, mister. We told you that. I swear. Me and Leonard hooked him up after he was dead… It was Leonard's idea."

Pork didn't say a word. He just stood there with one hand on the trunk lid looking at Farto. Farto looked at Pork, then the trunk, then back to Pork. Lastly he looked at Leonard, then climbed into the trunk, his back to Scott.

"Like spoons," Pork said, and closed the lid. "Now you, whatsit, Leonard? You come over here." But Pork didn't wait for Leonard to move. He scooped the back of Leonard's neck with a chubby hand and pushed him over to where Rex lay at the end of the chain with Vinnie still looking down at him.

"What you think, Vinnie?" Pork asked. "You got what I got in mind?"

Vinnie nodded. He bent down and took the collar off the dog. He fastened it on Leonard. Leonard could smell the odor of the dead dog in his nostrils. He bent his head and puked.

"There goes my shoeshine," Vinnie said, and he hit Leonard a short one in the stomach. Leonard went to his knees and puked some more of the hot Coke and whiskey.

"You fucks are the lowest pieces of shit on this earth, doing a dog like that," Vinnie said. "A nigger ain't no lower."

Vinnie got some strong fishing line out of the back of the truck and they tied Leonard's hands behind his back. Leonard began to cry.

"Oh shut up," Pork said. "It ain't that bad. Ain't nothing that bad."

But Leonard couldn't shut up. He was caterwauling now and it was echoing through the trees. He closed his eyes and tried to pretend he had gone to the show with the nigger starring in it and had fallen asleep in his car and was having a bad dream, but he couldn't imagine that. He thought about Harry the janitor's flying saucers with the peppermint rays, and he knew if there were any saucers shooting rays down, they weren't boredom rays after all. He wasn't a bit bored.

Pork pulled off Leonard's shoes and pushed him back flat on the ground and pulled off the socks and stuck them in Leonard's mouth so tight he couldn't spit them out. It wasn't that Pork thought anyone was going to hear Leonard, he just didn't like the noise. It hurt his ears.

Leonard lay on the ground in the vomit next to the dog and cried silently. Pork and Vinnie went over to the Impala and opened the doors and stood so they could get a grip on the car to push. Vinnie reached in and moved the gear from park to neutral and he and Pork began to shove the car forward. It moved slowly at first, but as it made the slight incline that led down to the old bridge, it picked up speed. From inside the trunk, Farto hammered lightly at the lid as if he didn't really mean it. The chain took up slack and Leonard felt it jerk and pop his neck. He began to slide along the ground like a snake.

Vinnie and Pork jumped out of the way and watched the car make the bridge and go over the edge and disappear into the water with amazing quietness. Leonard, pulled by the weight of the car, rustled past them. When he hit the bridge, splinters tugged at his clothes so hard they ripped his pants and underwear down almost to his knees.

The chain swung out once toward the edge of the bridge and the rotten railing, and Leonard tried to hook a leg around an upright board there, but that proved wasted. The weight of the car just pulled his knee out of joint and jerked the board out of place with a screech of nails and lumber.

Leonard picked up speed and the chain rattled over the edge of the bridge, into the water and out of sight, pulling its connection after it like a pull toy. The last sight of Leonard was the soles of his bare feet, white as the bellies of fish.

"It's deep there," Vinnie said. "I caught an old channel cat there once, remember? Big sucker. I bet it's over fifty feet deep down there."

They got in the truck and Vinnie cranked it.

"I think we did them boys a favor," Pork said. "Them running around with niggers and what they did to that dog and all. They weren't worth a thing."

"I know it," Vinnie said. "We should have filmed this, Pork, it would have been good. Where the car and that nigger lover went off in the water was choice."

"Nah, there wasn't any women."

"Point," Vinnie said, and he backed around and drove onto the trail that wound its way out of the bottoms.